Berkley Prime Crime titles by Laura Childs

Tea Shop Mysteries

DEATH BY DARJEELING
GUNPOWDER GREEN
SHADES OF EARL GREY
THE ENGLISH BREAKFAST MURDER
THE JASMINE MOON MURDER
CHAMOMILE MOURNING
BLOOD ORANGE BREWING
DRAGONWELL DEAD
THE SILVER NEEDLE MURDER
OOLONG DEAD
THE TEABERRY STRANGLER
SCONES & BONES

Scrapbooking Mysteries

KEEPSAKE CRIMES
PHOTO FINISHED
BOUND FOR MURDER
MOTIF FOR MURDER
FRILL KILL
DEATH SWATCH
TRAGIC MAGIC
FIBER & BRIMSTONE
SKELETON LETTERS

Cackleberry Club Mysteries

EGGS IN PURGATORY
EGGS BENEDICT ARNOLD
BEDEVILED EGGS

Anthology

DEATH BY DESIGN

Fiber &
Brimstone

LAURA CHILDS

BERKLEY PRIME CRIME, NEW YORK

THE BERKLEY PUBLISHING GROUP
Published by the Penguin Group
Penguin Group (USA) Inc.
375 Hudson Street, New York, New York 10014, USA

Penguin Group (Canada), 90 Eglinton Avenue East, Suite 700, Toronto, Ontario M4P 2Y3, Canada
(a division of Pearson Penguin Canada Inc.)
Penguin Books Ltd., 80 Strand, London WC2R 0RL, England
Penguin Group Ireland, 25 St. Stephen's Green, Dublin 2, Ireland (a division of Penguin Books Ltd.)
Penguin Group (Australia), 250 Camberwell Road, Camberwell, Victoria 3124, Australia
(a division of Pearson Australia Group Pty. Ltd.)
Penguin Books India Pvt. Ltd., 11 Community Centre, Panchsheel Park, New Delhi—110 017, India
Penguin Group (NZ), 67 Apollo Drive, Rosedale, Auckland 0632, New Zealand
(a division of Pearson New Zealand Ltd.)
Penguin Books (South Africa) (Pty.) Ltd., 24 Sturdee Avenue, Rosebank, Johannesburg 2196,
South Africa

Penguin Books Ltd., Registered Offices: 80 Strand, London WC2R 0RL, England

This is a work of fiction. Names, characters, places, and incidents either are the product of the author's imagination or are used fictitiously, and any resemblance to actual persons, living or dead, business establishments, events, or locales is entirely coincidental. The publisher does not have any control over and does not assume any responsibility for author or third-party websites or their content.

PUBLISHER'S NOTE: The recipes contained in this book are to be followed exactly as written. The publisher is not responsible for your specific health or allergy needs that may require medical supervision. The publisher is not responsible for any adverse reactions to the recipes contained in this book.

FIBER & BRIMSTONE

A Berkley Prime Crime Book / published by arrangement with Gerry Schmitt & Associates, Inc.

PRINTING HISTORY
Berkley Prime Crime hardcover edition / October 2010
Berkley Prime Crime mass-market edition / October 2011

Copyright © 2010 by Gerry Schmitt & Associates, Inc.
Excerpt from *Skeleton Letters* by Laura Childs copyright © by Gerry Schmitt & Associates, Inc.
Cover illustration by Dan Craig.
Cover design by Lesley Worrell.
Interior text design by Kristin del Rosario.

ISBN: 978-0-425-24402-9

BERKLEY® PRIME CRIME
Berkley Prime Crime Books are published by The Berkley Publishing Group,
a division of Penguin Group (USA) Inc.,
375 Hudson Street, New York, New York 10014.
BERKLEY® PRIME CRIME and the PRIME CRIME logo are trademarks of Penguin Group (USA) Inc.

PRINTED IN THE UNITED STATES OF AMERICA

10 9 8 7 6 5 4 3 2 1

This book is dedicated to Aunt Ger

Acknowledgments

Many thanks to Sam, Tom, Niti, Lance, Jennie, Bob, and Dan, as well as all my readers, scrapbooking friends, bloggers, reviewers, scrapbook magazine editors and writers, and scrapbook store owners.

Chapter 1

A GLOBULOUS giant head, evil grin stretched wide across its glowing orange face, teeth jagged as a buzz saw, bobbed and pecked at the air above Carmela Bertrand's head. Ten feet high, it dwarfed her five-foot-six-inch frame, seemingly oblivious to her concerned gaze. The bizarre creature hovered for a few more seconds, like a bad moon rising, then slowly sank to eye level.

"It's still not working," Carmela called to her friend Ava Gruiex. She retreated a few paces to the temporary table they'd set up in the Pluvius krewe's vast float den and bent low over her sketches. Some design flaw kept causing her giant puppet to deflate, and she couldn't quite put her finger on what was causing the implosion.

Carmela pursed her lips and frowned, allowing a few faint crinkles to appear at the corners of her mouth. Blue-gray eyes, with the same flat glint as the Gulf of Mexico, scanned

her notes and hand-drawn pattern, while one hand reached up to haphazardly tousle her caramel-colored chopped and gelled hair.

With a fair complexion, full mouth, and perpetually inquisitive expression, Carmela was quite lovely, even by New Orleans standards, where moonlight and magnolias seemed to be handed out by the bushel basket. But her physical traits, her attractiveness quotient to men, like current boyfriend Lieutenant Edgar Babcock, were the furthest thing from Carmela's mind right now. She was bound and determined to figure out this crazy puppet if it killed her. After all, Halloween was only six days away and this puppet, such as it was, was scheduled to march in the Monsters and Mayhem Torchlight Parade.

"Tell Miguel we're going to wrap for the night," Carmela called to her friend Ava, who'd offered to lend assistance as long as she didn't have to actually handle a needle and thread. Or ponder the puppet's inside hydraulics.

Ava nodded briskly, ran lethal red-lacquered fingernails down her tight red T-shirt to the waist of her skin-tight black leather pants, and nodded. She was a curvaceous almost-thirty, a few months older than Carmela, and a few inches taller. As she strode over to the monster, her four-inch stilettos clicking and clacking above the babble of other float designers in the vast float den, Ava drawled, in a voice dripping with honey, "Miguel, sweetie pie, Carmela says we're gonna bag it."

The strange yellow head seemed to bob in agreement on its stalklike neck, and then the puppet slowly bent forward. As if in slow motion, the creature collapsed into yards of parachute nylon, the fabric whispering softly, like banana leaves in a bayou breeze at midnight. And Miguel Angelle,

Ava's right-hand man at the Juju Voodoo shop, carefully emerged from his costume.

"Hot in there?" Ava asked him. Even though it was cool in the Pluvius float den, Miguel was sweating bullets inside the costume Carmela had designed and painstakingly constructed by hand.

"The mouth's still not working," Miguel told Ava. "Tell Carmela if she wants gnashing teeth, I have to get my hand all the way in there."

"Got it," said Ava as Miguel gathered up gigantic folds of nylon and pushed them at her.

Then Miguel gave a quick wave and was off across the den, dodging groups of other designers who were also putting finishing touches on their Halloween monster puppets.

Ava struggled to strategically fold the costume, finally decided she was fighting a losing battle, and ended up dragging the whole thing over to Carmela's table. "This is like trying to corral liquid mercury," Ava told her friend as Carmela reached out to help gather up the yards of flowing fabric.

"Need some help?" called a male voice.

Carmela recognized the voice instantly and executed a quick spin. "Jekyl!" she called, a grin lighting her face. "What are *you* doing here?"

Jekyl Hardy, one of New Orleans's premier Mardi Gras float designers and an art appraiser by trade, sauntered toward them. Rail thin, dressed completely in black, Jekyl wore his long dark hair pulled back in a severe ponytail, the better to accentuate his pale, oval face.

"In case you ladies hadn't noticed," said Jekyl, tucking his left hand into his black leather jacket and negotiating a slightly stilted bow, "I'm doing a little designing myself for

Monsters and Mayhem." Sidling closer to the two women, Jekyl delivered a chaste peck to Carmela's cheek and exchanged extravagant air kisses with Ava.

"Maybe I should turn this project over to you," said Carmela, looking a little glum.

"Not on your life, darling," purred Jekyl. "I'm positive your puppet's a marvel of magic and engineering. After all, you've got street cred; you're an experienced designer."

"Hardly," said Carmela, who had followed her heart a few years ago and opened Memory Mine, a cozy little scrapbook shop in the French Quarter. Fact was, she adored helping customers create meaningful scrapbook pages, memory boxes, and handmade cards, and would have been sublimely content with that alone, except for the fact that people kept asking her to tackle larger projects, too. Someday, someday soon Carmela hoped, she was going to learn to say no.

"C'mon, *cher*," said Ava, always the upbeat cheerleader. "You're a terrific designer. Remember that runway and backdrop you crafted for Moda Chadron's fashion show? Remember all your crazy ideas for Medusa Manor?"

"Mmm," said Carmela, "I think I'd rather not."

Ava glanced at a row of enormous heads that were stored on shelves against one expanse of wall: a six-foot-high smirking Julius Caesar, a goofy court jester, a medieval dragon, a beady-eyed horse, an Egyptian princess, Fu Manchu, and a Minotaur head, all looking like gigantic victims of a gigantic guillotine.

"Are all those heads going to be made into puppets, too?" Ava asked Jekyl.

Jekyl shifted from one foot to the other, looking reflective. "I hear the dragon's going to be incorporated into one of the Beastmaster Puppet Theater's puppets. And somebody's got

dibs on Julius Caesar, too." He paused. "That fearsome Minotaur head way down at the end was constructed in Hong Kong for *next* year's Pluvius float. As far as the others go . . . they're really just leftovers from past Mardi Gras floats." He made a snarky face. "Unless there's some change in plans I don't know about."

"Uh-oh," said Carmela. She'd just caught a glimpse of someone and instantly recognized his bandy rooster strut.

"What?" Jekyl asked, raising a single eyebrow.

"There's a possible change in plans right now," Carmela murmured under her breath.

The three of them watched as Brett Fowler, captain of the Pluvius krewe, strode arrogantly across the floor. "You people still here?" he called out in a high, reedy voice to everyone in earshot. His reputation as a tough, taciturn guy obviously preceded him, as groups of puppet builders hastily began to pack up.

"We were just leaving," Carmela called to Fowler, hoping to remain on his good side. She turned and said, under her breath, "Come on, guys, let's get out of here."

But Brett Fowler came huffing over to them anyway, his face as florid and red as his hair. "Ladies." He gazed with flat eyes at Carmela and Ava, then turned toward Jekyl. In a chilly tone he said, "Jekyl."

"Really," Carmela told Fowler, "we're going to take off. I know you're probably anxious to lock up."

Fowler glanced at his watch. "You got five minutes." His jowls sloshed from side to side as he talked. He was a man who'd turned to lard from too much of a good thing. That too much being oysters Rockefeller, fried catfish, pecan pie, shrimp bisque, sweet potato pie, and Jack Daniel's. Not necessarily in that order, but definite menu staples in New Or-

leans. "I have to take off," Fowler continued, "but I trust you folks will pull the door shut and set the security system?"

Carmela nodded. "We can do that." She was shocked Fowler hadn't just tossed them out on their ears. Brett Fowler, as Pluvius krewe captain, ran a very tight ship.

Ava dimpled prettily. "So lovely of you to let us use your float den," she trilled.

Fowler ignored her, seemingly immune to Ava's charms. "Just hurry it up," he snapped. Then he fixed his hard eyes on Jekyl again. "Jekyl? Can we have ourselves a conversation?"

"Sure," said Jekyl, although it was clear he really didn't care to. "Why not?" Jekyl shrugged, waggled his fingers good-bye at Carmela and Ava, and reluctantly followed Fowler across the den and out the door.

"Brett Fowler thinks he's so smart," sniffed Ava. "Just because he's rich." Fowler was the senior partner in Emerald Equities, a venture capital firm that had been going like gangbusters for the past couple of years. While everyone else in New Orleans was still dealing with the residual effects of Hurricane Katrina as well as the more recent recession, Fowler's firm seemed to pump out investment returns and continued success.

"But rich doesn't guarantee class," said Carmela. She'd married into one of the wealthiest families in New Orleans, the Meechums of Crescent City Bank notoriety, and they'd turned out to be a bunch of passive-aggressive infighting idiots. Mean as cottonmouths and perpetually snarly. Particularly her ex-husband, Shamus.

Flipping open the lid of a large cardboard box, the box that had once held her wedding dress, Carmela began layering in folds of puppet fabric.

"What do you want to do with the head?" asked Ava, regarding the large monster head.

"Probably leave it here," said Carmela. They'd transported the big goofy head in her car, top down, all the way from her apartment in the French Quarter to the float den in the Central Business District. And judging by the amount of stares and honking horns they'd garnered, had probably looked like some kind of *War of the Worlds* spectacle rolling down the road. Now it seemed far more practical to just leave the big head. After all, they'd be back tomorrow night to tinker with it again.

"So . . . just park it with the other heads?" Ava suggested.

"Sure," said Carmela, glancing around the den, noting the dozen or so enormous Mardi Gras floats that hunkered in the dim light. Adorned with purple and gold foil, the floats seemed to shimmer expectantly, as if they knew that very soon they'd be rolling down Napoleon Avenue, once again enthralling tens of thousands of people.

"Sure do like this monster fella," said Ava, reaching out to touch the jumbo papier-mâché creation.

"Hmm?" said Carmela, glancing around again. For some reason, they seemed to be the only ones left inside the float den. The slight babble of voices and hum of activity had faded away without either of them taking much notice.

Ava bent forward to hoist the bulbous head atop her shoulders. "I think I can . . ."

Without warning, a high, shrieking scream pierced the night.

Ava bobbled the head, almost dropping it, then gazed at Carmela with huge, saucer eyes. "Dear Lord, what was—"

Another pitiful scream rolled at them in excruciating

waves. A death knell of someone who'd been fiendishly attacked!

"Sounds like a banshee cry!" Ava shrilled.

Carmela gulped hard. Whatever it was, it was coming from right outside!

"You think we—" began Ava.

But Carmela was already dashing pell-mell for the door.

"Wait for me!" cried Ava, shrugging off the head. With her longer strides, she caught up with Carmela at the door. Together they pushed open the heavy sliding metal door and stumbled out into the darkness.

"What on earth?" said Carmela. Her eyes instinctively probed the empty parking lot and nearby warehouses.

"I don't see any—" began Ava.

And then Carmela, glancing down, murmured, "Oh no." She put out a hand and caught Ava, before she could take another step forward and contaminate the crime scene.

"What?" asked Ava. Then she followed Carmela's gaze downward. "Holy crapola!" Ava exclaimed in a quavering voice. "Is that who I think it is?"

Carmela nodded silently. Brett Fowler lay spread-eagled in the gravel, faceup, his mouth drawn back in a grim rictus of pain. Spread all around him was an enormous pool of darkness. Blood, Carmela supposed. Lots of blood. Carmela shivered as she took in the hideous details. At Fowler's feet lay the large, discarded Minotaur head. Its ugly, bullish snout was punched in; its glassy red eyes reflected madness. Its massive horns curled upward into nasty, sharp points.

"Dear Lord!" exclaimed Ava. "Somebody stuck Brett Fowler with that awful Minotaur head."

Carmela stared at Fowler's crumpled body, slowly leaking pints of blood. She took a couple of tentative steps forward

and reached out her hand. Touched the razor-sharp horns of the Minotaur head. Her fingers came away warm and sticky. "Not just stuck him," Carmela told her friend as she drew a single, shaky breath. "Gored him to death."

⟦ Chapter 2 ⟧

CARMELA did not call 911 like a good little girl. Instead, she phoned Lieutenant Edgar Babcock, homicide detective and her own personal snuggle bunny. Babcock arrived with a blat of sirens and a screech of vehicles. The cavalry coming to the rescue. Only there was no one to rescue, the murderous deed already a fait accompli. And once Babcock had hurriedly scoped out the murder scene and asked a few terse questions of Carmela and Ava, he didn't exactly give off cordial vibes.

"Did you touch the victim in any way?" Babcock asked them. Babcock was tall, lanky, and handsome. His ginger-colored hair was cropped short and neat, his blue eyes constant pinpricks of intensity. And he was always amazingly well dressed. A cop with a curious taste for designer duds.

Carmela shook her head. "No, of course not. I wouldn't do that. Disturb the crime scene, I mean."

"Definitely not," said Ava.

"Did you try to help him in any way?" asked Babcock. He stared at Carmela with a kind of grim determination. Probably the look most homicide detectives assumed once they were on the job. After all, their day at the office usually entailed firsthand knowledge of the Grim Reaper.

"No point in trying to help him," Carmela told Babcock. "Fowler was dead when we found him."

"How'd you know he was dead?" asked a plainclothes policeman who was kneeling over the body. He was young, dark-haired, dressed in a black jacket and chinos. Though he appeared cool and uninterested, he probably wasn't.

"Carmela, Ava," said Babcock. "This is Bobby Gallant."

"How do," said Ava, while Carmela nodded politely.

Bobby Gallant glanced up at them. "Nice to meet you." His gaze lingered on Carmela. "Finally."

"So how did you know Fowler was dead?" Babcock asked again, as gravel crunched and three men from the crime-scene unit came up behind him.

"Because," said Ava, lifting a hand to rapidly fan her face, "we heard him screaming like some kind of wild forest banshee."

"Understood," said Babcock. "But you said you perceived the victim as actually being *deceased* . . . why was that?"

Ava gazed at Babcock, looking perturbed. She licked her lips, then finally said, "How 'bout this? Because when we ran out here and found him, he was lying in a big old nasty puddle of blood?"

"And the horns on that Minotaur head were smeared with blood," Carmela pointed out. She was trying to be as helpful as possible, attempting to be as cool and professional as the detectives.

"Minotaur?" asked Gallant. As he clambered to his feet, his knees made little popping sounds.

"It's a mythical beast," Ava explained, gazing at Babcock, since he was the man in charge. "A half-bull, half-man that lived at the center of the Labyrinth, this mazelike—"

"I know what a labyrinth is," Babcock said, pulling a small spiral notebook from the inside pocket of his Harris tweed jacket. "I minored in classics."

"Gosh," said Ava, looking flustered. "And here I thought you got that nice shiny shield from one of those online cop shops."

"Sorry to disappoint you," Babcock said in a crisp tone. "Okay, how about the three of us move inside and finish this? Let Detective Gallant and the crime-scene boys do their work."

Carmela and Ava trooped back into the float den, with Babcock trailing behind them. He looked around the dimly lit float den and seemed to be formulating questions.

"Who else was here with you tonight?" Babcock stared at Carmela, carefully maintaining his professional distance.

Carmela, of course, wanted to throw her arms around Babcock and plant a great big old smooch on his handsome face. Instead, she hung tight to her composure and tried to answer his questions as best she could. She knew he had a job to do. "Jekyl Hardy was here at one point," she told him. "And maybe a dozen other designers and artists. Oh, and Miguel."

"Who's Miguel?" asked Babcock, jotting notes in his book.

"My assistant," Ava offered. "At Juju Voodoo."

The corners of Babcock's mouth twitched. "You need an assistant? To sell saint candles and voodoo trinkets?"

Ava wasn't amused. "You think selling fake bat's blood and love charms is easy in this economy? Listen, cupcake, I need a primo shtick that appeals to tourists. And lots and lots of help."

"I'm sure these are difficult times for all of us," said Babcock. "But let's get back to tidying up some details. There were other folks working here tonight?"

"Like I said," said Carmela. "Maybe a dozen or more."

"Or more," said Ava.

"Can you give me specific names?" asked Babcock, his pen poised.

Carmela and Ava stared at each other, thinking. Finally Carmela said, "Not really. We were pretty focused on our own project."

"Do you know what the others were working on?" asked Babcock.

"Kind of," said Ava.

"Then we can probably figure it out from there," said Babcock. "Now, you say Miguel left *before* your friend Jekyl Hardy arrived?"

Both women nodded.

"And did Mr. Hardy speak with Mr. Fowler?" asked Babcock.

Ava snorted. "If you could call it that."

Babcock's eyebrows shot up. "There was some sort of altercation?"

"Not really," said Carmela.

"I'll say there was," said Ava.

Babcock gazed at them. "Which was it?"

"They didn't get along," Carmela admitted. "Never have." *Oops, past tense.* "Uh, never did."

"And why was that?" asked Babcock.

"Oh," said Carmela, thinking, "Brett Fowler was always trying to bring in this other float designer, Jimmy Toups, that he deemed as being more creative and imaginative than Jekyl. Kind of dangled the guy over Jekyl's head. Plus Fowler hadn't completely paid Jekyl for his work on *last* year's floats."

"Are we talking a lot of money?" asked Babcock.

"Not sure," said Carmela. "But the rotten thing about Fowler was that he was always bragging about his company, Emerald Equities. He was constantly yammering about some hot deal he'd just engineered. And, of course, he'd been written up in the business section of the *Times-Picayune* a couple of months ago. And I'm pretty sure he was on several boards of directors. Face it, Fowler wasn't exactly low key."

"A real blowhard," muttered Ava.

Babcock kept his face relaxed and his tone neutral. "Can you think of anyone who might have wanted to kill Brett Fowler?"

"Business associates?" suggested Carmela. "He was pretty annoying."

"How about his wife?" suggested Ava.

"What about his wife?" asked Babcock.

Now Ava retreated a little. "I don't like to speak ill of the dead."

"Speak ill," invited Babcock. "Live dangerously."

"Well, according to local legend and lore," Ava said, in a conspiratorial tone, "Sissy tossed him out of his Garden District home a few months ago." Sissy Fowler was Brett Fowler's estranged wife, now widow.

"The rumor's always been that Sissy was the one with real money," added Carmela.

Ava nodded eagerly. "She's, like, always decked out in Dior and Prada."

"And Roberto Cavalli," added Carmela. Couldn't forget old Roberto Cavalli with his wild prints and gilded details.

Babcock looked interested. "Forgetting the designer aspect, what did you mean by *real money*?"

"Old money," said Carmela, enunciating carefully.

"The very best kind to have," agreed Ava. "Think rich great-granddaddies and trust funds. Silver spoons and private schools."

This time Carmela remained silent, thinking about her ex-husband, Shamus. He was old New Orleans money. And had money bought him a speck of happiness? Well, not exactly. Of course, money had bought him a great deal of comfort and some awfully spiffy toys. And her divorce settlement hadn't been all that shabby . . .

Babcock tapped his pen against the cover of his notebook, looking thoughtful. "Jekyl Hardy was here tonight . . . for what reason?" He cocked his head slightly as Bobby Gallant and a uniformed officer came trooping in to join him.

"Just kind of checking out the puppets," Carmela told him, trying to soft-pedal Jekyl's role in the whole thing.

"Puppets?" said Babcock. His eyes took on a slightly glazed expression while Gallant made a sound in the back of his throat.

"That's what tonight was all about," said Carmela. *Did he not see the Minotaur head? Doesn't he know what I was doing here?*

Ava put her hands on her shapely hips and slid a step closer to the three men. Her slinky movement was not lost on, or unappreciated by, any of them.

"Puppets for the big Halloween parade this coming

Sunday," Ava explained in a somewhat stern tone of voice. "Monsters and Mayhem is this year's theme."

"In case you gents aren't aware," said Carmela, "the French Quarter is staging a hearse procession, a Day of the Dead candle procession, and a Halloween parade with giant puppets." She halted her words and frowned. For some reason, this conversation (interrogation?) wasn't going as well as she thought it would. For one thing, she didn't like the way Babcock had quizzed her about Jekyl.

"We know all about the Halloween celebration," said Bobby Gallant. "In fact, we've already assigned some plainclothes officers to cover the French Quarter. Too many reports of tourists getting their wallets stolen."

"We're hoping to catch this pickpocket or ring of pickpockets before the big Halloween shebang," put in the other officer.

"That's mighty good to know," said Ava. She for one didn't relish having potential customers robbed of their money before she could lay a little voodoo sales patois on them.

"So you were working on a puppet, too?" Babcock asked. He hadn't taken his gaze off Carmela.

"We are," said Carmela. "For the New Orleans Art Institute. Angela Boynton, one of their curators, asked for our design help."

"Such as it is," said Ava, adding a little shrug. We're not like *real* designers or puppet makers. We just sort of fool around with papier-mâché and stuff."

Carmela decided she didn't need to mention to Babcock that her former marriage to Shamus Allan Meechum had landed her squarely in the Art Institute's big-buck Platinum Patrons Circle—which provided her with compli-

mentary tickets and invitations to all events, openings, and receptions where stuffed cherry tomatoes and cheap white wine were freely dispensed. Hence the connection to the Art Institute.

"Show me the puppet," said Babcock in a pleasant tone.

They all walked back to the far corner of the den where Carmela's table was still set up. She pulled out the fabric, draped it over Ava, then plopped the giant head on her friend's shoulders. Together they watched as internal mechanisms elongated the creature's neck and caused the head to tower above them.

"Wow," said one of the officers.

In the low light, the puppet, with its oversized skull and LED eyes, looked downright menacing.

"What's it made of?" asked Babcock.

"I fashioned the body sleeve out of parachute nylon," Carmela told him. "And the head's carved from urethane foam—the kind most often used for seat cushions. That way there's room for handholds and a few other tricks." With a touch of pride in her voice, she said, "I call it the Crunch Monster."

"Does it actually *do* anything?" inquired Babcock.

As if on cue, Ava flipped a switch inside the head. The misshapen head glowed orange, the mouth pulled back into a menacing gnash, the eyes lolled toward them, and a pair of skeletal arms seemed to float upward.

"Holy buckets," exclaimed Gallant, "your puppet's a real killer!"

"No," Carmela said, quietly. "That was the Minotaur head."

Chapter 3

BOO and Poobah, Carmela's two inquisitive dogs, met her at the door. Boo, a cutie-pie female Shar-Pei, lunged for the box in her arms and managed to snag a piece of nylon with her teeth. Poobah, a black-and-white mongrel, snapped at the fabric but hung back. The shy guy of the two.

"Boo, honey," Ava admonished, "your momma's gonna tan your hide if you rip any of that fabric." She shooed the dogs away and helped carry the carton into Carmela's living room.

Carmela dropped her hobo bag on the floor and pushed back a hank of honey-blond hair. "What a night."

"Kersplat," echoed Ava. Kicking off her stilettos, she padded across the floor in her bare feet and flopped down on Carmela's leather chaise lounge.

"First thing we have to do," said Carmela, "is call Jekyl."

Ava looked concerned. "You don't think a SWAT team stormed his apartment and hauled his skinny ass down to the station, do you? To, you know, whack him around a bit?"

"I certainly hope not," said Carmela.

Ava grimaced. "Or maybe they're waterboarding him."

"If they are, he probably conned them into using strawberry daiquiris," said Carmela, dialing the phone.

"Wouldn't put it past him," giggled Ava. "New Orleans being the drive-through daiquiri capital of the world. And thank goodness for that!"

"Jekyl?" said Carmela, when her friend answered. "You okay?"

"Did the police question him?" Ava asked in a stage whisper.

But Carmela was busy listening and nodding. "Okay, okay," she murmured into the phone. "Sure. Good luck. Call me when you can."

"No problem, huh?" said Ava.

"*Humongous* problem," said Carmela. "The police are there now."

"Aw, crap," said Ava. She fluffed her abundant mane of dark hair, looking more than a little concerned. "But Jekyl doesn't have anything to worry about, does he?"

"Not that I can think of," said Carmela.

"Just a slight matter of wrong place, wrong time," said Ava.

"Easily cleared up," Carmela agreed.

Ava nodded. "Of course Jekyl and Brett Fowler hated each other. *Despised* each other."

"There is that little detail," said Carmela.

"And everyone pretty much *knew* they were constantly at odds."

"It was no big secret," Carmela agreed.

"Oh man!" said Ava, looking glum. "Jekyl's in dippity-deep doo-doo, isn't he?"

"Exactly my thoughts," responded Carmela.

"Now I'm depressed," said Ava, splaying out her long legs on the lounger. "And when I get depressed, I get hungry. Ravenous, in fact."

"You want me to rustle up something to eat?" Carmela asked.

Ava's face lit up with excitement. "You have actual food?" Ava's notion of a well-stocked larder was a bottle of Dom Perignon and a plastic bag of miniature carrots in the refrigerator. Limp miniature carrots. Oh, and a five-year-old box of baking soda. Then again, pretty much everyone had that in their fridge.

"I can always find something," said Carmela. That smidgen of Cajun blood that flowed through her veins meant she also had a fine appreciation for food.

"When have you ever known me to turn down food?" asked Ava.

Carmela thought for a minute. "Never. Well, maybe once when you had the stomach flu."

"No," said Ava, "you still brought me shrimp chowder and cheddar cheese biscuits."

"Now that I recall, you wolfed down every bit of it," said Carmela, shaking her head at the memory. "Really amazing."

"I have a hardy constitution," said Ava.

Ambling over to her galley kitchen, Carmela pulled open the refrigerator door and peered inside. It wasn't jam-packed, but the cupboard wasn't entirely bare, either. "There's crawfish jambalaya and some corn bread," she called to Ava.

Ava perked up considerably. "Is the jambalaya from your own recipe with those spicy habanero peppers?"

"Uh . . . yup."

"Yum yum, you're a lifesaver!"

While Carmela heated jambalaya in a saucepan and popped squares of corn bread into the microwave, Ava spread out bright yellow plates and bowls and antique sterling flatware on Carmela's dining room table.

"*Cher*," said Ava, squinting at a stone lion. "You got a new piece of art."

"Picked it up at Preservation Antiques," said Carmela. "Like it?" The stone lion was at least two feet tall, ferocious looking, with one paw resting on a shield. "It's eighteenth-century French."

"Love it," said Ava. "And it's just perfect in your apartment." Carmela's one-bedroom garden apartment was a *tour de force* of antiques. Posh and elegant from dozens of forays through scratch-and-dent rooms of Royal Street antique shops, the living room was furnished with a brocade fainting couch, marble coffee table, and squishy leather chaise with ottoman. An ornate gilded mirror hung on one wall; lengths of handmade wrought iron that had once graced an antebellum mansion hung on the opposite red brick wall. The wrought iron made a perfect shelf for her bronze dog statues and collection of antique children's books.

"I picked up a new book, too," Carmela told Ava. "*The Border Boys with the Texas Rangers*. Published in nineteen twelve."

Ava pulled herself up, tottered across the room, and found the book on the shelf. She smiled. "I love this cover," she said, gazing at an illustration of a boy riding a bucking bronco. "It's got that authentic woodcut feel."

"Doesn't it?" said Carmela. "There's a whole series of those books, but that's my first one." She turned from where she'd been stirring a pot at the stove. "Do you think you should call Miguel?"

Ava bit her lip. "You think?"

Carmela nodded.

"What's wrong?" Ava asked, almost shouting into the phone. She listened for a few seconds, then turned to Carmela. "The police are at his apartment, too." Then she was back talking to Miguel. "Just tell 'em that you left early and that we'll back you up on it, okay? Okay. Sure. See you tomorrow." She hung up the phone, turned to Carmela, and frowned. "That's so not fair that they're questioning him. All Miguel did was help out and then leave early. I don't think he's ever met Brett Fowler."

"The police are just doing their job," said Carmela. Now that she was actually dating a member of the NOPD, she was somewhat forgiving in her assessment of law enforcement's tactics.

"No, they're not," argued Ava. "Not really. The police are basically wasting precious time when they should be out looking for the *real* killer."

"Who is . . . ?" said Carmela.

Ava shrugged. "Search me."

"You think he was there tonight?" Carmela wondered. "In the building? With us?"

"That's a cheery thought," said Ava, looking even more serious.

"C'mon," said Carmela, carrying food to the table. "Let's eat. You'll feel better about things once you get some food in your tummy."

"You know," said Ava, slipping into a chair, "I think you're right."

But as they chowed down on jambalaya and corn bread, they continued to ponder suspects.

"Sissy Fowler is a real character," said Ava, referring to the wife of the very dead Brett Fowler.

"But is she a crazy person?" Carmela asked. "Because it would take a crazy person to don a Minotaur head and then attack someone. Particularly if that someone was her husband."

"Thinking of all the Pluvius parades that Fowler has honchoed," said Ava, "he met with a very bizarre ending. Almost . . . poetic."

"Maybe if the poem is by Edgar Allan Poe," Carmela observed.

"Hah," said Ava, pointing a spoon at her. "Good one."

"I can think of a half-dozen guys who didn't like Brett Fowler," said Carmela.

"It's a big jump from 'didn't like' to killing someone," said Ava.

"Of course," said Carmela, "it could have been someone who wasn't even connected to the Pluvius krewe. Say, for instance, a business associate."

"You mean like a partner or something?"

"I was thinking more of a disgruntled client," said Carmela. "You've had disgruntled clients, right? I know *I've* had disgruntled clients."

"Oh yeah," said Ava. "I had one lady who bought a deck of tarot cards, then came back and threw them in my face. Claimed they were old cards and had lost their potency. When I gave her my 'for amusement only' spiel she really got mad!"

"So what'd you do?"

"I picked up the scattered cards and did a tarot reading on the spot. Told her she was filled with hostility and rage and that it would probably boomerang back at her, raining down bad luck." Ava smiled. "That did the trick. She got scared and ran out."

"Good save," said Carmela.

"This jambalaya is exquisite," said Ava, spooning it up like mad. "Someday you'll have to give me the recipe."

"Someday you might even learn how to cook," replied Carmela.

"Someday." Ava sighed. "Right after I learn how to hang glide and speak Croatian, which is never. Say, is Babcock gonna drop by tonight?"

"Why do you ask?"

Ava grinned. "Because he drops by almost every night?"

"You spying on me?" Ava lived directly across the court-yard in the second-floor apartment above her Juju Voodoo shop.

Ava shook her head. "Nope. I would never do that."

"Well, I doubt that he is," Carmela said slowly. "No, I'm pretty sure he's not."

"He say something?" asked Ava.

"Just a hunch I have," said Carmela. "A vibe."

"You have good vibes," said Ava.

Thirty minutes later they were chatting and watching TV. Ava sipped from a bottle of RC Cola as she nibbled a MoonPie.

"Uh-oh," said Carmela, glancing toward the phone. At which point it suddenly rang.

"Holy Toledo!" Ava exclaimed. "You just had one of your hunches!"

" 'Fraid so," said Carmela, grabbing for the phone.

"There was an accident," came a deadpan voice. "You were there."

Carmela dropped the receiver to her chest. "Bull-dingers," she said to Ava. "It's Shamus."

"What does he want?" asked Ava. "Can't that boy get it through his Cro-Magnon skull that you two are finally divorced?" She reached out and patted Boo on the head, then slipped her a crumb of MoonPie. "What's the problem, anyway? Did he drink and dial?" Poobah stuck his head toward Ava, and she slipped him a bit of MoonPie, too.

Carmela put the phone back to her ear. "Did you drink and dial?" she asked her ex.

"No," Shamus replied in a snippy tone. "You know I wouldn't do that."

"Duh," said Carmela. "What about last week?"

Shamus let loose an exasperated sigh. "That was me concerned about the dogs."

"That was you crocked," Carmela told him. "Wound up on Chivas Regal after you struck out on your date with Lilly what's-her-name."

"Listen, Carmela," Shamus said in his I'm-dead-serious voice. "I need to know what happened to Brett Fowler at the Pluvius den tonight." Shamus was a member of the Pluvius krewe and prided himself on his active participation. If you could call drinking, tossing beads, and dressing up in masks and togas active participation.

"How did you know I was even there?" asked Carmela. *How did he?*

"I have my ways," said Shamus. "So what I need to know is . . ." Shamus yapped in her ear for a few more seconds, and then his voice grew fainter as a competing cacophony of voices chattered in the background.

"Shamus?" said Carmela. "Are you still there? Or did you drift away on me?" *Like you did in real life?*

"Crappity-doo-dah!" Shamus cried, back on the phone with her now, sounding genuinely upset. "TV news already picked it up."

"It's on the news," Carmela told Ava.

"Good," said Ava.

"I heard that," said Shamus, "and it's *not* good! In fact, it's terrible! Brett Fowler's murder is going to be a terrible black mark against the Pluvius krewe!"

"Oh please," said Carmela, rolling her eyes. "You think the city of New Orleans is going to revoke your charter? Forbid a bunch of overgrown boys from building *floats*? Get real, Shamus, you're not so much worried about Brett Fowler's murder as you are about your boy-toy trappings."

"Tell Shamus his krewe already has a rotten reputation," Ava called out. "So what's a little more bad press?"

"I'll be the first to admit Fowler was no prize," said Shamus, "but for somebody to off the guy? That's absurd!"

"You sure we're talking about the same Brett Fowler?" Carmela asked him. "The one with the smart mouth and nasty streak? That one?" She was winding up now for a nice line drive down center field. "The one that got drunk at Antoine's during last year's Mardi Gras and ran around making donkey noises while trying to peer up women's skirts?"

"Yes, yes," said Shamus. "I appreciate that Fowler had a playful side. I also know you two never got along."

"That might be soft-pedaling it a tad," said Carmela. "I'm not sure *anybody* got along with him."

Shamus pretended he hadn't heard her. "Tell me about the murder," he demanded.

"No way."

"C'mon, Carmela, I need to know. It's important."

"I'm not at liberty to talk about it," said Carmela.

"To me?" asked Shamus, "or to anyone?"

"Anyone," said Carmela. "Police orders."

"Orders from any policeman in particular?" Shamus asked, his voice dripping with sarcasm.

Carmela kept her cool. Did Shamus know that she and Babcock were as cozy as they were? She didn't think so. Then again, Shamus was a schmoozer and a player around town. He could have easily found out, just the way he'd found out about Fowler's murder. "The police told us to keep a lid on," said Carmela. "While they conduct their investigation."

"Huh," said Shamus. Then he fell silent.

"Anything else?" Carmela asked, anxious to be rid of him.

"One thing," said Shamus.

"Hmm?"

"When are you moving into the Garden District home?"

He had her there. "Hmm?" she said, stalling.

"In case you don't remember, it's the great big house with the formal gardens in back that you coveted greatly. The one you were so magnanimously rewarded in our divorce decree."

Magnanimous, my butt, thought Carmela. *It took me three years of hard wrangling to finally get that piece of property.*

"I'll have to get back to you on that," Carmela told him. Truth be told, she was thinking of selling the place. It was

way too big for her, a mansion really, and the money from the sale, invested wisely, would go a long, long way.

"That home was in our family for years," said Shamus, his voice going hoarse and slightly weepy now. "Glory *gave* me that home." Glory was Shamus's tight-fisted, morally bipolar big sister. Vice president of Crescent City Bank.

"And then you gave it to me," said Carmela.

"Just for safekeeping," wheedled Shamus. "Think of it as a kind of stewardship."

"No," said Carmela, putting a little oomph in her voice, "it was payment. Payment in full for putting up with the likes of you."

The phone crashed down in her ear.

"Okey-doke," Carmela said to dead air. "You take care now."

"What's his *problema*?" asked Ava.

"Nothing earth-shattering," said Carmela. "Mostly he was being antagonistic."

"*Man*tagonistic." Ava sighed. "Typical." She paused. "He asked about the house, didn't he?"

"He did," said Carmela. Their recently signed divorce papers had been grinding their way through the court system. In another week or two, the place would be hers—lock, stock, and barrel. The spoils of war for her on-again off-again marriage to Shamus Allan Meechum.

"You going to live there?" asked Ava. " 'Cause if you up and move I'd miss you horribly." She leaned forward and grasped Boo's furry head between her hands. "Yes, I would, baby Boo. Auntie Ava would miss Carmela and her darling fur babies."

Boo grinned at Ava and wagged her tight, curly tail.

"I'm not sure I want to move in there," said Carmela. "Selling it would be the smart thing to do."

"Ho ho!" roared Ava. "Shamus would have a shit fit if you did that."

Carmela shrugged. "It would serve him right, after being such a demon about this divorce."

"Shave that boy's head and you'll probably find 666 carved into his skull," Ava chortled.

"Ava!" said Carmela. "That's a very creepy thought."

Ava let loose a little shiver and gave a sheepish smile. "Well, it *is* the week before Halloween!"

Chapter 4

THE next morning's headline in the *Times-Picayune* smacked Carmela right between the eyes: *Ponzi Scheme Partner Murdered.*

"Did you see this?" Gabby asked, thrusting the paper at Carmela. As Carmela's number one assistant, Gabby opened Memory Mine promptly at nine, while Carmela usually came flying in around nine thirty.

"I didn't just see it," Carmela told her, a little breathless now, "I was there!"

"What?" shrilled Gabby. She stood behind the front counter, behind the stickers and stencils and loops of fiber, holding a hand to her mouth.

"And, excuse me," continued Carmela, "but what exactly is this Ponzi scheme thing?"

"You really didn't read the article, did you?"

"No," said Carmela, slipping out of her suede jacket and

running a hand through slightly disheveled hair. She'd managed blusher and eyeliner, but a styling comb and mousse had somehow eluded her. Oh well, the bed-head look was in, wasn't it? "I don't take the morning paper anymore," Carmela explained. "Boo and Poobah kept ripping it to shreds, so I just gave up." On the plus side, the dogs were a great help in ripping up all those unwanted credit card offers that found their way to her mailbox each week. Who needed to spend sixty bucks on a paper shredder from Office Depot when dogs were so willing to shred gratis?

Gabby plunked the newspaper into Carmela's eager hands. "Read!" she commanded.

Carmela quickly scanned the front-page article. "My name is in here as witness to Fowler's murder!"

"Did you really see it?" asked Gabby.

"No," said Carmela.

"Keep reading," said Gabby.

As Carmela continued to digest the article, her heart sank and her blood pressure slowly blipped upward. Finally she said, "Fowler's company was *scamming* investors? Is this for real?"

"Read the whole thing," Gabby prompted. Her luminous dark eyes looked even more serious than usual, and she twisted a delicate hand in her flowing dark hair. Always dressed in her ubiquitous preppy style, Gabby today wore a yellow cashmere twinset with tailored khaki slacks and Tory Burch flats.

"Wait a minute!" said Carmela. "It also says here that Brett Fowler was *indicted* two days ago by the Securities Division of Louisiana's Office of Financial Institutions!"

"Yes!" shrilled Gabby. "Can you believe it?"

Carmela mumbled to herself for a few moments, then read aloud. "Investigators speculate that Fowler may have

funneled off millions of dollars from Emerald Equities to support his own personal, lavish lifestyle." She paused. "Holy magoomba!" Carmela looked up at a seriously distraught Gabby. "I'm stunned."

"*You're* stunned!" Gabby exclaimed. "We—Stuart and I—knew Brett Fowler socially, through the New Orleans Symphony and the Delta Foundation. Stuart even has . . . had . . . money invested with Emerald Equities!" Stuart Mercer-Morris was Gabby's slightly controlling husband and the Toyota King of New Orleans. "But after reading this," Gabby continued, "I'm worried sick at the possibility we might have lost our investments!"

"I think you should be darned nervous," said Carmela, still reading, still amazed. "Who would have guessed silly old Brett Fowler was such a pirate!"

"Looks like," said Gabby, starting to daub at her eyes.

"Which also means," said Carmela, jumping to what she deemed a fairly obvious conclusion, "that any number of people might have wanted Fowler dead."

"They would if they lost their money," said Gabby.

"Have you talked to Stuart about this?" asked Carmela. "I don't mean about Fowler being murdered, but about your investments? Do you know if you actually did lose money?"

Gabby shook her head, looking sorrowful. "No idea. Stuart had an early breakfast meeting at the Kingston Athletic Club, so he was gone when I got up."

"I think you better call him," said Carmela.

"Interrupt him?" said Gabby.

"Sure," said Carmela. "Why not? This is important."

"The thing is," said Gabby, looking timid, "Stuart takes care of all our investments."

"And I think it's really great that Stuart's so smart about

money and stuff," said Carmela. "But you're married, honey. And Louisiana, being a joint property state, says that half that money is *your* money."

Gabby fidgeted with her wedding ring.

"Remember your vows?" asked Carmela. "For better or worse. For richer or poorer?"

Gabby nodded with slightly more conviction.

"Good," said Carmela. "So you have every right in the world to know if you're suddenly poorer. To find out exactly how much of your money was hanging out there with Emerald Equities."

"You think?" asked Gabby.

"I know," said Carmela.

"Okay," agreed Gabby. "You're good at business, so I'll take your word for it."

Carmela pulled her cell phone from her bag. "You call Stuart while I give Edgar Babcock a jingle and see what he knows about this. He didn't mention a darned thing about it last night. Doggone him . . ."

Gabby stared at her bravely. "Meet you back here in ten minutes?"

"Count on it," said Carmela, heading for her office.

"Babcock!" Carmela sputtered, once she had him on the phone. "I just saw this morning's headlines!"

"That so?" came his casual reply.

"What's this about an Emerald Equities investment scam?" she demanded.

"Hmm?"

"Don't play coy with me," Carmela snarled. "You *knew* about it. You *had* to know about it."

"You're referring to . . ."

"The fact that Brett Fowler cheated investors and cooked the books. And you knew about this . . . this . . ." She quickly scanned the newspaper article again, looking for the precise word. "This indictment."

"You are quite correct, my dear."

"But you came waltzing to the scene of the murder last night, acting like it was some wacky incident out of the blue. And all along you were fully cognizant that Brett Fowler probably had a bull's-eye painted on his back. And . . . and . . . you didn't say word one to me!" For some reason she felt deeply betrayed.

"Carmela," said Edgar Babcock, sounding frustrated. But Carmela wasn't finished yet.

"Seems to me," said Carmela, "there must be a long list of New Orleans fat cats who got snookered by Fowler's slippery, slimy, financial impropriety. And once they figured out their investments were just smoke and mirrors, they might have wished him dead! Wanted him dead!"

"Okay," said Babcock, "now you know the full story. What do you want me to do about it?"

"For one thing," said Carmela, "lay off Jekyl Hardy. No way is he your killer."

"You know that for sure?"

"Of course I do," said Carmela. "And neither is Miguel Angelle."

"You sure about that, too?"

"Oh please," said Carmela, in a voice tinged with disgust.

"Listen," said Babcock, "you really need to stay out of this. To not get involved."

"I'm *already* involved," Carmela screeched. "I'm the un-

lucky lady who discovered Fowler's body. His dead, bloody, gored body."

"I understand," said Babcock. "You were there. But now you need to take a deep breath and step back. Let us do our work."

"*Us* being . . ."

"My team of homicide detective as well as the legal eagles at the Louisiana Securities Division."

"Something tells me it's going to be a mess," said Carmela.

"Of course it is." Babcock sighed. "It was a tangled web before the murder." Silence spun out between them, and then he said, "I'm swamped today with meetings. But what if I dropped by your place tonight?"

"For your little bit of R&R?" Carmela asked in an arch tone. "I'm not just your drop-by girlfriend, you know."

"It wouldn't be a booty call," promised Babcock.

"So you say," said Carmela.

Just as she was about to toss her cell phone back into her bag, her Lady Gaga ringtone chimed again. Carmela checked her screen, thumbed the On button, and said, "Jekyl?"

"Yeah," came his soft voice. "It's me."

"You okay? No more repercussions from last night?"

"Are you kidding?" Jekyl sighed. "I just came out of an hour-long meeting with two more homicide detectives."

That rat-fink Babcock, Carmela thought to herself. No way was she going to back off now. Not when one of her best friends was getting hassled. And no way was he coming over tonight for a little friends-with-benefits session.

"So the police are still on your case?" she asked him.

"And then some," said Jekyl. "Boo-hoo."

"Something's fishy," said Carmela. "What makes you *numero uno* on their suspect list?"

"Meet me for lunch and I'll tell you all about it," said Jekyl.

"Glisande's at one?" Carmela suggested. Glisande's Courtyard Restaurant was just across Governor Nicholls Street from Carmela's scrapbook shop.

"I'll be there with bells on," Jekyl promised.

"Good news," said Gabby as Carmela came barreling out of her office, riffling stacks of scrapbook paper as she passed by. "I just talked to Stuart."

"All quiet on the financial front?" Carmela asked, a hopeful note in her voice.

"He thinks so," said Gabby. She put a hand to her chest, made a big show of shaking her head, and breathed out a long *whew*. Then she added, "And if we *have* lost any money, well, it wasn't the entire ball of wax."

"Not the whole magilla," said Carmela. "Glad to hear it."

"You talked to Babcock?" Gabby asked, the Brett Fowler murder still obviously on her mind.

Carmela's brows knit together. "Tried to, but he was amazingly tight-lipped. Something tells me this is going to be a major, pull-out-all-the-stops investigation. Because it's not just about Fowler's murder; the whole Emerald Equities fraud is wrapped up in it, too."

Gabby nodded slowly.

"And for some reason," said Carmela, "the police are sniffing suspiciously at Jekyl's dapper little Cuban heels."

"Because he was at the float den last night?"

Carmela thought for a moment. "Yeah, but so were lots of people. I'm not sure being in the same *vicinity* is reason enough to grill Jekyl for a couple of hours."

"What do the police know that you don't?" wondered Gabby.

"I don't know," said Carmela, "but I'm going to find out."

"Good for you." Gabby grinned. "Dig around and do your sleuthing thing. Lord knows, you're good at it."

"I wouldn't say that," said Carmela.

"Oh, but you are," Gabby assured her. "You even pulled Shamus's fat out of the fire on more than one occasion."

"Don't remind me," said Carmela. She reached for a packet of eyelash ribbon, pulled it from its plastic package, and twined it around her fingers. Working off nervous energy.

"Of course," said Gabby, "this is going to be an awfully busy week. You've got the Fiber Arts seminar tomorrow, a couple of Halloween make-and-take classes, and your puppet project for Monsters and Mayhem. By the way, how's your monster puppet coming?"

"A genuine monstrosity," said Carmela. "Looks a lot like my initial sketches."

"And those were great," said Gabby. "Scary!"

"I think the actual puppet will be even better than the design."

"But you're not done yet."

"Ava and I were hoping to finish tonight," said Carmela.

"So you're going back to . . ." Gabby's voice trailed off.

"To the Pluvius den, yes," said Carmela.

"The scene of the crime," said Gabby. "Aren't you worried?"

"Not any more than I was last night," said Carmela as the phone on the front desk began to ring.

With her usual grace and efficiency, Gabby grabbed the phone and greeted the caller. She listened for a few moments, then turned to Carmela. "Do we have room for two more people tomorrow?"

"We'll make room," Carmela whispered. "Maybe slide the paper display into my office so we can add another table and chairs. Just remember to call the rental company and up our order."

"Of course you can come tomorrow," Gabby purred into the phone as Carmela glanced about her scrapbook shop. Tomorrow's Fiber Arts seminar was just one in a long line of specialty seminars she'd been sponsoring. Paper Moon had come first, showcasing all the wonderful mulberry, bamboo, vellum, lokta, and art papers. Then they'd done Arts d'Italia, using Italian-themed stamps and faux fresco techniques to create miniature Italian theaters, wine labels, carnival masks, and miniature books.

After that, Carmela had done a daylong seminar on keepsake boxes. That one had really been fun because it incorporated scrapping, stamping, decoupage, and design techniques on small wooden and metal boxes.

The seminars and special events were all carefully designed, of course, to funnel business into Memory Mine. That gigantic hiccup known as Hurricane Katrina was still making its presence felt in New Orleans and its surrounding parishes some six years later. Business was good and leaning toward better, but it still wasn't stellar, the way it had been in those halcyon pre-Katrina days. Memory Mine pumped out a living for Carmela, a fairly decent living at that, but after salaries, rent, and payments to suppliers, there wasn't

much of a profit. And in terms of business standards and practices, the difference between making a living and making a profit was enormous.

"Eighteen people," said Gabby, jotting a note to herself and looking pleased. "That's how many we've got coming tomorrow."

Carmela did her mental arithmetic. Eighteen people times fifty dollars per head was nine hundred dollars. Add in the extra paper, albums, fiber, ribbons, stamp pads, and charms that the scrappers would probably buy and you had yourself a very healthy day's sales.

"So what we need to do now," said Carmela, "is organize for the onslaught. Gather up all our fibers and ribbons and strings, then stash them in plastic bins for safekeeping. That way we can burst out of the starting gate first thing tomorrow."

"I hear you," said Gabby.

"And I've got to finish instruction sheets for all the projects."

"Are you going to demonstrate a couple of larger projects or mostly have make-and-takes?" asked Gabby.

"This and that," said Carmela. "A little of both."

"You're being very mysterious."

"I don't mean to be."

"Preoccupied, then," said Gabby.

"That must be it," said Carmela, who still hadn't quite shaken the gruesome image of Brett Fowler sprawled in a pool of his own blood.

Chapter 5

"CAR-MEL-A!" cried Tandy Bliss as she came flying through the front door of Memory Mine, her pink scrapbook tote bag slung across one skinny shoulder and bumping against her hip. Red hair was piled atop Tandy's head like a show pony and her high heels tapped rapid-fire castanet sound effects on the sagging wooden floor.

Right behind her breezed in Baby Fontaine. Cool, blond, and Grace Kelly demure. Baby was a socialite and Garden District matron who was perpetually named to the local best-dressed list. Like Tandy, Baby was also a scrapbooking fiend, the two of them being Memory Mine "regulars." As such, they were always accorded first dibs on all newly acquired paper, rubber stamps, punches, and clay that came into the shop.

"I didn't expect to see you two until tomorrow," said Carmela, surprise lighting her face.

Slinging her tote onto the large, battered craft table in the

back of the store, Tandy said, "We weren't going to come. But then we heard about the murder! And about you being Johnny-on-the-spot right there!" She gave a slight shudder and said, "So creepy!"

"Honey," said Baby, slipping an arm around Carmela's waist. "You actually *witnessed* Brett Fowler's murder?" This was asked in hushed tones. "It must have been awful."

"Not exactly witnessed," said Carmela. "More like, discovered the habeas corpus."

"Which is Latin for 'finding a nasty corpse,'" said Tandy. She rested a hand on one skinny hip. "Girl, what *did* you get yourself involved in this time?"

So, of course, Carmela had to tell them about working on the monster puppet at the Pluvius den, hearing the ungodly screams, and then running out to discover Brett Fowler's lifeless, battered body.

"Now toss in the whole Emerald Equities scam!" exclaimed Baby. "And wasn't that a shocker?"

"Sure was," murmured Gabby.

"Icing on the cake," said Tandy.

"That kind of financial hanky-panky will no doubt shatter more than a few lives," said Baby, always the straight talker.

"Since I spend every cent I have on scrapbooking supplies," said Tandy, "I obviously had nothing invested."

Gabby focused on Baby, who was generally acknowledged to be the wealthy one in their little group. "What about you, Baby? Did you and Del have money in Emerald Equities?"

"Not a penny," declared Baby. "I warned Del that any money he gave that scummy Fowler to invest would be over my dead body."

"And now it's Fowler's dead body," said Tandy in an ominous tone. "If I had to venture a guess, I'd say somebody lost their life savings and was freaked-out furious at him!"

"That's what I think, too," said Gabby.

"But who?" wondered Baby.

Tandy leveled a quizzical gaze at Carmela. "Who else was there last night? I mean besides you and Ava?"

"Quite a few designers," said Carmela, recalling the hum of activity in the den.

Tandy looked happy. "Maybe you were working alongside the murderer all along and didn't even realize it!"

"Chilling thought," murmured Gabby.

"I thought about the killer being there," said Carmela, "but I . . . I don't know. This whole thing kind of caught me off guard."

"More like somebody caught Brett Fowler off guard," said Tandy.

"There have to be dozens of angry investors," said Baby.

"Which also means dozens of murder suspects," said Gabby.

Baby languidly adjusted the Chanel scarf draped around her patrician neck. "Do we know how much money Fowler frittered away?"

"The *Times-Picayune* said millions," whispered Gabby.

Tandy frowned, considering Gabby's words. "Would you kill for a million?" she asked.

"No," said Carmela, "but a lot of people would." She paused, then added, "And have."

The steamed red snapper at Glisande's Courtyard Restaurant wasn't nearly as steamed as Jekyl Hardy.

"They're looking at me hard, Carmela," he complained. "And I don't like it one bit. Makes me *beaucoup* nervous!" As if to punctuate his sentence, Jekyl ran both hands along his sleek, dark skull, smoothing back his long hair. Dressed in black from head to toe—black silk shirt, black wool slacks, black high-gloss shoes—he looked brooding, agitated, and anxious. Like a second cousin to the Vampire Lestat.

"I don't blame you," said Carmela. She leaned forward in her wicker chair and took a sip of Chardonnay. The courtyard garden, where Carmela and Jekyl were seated, was elegant and relaxing. Bougainvilleas tumbled from jumbo clay pots and a three-tiered fountain pattered soothingly in the background. Overhead, wrought-iron carriage lamps and antique birdhouses dangled from a loosely latticed ceiling that was woven with tendrils of curling ivy. Even though it was late October, just the right amount of sunlight filtered through to lend some much-appreciated warmth.

Jekyl gazed at her with pleading, limpid eyes. "I need your help, Carmela."

"Of course," she said, lightly. "Anything I can do. You know that."

"No," said Jekyl. "I mean I *really* need some serious assistance. For one thing, I'd like you to tell your boyfriend to call off his slavering hounds." He shook his head. "They're running me absolutely ragged."

"Oh," said Carmela, toying with her snapper and a side dish of highly spiced mirlitons. "I'm not sure I can do that. Babcock pretty much has a mind of his own."

"Perhaps you could employ a few of your more persuasive techniques," said Jekyl, giving an impish grin.

Carmela set her fork down and took another sip of Char-

donnay to fortify herself. "I already tried," she told him. "I called Babcock this morning and asked him, pleasantly and politely, to back off."

"That's good," said Jekyl, looking pleased. "You're one step ahead of me. And I assume, that request coming directly from you, that Babcock agreed?"

"No," said Carmela. "He told me to mind my own business."

Jekyl's shoulders visibly slumped. "Seriously?"

Carmela nodded. "I'm afraid so."

Jekyl's fist hit the table, rattling silverware. "That's just not good enough," he said through clenched teeth.

Carmela frowned. In all the years she'd known Jekyl, she'd never seen him this upset. And they'd been through countless crazy float-building sessions, fund-raising drives for the Children's Art Association, and some pretty wild nights on the town. So . . . she had to wonder . . . was something going on that she wasn't privy to? Could Jekyl somehow be involved in Fowler's death? Not as the actual killer, but in some offbeat, peripheral way? Carmela stared at her plate and took another couple of bites, still unsure about the mirlitons, which were heavily doused with white pepper, Tabasco sauce, and garlic paste.

"What's going on, Jekyl?" she asked in a low voice. "This is me, Carmela. I'm on your side. Remember?"

Jekyl shoved his uneaten entrée aside, leaned back, and crossed his legs. Steepling his fingers under his pointed chin, he gazed at Carmela with a baleful look. Then his hands flew out in a gesture of futility. "Don't you get it? I designed the Minotaur head!"

"What?" said Carmela, not certain she'd heard him correctly.

"That's right," said Jekyl. *"C'est moi."* He curled one hand and touched his chest. "I designed the murder weapon. Now do you see why the police are sticking to me like a grubby roll of flypaper? Now do you understand why I've been questioned twice already? Practically flogged with rubber hoses? Because I'm involved in a bizarre coincidence that happens to look amazingly suspicious!"

"I had no idea," said Carmela, thinking it really *was* slightly suspicious. Or just an unlucky coincidence, like Jekyl said. She thought for a minute. "Did you . . . do you . . . have anything to do with Emerald Equities?"

"Are you serious?" said Jekyl. "You know I spend every available dollar on acquiring the most perfect antiques for my apartment. I've got my eye on a silk Oriental carpet right now as well as the most splendid mahogany English sideboard. There's a reason I've been featured in *Delta Living* magazine twice already."

"Good point," said Carmela. Jekyl lived in baronial splendor in a redbrick building known as Napoleon Gardens, once an eighteenth-century warehouse. Jekyl's oversized apartment boasted fourteen-foot ceilings, a pitted marble fireplace, an antique crystal chandelier, and a fanciful wrought-iron balcony that faced the broad ribbon of the Mississippi River. On nights when stars twinkled and a cool breeze wafted through the Quarter, you could hear the mournful toot of tugboats.

"However," Jekyl continued, holding up an index finger, "there may be a snicky, sneaky way to get a slight inside track on this entire investigation."

"How?" asked Carmela.

Jekyl's smile wasn't quite a smirk, but it was close. "That, my darling girl, is where you come in."

"What are you talking about?" Carmela asked. Hadn't she already tried her best with Babcock? Hadn't she pretty much exhausted her political cash as a girlfriend? Sure she had.

"Shamus," said Jekyl, springing the name on her in a sibilant hiss.

Carmela's head involuntarily jerked backward. "No!"

"Hear me out," pleaded Jekyl.

"No," Carmela said again. *No* meant *no*. No negotiation, no bartering, case closed.

But Jekyl was far from dissuaded. "Brett Fowler's murder is almost certainly related to misappropriation of investors' funds. And what better way to get an inside track on financial information than through Shamus?"

"You're way off base," Carmela told him. "Shamus wouldn't know an equity from a commodity to save his life." She gave a disdainful snort. "All Shamus has ever done is benefit from the perks of nepotism and receive a cushy job compliments of his wacky sister, Glory. Shamus's idea of a workday is lounging around his plush office listening to sports radio. Oh sure, he'll glad-hand an occasional fat cat customer, but he's still your basic dancing puppet."

"But he attends meetings," said Jekyl.

"Doubtful," said Carmela. Shamus in meetings? He was bored and fidgeting at their hour-long wedding. Which should have been a red flag to her, but hey, everybody makes a relationship boo-boo or two. Or three or four.

"What about this?" Jekyl asked, looking coy. "Shamus goes to lunch. Spends an hour or so at a couple of private, fat cat clubs, as well as French Quarter hotspots like Galatoire's, Antoine's, and Brennan's. Where he undoubtedly meets other financial personae."

"I suppose he might," Carmela allowed.

"Places where Shamus might *hear* interesting, privileged information," said Jekyl. "Which he could, if you schmoozed him daintily, repeat back to you."

"You have no idea what you're asking of me," said Carmela, looking glum. "It took me years to get rid of Shamus. Now you're asking me to invite him back into my life." Shamus, like the spicy mirlitons she'd just ingested, felt like a tight ball lodged in the pit of her stomach.

"Not back in your life for good," said Jekyl. "More like a quick visit."

"It's a bad idea," said Carmela. "Shamus could easily morph into one of those annoying shirttail relatives who come for a visit and never, ever leave." She was fairly certain Shamus would be flattered by her sudden attention to him after months of contention. No, it would not be a good scenario.

"Carmela," said Jekyl, his eyes burning with dark intensity. "Please?"

In the end, of course, Carmela yielded. Collapsed like a flimsy card table in the onslaught of Hurricane Katrina. Promised Jekyl she'd at least talk to Shamus. Pick his brain, what there was of it. See what information he'd acquired, if any, about Emerald Equities.

"You're a peach," Jekyl told her, smiling now, looking relaxed, and magnanimously offering to pick up the tab.

"Sure," said Carmela, her mood, like an eight-track tape clicking over to the B side, suddenly the polar opposite of his.

"Say now," said Jekyl, digging in his pocket. "I have a little gift for you. I was going to give them to you and Ava last night and then it completely slipped my mind."

He slapped two purple-and-black tickets down on the glass table. "Tickets. For the *Ballet Dracula* on Thursday night."

"That's right," said Carmela. "You're in the cast."

"Only a humble walk-on role." Jekyl smiled.

"Still . . ." said Carmela. "It's supposed to be a fun production." She recalled seeing a few posters around the French Quarter. And maybe a TV spot, too?

"Good," said Jekyl. "Then you'll come?"

"What have I got to lose?" said Carmela.

They strolled out together through Glisande's dining room. Decorated in a French palette of pale blue, eggshell white, and yellow, it was very posh and Old World. White linen tablecloths graced the tables; diners sat on plushly upholstered high-backed chairs. Windows were swagged with linen draperies, and bunches of dried lavender and white roses were arranged in enormous, white French crocks.

"Look who's here," said Jekyl, grabbing Carmela's elbow and steering her to a table where two men were seated, enjoying their lunch. "Hello, Boyd," Jekyl said in his cocky, man-about-town manner.

Boyd Hodney, chairman of the Pluvius krewe, set down his martini and struggled to his feet. "Jekyl! Hello." Hodney was sixty, silver haired, and wearing a two-thousand-dollar Armani suit. Compared to most of the hoteliers, restaurateurs, and shopkeepers who populated the French Quarter, Hodney looked beyond prosperous. He looked positively Wall Street. Before the bad old recession days, of course.

The two men shook hands, and then Jekyl said, "I'd like you to meet Carmela Bertrand."

"Shamus's wife?" asked the man seated across the table

from Hodney. He was a prosperous junior version of Hodney and seemed surprised to see her.

"Ex-wife," Carmela told him, smiling evenly.

"Shamus is a heck of a nice fellow," said Hodney, pumping Carmela's arm with hale-and-hearty vigor. "We're darned lucky to have him in our krewe."

"Whatever," said Carmela.

"Jekyl," said Hodney, in a conspiratorial tone, "you're all clear on this thing with Fowler, right?" He gave a slightly embarrassed laugh. "No police lineups? Ha-ha."

"Everything's ducky," said Jekyl, grinning like a maniac. "Shouldn't be a problem."

Not a problem? Carmela wondered. *Five seconds ago Jekyl was worried sick and pleading for my help. What just changed?*

"I wouldn't want anything to stand in the way of our number one float designer," Hodney extolled. He put a manicured hand on Jekyl's shoulder and said loudly to his dining companion, as well as everyone else in the room, "As far as I'm concerned, Jekyl Hardy has scored himself a lifetime contract with the Pluvius krewe. There isn't anyone who can design an entire Mardi Gras parade with as much flair and imagination as Jekyl."

"Thank you, Boyd," said Jekyl, grinning from ear to ear. "That means a lot to me. Especially coming from you."

Now who's the dancing puppet? Carmela wondered.

Chapter 6

"YOU'RE still here," Carmela murmured as she slipped in the back door of Memory Mine.

Tandy looked up from the table they'd dubbed Craft Central. "Of course we are, sweetie. We're waiting for you."

"Huh? What?" said Carmela, slightly befuddled. "Wait a minute, was I supposed to be teaching a class today?"

"Don't let her rattle you," said Baby as she shuffled through a stack of photos. "She's just hoping to get something going."

Tandy grabbed her pair of red half-glasses and popped them onto her nose, where they promptly slid down, giving her the look of a studious but fashionable owl. "You mentioned something about green scrapbooking last week?"

"Okay," said Carmela, sliding into the chair across from her.

"Anyway, it sounded kind of interesting," Tandy told her in a wistful tone of voice.

Carmela glanced at her watch and decided there was still plenty of time to get things lined up for tomorrow's seminar. "Would you like a quick lesson right now?" she asked.

"Would we ever," said Tandy. She dug a skinny elbow into Baby's side. "Wouldn't we, lovey?"

"That would be terrific," said Baby. "But only if Carmela has time."

"I'll make time," said Carmela. Glancing toward the front of the shop, she saw that Gabby was ringing up a customer while two other women were leisurely perusing floor-to-ceiling racks of scrapbook paper. Everything appeared to be under control.

"So what exactly do you mean by green scrapping?" Baby asked.

"Better if I show you," said Carmela. She disappeared into her office, then reappeared just as quickly, hefting a giant cardboard box. "It's basically working with recycled cards, old magazines, newspapers, corrugated cardboards, and . . . well, here, take a look." She dumped the contents of the box out into the middle of the table.

"Oh wow," said Tandy as paper, bubble wrap, and scraps of colored paper fluttered everywhere.

"It's repurposing items," said Baby, understanding instantly.

"That's right," said Carmela. "The trick is to take a snippet from a greeting card and work it into a meaningful design with some recycled ribbon, a scrap of paper, and maybe even a bit of raffia. You could even use a cool visual from a clothing hangtag."

"Gotcha," said Tandy, already digging into the pile and selecting a few items.

"For instance," said Carmela, grabbing a couple of items herself. "Take this sardine can label." She held up a shiny red-and-black label with a jumping fish on it. Very graphic and clean. "If you paired it with this bit of netting saved from a bridal shower favor bag, the design elements might just springboard you into a scrapbook page on fishing."

"I've got the headline," said Tandy. "Go Fish."

"Or how about Catch as Catch Can?" said Carmela.

"Figure one out for me," begged Baby. "What if I want to do a fun cover for a mini scrapbook highlighting my daughter's trip to England?"

"I think we could manage that," said Carmela. She grabbed a few more items from the generous pile. "How about . . . here it is . . . a bit of floral paper. What if we cut it into the shape of an English teacup? Then we'll cut one of your photos into a circle, place it against this white doily, and position it above the teacup."

"Well, that's pretty neat," said Tandy, squinting.

"Isn't it?" said Baby.

"Then," said Carmela, "maybe this little visual of a sparrow . . ."

"Obviously an English sparrow," said Baby.

"Placed against a castle backdrop that we'll undoubtedly find in one of our travel magazines," said Carmela, reaching for the stack.

"With Old English type," said Baby. "Got it. I'm off and running, thanks to you."

"You're welcome," said Carmela.

They all worked away for a few minutes, digging through the pile, figuring out designs, moving elements around, try-

ing new layouts. Finally, Baby circled back to the discussion they'd started this morning.

"Carmela," asked Baby, "has your sweetie mentioned much about the connection between Fowler's murder and this so-called Ponzi scheme that's been sprung on local investors?"

"By my sweetie, you're referring to Edgar Babcock?" Carmela asked. "New Orleans homicide detective par excellence?"

"Yes." Baby smiled.

"No," said Carmela. "When I tried to pry, he told me in no uncertain terms to mind my own business."

"It's a woman's God-given right to pry," said Tandy, twisting a piece of wire.

"Not when Babcock's concerned," said Carmela. "And apparently not when I'm the one who discovered the victim."

"But that's why he *should* keep you in the loop," said Baby. "Maybe you know more than you saw."

Carmela shook her head. "Translation, please?"

"Oh, you know," said Baby. "You ran outside, saw Fowler's body lying in a pool of blood, and probably panicked. Who wouldn't? But in the cold, clear light of day, rationality might return and you'll remember something important."

"Are we talking regressed memory?" asked Tandy. "Or is the term *repressed*?"

"Just plain old regular memory," said Baby. "There could be something Carmela saw or heard, but in the shock and panic of last night, forgot to mention."

"Interesting," said Carmela. "So I should . . . what? Relax and try to focus on last night's scene? See what bubbles up from my scarred psyche?"

"That sounds fairly plausible," said Tandy. "But also a little scary."

"Scary?" said Carmela.

"Sure," said Tandy. "Because you might remember something that points directly toward the killer. And if the killer figures out that you know something, you might become a target, too. Does that make sense?"

"Yes," said Baby.

"No, it doesn't," said Carmela. "This conversation just took a weird one-eighty-degree turn."

"Huh," said Baby. "Tandy might be right. Maybe you should be worried."

"What about Ava?" Carmela asked. "Should she be shaking in her high-heeled boots, too?"

"Probably," said Baby. She remained quiet for a few minutes, fitting some letters on her design. Then she said, "Can you remember who else was in the den last night?"

"The police asked about that," said Carmela. "And I was pretty foggy on that point. But now that I think about it, I'm pretty sure I saw Jimmy Toups wandering around at some point."

"The other float builder?" said Tandy. "Jekyl's big rival?"

"I think he was helping with a puppet," said Carmela. "And maybe . . . mmm . . . Fowler's business partner? I can't remember the guy's name, but I know I've seen them together at the Pluvius den. And, of course, their pictures have been in the paper."

"Roy Slayback?" said Baby, filling in the name.

"That's it," said Carmela, pointing a finger at her. "Gosh, I wonder if he's involved in the Emerald Equities scam, too?"

"Has to be," said Tandy. "Slayback was Fowler's partner."

"He was mentioned in the newspaper story," said Baby.

"So he's for sure being questioned," said Carmela. "Man, I really do have to talk to Babcock about all of this."

"Fowler's murder is just the tip of the iceberg," said Baby, who from her lofty perch in Garden District society knew quite a lot about the business community. "Like I said before, there's going to be some serious financial fallout, as well as a lot of people who'll find themselves in deep financial trouble, if not financial ruin."

"Probably so," said Carmela, thinking of Shamus and his Crescent City Bank connections.

"You're right about the business part," said Tandy, "but I think you're off base as far as suspects go."

"How so?" asked Baby.

"If I were the chief homicide investigator," said Tandy, "I'd find out what Sissy Fowler was doing last night."

"The wife?" said Carmela.

"Soon-to-be ex-wife," said Tandy. She leaned forward, a look of glee on her face. "I heard Sissy kicked Brett Fowler out of the house months ago."

"Ava mentioned that, too," said Carmela. "So Sissy had already severed her emotional ties."

"That's right," said Tandy. "But Sissy might have decided to sever any life ties, too."

"Tandy!" exclaimed Gabby, who'd just come back to join them. "That's so harsh."

"Life's harsh, kiddo," replied Tandy as she squirted a glob of glue on a piece of colored paper.

"Carmela," said Gabby. "Angela Boynton's on the phone. Your friend from the Art Institute?"

"I'll grab it in my office," said Carmela, getting up and making a quick dive around the corner. She snatched up the phone, settled into her purple swivel chair, put her feet up on a cardboard box that had just arrived, compliments of FedEx, and said, "Angie."

"Carmela," came Angie's worried voice. "Are you okay?"

"Fine and dandy," said Carmela.

"But last night . . ."

"Wasn't so great," admitted Carmela.

"And your name was in the paper," said Angie. "So . . . you found the body?"

"More like stumbled on it," said Carmela. "It's not like I was an actual witness or anything."

"Listen," said Angie, "I know you're probably embroiled in a police investigation . . ."

"Not so much," said Carmela. *Not as much as I'd like to be.*

"But I have to ask," continued Angie.

"About the status of your puppet," said Carmela. "Of course."

"I know the timing's lousy and the project isn't a particularly large commission for you . . ."

"But you need to stay on top of it anyway," said Carmela.

"Yes," said Angie. "Pressure from above. You know how it is with arts organizations. Especially now, with big-buck donors cutting back and our own bean counters frowning over every penny we spend."

"Rest assured," said Carmela, "that your monster puppet will be completed and fully functioning by the time Monsters and Mayhem rolls around this weekend."

"Aren't you a dear," said Angie, sounding relieved. "It's

the first time the Art Institute has participated in this type of festival, so everyone is on pins and needles . . ."

"My guess is we'll finish with the puppet body tonight," said Carmela. "And then take the next couple of days to tinker with the internal mechanism. Make sure everything's working perfectly."

"But the puppet will essentially be done tonight."

"Pretty much," said Carmela. "If you want to drop by the Pluvius den, feel free."

"I might do that," said Angie.

"Because we'd love to have you," said Carmela. *And hopefully that big old bloodstain will be cleaned up by then.*

"Problems?" asked Baby, when Carmela came back to join them.

"Nothing I can't handle," said Carmela.

"Carmela's our own little Nancy Drew," chuckled Tandy. "Always getting caught up in murder investigations."

"I thought she was our own Milton Glaser," said Baby. "You know, the guy who did the I Love New York campaign? Carmela's always so innovative when it comes to graphics and design."

"Carmela's a hybrid," said Tandy. "A Renaissance woman."

"Oh please," said Carmela, a little embarrassed now. She grabbed an editorial page from a garden magazine. A yellow-and-cream-colored water lily floated on a blue-black pond. She studied the picture. Maybe if she cropped it tightly and mounted the image on shiny gold card stock she could make a nice note card. A little embossed gold type on the front—lines from a poem, perhaps—and she might have a lovely piece.

"Hey," said Tandy, "what's the deal with this pickpocket guy who's been lurking in the French Quarter?"

"He's been mentioned on the TV news," said Carmela, eager to turn the conversation away from her. "Channel Seven is calling him the Slippery Dipper. Apparently he snakes his hand into your pocket or purse without your ever realizing it."

"What's so wild," said Baby, chiming in, "is that besides picking pockets, this guy steals your ID, then actually telephones your relatives and convinces them that you're a kidnap victim!"

"Oh my gosh," said Tandy. "A *virtual* kidnapping. I heard about that happening in South America, but I didn't know they were doing it here!"

"What?" said Gabby, drifting back again. "I didn't hear about the virtual kidnapping part."

"Oh yeah," said Baby. "It's like a double hit. You lose your money and your credit cards, and then your closest relatives get scammed, too. Imagine receiving a scary phone call telling you that Aunt Ida's been kidnapped. You'd panic and wire ransom money to this guy before you even know what's happening!"

"So many scams," murmured Gabby. "What's the world coming to?"

"Going to hell in a handbasket," muttered Tandy. "Face it, who can you really trust these days? Big government?" She gave a derisive snort. "The guys on Wall Street who caused the stock market meltdown? Yeah, right. Or how about the banks? Those are the guys I worry about. What a gaggle of slimy sh—"

"Shamus," said Carmela, her voice rising in a squawk. She'd happened to glance up just as her ex-husband waltzed through the front door.

"Exactly what we don't need today," Gabby murmured. "Want me to tell Shamus that you're busy?" she asked Carmela. "Teaching a class?"

"Tell him to buzz off," said Tandy, wrinkling her nose as if Shamus were some offensive odor.

"No." Carmela sighed. "I'll talk to him." *And try to get rid of him*, she thought to herself as she strode to the front of the store, intent on heading Shamus off at the pass. But he was already ensconced at the front counter, a look of befuddlement on his handsome face.

"Every time I come in here," Shamus said, his voice carrying to the back of the shop, "you have some new kind of gewgaw or rubber stamp for sale."

"That's called inventory," Carmela said, removing a packet of gold dragonfly charms from his hand and administering a light slap. "Believe it or not, it's rather common in the retail industry."

"There you go again," Shamus whined. "I've been here for something like five seconds and you're already giving me shots. For your information, Carmela, I know a lot about business. In fact, I understand the *intricacies* of business."

"Sure you do," said Carmela, planting her hands on her hips as she stood stolidly before him, a challenging look on her face. "What's a P&L, Shamus? Or how about an ROI? Too tough for you? Tell you what, I'll lob something easier at you. What's the difference between a C corp and an S corp?"

Shamus's face darkened. "What is this, Carmela, Twenty Questions? You never give me a break, do you? What is *your* problem? You always have to wear the pants? Men don't like that, you know. Men like a woman who's a little more . . ."

"Oh pleeeease," said Carmela. "Spare me your outmoded

notions about women as simpering little hothouse flowers. Save it for the barely legal debutantes you date, the girls who don't know any better."

Shamus looked supremely pained. "I didn't come here to pick a fight."

"Then why *did* you come here, Shamus?" Carmela was tiring of him. Life was too short to have Shamus back in her life, even if it was just for five minutes. She was about to give him the boot, the old heave-ho, when she remembered her promise to Jekyl. She had agreed to try to extract whatever financial rumor she could from Shamus. Doggone. Why did she have to go and promise that?

"I need to speak to you privately," said Shamus. He glanced back toward Gabby, Baby, and Tandy as though they were paid informants for the FBI. "Not in here."

"Fine," said Carmela. "We'll go outside. Stand on the sidewalk, and try not to frighten away customers or intimidate the tourists."

"Fine," Shamus huffed back. But when they got outside, he turned suddenly serious. "I need to find out about the murder investigation," he told her.

You and everyone else, thought Carmela. She gave a tiny shake of her head.

"I mean it," said Shamus, glowering. "I'm counting on you for some straight poop."

She fixed him with a determined stare. "You mean like inside information?"

"Yeah, yeah," said Shamus, nodding, clearly excited. "Stuff you've been able to pick up. You know, like . . . uh . . . pillow talk between you and your boyfriend." He winced at that last word.

Carmela downshifted into cool mode. Cool tone of voice,

steely eyes. "If I were to give you any information, then I'd have to receive some quid pro quo."

Shamus was suddenly baffled. "Quit what?"

"Quid pro quo. It's Latin meaning 'what for what.' As in an even, equitable exchange." Carmela hesitated. "Of information."

"Oh." Shamus's handsome face pulled into a frown. "I'm not sure I can do that."

"Good-bye." Carmela turned to go back inside her store.

"No, wait!" said Shamus, catching her arm.

Carmela hesitated, watching him shift from one foot to the other, pondering her words.

Shamus put a hand to his mouth and chewed viciously at his thumbnail. Finally he said, "You can't tell a living soul."

"Sure," said Carmela.

"You promise?" More chewing of nails.

"Let's just say my word is as solemn as our marriage vows," said Carmela, an evil grin dancing across her face.

"That's so not fair," protested Shamus.

"That's so how it is," said Carmela.

"Well . . ."

"Come on," said Carmela, waggling her fingers. "I'll trade information, but you have to go first. Tell me why your butt is suddenly caught in the wringer."

"The thing is," said Shamus, looking extremely nervous, "Crescent City Bank was . . . is . . . in bed, big-time, with Emerald Equities."

Carmela wasn't surprised. She'd pretty much guessed it. Why else would Shamus be sniffing around like a hound dog hoping for a handout? "In bed for how much?" she asked.

"A lot," said Shamus.

"What's a lot?"

"Something to the tune of seven or eight million."

Carmela let loose a low whistle. "And how did all this come about?"

Shamus shook his head as if he couldn't quite comprehend such bad luck. "It started with our bank brokerage services." He squinted at Carmela. "Have you ever heard the term *feeder fund*?"

"Of course." How could she not have heard it? The whole feeder fund debacle had been splashed all over CNN for weeks on end after Bernie Madoff was arrested.

"That was Crescent City Bank's first mistake," said Shamus. "Feeding our brokerage business into Emerald Equities." He drew a deep breath. "Of course, since the initial returns were so spectacular, we readily agreed to finance them in a couple of other ventures, too."

"Such as?"

"For one thing, Brett Fowler wanted a couple million bucks to finance a shipment of big-screen TV sets. Claimed he was getting them directly from a factory in Korea and had contracts in hand from several big-box stores."

"So there went another couple of million," said Carmela. "Funny how fast a few million can trickle through your fingers, huh?"

Shamus nodded.

"What else?" asked Carmela.

"We got caught up in foreign exchange rates, too. Riding the float . . ."

"Uh-huh," said Carmela.

"But now . . ." Shamus looked dour.

"Now the bank is really on the hook," said Carmela. "Okay, it's a terrible loss, but at least you can take solace in the fact that you're not the only ones who got defrauded."

"I don't imagine our customers and investors are going to be that understanding," said Shamus.

"Probably not," said Carmela. "So what is it you want me to try to find out?"

"Really just how the investigation is progressing," said Shamus.

Carmela stared at Shamus. He was smiling now, giving her his most sincere look. And something else. His blink rate had suddenly increased. A sure sign he was stonewalling about something.

"And that's it?" said Carmela.

"That's it," said Shamus. *Blink blink.*

"No," said Carmela, "you haven't quite told me the whole story."

"Sure I have," said Shamus. *Blink blink blink.*

Carmela folded her arms in front of her and said, "Shamus!" as though she were scolding a naughty puppy. Two passersby turned to stare.

Blink blink.

"All right," said Shamus, finally. "There's a little more."

"I thought so."

"About a week ago, the bank started getting wind of Emerald Equities' problems. He gave a wry grin. "We have friends in the Louisiana Security Division."

"I'm sure you do," said Carmela.

"So anyway," Shamus continued, "Glory decided to hire a private investigator. A guy named Mills Taggart."

"Oh no," said Carmela. Mills Taggart had an extremely shady reputation about town.

"Yeah," said Shamus. "Taggart had been dogging Brett Fowler's footsteps as well as digging for information."

"Dogging and digging," said Carmela. "That's just great.

But I'd say your hotshot investigator didn't exactly keep an eagle eye on Fowler. I mean, where was Taggart last night when Fowler was gored to death by Mr. Minotaur?"

"I don't know," said Shamus.

"Unless . . . ," began Carmela, then stopped. Let her mouth catch up with her brain. Then she spoke again and said, "Unless Taggart took matters into his . . ."

"He wouldn't do that!" Shamus cried. He knew exactly where she was going.

But Carmela wasn't so sure. What if Mills Taggart *had* taken matters into his own hands? What if Taggart was the one who'd murdered Brett Fowler? It was possible. Anything was possible. Of course, Taggart wouldn't have committed murder on this own. He would have been following orders from someone at Crescent City Bank.

Carmela inhaled sharply as she gazed at Shamus, feeling nervous and a little queasy. She stared at him as he met her gaze. No, she decided. Shamus would never issue an order like that. Shamus might be a doofus and a cad, but deep down he was a fairly moral character. At least where money was concerned.

But what about Shamus's big sister, Glory? Certifiably crazy and meaner than a rabid wolverine. Could Glory have ordered Mills Taggart to make the hit? Of course she could have. If somebody got between Glory Meechum and her money, she wouldn't hesitate to issue a kill order.

Chapter 7

"WHAT'S that heavenly aroma?" squealed Ava as she swished through Carmela's front door wearing a long, black, velvet cape. "*Cher*, is it what I think it is? What I *hope* it is?"

Carmela pulled off her oven mitt and asked, "Just what did you have your little heart set on?"

Ava's lovely face lit up with anticipation. "Your scrumptious Cajun shrimp bake?"

"Bingo," said Carmela. "Give that lady a fuzzy, plush puppy." She smiled as Boo and Poobah skittered across the floor, rushing to greet their aunt Ava. "In fact, you can take a plush puppy home with you right now. See one you like? Dog beds packed and ready to go in a heartbeat."

Ava knelt down and gathered Boo and Poobah into her arms. "What a funny momma you guys have. We know she'd *never* get rid of either of you. You're her little darlins."

"Hah," said Carmela, turning back to her oven to sneak a peek.

"Want me to set the table?"

"Sure," said Carmela. She unwrapped a French baguette, placed it on her cutting board, sliced it quickly, then piled the slices into a basket lined with a gingham napkin.

"That's good," Ava told her as she put out place mats, red Fiestaware plates, and knives, forks, and spoons. "You got plenty of bread for sopping up the juices."

"Fresh from the Merci Beaucoup Bakery," said Carmela.

"My most favorite place on earth," swooned Ava. "Their red-sugared jelly rolls are to die for, and their Doberge cakes are amazing." Doberge cakes were a special New Orleans creation, a confection consisting of multiple layers of cake and pudding swathed in butter cream and covered with fondant. Just *thinking* about one could give you a toothache.

"Well, I guess we know how you feel about carbs," said Carmela.

"Oh no," said Ava, looking worried. "I detest carbs. At least my hips and thighs do. See?" She stretched out a taut, toned leg, swathed in tight black denim jeans. "I'm really a fatso."

"That's right," laughed Carmela. "You've let it all slide since winning your last tiara." Ava had garnered beauty pageant fame by winning the Miss Teen Sparkle Pageant back in her hometown of Mobile, Alabama. Feeling that she'd attained her life's goal at age eighteen, Ava had graciously retired, leaving the world's stage open for other would-be beauty queens.

"I just can't find a lick of time to exercise," complained Ava, who was a size six in a tall, lanky body. In other words, perfection.

"You have a date every night," Carmela pointed out. "Maybe you could work in a little activity."

"Oh, I work in activity," said Ava, rolling her eyes. "Don't you worry about that!"

Chuckling, Carmela pulled her shrimp bake from the oven, then carried the bubbling and hissing casserole dish to the table.

"Now that's my idea of a hot dish," said Ava.

"You're a hot dish," Carmela joked.

"So many men, so little time," Ava murmured.

"What else?" asked Carmela, glancing at the table.

"Wine," Ava pronounced. "Food this fabulous deserves wine."

"Women as fabulous as we are deserve wine," said Carmela, grabbing a fresh bottle of pinot grigio.

Twenty minutes later, shrimp shells piled up on their plates, bread basket empty, and swirling a second glass of pinot grigio, Carmela and Ava were happy, sated, and deep into another discussion concerning the inconvenient and slightly messy demise of Brett Fowler.

"Know what I think?" asked Ava, pretending to sniff her wine like a connoisseur.

"What?" said Carmela, doing a little sniffing and tasting of her own.

"I think Sissy Fowler did it."

"Ah, that's what Tandy thinks, too."

"Tandy's a smart lady," said Ava, stifling a burp. "Yeah, I figure Sissy must have done it. Wives always kill their rich husbands. It's practically a cliché."

"Not really," said Carmela.

"Case in point," said Ava. "You wanted to kill Shamus."

"I did at times," Carmela admitted. "But I never would have. Not really."

"And the crazy thing," said Ava, "is that Sissy Fowler is rich in her own right."

"Then she really didn't have a motive."

Ava held up a finger. "But what if Sissy found out about Emerald Equities going belly-up? Maybe she couldn't face the humiliation and shame of having her husband's fraudulent business exposed?"

"Killing him would be one heck of a smoke screen," said Carmela, although she wasn't buying it. A crazed, defrauded investor, yes. Sissy, no.

"Okay, how about this?" said Ava, unwilling to let her theory go. "Maybe Sissy was afraid that if Fowler ended up broke, she'd have to pay him alimony? Support his fat, worthless ass for the rest of her life."

Carmela tilted her head from one side to the other. "It's a theory. But somehow I get the feeling Brett Fowler's murder was more business-related than personal."

"How exactly did you conjure this feeling?"

Carmela shrugged. "I don't know. It just . . . came to me."

"You mean like out of the blue? Like the proverbial lightning bolt?"

"Not quite that dramatic," said Carmela. "It's just been swirling randomly in my brain."

"You've had good hunches before," said Ava. "So . . . maybe."

"Maybe," said Carmela. She was also thinking about the conversation she'd had with Shamus this afternoon. "Hey, you know what I told you before about Glory hiring a private investigator?"

"Uh-huh," said Ava, pulling a copy of the *Times-Picayune* from her tote bag.

"Do you think Glory is crazy enough to order some sort of hit on Fowler?"

Ava looked up and frowned. "Heck yes, she is. For gosh sakes, Carmela, Glory throws a hissy fit if there's a single dog hair on the carpet. Imagine how insane she'd be if someone conned her out of eight million dollars!" Ava nodded to herself. "Yup, Glory's a total psycho. Look how she tried to cheat you out of alimony. And tried to keep Shamus from giving you the house."

"Good point," said Carmela. Good to talk smack about Glory, too.

"*Cher*," said Ava, smoothing out the newspaper, "have you been following the clues? For the Monsters and Mayhem treasure hunt?"

"I don't get the newspaper anymore." Carmela glanced at the dogs, who seemed to understand the subtext and ducked their heads in shame.

"Some lucky duck is gonna win ten grand if they find the Halloween medallion," said Ava. "No reason it shouldn't be us."

"No reason at all."

"So we should hunt for the treasure," said Ava. "Go for the big score!"

"Okay," Carmela said, agreeably.

"And we'll split it fifty-fifty? Pinky swear?"

"Pinky swear," said Carmela. They held their hands out, entwined pinky fingers, and shook meaningfully.

"Let me read you the first couple of clues," said Ava. "See if we can put our clever little heads together and figure something out."

"Shoot."

"Okay, this is the first one," said Ava. "Seductive and sprawling, you've got to come calling." She dropped the paper to her chest, furrowed her brow, and said, "What do you think?"

"Nothing pops out at me," said Carmela.

"This isn't going to be the cakewalk I thought it would be," said Ava, sounding slightly disgruntled. "Okay, let's move on to the second clue, the one that came out this morning." She cleared her throat. "Where treaties were signed, it's treasure you'll find." She paused. "Any of that ring a bell?"

"Still awfully vague," said Carmela. "That treaty thing could apply to lots of places in New Orleans."

"Maybe the treasure's hidden in the French Quarter," said Ava. "That could give us a huge leg up. Or maybe it's in Lafayette Square. Or along the St. Charles Avenue streetcar line."

"Maybe," said Carmela. "And maybe we'll just have to wait for the clues to home in a little closer."

"Hmm," said Ava.

"Ready for another fun diversion?"

"Hmm?" said Ava again. She was staring at the clues as if intense eye contact equaled divination.

"Jekyl gave us tickets for Thursday night's *Ballet Dracula*."

Ava looked up, pleased. "Really? Get out!"

"Yup."

"That's just peachy." She grinned. "What say we get ourselves all vamped up?"

"By vamped up, you mean . . ."

"Dress like vampires," Ava enthused. "You know, I could

wear my black velvet cape, some black stilettos, a long black dress with a plunging neckline."

"You'll look for any old excuse to wear a plunging neckline."

"You got that right," said Ava. "Daylight Saving Time? Plunging neckline. Bought a new lipstick? Drag out the plunging neckline." She giggled and hugged herself, loving her own quirky brand of humor.

"Then I think you should go all out," said Carmela, "in honor of this theatrical occasion." She, of course, had no intention of strutting around like she was offering herself up as Count Dracula's bride. But maybe she could don a little black dress with some sexy black ankle boots? That might be apropos. And she still had that crazy bat-wing purse Ava had prodded her into buying. Except, of course, she didn't want to come off looking like one of the cast!

Twenty minutes later Carmela and Ava strolled into the Pluvius krewe's vast float den. And even though they were exceedingly mindful of the violent murder that had taken place the night before, no one else seemed at all bothered. Lights were turned up, music blared from a boom box, and red-and-white coolers overflowed with Dixie longnecks and Turbodog beer. Designers and volunteer puppet builders chatted and laughed as they worked on various giant puppets.

"I thought this place would be all weird and subdued," said Ava, glancing around the cavernous den where merriment seemed to reign.

"Me, too," said Carmela. "But all the puppet builders are acting like nothing happened."

"Maybe they don't know?" asked Ava.

"Oh, they know," said Carmela.

"So it's like whistling in the dark," suggested Ava. "Or dancing on a grave. Wait, is that right? The dancing part?"

"Dancing works for me," said Carmela, sliding a large box that held her puppet body onto the table.

"Do you think the bull's head is still here?" Ava asked, quietly.

"The Minotaur?" Carmela shook her head. "I'm pretty sure Babcock confiscated the darned thing. Murder weapon, you know."

"Oh." Ava thought for a moment. "Do you think they, like, checked it into the property room, like the cops do on *Law & Order*?"

"I suppose."

"Ask Babcock about that, will you? I'm curious."

"If I ever see him again," said Carmela, taking the cover off the box.

Ava's brows arched sharply upward. "You two lovebirds can't be feuding! *Cher*, you're my role models. You're what I strive for in a relationship."

Carmela pulled the yards of fabric out and shook them. The costume fell in luscious golden ripples. "You mean just dating, no real commitment, never sure when he's going to turn up on your doorstep? Your basic laissez-faire relationship?"

"When you put it that way, it doesn't sound so glamorous," said Ava. "A gal can get that kind of treatment any old day from any old guy."

"See?" said Carmela. "Now you'll have to find a different role model."

"Now I have to find a serious *boyfriend*," said Ava, putting

a finger in her hair and twirling it languidly. "I really figured I'd be married by the time I turned thirty. No way do I want to end up as the crazy old voodoo lady with a bunch of snarling cats."

"You only have Isis, who's a complete and utter love, plus you still have plenty of time."

"No," said Ava, "it still feels like some kind of millennium clock is ticking constantly inside my brain. I dream about giant, flickering LED numbers. And time just slipping away."

"Maybe, when you least expect—"

"Helloooo," said Ava, turning and suddenly thrusting a hip forward as she projected a megawatt smile.

"Hey there, pretty lady," said Boyd Hodney, suddenly stopping in his tracks to focus his complete attention on Ava.

Ava cocked an index finger and said, "I've seen you around here before, haven't I?"

Hodney didn't stand a chance. It was as though Ava were pulling him in with a tractor beam. A beauty tractor beam. Carmela, of course, was completely ignored, even though they'd just talked at lunch today.

"And you are . . . ?" Hodney asked Ava, his eyes roving up and down her well-endowed figure.

Ava dimpled prettily. "Ava Gruiex." She extended a fluttering hand. "Proprietress of the French Quarter's Juju Voodoo shop. And who do I have the pleasure of . . . ?"

"Boyd Hodney," said Carmela, cutting in, wondering what he was doing here tonight. "Boyd's the illustrious chairman of the Pluvius krewe."

"A man with a title." Ava sighed.

"I see you girls are working on one of the puppets," Hodney stammered, still struck by Ava's charms.

"Ladies," Carmela corrected. "Girls, on the other hand, have pigtails and wear braces."

"Of course," said Hodney, grinning maniacally as if Carmela had just shared some marvelous inside joke with him.

Ava oozed a little closer to Hodney. And, Carmela had to admit, with his silver hair, tapered Burberry sport shirt, and neatly pressed tan slacks, he did cut a handsome figure.

"Say now," said Hodney, dropping his voice to a lower, more conspiratorial register. "What say we get together for a drink afterward? Maybe meet at Zebo's down the block? They have live music." He glanced at his watch, then back at Ava. "I have some business to attend to, but if we rendez-voused around ten I could get to know you better." He shot a sideways glance at Carmela. "Bring your friend here, too."

"Big of you," said Carmela.

"Maybe we'll do that," said Ava.

"And maybe not," said Carmela as Hodney moved off.

"Bye-bye," sang out Ava. "See you later."

"He's married!" Carmela hissed as soon as Hodney was out of earshot.

"He didn't look married," said Ava, all innocence. "He wasn't wearing a wedding ring."

"Trust me, he is," said Carmela. "To a crazy lady named Tallulah who grows orchids and adores skeet shooting."

Ava shrugged. "Maybe they're getting a divorce?"

"I hear Tallulah's a crack shot."

"Spoilsport," said Ava, pretending to sulk.

"Carmela put a hand on Ava's shoulder. "Even if he was in the throes of divorce, you don't want some crazy lady's seconds. Hodney's basically distressed merchandise."

"Maybe he's a scratch-and-dent guy," said Ava. "Used but still serviceable."

"Trust me," said Carmela, "a married man is never a good deal."

"Married?" said a voice behind Carmela. "Who'd want to go and spoil all the fun of being single in this crazy, clubbing town?"

Carmela whirled around to find that Jekyl Hardy had slipped in behind them, moving like a stealthy vampire. In his tight black jeans and black leather motorcycle jacket zigzagged with silver zippers, he looked just this side of dangerous.

"Ava was just flirting with Boyd Hodney," said Carmela. "But I told her he was married."

"Boyd's a good guy," Jekyl said instantly, a curious, crooked smile on his face.

Carmela reared back. "Since when did you and Hodney become fast friends? You used to call him Mr. Slicko. And what was with the Hardy Boys act today at lunch? I expected you two to pull out decoder rings and trade vital secrets."

"We're friends," said Jekyl, "ever since Boyd Hodney named me head designer for the Pluvius krewe and gave me a three-year contract!"

"Really?" said Carmela.

"Jekyl, that's wonderful!" enthused Ava. "You found legitimate work! I mean, aside from your antique consulting." She grabbed him by his leather lapels and planted a big kiss on his cheek.

"When did all this take place?" Carmela asked, reaching out and wiping away the red smear Ava had left. "I thought you were on the outs with the Pluvius krewe? That they still owed you money from this past Mardi Gras? In fact, last time we swirled Cosmos together at Yellow Bird, you were threatening to take the Pluvius krewe to court!"

"Water under the bridge," said Jekyl, waving a hand. "All is forgiven."

"Shazam, we're friends?" said Carmela. "Just like that?" Something sounded fishy to her.

"Hodney called me first thing this morning and made the offer," said Jekyl, explaining. "Obviously I accepted."

"Wait a minute," said Carmela. "I thought first thing this morning you were being interrogated by the police."

"After that," said Jekyl.

"After that," repeated Carmela. Things sure were happening at warp speed. "And you accepted Hodney's offer in a heartbeat," said Carmela, snapping her fingers.

"Of course," said Jekyl. "It's a wonderful deal. Gives me complete security."

Carmela refrained from giving Jekyl her standard lecture that there was no such thing as complete security. She knew for a fact that life had a quirky way of turning on a dime.

"What about Jimmy Toups?" asked Ava. Jimmy Toups was a rival float designer and Jekyl's self-proclaimed nemesis. Everyone knew there was no love lost between the two of them, even though Jekyl and Toups had been forced to grudgingly work together on more than one occasion.

"Actually," said Jekyl, his eyes roving across the den. "I just saw Jimmy Toups. A couple of minutes ago."

"That's not what I was asking," said Carmela. She gazed toward the center of the den, where a group of puppet builders were popping beers and talking loudly. Not getting much done except enjoying an impromptu party.

"I know what you were asking," said Jekyl, "and I'm here to say it isn't a problem. If we have to work together, then we work together."

"So now you're best buds?" Carmela asked, still incredulous.

"If we have to be," said Jekyl. But he didn't sound enthusiastic.

"Excuse me," laughed Carmela, "just when exactly did you stop being a prima donna? When did you hang up your tutu?"

Jekyl clicked his heels together and bowed deeply, like a fencing master addressing his class. "Never. I hope." He looped an arm around Carmela's waist and pulled her aside. "Aside from all that, cookie . . . do you have any news for me? Concerning the, uh, investigation?"

Carmela quickly related to Jekyl all the details surrounding her conversation with Shamus, including the information about Mills Taggart, the private investigator.

"And you say this Taggart fellow is working directly for Crescent City Bank?" Jekyl asked.

Carmela nodded. "According to Shamus, yes."

"I'd say that's very good news," said Jekyl. "It means the bank smelled a rat in their financial dealings with Fowler."

"Well . . . yeah," said Carmela. "Obviously not right away, because they got in pretty deep. But something tipped them off more recently."

"Do the police know about Taggart?"

"You're asking me if Edgar Babcock knows?"

"Right," said Jekyl.

"I'm not sure."

"Then you're going to have to plant the proverbial bug in his ear," Jekyl told her, excitedly. "Because if the bank was suspicious of Fowler, it pretty much gets me off the hook."

"I didn't think you were exactly *on* the hook," said Car-

mela. She stared thoughtfully at Jekyl. "Is there something you're not telling me?"

"No," replied Jekyl. But at the last moment his eyes slid away.

Chapter 8

"LUCKY me," trilled Ava. "I get to climb inside this shapeless, weird puppet body again."

"Would you rather play the role of seamstress?" Carmela asked. "Loop a tape measure around your neck and make judicious tucks and stitches here and there?"

"I'd probably just sew my fingers together," said Ava, reaching for the costume.

"Okay, then, that matter's settled."

Ava slipped the fabric over her head, then did a sexy little shimmy so it slithered down over her hips. "I'll just pretend to be one of the fit models for one of those fancy French ateliers," she laughed. "Or, better yet, you can play Karl Lagerfeld and I'll be your creative muse."

"Dream on, darlin'," said Carmela as she tucked and draped and pinned some more.

"Don't stick me," said Ava, fidgeting.

"The only thing you're gonna be stuck with tonight is a married man," Carmela told her.

"You don't like him." Ava gave a little pout.

Carmela stood her ground. "Uh, no . . . not for you, I don't."

"Can we still meet for drinks? Maybe just pal around?"

"We'll see," said Carmela, thinking that when this day was done she just wanted to head straight home and snuggle with her dogs. Or whatever sexy detective might show up on her doorstep.

"Hey, that's looking great!" called a woman's voice.

Carmela looked up, straight pins protruding from her mouth, and managed a strangled grin. She hastily spit pins into her left hand and said, "Angie, glad you could make it."

A woman with shoulder-length light brown hair, green eyes, and a slight bump on her nose ambled toward them. Usually dressed in conservative suits with a single piece of good jewelry, Angie was casual and comfy in blue jeans and a heather-blue sweater.

"Like my prom dress?" Ava asked, flapping her arms, causing yards of fabric to gently billow out. "There's enough material here for three people to hide in!"

"Very stylish," Angie chuckled. "But how does it work with the head?" She glanced around. "Where's this dreaded monster head I've heard so much about?"

Carmela pointed an index finger at Angie. "One minute and we'll show you."

"In fact," Ava suggested, "why don't you turn around and let us do a dramatic reveal. A big ta-da. Hopefully, the full effect will blow your socks off."

"Let's go for it," agreed Angie.

Carmela hoisted the puppet head down from the shelf and positioned it on Ava's head and shoulders. "That's it," she told her friend, "stick your hands in right there. Then when I give the signal, just flip the switch."

"Got it," said Ava.

"Okay," Carmela called to Angie.

Angie turned, gaped, and took a slow step backward. "Wow." She ran a hand through her hair, taking it all in.

"Now for the action sequence," said Carmela. "Ava?"

Slowly, the puppet head elongated on its stalk neck. Enormous eyes whirred crazily, and a mouth opened to reveal a snaggle of sharp teeth.

Angie's mouth dropped open as she watched the puppet go through its motions. "That's fantastic," she murmured. "Almost . . . unbelievable."

"You like it," Carmela said, pleased.

"No, I *love* it," said Angie, who was close to jumping up and down. "Your design was fantastical on paper, but I never dreamed you'd pull it off so beautifully. Now . . . well, I think our puppet's going to be the hit of the parade!"

"We certainly hope so," came Ava's muffled voice.

Angie stepped closer to the puppet, reached a hand up, and gently stroked the giant head. "You okay in there?" she asked.

"Okay," came Ava's muffled reply.

"Will Ava carry it in the parade?" Angie asked Carmela, who was busily adjusting fabric.

"No, no," Carmela told her. "We've already tapped Ava's assistant, Miguel, to do that. Miguel's been working with us right along."

"Like I said, fantastic," said Angie.

"Can I come out now?" Ava pleaded.

* * *

"Angie was really pleased, huh?" asked Ava. After assuring Angie that all puppetry-related activity was a go and walking her to the door, Carmela had come back to lift the head off Ava. Now it was positioned on their worktable so they could make a few minor refinements.

"She pretty much flipped over it," said Carmela.

"Wouldn't be bad if we scored a few more projects from the Art Institute."

"Wouldn't be bad at all," agreed Carmela. Freelance design projects were one of the things she thrived on. These days, who couldn't use a little extra money?

"You're a graphic artist," Ava pointed out, "so you could probably design some whiz-bang posters or invitations. While I . . . I could . . ." She thought for a moment. "Hmm."

"Pretty much do anything," said Carmela, finishing her statement. "Because you have a very creative mind."

"That's it," said Ava, agreeing. "I'm a concept person. A big-picture gal."

"Easy, babe," said Carmela. "You don't want to sound like Shamus. He was always yapping about the big picture."

"When all he did was take little pictures," giggled Ava, referring to Shamus's endless photography projects.

"Even then, it took him three years to pull together an actual exhibition," said Carmela. "Which is a real kick, because sometimes we do six or seven different projects in a single day at Memory Mine."

"*You're* the big-picture person," said Ava. "You always see things one step ahead."

"Except when I married Shamus."

"Nobody's got a perfect track record," said Ava. She shook

her mass of dark hair back, arched her back, and muttered, "Oh crap."

"What?"

"Jimmy Toups," Ava whispered as a tall, barrel-chested man in a khaki jumpsuit came bounding over to them.

"So this is the fabled Crunch Monster," said Jimmy, poking a fat finger at Carmela's puppet head. Even though Toups was pushing fifty, he wore his thin blond hair in a gelled faux-hawk and wore a jumpsuit outfitted with pockets, zippers, and epaulets. He enjoyed a so-so reputation as a sculptor, but the only piece Carmela could recollect was a stylized bronze alligator in Audubon Park.

"Kindly do not touch the merchandise," Ava told Toups in an icy tone.

Toups held up his hands and said, "Just being neighborly, didn't mean to interfere."

"You're working on a puppet head, too?" Carmela asked, even though she didn't remember seeing Toups at the den during the last week. Then again, she hadn't exactly been on the lookout for him.

Toups cocked his head to one side as if considering her question. "I've been doing consulting, mostly," he said finally. "Got lots of projects in the hopper right now."

"That's great," said Carmela. She wanted to stay on the good side of Jimmy Toups just in case he and Jekyl did have to work together. Besides, it was always more convenient to have an ally than an enemy. Well, most of the time it was.

"How goes the scrapbook business?" Toups asked her.

"Good," Carmela told him. "Holding its own."

Toups gave a little chuckle, then said, "I'm probably going to drop by your shop in the next couple of days."

"Oh?" said Carmela.

"Pick up some materials," Toups added, trying to sound mysterious.

Ava smoothed a piece of fabric, then said, "You getting into scrapbooking, Jimmy?"

That was the opening Toups was looking for. He rocked back on his heels, and a slow, smarmy grin creased his face. "Fact is, I'm cataloging photographs for a Mardi Gras book that I'm writing."

"What?" said Carmela, almost sticking herself with a pin. She knew darned well that Jekyl Hardy was writing a Mardi Gras book, too.

"Yeah," said Toups, enjoying his little bombshell. "It's going to be the definitive history of Mardi Gras."

"Wow," said Ava, looking stunned. "You have a book contract and everything?"

Toups frowned at her, highly offended. "You seriously think I'd do all that hard work on spec? Of course I have a book contract. From Peregrine Publishing. Which is why I'm in the middle of organizing a huge collection of photos. Have to get 'em into a meaningful sequence, so I can flesh out the various chapters."

"You're using your own photos?" asked Carmela, intrigued now.

"Some are my own," said Toups. "Most belong to Sissy Fowler."

"Say what?" said Ava, looking even more surprised.

"Notwithstanding the tragedy of the other night," said Toups, "Sissy has been working with me rather closely. In fact, she's been an absolute love. We've literally fallen head over heels for each other."

"You don't say," said Carmela. Now she was just plain stunned.

"Oh yeah," continued Jimmy. Sissy's shared all sorts of vintage photos and memorabilia with me, stuff that goes back more than fifty years." He paused. "Sissy's father was captain of the Pluvius krewe long before the torch was passed to Brett."

"Did, uh, Brett Fowler know about your little project with Sissy?" Carmela asked.

"He did," said Toups. "But I can't say he was hopping up and down over it." He shrugged. "Of course, now Brett Fowler doesn't have much to say about anything!"

"Wow," said Ava, "Jimmy Toups just sort of passed over Brett Fowler's murder like he was a bug on a windshield. No regret, no respect."

"Toups is a cold, callous guy," agreed Carmela. "Always has been."

"No wonder Jekyl's always been so wary of him." Ava paused. "You don't suppose Jimmy Toups and Sissy Fowler are truly romantically involved, do you? He was just speaking metaphorically, right?"

"I don't know *what* to think. I'm still spinning about his book deal, especially coming on the heels of Jekyl's book deal."

"I hear you," said Ava.

"And I imagine that whichever book comes out first will be the big seller." Carmela grimaced. "While the second book . . ." She paused. "Will be the also-ran."

"Jekyl better get his tail in gear," said Ava as she began shrugging out of the costume, "before he gets one-upped." Once the fabric lay in a puddle around her feet, she added, "But if Toups really *is* involved with Sissy, he could actually be considered a suspect."

"In Fowler's murder?"

Ava nodded.

Carmela considered this. "You think Jimmy Toups really had a motive for murder?"

"Think about it," said Ava. "Toups is getting cozy with Sissy Fowler while her estranged husband is running amok in bad debt and a faltering Ponzi scheme . . ."

"And if Toups really is crazy for Sissy—or for her money—maybe all he needed was a little creative coaching," Carmela postulated.

"Coaching and canoodling," said Ava.

"Never in a million years would I have considered Jimmy Toups a suspect," said Carmela. "Until he waltzed in here tonight and started running his mouth. And *you* put it together."

"Nancy Drew did have a sidekick," said Ava, pleased. So . . . is this something you should mention to Babcock? Maybe help steer the investigation in Toups's direction?"

"It's something to think about," said Carmela. "At least it would get Babcock focused in a different direction. And by that I mean away from Jekyl."

"That'd be good, right?" said Ava.

"Right," said Carmela. Except, of course, for the fact that Jekyl seemed to be hiding something.

"I just had another thought," said Ava. "Do you think Jekyl knows about Jimmy Toups's book?"

"No idea. But you can bet I'll mention it to him."

In the end, Carmela dropped Ava off at Zebo's so she could meet Boyd Hodney, then drove on home. Feeling at odds and ends, endless permutations of theories and suppositions

running through her brain like chase lights on a theater marquee, Carmela walked the dogs up and down the back alley a couple of times, puttered around her apartment, then laid out her clothes for tomorrow. Finally, she pulled back the covers and slithered into bed.

Just as she was about to drift off to sleep, images of monster puppets swirling in her brain, she was cognizant of a soft rap at the front door.

What?

The noise registered in her slightly fogged brain, but didn't seem to telegraph to the rest of her zonked-out body.

Knock knock.

Now Boo and Poobah were up and padding to the front door. A whine and a couple of dog grumbles followed. Sighing to herself, Carmela swung her legs out of bed and rubbed her bare feet on a white flokati rug, enjoying the tickle of the soft wool.

Babcock? Has to be.

Carmela pulled on a white terrycloth robe and bumped her way through the darkness to the front door.

"Hiya," said Babcock, when the door creaked open. "You asleep?"

"Not any more," Carmela told him, scratching at her hair that had to be sticking straight up, wishing she'd worn eyeliner to bed.

"Can I come in?"

Carmela hesitated for a millisecond, then swung the door wide open.

"Hey, kids," said Babcock, kneeling down to greet the dogs. Fully awake and eager for attention now, Boo and Poobah crowded around him excitedly. After he'd paid them

sufficient doggy tribute, he stood up and gave Carmela a quick kiss.

"I guess I know where I stand in the pecking order," she told him.

"You're my number one," he said, circling his arms around her and pulling her close.

"We need to talk," she told him.

Babcock grimaced. "Ooh, I don't like the sound of that."

Carmela took him by the hand and led him over to the chaise lounge. They plopped down, the leather squishing amiably beneath them. "Shamus used to say that whenever a woman says *we* need to talk, it means *she* needs to talk."

He gazed earnestly into her eyes. "I'm not Shamus."

"And thank goodness for that."

They snuggled closer, pressing tightly against each other, hip to hip, shoulder to shoulder.

"Tough day at the office, honey?" Carmela asked.

Babcock's quick laugh turned into a cough.

"Sorry, sorry," she told him.

He waved a hand at her. "No, it's just . . . you caught me by surprise."

"When I stop surprising you, that's when I'll start to worry."

He took her hands in his, stroking them gently and twining them between his larger paws. "You look worried."

"Are you still investigating Jekyl?"

Babcock took a deep breath, then said, "No. Not so much. The investigation is focused in other directions, too."

"Toward Sissy Fowler and Jimmy Toups?"

Curiosity rose like a flame in Babcock's eyes. "How'd you know about that?"

"I'm plugged in," said Carmela.

"Huh," said Babcock. "The French Quarter Mafia?"

"Something like that."

"So what else is on your troubled but highly creative mind tonight?" Babcock asked. "I sense there's more."

"You have to keep this under your hat," said Carmela.

Babcock squinted at her. "Carmela. You know I can't always . . ."

"As much as you can."

"Okay."

"I found out that Crescent City Bank hired a private investigator."

"They *what*?"

Carmela smiled. He hadn't known. Well . . . good. She *was* valuable in this investigation after all. "The bank hired a private investigator to tail Brett Fowler. It seems they funneled some investment money his way and then got wind that his hedge fund was all smoke and mirrors."

"Who was this investigator?"

"A guy by the name of Mills Taggart."

"Oh," said Babcock.

"You know him?"

"Know *of* him," said Babcock. "Taggart doesn't exactly have a sterling reputation." Babcock withdrew a hand, put it to his face, and stroked his cheek, thinking. "Taggart was tailing Brett Fowler," he recited slowly to himself.

"So I'm told." Carmela watched him in the darkness, thinking how handsome he was, how focused he was.

"Taggart didn't do a very good job of it, did he?" mused Babcock.

Carmela thought for a minute, then said, "I don't know. Maybe events turned out *exactly* as planned."

Chapter 9

EIGHTEEN curious faces stared at Carmela in anticipation of today's Fiber Arts seminar. But Carmela was carefully prepped and ready to kick it into high gear. Skeins of mohair and loops of Lurex, ribbon, and jute lay on the table before her. Both she and Gabby had arrived super early this morning to set up tables and chairs, spread out craft materials, and arrange for delivery of boxes of tasty beignets from the Café du Monde as well as *geaux* cups of good strong chicory coffee. Carmela figured the sugar high and the coffee jitters would help fuel the creativity. And she was pretty much right.

"What I thought we'd do in our morning session," said Carmela, standing at the head of the table, bouncing on the balls of her feet to dispel any nervous tension, "was take a look at some of the amazing fibers that are available and then incorporate them in a couple of projects."

One woman raised her hand. "Scrapbooking projects?"

"Sure," said Carmela. "But remember that scrapbooking really dovetails with card making and rubber stamping, as well as designing cards, hangtags, mini albums . . . well, you get the picture."

"Pictures," murmured Tandy, who was seated to her left, champing at the bit.

Carmela dumped out a plastic box of fibers and talked a little bit about each one. Jute, string, leather cord, eyelash yarn, mohair, fringed ribbon yarn, Lurex fibers, knotted flag fiber, bouclé, chenille, and a few more. Once she did a quick introduction of each fiber, she passed a loop of it around the table so all the women could see, touch, and enjoy. Because that was the thing about fibers: besides being a delight to the eye, they were also so deliciously tactile.

The fiber introduction took a good half hour, with the ladies sipping coffee and oohing and ahhing over the various types. Then, paper plates and coffee cups were collected into a big black trash bag and Carmela got down to the serious business of having fun.

"Some of you have probably been using fibers already in your scrapbooking," said Carmela. She held up a roll of black velvet chenille. "This chenille ribbon, for example, is perfect for creating a photo border. In fact, it lends an elegant formality." She picked up a skein of soft, pastel yarn. "Now baby pictures, on the other hand, look great when outlined in a soft, pastel mohair. The more snuggly, the better."

The women all nodded, and then a woman in a pink frilly blouse held up a hand and asked, "And you can sew them right onto your scrapbook page?"

"Sewing works well," said Carmela, "but you can also stick fibers on using tiny glue dots. Or you can draw a de-

sign with glue . . . a flower, for instance . . . then press your fiber down over your glue outline."

"So you have a furry flower," said Baby.

"You will if you use mohair or bouclé," said Carmela. "And remember, fibers are ideal for attaching buttons, charms, and beads to scrapbook pages and craft projects." She looked up and nodded at Gabby. "Gabby's going to give each of you a piece of twenty-gauge craft wire, and then we're all going to make a fiber letter." Carmela took a piece of wire and fashioned it into a capital A. "Do any letter you want, uppercase or lower, free-form or formal. For demonstration purposes, I'm going to do an A." She held her wire A up for everyone to see. "Then I'm going to take a piece of red-and-blue yarn and start winding it around the letter. I tuck one end under the wrapped yarn, then work my way around my letter."

As Carmela talked, her nimble fingers wrapped fiber around and around her letter A. Other heads bent intently as they fashioned letters from wire and worked intently with their chosen fibers.

"When I get to the end," said Carmela, "I use a dab of glue to keep the whole thing from unraveling. Now the letter can be bent slightly, making the shape even more perfect, or I can just play with it and achieve a wavy shape."

"Love it," declared Tandy.

Carmela went around the table, helping out, giving encouragement, and having fun. This was what it was all about, of course: teaching crafty ladies to be even craftier.

With the fiber-wrapped letters a success, Carmela moved on to page and photo borders. This entailed wrapping leather strips around preformed photo borders as well as punching holes in strips of card stock and then weaving in Lurex and knotted flag fibers for color and textural interest.

"Remember," said Carmela as everyone worked away, "these fibers are all acid free, made specifically for use in scrapbooks."

"But how do you keep them all organized?" one of her customers asked.

"Ziplock bags," Carmela told her. "And since some of the fibers, particularly mohair, shed slightly, you do want to keep them from getting all over the place."

An hour later, they moved on to wrapped hearts.

"These are always a fun way to showcase fibers," Carmela told her audience. "You take a die-cut heart—Gabby, will you pass those out?"

Gabby nodded and moved around the table, handing out die-cut hearts in various sizes.

"What you want to do," said Carmela, "is decorate your heart first. Maybe brushing a little gold paint on a red heart. Or taking a plain card stock heart and covering it with brocade paper . . ."

"Do one for us," urged the woman in the frilly blouse. "It's always easier to make something after you've seen a demo."

"Gladly," said Carmela, grabbing a heart that had been cut from dark purple card stock. "First I'm going to dab on a little gold paint as a backdrop." She dabbed away as everyone watched. "Not too much, just enough to lend a faux-finished feel. Then I'm going to use a rubber stamp—in this case, one that's an old-fashioned portrait of a woman. I'll press it against my bronze ink stamp pad . . ." She pressed her stamp against the bronze stamp pad. "Then stamp right on my heart. Now I'm going to wrap my heart with a small bit of copper wire. Not completely, just a couple of strands. Wrap them diagonally or create a tiny cage design. That way the design still

shows through." She finished wrapping her wire, then twisted a loop on top. "Now I can turn my heart into a tag or a scrapbook page embellishment, or even attach it to a bookmark."

"Splendid," breathed one of her customers.

"Good," said Carmela, "now you all give it a go. Use any rubber stamps you want, and any of the fifty or so fibers or types of wire on the table."

The women worked for a good thirty minutes or so, with Baby creating a dimensional heart using three different-sized pink and orange hearts glued one on top of each other, then finishing them off with a narrow strip of pink gauze ribbon.

"That's really breathtaking," Gabby told Baby, while all the other women seemed to agree.

"You don't need me," laughed Carmela. "You should be teaching this class."

"Oh no," Baby demurred. "Never."

"Did you know," Carmela said to her group, "that you can even do fiber earrings?"

That brought out even more enthusiasm, so she did another quick demonstration.

"You start with felt beads," she told them, pulling two purple and two gold felt beads from a packet. "Then run a two-inch eyepin through them, add a glass bead or two, then attach to French hook ear wires."

"Earrings," said one of the women, obviously delighted. "Who would have thought!"

At which point Gabby began circling the table, taking orders for lunch, and Carmela slipped into her office to check her notes for the afternoon session. After five seconds of reviewing, she received a phone call from Ava.

"Get over here fast," Ava trilled. "Sissy Fowler just came in and she's buying out the store."

"*The* Sissy Fowler?" asked Carmela.

"That's right," said Ava. "Wife of the highly unpopular, still-under-indictment dead guy."

"What on earth is she doing at your place?" asked Carmela. "Shouldn't Sissy be in hiding or mourning or something like that?"

"She ain't wearing black, and she sure isn't hanging crepe," said Ava.

"So what *is* she doing?" asked Carmela.

Ava chuckled. "Get over here and find out, girlfriend!"

After checking with Gabby and being assured lunch was in her very capable hands, Carmela ducked out the back door and scurried the few blocks to Ava's voodoo shop.

Hesitating at the high-gloss red front door where fat, bouncy black letters spelled out *Juju Voodoo*, Carmela tried to catch her breath. After all, she didn't want to appear too anxious.

Carmela peered at her reflection in the multipaned front window and fluffed her hair. Below her reflection, a neon sign glowed bright red and cool blue, illustrating a palm with its basic head, heart, and life lines. A wooden shake roof, slightly reminiscent of a Hansel and Gretel cottage, dipped down in front.

"Ava?" Carmela called as she pushed her way into the dark interior, and was immediately greeted by flickering red votive candles and the fragrant aromas of sandalwood and patchouli oil.

Juju Voodoo was, of course, the premier voodoo shop in New Orleans. If you had your heart set on a life-size (death-size?) jangling skeleton, Ava could hook you up. Same went for voodoo dolls, evil-eye necklaces, love charms wrapped in netting and lace, saint candles, incense, shrunken heads,

and necklaces hung with carved teeth and bones. Inventory was key here, and Ava prided herself on having the perfect juju magic for whatever ailed you. Of course, most of the love charms were really herbs and spices and the rest were fun tourist souvenirs. But Ava did a land-office business and even offered a reading room in back where, should you care to take a chance with spirits from the great beyond, you could have a reading from tarot cards, the *I Ching*, an astrology chart, or any other popular form of divination.

"*Cher*," said Ava, popping up from behind the counter. "How fun of you to drop by."

"I was just in the neighborhood," said Carmela, following Ava's cue and noting her sideways glance at Sissy Fowler.

Sissy Fowler was indeed shopping up a storm. A large wicker basket dangled from one arm as she busily selected saint candles for her husband's funeral tomorrow. St. Rita, the patron saint of difficult marriages, was balanced in one of Sissy's hands, while St. Titus, patron saint of stomach disorders, had just been set back on the shelf.

Wearing a salmon-pink pantsuit with a gigantic pearl cluster pin, Sissy looked well off, well fed, and well rested. Her pinkish-blond hair was carefully coiffed and swirled atop her head like strawberry cream strudel. Gold charm bracelets clanked on both wrists, and Sissy's lip-glossed mouth was drawn into a tiny pout.

"Do you two know each other?" Ava drawled.

Sissy turned and smiled, then stuck out a pudgy hand. "Carmela?"

"Nice to see you again, Sissy." Carmela had met Sissy at a meeting of the Garden District garden club, back when she was a new bride trying desperately to fit in with the old guard. "And may I extend my deepest sympathies," Carmela added.

"Deep, deep sympathies," intoned Ava.

Sissy blinked rapidly, spattering little flecks of mascara across carefully rouged cheeks. "Ava and I were just talking," she said. "About how the two of you discovered my dear, departed husband. And now . . . here you are again!"

Sissy's expression was so pained, her voice so shrill, that Carmela wasn't sure if Sissy was troubled by the coincidence or tickled. Turns out, it was the latter.

"I wanted to express my sincere thanks to the both of you," said Sissy, "for callin' 911 and all."

"Think nothing of it," said Ava. "It was the least we could do."

"It was the only thing we could do," said Carmela. She was surprised at how calm and collected Sissy appeared. Not exactly the portrait of a tearful, grieving widow. But maybe all that would come later, along with a dose of posttraumatic stress tossed in for good measure. Maybe.

"I'd be honored if y'all came to the funeral tomorrow," said Sissy. "In fact, it would truly warm my heart."

"Then we'll certainly be there," said Ava. She glanced at Carmela. "Won't we?"

"With bells on," said Carmela.

Sissy held up the St. Rita candle she clutched in her hand. "Do you have twelve of these all together? I thought it might be nice to line the center aisle of the church."

"Four more and you've got yourself a case," said Ava. "Which means a fifteen percent discount."

"Sold," said Sissy as overhead a dancing skeleton clicked and clacked in the slight breeze.

Carmela cleared her throat. "We were . . . uh . . . talking to Jimmy Toups last night."

"Dear Jimmy," said Sissy, clapping a hand to her ample bosom.

"He mentioned that the two of you were working on a book together," continued Carmela.

"We most certainly are," said Sissy. "On the history of Mardi Gras. And Jimmy and I have grown quite close in the process. The dear fellow even wants me to have editorial credit. Imagine that, little old me!"

"That's wonderful," said Ava, slamming the case of saint candles down on her wooden counter.

Looking pious, Sissy cast her eyes downward for a moment, then said, "Of course, we've put the book on hold for the time being."

"Naturally," said Carmela, thinking the poor woman must be grieving after all.

"But we'll be back at it bright and early come Monday," Sissy assured them, whipping out her Visa card and handing it to Ava.

So much for being prostrate with grief, Carmela decided.

"You need help carrying the candles out to your car?" asked Ava, once Sissy's transaction was complete.

"I can manage," Sissy assured her. "Now's when all those Pilates classes pay off."

Carmela watched Sissy heft the case of candles and wondered, had Sissy's Pilates classes given her enough strength to hoist a Minotaur head and ram it through her husband's heart? Maybe so, since Sissy looked like she could be a formidable opponent. The question was—did she really have a motive?

"Do you know . . . ?" began Carmela. "Are the police any closer to finding your husband's killer?" A blunt question,

maybe even impertinent, but she was dying to hear Sissy's answer.

Sissy narrowed her eyes and set her jaw so firmly Carmela could hear her mandible click into place. "You better believe they are," exclaimed Sissy. "Because I gave them a good, hard nudge in Tanya's direction!"

Carmela and Ava gazed at each other, a little confused. Who?

"Tanya," said Ava, enunciating carefully. "Who, pray tell, is Tanya?"

Sissy shifted the box in her arms and rolled her eyes expressively, as if she had an enormous secret she was bursting at the seams to reveal. So, of course, she did.

"Tanya, dear ladies," announced Sissy, "is my late, philandering husband's girlfriend du jour!"

"Tanya," said Carmela, once Sissy had bumped her way out of Juju Voodoo and the hinged door had whapped her on the backside. "Imagine that. Fowler had himself a chickie-poo."

Ava scratched her head. "Frankly, I'm shocked Brett Fowler even found a wife, considering he was such a major oinker. And I don't mean to speak ill of a paying customer, but Sissy wasn't exactly a prize catch, either."

"Fowler thought she was," said Carmela. "At one time, anyway. Although that may have been because she was rich."

"Sissy's real rich?" asked Ava.

"Rich enough," said Carmela, recalling Sissy's ginormous Garden District home and the dove-gray Bentley parked in her driveway.

"Must be nice," said Ava, resting both elbows on the counter and dropping her chin into her hands.

"Alone with all that money?" said Carmela. "Maybe not so great after all."

"You know what's so exasperating?" asked Ava, looking thoughtful. "Men can *always* find some woman who'll adore them, no matter what. There are, like, eight-hundred-pound guys who haven't left their bedrooms in six years, yet they still have multiple women swooning over them."

"It is a weird phenomenon," agreed Carmela. She'd seen a TV show about a guy who'd been hefted out his window in a whale sling, then transported to his wedding on a tractor trailer.

"And the other crazy thing," said Ava, "is that prisoners seem to attract women like flies."

"Gotta be the bad-boy syndrome," said Carmela.

Ava looked mystified. "But we're talking *really* bad boys. Murderers serving life sentences in hellholes like Angola and Sing Sing. Some of 'em have to beat women off with a stick. Some have even gotten married while serving life terms!"

"What's your point?" Carmela asked in a droll tone.

Ava shrugged. "I don't know. Maybe that when it comes to relationships, life is basically unfair?"

Carmela chuckled. "Lady, you just said a mouthful."

Ava picked up a string of skull beads and ran them through her fingers, her red nail polish glinting in the dim light. "Babcock came over last night?"

"He did."

"You guys talk about the murder?"

"Some."

"He tell you any more about the investigation?"

"He's playing it pretty close to the vest," said Carmela.

"Typical," said Ava. "Think he knows about Fowler's little dolly? Tanya?"

A smile played at Carmela's mouth. "He will shortly."

"Ah, good girl."

"How'd your, um, *date* go last night?"

"With silver fox Hodney? He was nice. Even ordered a bottle of Cristal."

"Expensive," said Carmela. They'd served Cristal at her wedding, and Shamus had grumped endlessly about the cost. He'd quaffed multiple glasses, of course, but had still grumped about it.

Ava rubbed her nails against her blouse. "Hodney can afford pricey champagne."

"But can you afford Boyd Hodney?"

Ava pursed her lips, about to say something, then didn't.

Carmela figured she'd better put a lid on the Hodney talk. Ava was a smart cookie; she'd figure things out for herself. Especially when Mrs. Hodney stepped in like a drill sergeant to short-leash her roving-eyed husband.

"Here, *cher*," said Ava, sliding a pair of black enamel bat-wing earrings across the counter. "These are for you."

"What a coincidence," said Carmela. "I got up this morning, put on my tweed jacket, and thought to myself, *Pearls are so boring. What I really need to bling things up is a nice pair of bat-wing earrings.*"

"Now you've got them," laughed Ava.

Carmela pulled off her gold hoop earrings and slipped on the bat earrings. "Who doesn't love *die Fledermaus?*"

"Have a skull bracelet, too," said Ava, pushing a carved bone bracelet across the counter.

"What's with all this sudden generosity?" asked Carmela. "Are you having inventory issues?"

"I was kind of hoping you'd wear the jewelry Friday night."

"Dare I ask what's on the agenda for Friday night?"

Ava hooked a thumb and pointed toward a black-and-red poster that rested on her counter.

Carmela scanned the poster, then said, "Holy crapola, you're leading a vampire tour?"

Ava gave a bright smile. "Fun, huh?"

"I don't know," said Carmela. "I've never been on one."

"Got any ideas?"

Narrowing her eyes, Carmela said, "What kind of con are you running? I mean, on *me*?"

"I . . . well, here's the thing." Ava shrugged. "I had a few requests from customers to do a vampire tour, and I sure as heck didn't want to say no, the economy being what it is. Then, suddenly, everything sort of . . . *kapow*!" She clapped her hands together. "Spiraled."

"Spiraled out of control?"

Ava looked thoughtful. "Veered off course, anyway."

"How many people did you promise to lead on this tour?"

Ava hunched her shoulders and said in a small voice, "Twenty?"

"What!"

"I'll give you half the take. It's only fair."

Carmela thought for a few seconds. "What would be the take?"

Twenty people times twenty-five bucks, that's . . ." Ava scrunched up her face, trying to run the numbers.

"Five hundred bucks," supplied Carmela.

"Right," said Ava, brightening. "So you'd get two hundred and fifty. For a couple hours' work."

Carmela tapped her foot on the floor, thinking. "And all I have to do is help lead this vampire tour?"

"That's it." Ava paused. "Chat up the tourists with me and wear a long black gown and smear a little fake blood around your mouth."

"Anything else?"

Ava dug under the counter, pulled out a plastic box, and slid it across the counter.

"What's that?"

Ava gingerly opened the lid.

Carmela lifted a single eyebrow and let it quiver. "You want me to wear vampire fangs?"

"Sure," said Ava, "it'll be fun."

"You think?"

"As long as you get 'em settled in okay," said Ava. "Otherwise you kind of spit on people when you talk."

"Nice," said Carmela. She made no move to grab the box. The fangs sat between them in a kind of no-man's-land.

"Maybe chalk it up to a crazy experience?" said Ava, looking hopeful.

"But why does it have to be *my* experience?"

Ava pushed the box toward Carmela. "Take a saint candle, too. I'm stocked to the rafters."

Carmela pocketed the fangs and glanced around. "What's with all the gold-and-green saint candles? You got some kind of sale going on?"

"Oh," said Ava, pulling one down and setting it on the counter in front of Carmela. "You're talking about St. Erasmus. He happens to be our most popular guy."

"Patron saint of . . ."

"Storms and hurricanes," said Ava.

"No wonder he's a big seller," said Carmela. "Maybe

I should take him home with me. Think of it as flood insurance."

"Couldn't hurt," said Ava, grabbing a second candle.

Carmela gazed at the upturned countenance of St. Erasmus. The paper on the outside of the candle had crinkled, and poor St. Erasmus was looking a little under the weather. "Anything else I should know about him? Like how he came to be a saint?"

"Let me think," said Ava, staring thoughtfully at the candle for a few seconds. "Do I know any fun factoids?" Then she snapped her fingers. "Oh sure! He was disemboweled in Italy back in 303!"

Chapter 10

"THERE'S a girlfriend?" Gabby whispered. Carmela was back at Memory Mine, standing at the front counter with Gabby. All the Fiber Arts attendees were busily conversing with each other as they dug into their catered lunches from the Pirate's Alley Deli.

"Kind of blows your mind, huh?" said Carmela.

"I've met Brett Fowler quite a few times," said Gabby, "and I never pegged him for a . . ." Gabby stopped, suddenly looking uncomfortable.

"Philanderer?" filled in Carmela. "Cheater? Adulterer?"

"Now the whole thing really does sound sordid," said Gabby.

"You can put your criticism of Fowler on the back burner for now," said Carmela, "because—get ready for this—his wife, Sissy, is seriously involved with Jimmy Toups."

"What?" said Gabby. "Sissy and the float builder? The

one who wears those wacky, eighties-looking jumpsuits?" Now Gabby really seemed blown away.

"I think Toups must have bought out an army surplus store or something," said Carmela. "Then had his jumpsuits tailored to fit."

"That's just weird," muttered Gabby.

"The jumpsuits or the affair with Sissy?"

"Both," said Gabby, gathering up rolls of sisal and jute.

"Okay, here's the real kicker," said Carmela. "Sissy and Jimmy Toups are collaborating on a Mardi Gras book."

"Excuse me?" Gabby's eyes grew wide. "But isn't that Jekyl's pet project?"

"Not anymore," said Carmela. "Now it's Sissy and Jimmy Toups's pet project. They claim to have an actual book contract from Peregrine Publishing."

"Holy cow," said Gabby. "Jekyl's going to be freaked."

"Uh . . . yeah, he is," said Carmela. "And I've been trying to figure out how to break the wretched news to him."

"You've got to just *tell* him straight out," said Gabby. "But please . . . sugarcoat it a little bit. You know how deeply sensitive Jekyl is."

"Maybe if I try to present it more as a heads-up sort of thing," said Carmela.

"A motivator," said Gabby.

"And a swift kick in the keister," said Carmela. "So Jekyl gets his act in gear and finishes his book *first*."

Gabby looked thoughtful. "How much of his book does Jekyl have completed, anyway?"

"No clue," said Carmela. "But I happen to know he spent his entire advance." Six months ago Jekyl had found a French armoire at Bayou Baubles that he just *had* to have.

"Better call him right away," suggested Gabby.

* * *

"Carmela, my love," Jekyl chortled, once she had him on the phone. "What have you been up to? Designing menus for some lively new bistro? Decoupaging foreign stamps onto a picture frame?"

"No," said Carmela. "But I ran into Sissy Fowler over at Ava's shop."

"Do tell," said Jekyl, sounding flippant.

"Jekyl," said Carmela, "I've got some weird news for you. Are you sitting down?"

"No, darling," said Jekyl. "At this moment I'm strolling down Magazine Street heading for the Bluebeard Gallery. They have a marvelous collection of sterling silver candlesticks and things that just came in, and yours truly is getting first look. But tell me quick, love, what's your big news?"

"Okay," said Carmela. "Uh . . . Sissy Fowler claims to have a book deal going with Jimmy Toups."

Silence spun out for a few moments. Carmela could just imagine Jekyl's brows knitting together. Finally he said, no longer flippant and in a tone bordering on icy, "What *kind* of book deal?"

Gulp. "I'm a little foggy on the whole thing," Carmela said, backing off a bit. "But I've been told it has something to do with the history of Mardi Gras."

Jekyl's voice suddenly switched to deep-freeze mode. "Excuse me, that's *my* project."

"I know it is," said Carmela. "Because you, of all people, are the hands-down Mardi Gras expert. And that's why I'm giving you this heads-up." Carmela paused, listening to Jekyl's breathing. She hoped he wasn't spinning into cardiac arrest or something. "I know it sounds crazy and steps on

your toes like crazy," she continued, "but Jimmy Toups and Sissy Fowler both claim they're busy selecting photos and writing text."

"Well . . . shit," said Jekyl. Then more silence. "How did you find out about this?"

"Directly from the horse's mouth. I ran into Sissy at Juju Voodoo."

"So more like the horse's ass," snarled Jekyl.

Carmela let his remark zip over her head. "So what I was wondering was, how far along are you with your book? Is there any chance you can hurry things up and eclipse those two dunderheads?"

"Possibly."

"Jekyl," said Carmela, "I say this to you as a friend with *beaucoup* love in my heart. In the immortal words of Captain Jean-Luc Picard from *Star Trek*, 'Make it so.'"

Carmela's afternoon session had settled into more techniques on wrapping fibers around die-cut letters and numbers when Quigg Brevard sauntered into her shop.

Quigg was a handsome restaurateur and owner of Bon Tiempe Restaurant in the Bywater district and Mumbo Gumbo in the French Quarter. Carmela had dated Quigg a couple of times, back when she and Shamus had separated for the second time. She and Quigg had seemed to simmer for a while, and then the relationship had slid to the back burner, where it rapidly cooled.

Now Carmela thought of Quigg as a friend. A good, handsome friend. Still very easy on the eye.

"Hello, beautiful," Quigg said to Carmela. It was his standard greeting to all women.

Some of the women glanced up at Quigg and smiled. A few melted. And more than a few of them watched him with cool appraisal as Carmela led him back to her office. Quigg's olive complexion, dark snapping eyes, broad shoulders, and casual, almost lazy manner could almost take your breath away.

"You've got a project," she said to him, once they were both seated, she in her swivel chair, he in the red leather director's chair, their knees touching slightly.

"Always," said Quigg, fidgeting because he didn't quite fit in the director's chair.

"What is it this time?" Carmela asked. Quigg was a dyed-in-the-wool entrepreneur. Always opening restaurants, launching new products, coming up with new business angles. Last year he'd even invented a new type of corkscrew.

Popping open his leather attaché case, really a messenger bag, Quigg pulled out a bottle of wine and placed it on Carmela's desk. Red wine, no label, with a handsome gold foil seal covering the cork.

"Wine," said Carmela. "And from the looks of that bottle . . . a Bordeaux?"

"Exactly," said Quigg. "Produced solely from grapes in my vineyard."

Carmela grinned. This was an offbeat surprise. "You have a vineyard? Seriously?" This was a new wrinkle in the Quigg empire.

"St. Tammany Vineyard," Quigg told her. "My newest enterprise under the corporate umbrella of Quigg Brevard LLC. We're fifteen miles north of Lake Pontchartrain with twenty acres already under cultivation."

"Impressive."

"Not really, you haven't seen my production center yet.

It . . . well, it still needs work. We're basically one step be-yond stomping grapes with our feet." He handed the bottle to Carmela. "But the quality's good. Better than good."

"And let me guess," she said, spinning the bottle around. "You need a label."

"A logo and a label," Quigg told her. "In fact, several labels for my different varietals." He paused. "Are you interested?"

"I have to say I'm intrigued," said Carmela. She glanced out the door of her office, where her paying customers were working away. Probably anticipating the next project. "But I'm also a little busy right now. I've got more semi-nars scheduled in the next couple of weeks, and I'm kind of crashing on a project for the Art Institute."

"You're always busy," said Quigg, the corners of his mouth twitching. "That's what keeps you so young and gorgeous."

"You figured out my secret," said Carmela. *That and eight hours of sleep and gooping on lots of heavy-duty moisturizer.*

"Tell you what," said Quigg. "Why don't you drop by Bon Tiempe tonight and taste some of my wines? Make up your mind then."

"Maybe," said Carmela, hedging.

"Bring your crazy friend, Ava," said Quigg. "I'll have Chef Daniel whip up something really special." He leaned forward and gave her a sly, heart-tugging grin. "Deal?"

"Okay," Carmela agreed. "Deal."

When Carmela returned to her seminar, Tandy was telling the women sitting next to her all about Baby's upcoming Halloween party.

"They're the best parties in the world," Tandy raved.

"Baby has a love affair with Halloween, so she always decorates to the nines. Plus she serves the most amazing food." Tandy dropped her voice. "Catered, don't you know?"

Looking a little embarrassed, Baby quickly changed the subject. "Has anyone heard anything about Roy Slayback?" Roy Slayback was, of course, Brett Fowler's partner in Emerald Equities. According to the ongoing stories in the *Times-Picayune*, Slayback was claiming to have no knowledge of Fowler's financial improprieties.

"Slayback had to know," said Tandy. "After all, he sat in the office next to Brett Fowler." She gave an exaggerated eye roll. "Nobody's that dense."

Carmela joined the conversation. "I understand Roy Slayback usually handled the venture capital part of Emerald Equities. In fact, that's where Emerald Equities got its first foothold. In venture capital."

Tandy blinked. "What's that?"

"Financing and underwriting businesses," said Carmela. "Helping them launch new products, go public, that sort of thing."

"Interesting what you learn when you've been married to a banker," said Tandy.

Carmela smiled to herself. She hadn't learned those things from Shamus. She'd learned them all by herself reading *Forbes*, *Business Week*, and the *Wall Street Journal*. She was a firm believer that all women should strive to be financially independent. And learning as much as you could about business and finance was the first step. Even if you never actually traded stocks or bought bonds, knowledge about them gave you a certain amount of power. And it sure as heck made it easier to carry on a conversation in the company of men. Men who thought you understood

business accorded you a grudging respect. Sometimes even just plain respect.

"I know Roy Slayback quite well," said Baby, "and I can't imagine he's involved in any sort of Ponzi scheme."

"Maybe," said Tandy, sounding doubtful.

"In fact, I'm going to call him and make sure he comes to my party Saturday night," said Baby. "He could probably use a little support."

"Unless he gets hauled off to jail," snorted Tandy.

When Carmela had a couple of free moments, she slipped into her office and called Edgar Babcock.

"Carmela," he said, right off the bat. No hello, no howdy-do.

"You're on your cell phone?" she asked. "Caller ID?"

"Of course."

"Good," she said. "I didn't think you'd suddenly developed the power of ESP."

"What's up?" Babcock asked, sounding police-officer-hurried now.

"Just wanted to see what's new," said Carmela. "As in how goes the investigation?"

"Moving along," said Babcock. "Nothing earth-shattering, but we're still putting together pieces and inching forward. Shouldn't be too long before we issue an arrest warrant."

"Do you still have Jekyl Hardy's name on your most-wanted list?"

"Mmm, maybe." Babcock put his hand over the phone, mumbled something to someone named Andy, then came back on the line again. "One little detail *has* come up," he

told her. "We found out that your friend Jekyl Hardy designed the Minotaur head."

"Ah," said Carmela, trying hard to sound casual.

"A rather interesting coincidence, which I'm guessing you knew about," said Babcock.

She stalled again. "Mmm . . ."

"Carmela, have you told me everything?"

"Everything I know." Carmela took a deep breath, then said, "I ran into Sissy Fowler earlier today. Over at Ava's shop."

"Okay, that's one way to change the subject."

"Sissy was not prostrate with grief or gnashing her teeth."

"So few women do that anymore," said Babcock. "Kind of makes one pine for the good old days."

"Is that cop humor?"

"Nope, just my own droll brand, which seems to be grossly underappreciated."

"The thing is," said Carmela, "Sissy was rambling on about a Mardi Gras book she's working on with Jimmy Toups."

"How nice for her."

"You don't find that a tiny bit suspicious?" asked Carmela. "The bereaved widow teaming up with one of the Pluvius krewe's float designers?"

Babcock sighed. "I find everything suspicious, Carmela. That's why I carry a gold shield. But the thing is, I practice deductive reasoning coupled with restraint and a healthy dose of skepticism. I don't go lunging after every little clue or snippet of information."

"And you're implying I do?" Carmela put a serious chill in her voice.

"You're a civilian," said Babcock. "It's only natural."

"And sometimes you have tunnel vision," Carmela shot back.

"Touché," said Babcock. "Now let's get our conversation back to a more personal level, where it belongs. What are you doing tonight?"

"For your information, I have a date to do some wine tasting."

"What?" said Babcock. "Where?"

"Bon Tiempe Restaurant."

"With that greasy Quigg character?" Babcock asked, his voice tinged with what Carmela thought must surely be jealousy.

"Quigg's a highly respected restaurateur," replied Carmela. So there.

"Hah," snorted Babcock. "Just for that, I'm going to call you tonight precisely at ten o'clock. For bed check."

"And I might not be home," said Carmela, hanging up on him.

Just as Carmela was demonstrating some techniques for using raffia, the bell over the front door dinged noisily, and Tandy squealed, "Good heavens, is it Halloween already?"

All eyes suddenly turned front and center as a bizarre apparition—really a man in a silky black-and-white skeleton costume—came swaggering into Memory Mine. But it was his head that drew the real attention. A black hat perched atop a skull that had been painted powdery white. White theatrical paint covered the man's entire face. Pinprick nostrils and a wide mouth had been drawn crazily with black grease paint. And his eyes had been fitted with red

contact lenses. All in all, a very professional costume that lent a scary, gruesome look!

Gabby sought to head the errant skeleton off at the pass. "I'm sorry, but we have a private event going on today . . ."

"No problem, cutie pie," replied the skeleton as he sidestepped her. "I just dropped by to pass out a few souvenir doubloons."

"Goodness," said Baby, "it's Mr. Bones! I've been hearing about him." She waved for him to come on back and join them. "Hello there, Mr. Bones."

Mr. Bones swept his black fedora from his smooth, white skull and bowed deeply. "Mr. Bones at your service, ladies. I don't mean to disrupt your class, but I am a man, albeit a dead man, on a rather important mission."

"What kind of mission?" asked Carmela as all the women turned their full attention on Mr. Bones.

"He's been hired by the French Quarter Business Association," explained Baby. "To wander around the Quarter and drum up business for the big Halloween celebration."

"It is also my good fortune to pass out beads and doubloons," said Mr. Bones, suddenly digging in the hidden pockets of his skeleton suit and pulling out strands of purple and gold beads.

"Ooh, beads!" exclaimed Tandy. "Throw me somethin', mistah," she cried, echoing the chorus that resounded from the onlookers during raucous Mardi Gras parades.

"I want to extend a most cordial invitation to all our big Halloween events," said Mr. Bones. "As you probably know, our treasure hunt has already begun, as have ghost train rides on the St. Charles Avenue streetcar line."

"That sounds like fun," said one of the women, letting loose a little shiver.

Mr. Bones held up a bony index finger. "And Sunday night's big event on Halloween will feature live zydeco music and food booths in Lafayette Square, plus our Monsters and Mayhem cavalcade of hearses, Day of the Dead candle parade, and the much-heralded giant monster puppet parade!"

"I guess we know about that," murmured Carmela.

"Who are you really?" asked Tandy, being slightly flirtatious. "Do I know you?"

"Possibly," said Mr. Bones, giving her a wink and a ghostly grin.

"Have *we* met?" asked Baby.

Mr. Bones paused to think for a moment. "I'd say . . . perchance we have."

"You're being very cagey about your identity," said Tandy. "Do you work in the French Quarter?"

"Sometimes," said Mr. Bones.

"Maybe in one of the antique shops?" asked Baby.

"Mmm . . . no," said Mr. Bones.

"Hmm," said Tandy, looking puzzled. "We need a better clue."

Mr. Bones sidled over to Carmela and pressed a large silver doubloon into her palm. "Try this," he told her, then squirted away, dancing and doing an almost Charlie Chaplin–type walk.

"I know him," mused Baby. "I really think I do."

Gabby nudged an elbow at Carmela. "Who do *you* think he is?" she asked. "I mean . . . really?"

Gazing after the departing Mr. Bones, Carmela said, "No idea."

Chapter 11

"YOU think we're gussied up enough?" asked Ava as they stepped up to the hostess stand at Bon Tiempe.

"I think we're gussied just fine," said Carmela. She was wearing black slacks and her almost-Chanel black jacket with its tailored look and slight bit of fringe. Ava was dressed in a floor-length black velvet dress with a plunging neckline. Strange attire anywhere else, but in New Orleans, the week before Halloween, almost perfect.

"Sorry to keep you waiting," said the hostess, who'd just returned from seating a large party. "You have reservations?"

"Concerning this dinner, yes," Carmela quipped.

The young, college-age hostess stared blankly at her.

"We're here as special guests of Quigg," Carmela quickly amended. She waved a hand in the air as if to scrub away her previous words. "Sorry, bad joke. Reservation for Bertrand?"

"Oh, of course," gushed the hostess. "You're Mr. Brevard's wine-tasting guests! Please step right this way." She picked up two tall parchment menus that Carmela had designed earlier in the year, then hurriedly set them back down. "Oops, you ladies won't be needing menus tonight. I understand Chef Daniel has prepared a special tasting menu."

"Special," murmured Ava as she shook back dark, curly hair and glided into the dining room. "We're very special."

"Try to get over yourself," laughed Carmela. "It's only Quigg."

"And Chef Daniel," said Ava. "He of the tasting menu."

"Here's your table, ladies," said the hostess, plucking a *Reserved* sign from the white linen tablecloth and deftly sliding out two brocade-covered chairs.

"Lovely," said Carmela as they sat down to a beautifully set table with an elegant tablescape. A low silver bowl contained a tumble of white orchids and sprigs of ivy. A pair of white, flickering tapers stood in silver candleholders that had ornate stag's-head bases. Silver charger plates were flanked by gleaming sterling silver flatware. Three Baccarat crystal wineglasses and a champagne flute were lined up with great precision at each place setting.

"Fabulous," said Ava, grabbing Carmela's hand and giving a conspiratorial squeeze. "Thanks for inviting me, *cher*, because I do love this place. And this kind of service!"

Housed in a crumbling old mansion in the Bywater district, Bon Tiempe exuded an aura of class and Old World charm. Antique chandeliers tinkled and sparkled overhead; oil paintings crackled with age hung on brocade-covered walls. Sagging wooden floors were covered with lush Oriental carpets. And to make the dining experience even more intimate, lush velvet draperies with fat tassels

sectioned off various parts of the restaurant to create cozy dining nooks.

"Bon Tiempe is a little over the top," said Carmela. "Even for New Orleans."

"Are you positive you're not even a teensy bit interested in Quigg?" asked Ava. "Because if you showed him the skimpiest scrap of affection, I'll bet we could dine here all the time."

"Aside from the fact that we'd both probably gain twenty pounds, I hear what you're saying," said Carmela. "And I like the basic concept."

"There's a *but* coming," said Ava.

Carmela nodded. "But with Babcock in the picture, there's no chance of a big spark happening between Quigg and me. We had our little go-round, and it was a no-go."

"Just didn't feel it, huh?"

"Not really," said Carmela.

"Okay."

"Why don't *you* flirt with him?" Carmela suggested.

Ava tilted her head to one side, and her gold and crystal hoop earrings caught the light and reflected tiny pinpoints of brilliance. "I've tried"—she sighed—"but Quigg treats me like last century's wallpaper. His beady little eyes are always riveted on you!"

"Come on," said Carmela, "you practically invented Flirting 101!"

"I know!" wailed Ava, "and that's what scares me. What if I'm losing my touch? Maybe I'm getting too old. Or too fat." She sighed again. "Men just don't respond to me like they used to."

"Not true," said Carmela, crooking a finger at the busboy. "Could we get some lemon wedges for our water?" she

asked him. The busboy nodded, turned, then caught himself. He gazed back at Ava, his face suddenly going slack as if dumbstruck by her beauty. "Is lemon okay?" he asked her. "Because I could bring you a lime if you want." Color flared in his cheeks. "Or . . . anything you want."

"See?" Carmela murmured. "You've still got the old razzle-dazzle."

"Thank goodness," said Ava. She turned a sloe-eyed smile on the busboy and said, "Lemon's just fine, darlin'."

"Right away," he said, practically tripping over his feet.

"Catch and release," laughed Carmela.

Ava slid her dress down, revealing one bare shoulder. "You've restored my confidence."

"Think of it as warped encounter group therapy," said Carmela. Then, under her breath, added, "Here he is."

"Ladies!" exclaimed Quigg Brevard as he sped over to their table. "Welcome!" Dressed in a slim-fitting Italian tuxedo, Quigg certainly looked the part of the successful restaurateur and debonair man-about-town. Albeit one direct from central casting.

"Mr. Brevard," drawled Ava, extending a hand and fluttering her false eyelashes, "so very kind of you to invite us."

Quigg bowed deeply and planted a quick kiss on the back of Ava's hand, then immediately turned his full attention on Carmela. "Delighted you ladies could make it." His eyes remained glued on Carmela.

"See?" said Ava, giving a little shrug. "Exactly my point. Wallpaper."

Quigg continued to focus on Carmela. "I took the liberty of having Chef Daniel prepare a special tasting menu that should pair nicely with my wine offerings."

"I could be undressed," Ava murmured, "and he wouldn't notice."

"Knowing you're an aficionado of fine Louisiana oysters," Quigg said, grinning at Carmela, "I had some of the tasty little mollusks shipped in just this morning from Bayou du Large. They're cold and salty with just the perfect modicum of brine. An ideal starter course."

"You're very kind," said Carmela.

"Arnault," said Quigg, stepping aside for their waiter, a tall, thin, stoop-shouldered man with a thin comb-over. "You've brought the champagne."

"Yes, sir," said Arnault. He covered the top of the bottle with a white bar cloth and worked at the cork until there was a delicate pop.

"Music to my ears," said Ava.

"This is my St. Tammany Vineyard champagne," said Quigg. "I call it Bayou Sparkler, and it's truly made in the traditional French *méthode champenoise*."

Carmela took a sip. "Delicious."

"Feel those tiny bubbles bursting on your tongue?" asked Quigg. "Can you taste the delicate champagne mousse?"

"You're really into this, aren't you?" said Carmela.

Quigg seemed filled with pride. "I'm a vintner now. I finally found my true passion in life."

"While some of us are still looking," said Ava, under her breath.

"Enjoy, ladies," said Quigg, giving a giant Cheshire-cat grin as he edged away from them.

"Such an elegant man," said Ava. "And he doesn't even notice me."

"He noticed you," said Carmela. "He kissed your hand."

"While his eyes were lasered on you," said Ava. "Again, I make my point." She adjusted her neckline downward and glanced about the restaurant. "However, there are so many other attractive gentlemen here."

"Always are," said Carmela. "Bon Tiempe was a power lunch spot from the get-go, and now it's a power dinner spot, too."

"Ladies," said Arnault, "may I present you with your first course? Oysters on the half shell with a small dab of osetra caviar on the side." He set silver platters in front of each of them, filled with crushed ice and topped with a half-dozen fresh oysters quivering in their own brine. On a flat silver tray was a mound of fresh shaved horseradish, a puddle of hot sauce, and a small dab of osetra.

"Wow," said Ava.

"Smashing," said Carmela. Not only was she an oyster freak, but caviar was one of her guilty pleasures.

"Enjoy," said Arnault.

Ava picked up an oyster, tilted it toward her mouth, and slurped delicately. "Fantastic!" she declared.

Carmela, on the other hand, grabbed a tiny seafood fork and speared her oyster.

"Oh, you're eating fancy tonight," said Ava. "Not like a real oyster-eatin' party." Traditional Louisiana oyster feasts dictated that oysters be carried in bushel baskets to your picnic table, then dumped out on newspapers. From there you shucked your own oyster, doused it with hot sauce, and let it slide.

"Not fancy," said Carmela, "just easier to dip them that way."

"I forgot, you're a hot sauce fan."

"The hotter, the better. Of course, I'm partial to Sweet Cajun Fire, produced over in Prairieville."

"I'm an oyster shooter gal myself," laughed Ava. "Tip 'em up to your mouth and let them slide down your gullet."

"Efficient," agreed Carmela.

Ava helped herself to a second oyster, then said, "Did you get a chance to tell Babcock about our close encounter with Sissy Fowler today?"

"Sure did."

"Any reaction?"

"You mean did he leap into his unmarked car and rush, lights and sirens blaring, to Sissy's house to slap a pair of handcuffs on her?"

"That would be pretty dang exciting," said Ava.

"Well, it didn't happen," said Carmela. "In fact, Babcock was dreadfully ho-hum about the whole thing."

Ava's brows knit together. "Then he's awfully short on gratitude. We practically handed him another suspect on a silver platter." She glanced down. "Kinda like these oysters."

"Babcock insinuated that we were overly suspicious and trying way too hard," said Carmela. "Then he said it was understandable since we were civilians. And the way he said *civilian* made it sound more like *dummkopf*."

"Ouch," said Ava. "Doesn't he know you're *good* at this investigating stuff? You've got a couple of crime-solving notches on your belt, which means you're practically a pro!"

"I don't think Babcock will ever see it that way," said Carmela. She took another sip of champagne and decided it was awfully good. Not up there on the Mount Olympus of champagnes with Perrier-Jouët or Dom Perignon, but still tasty with an elegant, dry finish.

Ava grimaced. "The fragile male ego. Gets in the way every time."

"So we'll just keep things on the QT," said Carmela.

"Gotcha," said Ava. "Hey, I bet you were so busy with your fiber seminar today you didn't see this morning's clue. So if you're interested, I brought it along."

"Dig it out," said Carmela, spearing her final oyster. "If we can't solve this murder, maybe we can unravel the treasure hunt clues and win that money."

Ava fished in her purse and pulled out a scrap of newspaper. She scanned it, holding it out at arm's length. "Teensy-weensy typeface," she muttered.

"Perhaps you're in need of glasses?"

"Never!" scoffed Ava. "Remember what Dorothy Parker said?"

"Men seldom make passes at girls who wear glasses," finished Carmela. She hesitated. "Think that's really true?"

"I'm not gonna risk it," said Ava, squinting like crazy. "Okay, listen up. This is clue number three. 'From clubs to greengrocers, come on and get closer.'" She bit her lip and stared at Carmela. "What do you think?"

"Maybe near the French Market?" said Carmela. "There are a few clubs there, plus the farmers' market."

"We're a couple of smart cookies. We should be able to figure this out."

"I think the Monsters and Mayhem organizers are trying to bring everyone down to the wire at the last possible moment. Create a lot of treasure-hunting buzz."

Suddenly, Quigg was back at their table. "Oysters to your liking, ladies?"

"Wonderful!" they both exclaimed at once.

Quigg leaned toward them in a conspiratorial manner. "It's been said Louisiana has four seasons—crab, crawfish, shrimp, and oyster."

"Hah," said Carmela, giving a polite guffaw. It wasn't the first time she'd heard this little ditty. It wouldn't be the last.

"Good one," said Ava, who was also familiar with the Louisiana war cry.

"Ready for a second round of wine tasting?" Quigg asked.

"Bring it on," said Carmela.

Quigg produced a bottle of white wine and deftly poured it into their tulip-shaped glasses, while Arnault whisked away empty platters of oyster shells. "This is my blend of Sauvignon Blanc and Blanc du Bois, a hybrid grape," he told them. "Crisp but slightly fruity at the same time."

"Does the wine have a name?" asked Ava.

"I'm still toying with that," answered Quigg. "Maybe . . . Indigo White or Sauvignon Silver?"

"Could work," said Carmela.

"If you come up with something better, let me know," said Quigg. "Put it on my tab."

"I haven't decided if I'm going to do the project yet," Carmela told him.

"Oh, you will," he said over his shoulder.

"Ego," muttered Ava.

Their second course consisted of mustard crusted salmon medallions, barely seared and served with a tiny dollop of crème fraîche.

"Really wonderful," said Ava. "His menu has improved by leaps and bounds."

"Quigg made his name by serving fried oysters and jambalaya," said Carmela, "but he's pretty much shifted those dishes over to Mumbo Gumbo." Mumbo Gumbo was Quigg's more Cajun-style restaurant in the French Quarter.

"Watch out, Emeril," said Ava.

"And after a couple of trips to New York," continued Carmela, "where he dined at Le Bernardin, Per Se, and Adour Alain Ducasse, Quigg came back bound and determined to put a fine dining spin on Bon Tiempe."

"Well, he certainly succeeded," enthused Ava. "This food is to die for. Too bad we just get a small taste and not a whole entrée."

"Then it wouldn't be a tasting menu," Carmela reasoned.

"At least there's more good stuff on the way," giggled Ava.

"You know what?" said Carmela, "I think I might have another clue."

"What are you talking about?" asked Ava.

"I just remembered. Mr. Bones, this crazy skeleton character whose job is to get a buzz going for Halloween weekend, came waltzing into Memory Mine this afternoon. While he was handing out beads he gave me . . . wait a minute . . ." Carmela grabbed her bag and dug quickly into her coin purse. "Yeah, here it is. I think it might actually have a clue on it."

"Hand it over," said Ava. "This could be the leg up we need."

"Hard to read," said Carmela, eyeing the tin doubloon, then passing it to Ava.

Ava screwed up her face, moved her lips, then held the coin at arm's length. She shook her head. "Nope, that doesn't work."

"Maybe . . ." Carmela moved a candlestick closer. "If we shed a little light on the subject?"

"Oh yeah," said Ava. "I can read it now."

"What's it say?"

"Huh," said Ava, looking a little startled. "It says, 'Come knock on the door, there's room for one more.'" She paused, then took a sip of wine. "What do you think?"

"Cemetery?" asked Carmela. "One of the old marble aboveground crypts?"

"Sounds more like they mean *inside* a crypt," said Ava, looking a little nervous.

Chapter 12

"CHICKEN Marengo," said Quigg, "happened to be the Emperor Napoleon's absolute favorite dish." He lounged against the pillar by their table, holding a bottle of red wine, watching Arnault the waiter place their third tasting course before them.

"Love the French cuisine," said Ava.

"And our take on Napoleon's chicken is accompanied by a wine I call my Mardi Gras Medley," said Quigg. "A blend of Syrah and Shiraz." He poured the wine into their tulip-shaped glasses.

Carmela picked up her wineglass, swirled, sniffed, and took a tiny sip. "Now this," she said, "is spectacular."

"You like?" asked Quigg, flashing his trademark quirky grin.

"I like it a lot," said Carmela. "It's mellow but with great body. This wine could really catch on. I mean, it could be

the star attraction among all your varieties, especially if you marketed it to other restaurants and some of the specialty wine shops."

"I knew I could count on you to sprinkle a little of your marketing fairy dust," said Quigg.

"Maybe do a press party," said Carmela, thinking. She was charged up, and her brain was suddenly cranking out ideas. "Either here or at your winery. Invite the media—print, TV, and radio. And try to round up as many prominent restaurateurs and Louisiana wine shop owners as you can."

"And friends," said Ava. "Friends are always good."

"You think it's too late in the year to do a splashy introduction?" Quigg asked.

Carmela shook her head. "Not if you've got inventory."

"I have enough," said Quigg, nodding.

"Then I think you should schedule it toward the end of November," said Carmela. "Maybe tie in a kind of harvest or holiday theme."

"I like that," said Quigg, stroking his chin and looking thoughtful. "Will you honcho the event? Pull all the loose ends together?"

"No, no," said Carmela, "not my forte at all. But I do know some terrific event planners."

"But you'd work with them?" Quigg persisted. "Lay out a basic blue print?"

"Maybe Carmela could trade out her time for cases of wine?" prompted Ava.

"Might work," said Quigg. "Hey, don't let your chicken Marengo get cold!"

"Mmm," said Ava, who was already eating, "it's wonderful. But I gotta ask, is it really okay to drink red wine with chicken?"

"Napoleon did," Quigg said with a poker face.

"When in France . . . ," chuckled Ava.

"No, no," said Quigg, "it's fine. Better than fine. Don't let those stodgy old-school rules about wine hold you back. They've basically been tossed out the window. Now wine lovers drink white Bordeaux with beef, Cabernet with fish, and even sparkling wine with Chinese food."

"Never cared for rules anyway," chortled Ava.

"Except in the kitchen," said Carmela. "Where I imagine Chef Daniel's recipes are written out to the ounce."

"Down to the milliliter," said Quigg. "But there's a dandy payoff. Bon Tiempe was just awarded three stars by Michelin. That ain't bad apples."

"So the chicken Marengo," said Ava, forking up her last piece, "this is a fairly new addition to your menu?"

"As is the panko-crusted shrimp and lemon-pepper duck breast."

"You're a smart guy," said Ava. She prodded Carmela with an elbow. "Isn't he a smarty?"

"Got the savvy to spot trends," agreed Carmela. "Quigg always keeps an eye on both coasts."

"Aren't you sweet," said Quigg, giving Carmela a lingering glance.

"Whew," exclaimed Ava, some ten minutes later. "Another course." She reached down and discreetly patted her tummy. "Good thing I wore a stretchy dress." Arnault had just served and explained the finer points of their final entrée course, what he called a lamb chop lollipop served with a slightly sweet tomato-corn relish. The accompanying wine was Cajun Cabernet, a full-bodied, dry Cabernet with just a hint of oak.

"Isn't it interesting how the sweetness in the corn relish complements the lamb chop?" said Ava.

"Food chemistry," said Carmela. "There's something about a taste receptor pathway."

"In your brain?" asked Ava.

"On your tongue," said Carmela, taking another bite.

"You're a smarty, too," said Ava. "You know so much about food chemistry. To say nothing of your prodigious cooking and baking skills."

"My cooking's passable," said Carmela, "because when you create a jambalaya or gumbo, you can toss in a dab of this, a dash of that. And somehow it always turns out. But baking's a whole 'nother thing. It requires very precise measurements."

"Like scrapbooking?" asked Ava.

"No, scrapbooking's a bit of a mishmash," laughed Carmela. "At least it is for me. The fun is in cobbling together a few scraps of paper, showcasing a photo, then adding a smidge of lace or ribbon and using whatever stickers or brads I have on hand."

"Fun," said Ava.

Loud, jovial voices suddenly erupted at the table next to them, and both Carmela and Ava turned to see what was going on. But it was only a group of four businessmen, dining and drinking. Although the dining portion of the evening seemed to have pretty much concluded, while the drinking part was seriously under way, probably putting a good ding in their expense accounts.

"I have a red wine I want you to try!" Quigg called to the men. He made a beeline for their table and poured out generous servings. "From my St. Tammany Vineyard. A blend of *Ison* muscadines and Norton grapes."

"More wine?" Ava drawled, and in so doing caught the attention of the four men.

"Come join us," one of the men beckoned to her. "We're lonely."

"A lonely hearts club," chimed in a second one.

"Should we?" Ava whispered to Carmela, who shook her head no.

"Sorry," Ava told them, "it's a school night."

But with corks a-popping, Quigg was suddenly the ebullient, proud vintner, pouring wine for everyone at the surrounding tables. Which got them all chatting and clinking wineglasses and served as Ava's introduction to Tom Travers, one of the four men sitting at the neighboring table.

"I know you," Ava told him, pushing a mass of curly hair behind one ear and hunching one enticing shoulder forward. "Not personally, but I've seen your photo in the business pages. You're Tom Travers. And you run an import company."

Travers, flattered by Ava's attention, said, "That's right, pretty lady. I own Delta Imports. Mardi Gras beads and masks are my particular specialty."

"Don't let him kid you," said one of his sidekicks. "Delta Imports deals with some of the largest U.S. corporations. Fact is, Tom's company is a major fashion importer, too."

"You ladies ever hear of Dongguan?" Travers asked "In mainland China?"

"Sure," said Ava, though she probably hadn't.

"It's one of China's largest factory cities," Travers explained. "Located in the Pearl River Delta near Hong Kong. Dongguan turns out sneakers, clothing, even designer goods."

"Is that so?" asked Ava as she pursed her lips and turned

curious, mischievous eyes on him. "Always enjoy the designer goods."

"And my company," said Travers, giving a slight bow of his head, "Delta Imports, has been fortunate to score contracts with a number of exclusive retailers."

"From China's delta to ours," quipped Carmela.

"Something like that." Tom grinned. He was sandy-haired and handsome, dressed in a dark blue suit, light blue shirt, and loosened red rep tie. Maybe late thirties. He wore no ring on his left hand, third finger.

"So beads are just a sideline," said Ava, flirting shamelessly.

Travers stood up and pulled his chair a few feet closer to Carmela. "That and a few other Mardi Gras items."

"Like what?" asked Carmela.

"You know the guy who got stabbed with the Minotaur head?" Travers asked in a low voice.

"Brett Fowler," said Carmela. "Yeah, we know all about it. Firsthand."

"We were there that night!" added Ava.

"Really?" said Travers, looking concerned. "How awful."

"You were mentioning the Minotaur head," said Carmela.

"Well . . . we imported it," said Travers. "Used to be so many of the large heads and animated characters were constructed in Italy, but now China is turning out great stuff, too."

"Our friend Jekyl Hardy designed that Minotaur head," said Ava.

"Sure"—Travers nodded—"I know Jekyl. He helped me locate a pair of crystal lamps for my town house. He must feel as awful as I do about the head."

"You mean you feel like an accomplice?" asked Carmela.

"Something like that," said Travers, grimacing. "Seeing as how Delta Imports conveyed the specifics to the manufacturer, then had it shipped back here."

"Not your fault," said Carmela. "Nothing you can do about it."

"Just feel sorry for Fowler," said Travers.

"Only if you got paid," said Carmela. "I hear lots of people were burned rather badly in his Ponzi scheme."

"Not I," said Travers. "After that whole Madoff fiasco I'm wary of *any* type of investment fund."

"As well you should be," said Carmela.

"I hope the police are close to arresting someone," said Travers. "Although the article in this morning's *Times-Picayune* was vague. But maybe purposely so; maybe they're holding back at the request of the investigators."

"Maybe," said Ava, glancing at Carmela.

"If I were going to take a hard look at someone," said Travers, glancing over at his buddies and seeing that they were deep in conversation, "I'd look at Boyd Hodney." When Travers saw the startled looks on Carmela's and Ava's faces, he said, "You know Hodney?"

"Um . . . sort of," said Ava.

"Why point the finger at Hodney?" Carmela asked.

Now Travers looked like he might have said too much. "Please don't quote me on this, but Hodney and Fowler *never* got along."

"But Hodney's chairman of the Pluvius krewe," said Carmela.

"And Fowler was captain," replied Travers. "Sure. But ask anyone in the krewe and they'll tell you the two men were always at each other's throats."

"Funny," said Ava. "Fowler kind of did get his throat ripped out."

"Along with a few other choice body parts," added Carmela.

"*Cher*," said Ava, "are you okay to drive?"

"I'm okay," said Carmela as they bumped down Royal Street. "I kind of dogged it on those last two glasses of wine. Took just a sip versus actually imbibing."

"You're such a good girl."

"Not really," said Carmela, grinning to herself.

"What did you think of Tom Travers?"

"Cute guy," said Carmela. "Seemed nice."

"And he's unmarried."

"That's a major point in his favor," said Carmela.

Ava fiddled with her hair. "He asked me to go out with him."

"Then I think you should."

Ava pulled her face into a pussycat grin. "I think I will." They drove for a couple more blocks, then Ava said, "What say we take a slight detour and look for the treasure medallion?"

"What sort of detour did you have in mind?" Carmela asked, hoping it didn't entail cemeteries or bayous.

Ava scrunched her face up as if she were thinking hard. "You know those last two clues about 'clubs to greengrocers' and 'knock on the door, there's room for one more'?"

"Uh-huh."

"What if they refer to the French Market, where there are lots of vegetable stalls?"

"Might apply," said Carmela. The French Market, right

along River Walk, was a tin-roofed, open-air market where you could buy mirlitons, peppers, gourds, peanuts, strings of chilies, and whatever was in season. "But what about the 'knock on the door' part?"

"The Chantilly Hotel's only a block away," said Ava.

"So . . . ?"

"It's really old," said Ava. "More than a hundred years old, and it started out as a speakeasy. You know, the kind of place where you really had to knock on the door?"

"Ah," was Carmela's measured response.

"T-S-T-E-C?" asked Ava.

"Huh?"

"Too stupid to even consider?" deciphered Ava. "Or . . . ?" She paused. "Maybe a germ of an idea?"

"My vote's for the germ," said Carmela. "In fact, I think you're very clever in putting those clues together. Sure, we can go take a look."

"What can it hurt?" asked Ava, snuggling back in the passenger seat of Carmela's two-seater Mercedes.

Carmela zipped up North Peters Street, past a couple of hulking warehouses, and finally emerged on the fringe of the French Quarter. The original heart of New Orleans, or Vieux Carré as it was originally called, was a crazy cacophony of old brick buildings, art galleries, gourmet restaurants, souvenir shops, narrow streets, boutique luxury hotels, jazz clubs, strip joints, and a couple of churches thrown in to help balance things out.

"So a right turn on Dauphine," Carmela murmured, pausing at a red light.

A slight fog had eased north from bayou country, giving everything a softer, hazier edge. Buildings were shrouded, noise was damped, neon was subdued, and the flickering

wrought-iron streetlamps were even more reminiscent of eighteenth-century Paris.

"Just up the block," said Ava, peering out the side window. "There. There it is!"

Carmela maneuvered her car to the curb, miraculously finding a parking space.

"I'm never moving," she told Ava. "This is a first."

"Oh, you're moving," said Ava, pushing open the door and clambering out. "C'mon, let's go!"

With a backward glance at her car, the car Shamus had given her a few years ago, Carmela followed Ava toward the Chantilly Hotel. The place was, of course, adorable. Three stories high and constructed of dark brick, the building oozed charm and history. Brass lamp fixtures glowed on either side of the double mahogany wood doors, and a small brass plaque discreetly proclaimed *Chantilly Hotel*.

Inside was just as charming. Exposed brick walls, polished marble floor, giant white ceramic pots of banana trees, and plush aubergine club chairs.

Sashaying up to the front desk, where a youthful desk clerk looked up from his papers, Ava proclaimed, "Howdy."

"Good evening," said the young man, who was barely in his twenties. With his dark, slicked-back hair and dark gray suit he looked like he'd just stepped out of a 1930s movie. Film noir.

Ava touched a finger to her collarbone. "I'm Ava Gruiex and this is Carmela Bertrand. Perhaps you've heard of us? We both have shops here in the French Quarter."

The desk clerk gave a slight nod. Not quite acknowledging the fact, but certainly not dismissing them, either.

"We have friends coming to visit in a few weeks,"

said Ava, "and we were thinking of recommending your hotel."

"Splendid," said the desk clerk, animated now. He reached for a stack of brochures, fumbled one, then handed it to Ava. "Perhaps you'd like to pass along one of our brochures."

"Good idea," said Ava. She accepted the brochure, tapped it with a lacquered fingernail, then passed it to Carmela. Looking around, she noted a circular stairway tucked behind a baby grand piano, and said, "Did I hear right? You have a roof garden?"

"Indeed we do," said the clerk. "A postage stamp–sized garden, but the view is quite lovely. You're certainly welcome to take a look."

"And you have a courtyard out back," said Carmela, quickly thumbing through the brochure.

"Where we serve tea at four and cocktails at six," said the desk clerk. "Complimentary, of course, for our guests."

"That's something to keep in mind," said Ava.

"Thank you," said Carmela. "We'll look around and then get out of your hair."

"Take your time," said the desk clerk, giving Ava an appreciative smile.

"This is cool," breathed Ava, once they were standing on the roof deck. The raised wooden deck, maybe fifteen by eighteen feet, was surrounded by a tangle of banana trees, dogwood, and magnolias. Two elaborate wrought-iron benches fashioned in an S-curve held plush velvet cushions. A cool breeze swept across the building tops, rustling leaves and stirring the air. The dark ribbon of the Mississippi River sparkled just a couple of blocks away.

"The desk clerk was right about this place being awfully small," said Carmela. "So I'm not sure the merchants association would hide the treasure medallion up here. The hotel wouldn't want people tromping through."

"The courtyard in back?" said Ava.

"Let's take a look."

The courtyard was much larger. Large trees, lighted fountain, wrought-iron chairs and tables, and a zigzag pattern of bricks that added to the charm but made walking difficult.

"Hard to walk on these things," complained Ava.

"Try walking on your tiptoes," cautioned Carmela as they crossed the treacherous bricks. The courtyard was moody and deserted, except for two macaws in a large cage.

"Poor birds," said Ava. "Maybe we should let them go."

"It does seem wrong to imprison such beautiful birds," said Carmela.

"It's not like they're hand-raised parakeets," said Ava. "These birds belong in a jungle."

"Or maybe a bayou?" Carmela murmured. They both stared into the cage, where the two macaws stared back at them with inquisitive, shiny oil-spot eyes.

Ava glanced sideways at Carmela. "You think?"

"Let's not be too hasty, okay?" suggested Carmela. "If we do anything tonight, that desk clerk will know it was us."

"Good point." Ava looked around the courtyard, seemingly deep in thought. Then she said, "So what do you think? Could the medallion be hidden here?"

"Possible," said Carmela, "but not probable. Again, I think you had a great brainstorm about this place, but management . . ."

"Doesn't want every looky-loo tromping through here," said Ava.

"Like us," added Carmela.

"So no go," said Ava. She tottered back to the birdcage and bent in close. "Hang tight, kids," she whispered to the macaws. "There could be a jailbreak yet."

Chapter 13

BELLS chimed overhead as Carmela nosed her car into a parking space and scurried, as best she could in high heels, toward the historic Trinity Episcopal Church. Set in the Garden District at the corner of Jackson and Coliseum streets, the old church had originally been constructed in 1852. But like so many buildings in New Orleans, where the watchword was *fanciful*, the church had been embellished and enriched over the years. Thus a soaring bell tower and new facade had been tacked on to the original design, giving it a distinct Gothic Revival style.

Padding silently down a side aisle, Carmela searched for Ava, found her, then slipped into the pew next to her.

"*Cher*," whispered Ava. "You made it. I was beginning to worry."

Carmela motioned to her hair. "Hair," she whispered back. The omnipresent heat and humidity in New Orleans

weren't always kind to one's coiffure. And Carmela wasn't a morning person.

"You look cute," mouthed Ava.

"That's because I'm wearing a hat," murmured Carmela. Worried that her hair resembled an artichoke, Carmela had put on a small black velvet cap, complete with curled black feather. Along with her sedate black suit, she felt it lent a sort of Lauren Bacall look. Channeling the forties and all that.

Ava nodded again. Okay.

Carmela leaned back, slipped off her pinchy black high heels, and gazed around. Trinity Episcopal was a stunning church. Lots of meticulously carved wood; a series of amazingly tall, arched stained glass windows; and the five-thousand-pipe Trinity Tracker organ. On Tuesday evenings, the church presented what they called their Organ & Labyrinth program, which was basically a lovely organ recital done by candlelight.

As notes suddenly flooded from that organ—Handel's *Largo*—Carmela leaned sideways and glanced toward the front of the church, craning her neck, trying to see exactly who was in attendance.

There was Sissy Fowler, of course, sitting up in the front pew. Carmela recognized Sissy's strawberry-swirl hair and primly expensive St. John knit jacket and skirt. And, lo and behold, was that Jimmy Toups sitting to Sissy's left? Oh yes, it was. And who was the silver-haired man in the dowdy brown suit on Sissy's right? Hmm. Probably a relative.

So who else was here? Because there was certainly a large contingent of mourners. Or were they mourners? Carmela wondered. Maybe they were unlucky investors who'd lost considerable sums of money and were here to witness the finality of it all.

Eyes roving the crowd, Carmela picked out Jekyl Hardy, sitting with some of his fellow antique dealers. And there was Shamus, stifling a grin as he fidgeted among fellow members of the Pluvius krewe. And, interestingly enough, she also picked out Edgar Babcock. Way across the aisle from her on the right side of the church and one row ahead.

Well, hello, sweetheart. Come to give the suspects a once over?

Of course he had. Which probably meant his investigation hadn't made as much progress as he'd let on. Interesting.

Creaking noises and the sound of a muffled shuffle took Carmela's mind a few seconds to process, and then she realized the entire congregation was getting to its feet. The coffin had arrived. Struggling to jam her feet into her heels, Carmela pulled herself upright just as Brett Fowler's gunmetal-gray casket slid silently past her like some kind of miniature nuclear sub, pushed by a grim-faced funeral director in a too-tight black suit.

Not a big fan of funerals in general, Carmela had one bizarre, giddy moment where she imagined the funeral director struggling into one of the roomy, cut-up-the-back suits he used to dress his clients. Then she pulled herself back to the here and now, sat down again with the rest of the mourners, and focused on the actual memorial service.

Only she really didn't focus all that well. Carmela's mind continued to drift back to that night at the Pluvius den when she and Ava stumbled out the door to find Fowler lying in a pool of blood.

She thought about Jimmy Toups, suddenly cozy as a bedbug with Sissy. Of Jekyl's long-standing feud with Brett Fowler. Of their dinner last night where Tom Travers had pointed an accusing finger at Boyd Hodney, the Pluvius

krewe's chairman. Who knew Fowler and Hodney were mortal enemies? Not her. Maybe not even Edgar Babcock. She also thought about Mills Taggart, the private detective, who was paid, and probably paid well, to do Glory Meechum's callous bidding. And all the hedge fund clients who had to be seething over their considerable losses.

And finally, there was Sissy Fowler herself. Brash, used to getting her way, stuck in a loveless marriage. And more recently, Sissy playing out her final role as the cast-aside wife whose husband was involved with a much younger woman.

Or *was* it Sissy's final role?

Could she have played another part? A more insidious, evil role?

Carmela sighed. Lots of suspects, lots of suppositions, but no hard evidence.

Ava touched Carmela's arm. "Don't the candles look nice?"

Carmela nodded, even though she'd completely forgotten about the saint candles Sissy had purchased yesterday. She glanced down the aisle, noticed the flickering lights dipping and swaying hypnotically. A nice touch? Sure. Whatever.

Carmela bowed her head during the prayers and fidgeted slightly while someone—a relative, she guessed—gave a somewhat somber and carefully worded speech about Fowler.

And then the organ chimed out its mellow notes again.

Sissy struggled to her feet, walked to Fowler's casket, touched it gently with one hand, then placed a spray of lilies atop it. Then it was only a matter of moments before the funeral director seesawed the casket back and forth and pointed it down the aisle.

Carmela watched it zip by again and relaxed. The service

was concluded, and she and Ava had been in attendance just as they'd promised Sissy.

"Who's the girl with the blond bouffant who's cryin' her little eyes out?" Ava whispered as the mourners filed past them.

Carmela only caught the back of the snuffling girl's head. "No idea."

"Maybe a relative?"

"Could be."

"Gonna have a bad case of the puffs," observed Ava. "Need a couple cucumber slices for those swollen eyes."

"That's what you use?"

"Sure," said Ava. "Works like a charm."

"But you *never* have cucumbers in your refrigerator," commented Carmela. "All you have is wilted lettuce and champagne."

"And cat food," added Ava.

"Cat food," said Carmela. She supposed a chilled, un-opened can of cat food might yield the same depuffing benefits.

"Think we should stick around and deliver more condolences to Sissy?" asked Ava. "Or is that just way too redundant?" She looked hopeful. Like she wanted to skedaddle out of there.

"Let's stay and talk to her," Carmela suggested. But condolences were the last thing on her mind.

Waiting until most of the mourners had filed past, Carmela and Ava rose from their seats and walked slowly down the aisle.

"A lovely service," murmured Ava.

"Wasn't it?" said Carmela, though she could barely remember it.

Cool air washed across their faces, and then they were out on the steps, mingling.

"Cute shoes," Ava cooed, nodding at Carmela's pointy-toed heels.

Carmela glanced down. "They're killing me."

"Of course," Ava said pleasantly. "That's the sacrifice we girls make to look sexy. Ooh, look at that line. I guess everybody wants to offer condolences to Sissy."

Or inquire about their money, thought Carmela.

"That's okay," said Carmela. "We can wait." *And look around, too. See who showed up for this gig.*

"Did you see Jekyl?" Ava asked. "He was actually wearing a suit!"

"Spiffy," agreed Carmela. "Did you notice Shamus?"

Ava frowned. "He acted like he was at a fraternity party. I expected him to high-five somebody at any minute."

"Story of his life," Carmela replied.

As the line edged forward toward Sissy Fowler, so did they. Finally, they were in earshot of Sissy, who was still flanked by Jimmy Toups and the brown-suited man.

"Toups didn't wear his trademark jumpsuit today," Ava sniggered.

"He'll probably change in his car," said Carmela, enjoying their snarkiness.

"Who's the other guy standing next to Sissy?" asked Ava.

"That's what I've been wondering."

They found out soon enough.

"Car-*mel*-a!" exclaimed Sissy, throwing her arms wide. "And Ava!" She grabbed them, pulled them in closer. "Y'all know Jimmy here?"

Carmela and Ava gave perfunctory nods while Jimmy voiced a grudging hello.

"And this here's Roy Slayback." Sissy dropped her voice. "Brett's partner in the . . . uh . . . business."

"Holy cripes," Ava exclaimed, "I bet *you're* in the soup."

Carmela almost laughed out loud, but Slayback recovered quickly. He ran a quick hand across his comb-over as he managed to put a pinched, neutral look on his pinched, neutral face.

"I've offered complete cooperation to the police," Slayback told them. "Any information that helps get to the bottom of this mess." He shook his head and added, "Of course, I had no idea."

"Neither did I," offered Sissy. "The awful thing is, we're *both* victims of my late husband's fraud." She batted her eyes, mustering a few tears and managing to look earnest.

Slayback hunched his thin shoulders forward, doing his best to project innocence as well. "Our business records are all in the capable hands of the Securities Division, and I've been attempting to get in touch personally with each and every Emerald Equities client."

"He has," echoed Sissy. "It's been a tough go these last few days, but Roy's performed magnificently."

"As far as corporate records and even my personal finances go," said Slayback, "I've completely opened the kimono."

"I did that once myself," Ava murmured.

"Aren't you a card!" Sissy guffawed as she reached out and tapped Ava on the shoulder. Then, in one swift move, Sissy swiveled around and pulled Jekyl Hardy into their little circle.

"Hello, all," said Jekyl, giving a short wave.

"Jekyl," said Sissy, pushing out her lower lip and looking slightly pouty, "I am sorely in need of your art expertise."

"How can I help?" asked Jekyl, looking suddenly solicitous.

"I would dearly love for you to come to my home and take a look at some of the antiques Brett has collected," said Sissy. Then, looking slightly discombobulated, she said, "I fear there may be lawsuits pertaining to my personal estate and that I might have to sell off some antiques in order to raise capital."

"I'd be happy to take a look," said Jekyl, steadily ignoring Jimmy Toups.

"That would be splendid," Sissy replied. "Let me, uh, check my calendar and give you a call. But the sooner the better."

"As you wish," said Jekyl. He smiled at Carmela and Ava. "Ladies?" He hooked arms with both of them and led them away.

"Our condolences," Carmela called over her shoulder. "Again."

"Ditto," said Ava.

When they were out of earshot, Ava said to Jekyl, "Wouldn't Brett Fowler just go crazy? Sissy asking you to appraise his antiques?"

"He's probably turning over in his grave right now." Jekyl smiled.

"He's not quite in his grave yet," Carmela pointed out.

"He will be soon," said Jekyl.

Noticing Shamus nearby, Carmela said to Ava, "You two run on ahead, okay? I have to talk to Shamus, then zip back to the shop."

"You gonna be okay?" asked Ava.

"Perfectly fine," said Carmela. "We're divorced, remember?"

"I know that," said Ava. "But does he?"

Shamus was bumping knuckles with his buddy Sugar Joe when Carmela caught up to him. "Shamus, do you have a minute?"

"Babe!" said Shamus, seemingly happy to see her. "For you, anytime is good."

Right, thought Carmela.

"See ya, buddy," said Sugar Joe.

"Back at ya," said Shamus, giving a big thumbs-up.

"What are you, ten?" said Carmela. "You two act like you're about to hop on the bus to summer camp."

"We're krewe members," said Shamus, looking a little less thrilled to see her now. "Pluvius krewe. Best ever."

"I'm sure Comus, Rex, Endymion, and Bacchus would have something to say about that," said Carmela, naming some of the major Mardi Gras krewes. "But I digress. What I really wanted to ask you is why Brett Fowler and Boyd Hodney were such sworn enemies?"

Shamus frowned. "Who told you they were?"

"It's no secret," said Carmela, taking a stab in the dark.

"Well, you're right, they despised each other," said Shamus.

"And the reason for this was . . . ?"

Shamus seemed to ruminate for a few seconds. "I think it goes back to a bad business deal." He thought for a minute. "Or maybe it was a real estate deal."

"Whatever," said Carmela. "Question number two is about Mills Taggart, Glory's private investigator. Is he still on the job?"

"Sure," said Shamus. "This Emerald Equities scam is a total mess!"

"And he's looking into it? I had no idea Mills Taggart had forensic accounting skills."

"Accounting?" Shamus frowned, then screwed his handsome face into an expression of deep thought. Finally he said, "That'd pretty much be Glory's area of expertise."

"Get a clue, Shamus," said Carmela. "Glory's only area of expertise is being the local banking ogre. Or would it be ogress?"

"Be nice, babe," said Shamus. "You can afford a little civility." He paused. "Now that you've got my house." He stuck his hands in his pants pockets and rocked back on his heels, looking boyish and casual. "You'll have to admit, Glory was totally magnanimous in giving you the house as part of our divorce settlement."

"Glory hung on to that house tooth and nail," Carmela said, correcting him. "Her fingernails are probably still embedded in the siding. *You're* the one who finally swayed her."

Shamus grinned and put both arms around Carmela, ready to pull her into a warm embrace.

"No!" said Carmela, reverting to her disobedient puppy voice. "None of that. No way."

"Babe . . . ," whined Shamus. "I still have feelings . . ."

Carmela shook an index finger at him. "No, no, no. No feelings. Feelings . . . bad! You and I are kaput."

"Couldn't we still be friends?"

Carmela considered this. "Friends?" *How would that work, anyway?*

Shamus crinkled his eyes and gave her a sly look. "Friends with benefits?"

"No benefits for you," Carmela snapped. "You've had more than your share of benefits. Double benefits, in some cases. Certainly enough to last you a lifetime—or until you woo your next eighteen-year-old girlfriend."

"Young chicks *are* hot," Shamus admitted, with a wolfish grin.

"Incorrigible," muttered Carmela as she stomped away.

"You hag!" suddenly rose above the mumbled quiet. A piercing scream of accusation that drifted above the mourners, rooting them to the spot where they stood.

"Adulteress," came a shrill retort.

Whirling around, Carmela saw Sissy Fowler and the tearful blond with the puffy eyes facing off against each other like two alley cats. Their mouths were drawn into snarls, eyes locked murderously upon each other, and hands clenching and unclenching, ready to gouge out eyes and yank hair. A group of stunned funeralgoers circled them uneasily. It was a cross between *Maury* and *Extreme Cage Fighting*.

That has to be Tanya, Carmela decided. The Tanya that Sissy had insinuated was Fowler's girlfriend and had even pointed an accusing finger at the other day.

"You schemed and plotted and finally murdered your own husband!" screamed Tanya, screeching like a crazed banshee. "Because you didn't want *me* to have him!"

"You're utterly berserk!" shrieked Sissy. "*You're* the one who killed my husband! You should be locked behind bars! Dragged to jail and thrown in the hole!"

"Brett despised you!" spat out Tanya. "Said you sucked the life out of him!"

Sissy suddenly advanced on the younger woman, jaw locked tight, eyes ablaze, her pinkish hair swirling about her head like a vengeful, tutti-frutti Medusa!

"Ladies, please!" said Jimmy Toups, trying to insinuate himself between the two women.

But Tanya just pulled off a black ballet flat and whapped him hard on the shoulder.

Toups jumped back and yelped a feeble, "Help," but everyone pretty much ignored him, so mesmerized were they by the drama being played out before them. It was a mélange of street theater, daytime soap opera, and a bit of Japanese game show thrown in for good measure.

"Gold digger!" seethed Sissy as tiny particles of spit flew from her mouth. She was having a veritable hissy fit. Or, in her case, a Sissy fit.

"Old hag!" screamed Tanya, swinging her shoulder bag at Sissy and whomping her a good one on the upper thigh.

"Whoa, whoa," came the reasonable voice of Edgar Babcock. He put out a hand, stepped between them, and reached into his jacket pocket. Pulling out his gold detective shield, he held it up high. When he did so, his jacket fell open, revealing his shoulder holster and sending the message that he was armed. And possibly even dangerous. "This is neither the time nor the place," he firmly reprimanded the two women. "If you have differences, I suggest you engage legal counsel."

"Differences . . . ," hissed Sissy as Jimmy Toups tugged at her arm again. But Sissy shrugged him off like an insignificant gnat. "I'd say we have . . ."

"Enough!" said Babcock at the top of his lungs, although he managed to maintain a look that was cool and unaffected. "That's it. We're done with this happy crap."

"But I'm not finished with her," snarled Sissy, stalking off. "Just you wait . . ."

"Just *you* wait till I spill the beans about what I know," spat back Tanya, still waving her shoe—which Carmela thought might be a Capezio—as she stomped away.

It wasn't a clean end to a clean fight, but order had been restored. Sort of.

"Babcock," said Carmela.

He spun around and his eyes lit on her. Then he gave a tired, crooked smile. "You."

"You didn't see me in church?" Carmela asked.

Babcock shook his head.

"Too busy looking for suspects?"

"Something like that." He put an arm around her shoulders, and they moved away from the shocked crowd that was still shaking their heads and mumbling to each other. Possibly they'd never seen a funeral quite so raucous. On the other hand, New Orleans boasted plenty of jazz funerals, alcohol-fueled wakes, and strange burials in family crypts where old bones were shoved down metal chutes to make room for new family members. So maybe this was just par for the course.

Carmela was about to ask a question when Shamus came shambling up to them.

Oh no, thought Carmela. *This is one of those worst-case scenarios you hope never happens. What do I do now? Faint dead away? Run away? Stand my ground to grin and bear this?*

"We haven't met," said Shamus, smiling widely and sticking out a hand. "I'm Shamus Meechum."

Edgar Babcock's brows rose imperceptibly as they shook hands. "Ah, the ex."

"I like to think I still play a part in Carmela's life," said Shamus.

"I don't," said Carmela.

Shamus ignored Carmela and focused on Babcock instead. "You've got yourself a great girl."

"Really," said Babcock, "because I don't think I've got her at all. Carmela's very much her own person."

Shamus looked nonplussed. "You know what I mean . . ."

Babcock put an arm around Carmela's shoulders and pulled her away. "No, I really don't," he said to Shamus over his shoulder.

"I could kiss you," said Carmela as they walked down the block in lockstep.

"Then please do," replied Babcock.

"Maybe not right here."

"Then where?"

"Tonight? Oh wait," said Carmela. "I'm supposed to go to the *Ballet Dracula*."

"Babcock grimaced. "Seriously?"

"Sure," said Carmela. "We're thinking it might be fun. And Ava's all whipped up about dressing like a vampire."

"Then have lunch with me now," said Babcock.

"I really should get back to the shop."

"A quick lunch," urged Babcock. He lifted a hand, gesturing. "Commander's Palace is just down the block."

"Mmm," said Carmela, thinking about their spectacular bread pudding soufflé. "I think you just convinced me."

Commander's Palace, a fanciful white and aqua-blue Victorian mansion, was hands down one of *the* best places to dine in all of New Orleans. First opened in 1880, the venerable restaurant sat center stage on Washington Avenue, directly across from Lafayette Cemetery. Jefferson Davis spent his last days

there, Mark Twain dined there, and Emeril presided over its kitchen for several years. In fact, Commander's Palace was so beloved and had become such a New Orleans institution that it closed only two days a year—Christmas and Fat Tuesday.

Comfortably seated in the Garden Room, amid plants, trellises, and paintings, Carmela ordered the Creole blue crab salad with rum-Creole mustard vinaigrette. Babcock chose the black pepper–seared shrimp.

"What did you think of the catfight?" Carmela asked, smoothing the crisp linen napkin in her lap.

"Unfortunate," responded Babcock.

"Did you believe what either of them was saying?"

"They were both upset and overwrought," said Babcock.

"That's not what I asked."

"I know exactly what you asked," said Babcock, "and why you asked it. And you know my standard answer. I'd prefer you stay out of this investigation."

"That's not an answer," said Carmela, "that's a . . . um . . ."

"Tired old request?"

"Bingo," said Carmela. She hesitated as two waiters approached their table with silver covered dishes, paused, then removed the covers with a choreographed flourish and placed their entrées before them.

"Wonderful," pronounced Babcock as the waiters discreetly departed.

"Not really," said Carmela.

Babcock peered at her blue crab salad. "Something wrong with the crab?"

"You're the crab," said Carmela. "Always waving me off, keeping me at bay even when I have information to feed you."

"And I thought this was just lunch," said Babcock, digging into his shrimp dish.

"It *is* lunch," said Carmela, "but I thought we could have an exchange of ideas, too."

"Okay," said Babcock, "I'm a reasonable man. Let's exchange ideas. You go first."

Carmela leaned forward and said in a conspiratorial whisper, "Did you know that Brett Fowler and Boyd Hodney were mortal enemies?"

He stopped chewing. "How do you know that?"

"I just know."

"Come on, Carmela."

"You know what?" said Carmela as she stabbed viciously at a hunk of crabmeat. "Why take my word for it? Why not talk to a few members of the Pluvius krewe? Go out and scrounge for your own answers, get the 411 from them."

The corners of Babcock's mouth twitched. "Actually, I'm getting a lot of information from you."

Carmela brightened. "Really? Then why won't you let me play a more active role?"

"Because I don't want you to get hurt," responded Babcock. He set his knife and fork down and gazed at her with serious intensity. "Listen to me, Ms. Carmela Bertrand, my sweetheart. There's a stone-cold killer running amok in the Big Easy. And the more questions you ask, the deeper you get involved and the more you distinguish yourself as a target."

"So?" said Carmela, giving him a big-eyed gaze.

"So if anything happened to you, I'd never forgive myself." Babcock paused, looking more serious than Carmela had ever seen him. "You're it, lady. You're the best I've ever met."

"Really?" Her voice rose in a self-satisfied squawk.

Twenty minutes later, after a great lunch, intense conversation, and strong chicory coffee, they whispered together over a shared bread pudding soufflé.

Chapter 14

"YOU'RE back!" exclaimed Gabby as Carmela slipped into Memory Mine. She lowered her voice as concern bloomed on her face. "How was the funeral?"

"A little on the strange side," said Carmela. She was glad to see that Memory Mine was fairly busy. A half-dozen customers picked through paper and perused albums, beads, brads, and rubber-stamp displays.

"How do you mean?" asked Gabby. "You mean like weird prayers or music selection?"

"Hah," said Carmela, "we should be so lucky." And so she told Gabby about the postservice go-round between Sissy and Tanya.

"A catfight?" exclaimed Gabby.

"Let me put it this way, the fur was definitely flying."

"So there really was . . . is . . . a girlfriend," said Gabby, looking a little embarrassed. She was a strict Catholic who

believed in the sanctity of marriage and a lifetime of commitment. In fact, Gabby had worked tirelessly to try to keep Carmela and Shamus together. But after a while, even she'd thrown in the towel.

"Definitely a girlfriend," said Carmela. "Little Miss Tanya Perdue." She paused and ran her fingers through what surely must be "hat hair" by now. "Over lunch with Babcock, I tried to get him thinking about this Tanya person."

"You think Tanya killed Fowler? I thought she was in love with him."

"We don't know all the details," said Carmela, picking up a stack of mail from the counter and sifting through it. "But I'm sure she has a story to tell."

"Wow," said Gabby.

"I also tried to point Babcock in the direction of Boyd Hodney. You know Boyd Hodney?"

"The Pluvius chairman?"

"Ayup."

"How does he figure into this?"

Carmela drew a deep breath. "I found out that Hodney and Fowler were sworn mortal enemies."

Gabby looked pained. "I don't like to think of anyone as being mortal enemies."

"I know you don't, sweetie," said Carmela. "You always look for the good in people."

Gabby ducked her head. "You make it sound kind of simplistic. Like I'm some kind of Pollyanna."

"Sorry," said Carmela, "I sure didn't mean it that way. I just meant that you're one of those genuinely nice, honest people who always sees a silver lining amid the dark clouds."

Gabby laughed. "Whereas you . . ."

"Always see dark clouds and worry too much about my hair," laughed Carmela.

"No, you're a good person, too," said Gabby, giggling a little, her humor restored. "Look how you're trying to get Jekyl untangled from this whole Fowler murder mess. Standing up for Jekyl is a very kind act on your part."

"Really?" said Carmela. "And here I thought I'd just been shanghaied."

"Jekyl does have a way . . ." began Gabby, just as the bell over the front door tinkled and, lo and behold, Jimmy Toups came waltzing in.

Both women stopped talking and stared pointedly at him, though Jimmy acted totally nonchalant.

"Ladies," he said. "Good day."

Gabby nodded politely, while Carmela said, "That was quite the scene today, huh?"

Which launched Jimmy into a crazy tirade. "That Tanya person was simply horrible!" mourned Jimmy, "to accost poor Sissy after such a terrible, heart-wrenching loss."

Carmela wondered if Jimmy meant Sissy's loss of a husband or her loss in finances.

"Simply unforgivable," continued Jimmy.

What was really unforgivable, of course, was the murder of Brett Fowler. But Carmela kept that to herself for now.

"How can we help you?" asked Gabby, stepping in.

"Oh," said Jimmy, as if he'd suddenly remembered why he was there. "Like I was telling Carmela the other day, I'm writing a book on the history of Mardi Gras and I'm absolutely swimming in way too many photos."

"So you need help with organization," said Gabby, coming around the counter.

"You read my mind," said Jimmy.

If only, thought Carmela.

"Do you want to organize and store your photos?" asked Gabby, "or use some type of album to help arrange them according to your chapters?"

"I think . . . both," said Toups.

"In that case," said Gabby, reaching for a large black leather album, "I'd recommend a couple of these. They'll hold almost one hundred sheets of photos and are acid free."

"And what about just storing photos?" asked Toups.

Carmela pulled a blue cardboard box from the shelf and handed it to him. "You can't beat these. They're inexpensive but hold tons of photos. You can even add file tab organizers."

"I knew I could count on you ladies," said Toups.

"We're here to help," said Gabby.

"How's the book coming?" asked Carmela.

Both Gabby and Toups stared at her.

"I assume you've already penned your book prologue," said Carmela.

"I have," said Toups, "written a few chapters, too."

"Wonderful," enthused Carmela. "How many chapters?" She was dying to find out, so she could tell Jekyl.

"A few," said Toups. He seemed to have an inkling that Carmela might be trying to pry information from him.

"Chapters you wrote?" Carmela asked, "or that you co-wrote with Sissy?"

Gabby looked suddenly uncomfortable. "I think it's just wonderful that you two are collaborating." She seemed to want to defuse a tense situation.

"I do, too," said Carmela, feigning enthusiasm. "Must be fun to put your heads together. Especially on something as near and dear to your hearts as Mardi Gras."

"Oh, we're having an absolute ball," said Toups, relaxing now. "We're like a couple of crazy conspirators."

"I'll bet you are," murmured Carmela, wondering if they could have also been co-conspirators in Brett Fowler's murder.

Twenty minutes later, Carmela sat at the back table with three customers, all of them gazing at a pure white skull that occupied the middle of the table. This wasn't biology or a med school lecture. Rather, Carmela was about to demonstrate techniques for decorating sugar skulls. One of the women, Byrle Coopersmith, was a so-so regular and looking forward to carrying her finished skull in the upcoming Halloween parade.

"I've heard about sugar skulls," said Byrle, "but I don't know too much about them."

"They're an art form that originated in southern Mexico," said Carmela. "Families make their own sugar skulls, then decorate them using colored frosting, paints, beads, and feathers. Then the skulls are carried to the cemetery to celebrate the Day of the Dead, which is basically November first to the second."

"The skulls are a way of honoring ancestors," added Gabby. She had finished with Toups and was greatly interested in the sugar skulls. Of course, decorating skulls wasn't scrapbooking per se, but it sure was a dandy, offbeat craft!

"Traditional sugar skulls are made from sugar, meringue powder, and water," Carmela told them. "And you can easily make your own if you have a special mold. But today we'll use prepared sugar skulls along with ready-made icing from

the grocery store." She stood up, grabbed a box that was sitting atop a flat file, and carried it to the table. It contained a
half-dozen white sugar skulls.

"All together like that, they look kind of creepy," giggled
one of the customers. "Like something you'd find in Lafayette
Cemetery." That prompted nervous giggles from all of them.

"Hopefully not," said Gabby, who was an active member
in the cemetery's preservation society.

"So what we're going to do right now is decorate these
babies," Carmela told them, "using colored mist food sprays,
ready-made icing, and even some write-on gels."

Gabby tossed a handful of tubes filled with icing onto the
table. "And we have sparkle gels, too. Which look a little
like tubes of lip gloss."

"And probably taste even better," added Carmela.

"What's the best way to start?" Byrle asked Carmela. "I
mean, they really are blank canvases."

Carmela gave her skull an appraising look. "Want me to
do one quickly?"

Everyone around the table nodded.

"Okay," said Carmela, reaching for a bottle of pink
food spray. "I'm going to give this guy a slightly pinkish
tinge first." She depressed the plunger, and a fine pink mist
settled across the top of her skull, almost as if it had been
airbrushed.

"Cool," said Gabby.

"Blusher," said Byrle.

"Then I'm going to build up a few layers," Carmela told
them.

"Oh," said Byrle. "Kind of like you do with scrapbooking."

"Exactly," said Carmela as she grabbed a tube of orange

icing. "Now I'll outline this guy's eyes in orange . . ." She squeezed out two raccoon circles. "Then his mouth as well." She finished that, then grabbed a tube of sparkle gel. "Now I'm going to put a little war paint on the side of his face and the top of his head. Using the red sparkle gel to make a couple of squiggles, then the yellow sparkle gel to give him some eyebrows and . . ." She squinted at her skull. "Maybe some yellow teeth, too."

"He's starting to look pretty good," offered Byrle.

"Thank you," said Carmela. "But the real fun comes in smoothing on gold foil, popping in a couple of sparkly beads for eyes, and adding a few feathers on top of his head."

"Love it!" exclaimed one of the women.

"So you get the idea?" asked Carmela.

They all nodded as they grabbed for food spray bottles and gel tubes.

Yes, Carmela decided, they got it.

For some reason, the shop got crazy busy then. Customers rushed in to buy black and orange scrapbook paper as well as skeleton, bat, and witch rubber stamps.

Then Gabby dragged out some finely cut vellum spiderwebs that had just arrived, and those were a big hit, too.

And just when Carmela didn't think they could fit any more people in her shop, Baby and Tandy showed up!

"Tootles, possums," sang out Baby as the two of them plowed their way toward Carmela, who was busy at the cash register. "Guess where we're just back from?"

"The Haunted Harvest Market," exclaimed Tandy, answering the question herself. "And boy, do we have loot!"

They hoisted their brown shopping bags up onto the front counter and dug in, eager to show and share.

"Fresh Cajun chèvre," said Baby, brandishing a plastic-wrapped roll of goat cheese. "And some fresh-baked pumpkin bread."

"Plus roasted peanuts," said Tandy, "and genuine alligator sausage and a jar of pear butter."

"Which is actually scrumptious on a toasted baguette along with the chèvre," said Baby.

Tandy took a moment to survey the shop. "Boy, are you guys ever busy." Then, peering toward the back, she asked, "Hey, are those sugar skulls I see?" Which sent Baby and Tandy hustling to the back table to inspect the work so far.

Carmela followed them back. "If you two want to decorate skulls, I can order a few more."

"Actually," said Baby, "we were wondering if we could scrapbook some bangles." She eyed the table. "But I don't think there's much room for us to work."

"Nonsense," said Byrle, "the more the merrier. "Come on, ladies, scrunch down a little. Scrapbooked bangles sound interesting, too."

"They're really a snap to make," Carmela told them. "You take old wooden and plastic bangle bracelets, then cover them with snippets of paper, stickers, or whatever, then apply a layer or two of Mod Podge."

"Here are a few bangles," said Gabby, tossing some wide plastic bangles onto the table. And I'll get our box of paper snippets." She glanced at Carmela. "And Carmela, you've got a phone call."

Carmela slipped into her office and grabbed the phone. "Hello?"

"You all set for the winery tour tomorrow?" asked Quigg.

"I haven't agreed to doing your project yet," said Carmela.

"Come on," Quigg growled, "you know you want to. Besides, it'll be fun to work together again."

"It'll be fun to do the logo and package designs," said Carmela.

"So you'll do it?" Quigg enthused.

"I suppose," said Carmela, suddenly feeling mouse-trapped.

"Excellent. I'll call the winery and tell them you'll be there around ten tomorrow, okay?"

"Okay, sure," said Carmela.

"And I'll make sure you get the grand tour."

"The fifty-cent tour will be just fine," said Carmela.

"Love to get those discounts," chuckled Quigg.

By four forty-five, sugar skulls had been cleverly decorated and bangles adorned, and a purple twilight haze was settling over the French Quarter. This was the golden hour, the time of day Carmela liked most. A hush between the daytime hustle-bustle of tourists and the go-go nighttime when clubs and cafés pulsed with thumping music. Lights winked slowly on, lacy wrought-iron balconies and gates caught the glint from a setting sun, and you could hear the patter of secluded garden fountains behind old brick walls.

"Goodness, look at the time," exclaimed Baby. She jumped up and began stuffing her bangles and farmers' market goodies into her Gucci tote bag. Which set off a chain reaction among the other customers, too.

"Know what we should do?" said Gabby, carrying Carmela's demo skull up to the front counter.

"Hmm?" said Carmela. She was gazing out the front window at the soft glow of gaslights in the dusk.

"We should put a lighted candle inside your skull and leave it burning in the front window."

Carmela smiled. "A sneak preview of the Day of the Dead procession."

"Something like that," said Gabby. "If we use a tiny vigil light, the candle should just burn out by itself in a couple of hours."

And in a couple of hours, Carmela thought to herself, *I'll be at the* Ballet Dracula.

Chapter 15

"THAT'S what you should wear," said Ava, pointing at a long, black, frilly gown she'd hung on the door of Carmela's closet.

Carmela, standing in her bedroom in her slip, wrinkled her nose. "Awfully froufrou."

"How dare you call that gown froufrou, when it's really classic Goth," said Ava.

"But I was just going to wear my LBD," said Carmela, using the common shorthand for *little black dress*.

"All fine and good," Ava argued, "except it should be an LBSD. A little black spooky dress."

"I'm not so big on spooky," said Carmela, wondering if she should tease her hair into a spiky artichoke look or leave it smooth.

"I've noticed," said Ava. "Which is why, ta-da, I brought

you one of *my* best Goth gowns to wear. Come on, slip it on, see if it fits."

"Gonna be too long," said Carmela, struggling into the dress.

"No problem," said Ava. "I brought along a silver skull pin. We'll just gather the skirt up on the diagonal, pin it, and have you wear some really high heels."

Carmela stared at herself in the full-length mirror. "You thought of everything, didn't you?"

Ava gave a cat-that-swallowed-the-canary grin. "I thought you'd probably try to weasel out of dressing like a vampire."

"I couldn't just carry my bat-wing purse?" asked Carmela, still studying herself. Actually, the dress looked awfully darned good on her.

"It's a copy of a Dior couture," said Ava, gathering fabric and placing the skull pin just so. "Dior always does luscious layers of ruffles. Only when you rework it in black, it comes out Goth."

"I'll buy that," said Carmela. Ava, after all, was the resident expert on Goth.

"Now your hair," said Ava.

"Always a problem," agreed Carmela.

"No, it looks good," said Ava. "But let's gel it up a bit more."

"So an artichoke look," said Carmela. "Have at it." After all, Ava had spent six months in residence at Mr. Gary's College of Hairdo Knowledge. Higher education to be sure.

Ava squirted a huge glob of gel into her palm, briskly rubbed her hands together, then worked it through Carmela's hair for a couple of minutes. Peering into the mirror,

Carmela saw that her hair now stuck up in chunky waves, not unlike the bride of Frankenstein.

"Now comb it out?" she asked in a small voice.

"Nope, we just give it a good tousle," said Ava, really poufing up Carmela's hair to heroic proportions. "And, as the pièce de résistance, we'll add a feather accessory." Ava whipped a tangle of black feathers past Carmela's face and pinned it in her hair.

Carmela stared into the mirror again. "I look like I'm wearing a bird on my head. A raven."

"Cool, huh?" said an enthusiastic Ava.

"I guess," said Carmela, slightly aghast, wondering who she'd run into tonight.

Ava, of course, wore a long, slinky, low-cut gown, slit thigh high and ornamented with black spangles and seed pearls. To give herself an exaggerated hourglass figure, more exaggerated than it already was, she'd laced a black leather corset over her dress. On her head, she'd perched a sort of top hat, the kind Johnny Depp had worn in *Sleepy Hollow*, only Ava's hat had a black net veil attached.

"You look like a cross between a vampire bride and a thirties jazz singer," Carmela told her.

"Thank you," said Ava, digging into her black snakeskin clutch purse, then applying a generous dab of bright red lip gloss.

"Thank heavens we're not the only ones, besides the cast, who are wearing costumes," said Carmela. All around them, on the street outside the theater, women swooshed past them in whispering long black gowns.

"Isn't it fun?" said Ava, giving a little shiver. "Don't you feel over-the-top glam?"

"Maybe and yes," answered Carmela as they stepped into the glittering lobby of the historic Vieux Carré Repertory Theatre.

It was an old vaudeville theater, well over a hundred years old, that had fallen into wreck and ruin and only recently been renovated. Now, the lobby was a mixture of Renaissance and Florentine style, with antique marble statues, cut crystal chandeliers, plum-colored velvet draperies, and plush carpeting to match.

"There's your Mr. Bones!" squealed Ava as the skeleton-costumed performer jumped out from behind a potted plant and casually tipped his hat at them.

"Fancy meeting you here," said Carmela.

"Maybe you have a clue for us?" Ava begged.

In answer, Mr. Bones waggled a finger and shook his head. Not tonight.

"Too bad," said a disappointed Ava as they followed the crush of people toward their seats. "I'm still not making much progress on finding the treasure medallion." Then, as they entered the theater proper, her mood shifted dramatically. "Wow, will you take a look at this renovation? Gorgeous!"

Dove-gray velvet theater seats sloped steeply down to the stage. Overhead was another large chandelier set against an azure-blue ceiling that was embedded with tiny, twinkling stars.

"The Repertory Theatre must have some angel," commented Carmela.

"You mean like a guardian angel?" asked Ava.

"I mean a financial angel," Carmela replied. She had served on the boards of several nonprofit arts organizations, and a financial angel, a wealthy person who could be counted on for continued financial support, was always a coveted find.

Hobbling down the treacherously steep steps, Carmela and Ava found their row and eased their way past a half-dozen seated guests, murmuring "Excuse me" all the way. Settling into narrow seats, they immediately opened their programs and scanned for Jekyl's name.

"Do you see it?" asked Carmela.

Ava continued scanning. "No, but . . . hey, this is kind of weird. Jimmy Toups is listed in the credits."

"You're kidding! What for?"

"Says here he's one of the set designers."

"Interesting," said Carmela.

"Oh, here's Jekyl's name," said Ava.

Carmela squinted at the spidery type. "What's it say? What's his role exactly?"

"He's in the chorus," said Ava.

"So a nondancing role."

Ava looked suddenly disconcerted. "Dancing?"

"It's a ballet," Carmela pointed out. "Remember? The *Ballet Dracula*?"

"Son of a gun," murmured Ava.

And then the lights dimmed, the curtain rolled up, and the drama began. Three writhing female dancers, Dracula's brides, slithered and jumped in a sensuous, eerie dance number that featured a crumbling castle backdrop and a coffin center stage. When Dracula finally emerged from his cof-

fin, the audience collectively inhaled. Dressed in black, face painted Kabuki theater–white, the principal dancer stalked the stage, then came alive with twirling, dazzling motions. Slashing wildly with his cape, he made leaps so amazingly high that he seemed to hang motionless in midair on the moody blue-lit stage.

"Wonderful," whispered Ava. "I really like it!"

Carmela had to agree as the whirlwind first act continued. Scenes changed, backdrops slid magically into place, and the dancers who played the roles of Jonathan Harker, Van Helsing, Renfield, Mina Harker, and Lucy Westenra were masterful.

When the plush curtain descended on the first act, Carmela and Ava joined in the thunderous applause. Then Ava whispered, "Time for a drinky-poo? I think there's a cocktail bar."

"Lead the way," said Carmela, gathering up the voluminous folds of her skirt.

Together they crab-stepped their way to the aisle, huffed their way up the steep steps, and emerged in the mezzanine level, where a small, temporary bar had been set up.

"Whatcha got?" Ava asked the tuxedo-clad bartender as other theatergoers pressed around them.

"A limited drink menu," said the bartender. "Red wine or Bloody Marys. But"——he held up a finger—"should you choose to go the Bloody Mary route, we have a complete garnish bar."

"What's a . . . ?" began Carmela.

The bartender pointed to the left of the bar. "Pretty much anything your heart desires as garnish for your drink. Shrimp on skewers, giant dill pickles, celery sticks, red pepper rings, jalapeños, pickled onions . . . you name it."

"Perfect!" proclaimed Ava. "A Bloody Mary for each of us." She reached into her clutch purse for bills.

"Maybe you'd let me take care of that," boomed a friendly male voice.

They turned and found Tom Travers, their acquaintance from last night, smiling broadly at them.

"Fancy meeting you here," purred Ava. She fluffed her hair and stuck out an angular hip.

"Likewise." Travers grinned. Her moves, and the black leather corset, were not lost on him.

"Are you here with someone?" Ava asked.

Travers dipped his head and said, "Promise you won't laugh?"

Carmela and Ava promised.

"I'm here with my brother-in-law," said Travers. "Something came up at the last minute and my sister couldn't attend, so I'm the amusing theater companion for the evening."

"How lucky for us," said Ava. The bartender slid their drinks across the bar, and all three of them moved toward the garnish bar. "Pickles," said Ava. "They're my downfall." She wrinkled her nose. "All that sodium."

"Say," said Travers, "you ladies are coming to the backstage party, aren't you?"

"Jekyl mentioned something about it," said Carmela.

"Anyway," said Travers, "I'm going to the backstage soiree because my brother-in-law is on the benefactors' committee. But you guys come too, okay?" He began backing away from them. "Opening-night hijinks and all that?"

"Okay," said Ava as the crowd closed in like waves.

"We'll see you there," said Carmela, who was definitely starting to enjoy the evening.

Ava stirred her Bloody Mary with a pickle spear while Carmela cadged another shrimp.

"I'm definitely having a good time," said Ava.

"I can see that," said Carmela, her eyes twinkling.

"He's nice, isn't he?" asked Ava. "Plus he's handsome and funny. He could be the one, *cher*. He could be the perfect man for me."

Carmela gave her friend a one-armed hug as they moved out of the way. "I hope he is," said Carmela.

"Don't you just love all the wild costumes?" asked Ava, surveying the crowd.

Carmela had to agree. As an homage to the opera and in the spirit of Halloween, many theatergoers wore long black dresses, short black dresses, black tuxedos, jet jewelry, and skull jewelry. There were even a few silver-tipped canes and satin-lined capes thrown into the mix.

"Do you see the cameo that woman is wearing?" asked Carmela, nudging her friend. "I bet it dates back—"

"Don't look now," Ava hissed, interrupting her. "But Shamus and Glory are here."

So, of course, Carmela looked.

"Should we turn tail and run?" asked Ava. "Try to melt into the crowd?"

"Too late." Carmela sighed. She'd just noticed that Shamus had just noticed. "They're headed our way."

"Should I be cordial or catty?" asked Ava. "Give me a clue, *cher*. Hey, wait a minute, who's that lug they've got in tow? Looks like a Mafia hit man."

"I'm making an educated guess here," said Carmela as Shamus's big sister, Glory Meechum, and a stocky, bull-necked man advanced on them, "but I think it's probably Mills Taggart, Glory's personal PI."

Turns out, Carmela was right. And once stilted greetings and introductions had been made, Taggart took his place stolidly behind Glory.

"Expecting assassins?" asked Ava.

Carmela almost choked on her drink.

"Or perhaps a hail of silver bullets?" Ava continued.

Glory's full bulk, including helmet hair, Easter Island face, and crazy, wonky eyes, descended on them like an evil weather balloon. "You think this is funny?" she shrilled. "That I need personal protection as well as a private investigator? *You* try losing a small fortune in this Emerald Equities scam! You try sorting through the fallout! I haven't had a wink of sleep in days! And those good-for-nothing New Orleans police aren't doing a single *thing* except standing around scratching their behinds and asking stupid questions!" She threw an angry look at Carmela, which Carmela supposed was Glory's not-so-subtle show of disapproval against Detective Edgar Babcock's detecting skills. Oh well.

"Been tippling tonight?" Carmela asked Glory. The way Glory was carrying on, she must have skipped the first act to hang out at the bar.

"Maybe she has a flask strapped to her hip," Ava added, trying to be helpful.

"Don't antagonize her," whispered Shamus. "She's been through enough already."

"Look! Look!" spat out Glory, pointing a finger. "Look who had the audacity to show up tonight!"

They all glanced past Glory's quivering fingertip to see Sissy Fowler hanging on the arm of Jimmy Toups. Dressed in a long pink gown with insets of black lace, Sissy looked like an aging vampire wannabe. Toups was in one of his trademark jumpsuits. Black, of course.

"And her own husband just buried today," snarled Glory. "Hussy." She took a quick suck of her drink. "Trollop."

"Hers wasn't exactly a marriage made in heaven," allowed Carmela.

"Know what I heard?" asked Shamus, a smug, self-satisfied smile creeping across his face.

"What's that, Shamus?" Carmela asked in a tired voice. Shamus was as bad as Glory, and Carmela was beyond weary of the Looney Tunes Meechum clan.

Shamus managed to look both smug and disapproving. "I heard that Sissy Fowler was bankrolling Jimmy Toups's book."

"Bankrolling?" said Carmela, with a quizzical expression.

"As in *financing*," said Shamus, as though he were administering a remedial arithmetic lesson.

"I thought Jimmy Toups had a contract," said Carmela. "With a legitimate publisher." At least, that was Jimmy's story.

Shamus let loose a loud snort. "Can you say *vanity* press? I mean, come on, what publisher in their right mind would give a book contract to those two goofballs?"

"So yet another scam," said Carmela, just as the overhead lights winked on and off.

"Second act's gonna start," said Ava, tugging at Carmela's sleeve. Got to get going." She flashed a cheesy smile. "Hey, folks, it's been a blast."

Shamus peered at Carmela. "You're wearing a bat on your head?"

"Raven," Carmela snapped.

"Fooled me," said Shamus as he turned toward Glory. "You ready to go, big sis?"

Glory thrust her arm out, handed Shamus her empty glass, and said, "Get me another one."

"Glory's mean as cat pee, isn't she?" asked Ava as they bumped their way back to their seats.

"You don't know the half of it," said Carmela. "Fact is, all the Meechums have a distinct mean streak. Just not as pronounced as Glory's."

"Wonder why?" said Ava.

"Gotta be about the money," said Carmela. "None of them can wait to get their sticky hands on it." Besides founding Crescent City Bank, great-granddaddy Meechum had also spawned a dynasty of money-grubbing ingrates.

The second act of *Ballet Dracula* was even more exciting than the first. An entire company of dancers in Victorian dresses and frock coats whirled and swirled onstage, while Dracula performed his semi-amorous, hypnotic dance with the supple-necked Mina Harker.

Then Jekyl finally made his appearance as a member of a sort of Greek chorus, although in this case, it was more of a Transylvanian villager flashback chorus.

In a cacophony of dance and music, blue-black lighting flickered onstage, interspersed with smoke from dry ice, a burst of red lights, and any number of swooning women. And when the heroine was rescued, the wooden stake pounded, and the lovers finally reunited, the curtain crashed down to a thunderous ovation.

Clapping a hand to her chest, Ava exclaimed, "*Cher*, that was magnificent. I can hardly draw a breath, I'm so moved."

"You don't think it's from being pinched into that corset all evening?"

"Oh you," said Ava, waving a hand. "There's really just the teensiest sense of restriction." She winked. "You might even enjoy it."

"No, thanks," said Carmela. "I had enough restriction when I was married."

"So now we go backstage?" asked Ava. "To join the cast party?"

"Let's do it," Carmela agreed. "Jekyl invited us, and so did your new boyfriend."

"Not my boyfriend yet," said Ava.

"*Yet* being the operative word," said Carmela.

They waited until the theater was practically empty, then descended the steps all the way down to the bottom. When they hit the footlights, they followed two other women around the rounded stage and ducked through a side curtain.

The cast party was already in full swing. Actors mingled with costumers, makeup artists, and set designers amid a jumble of scenery, folding chairs, and hastily arranged tables. A temporary bar had been set up with champagne, wine, sandwiches, and a couple of large pots of steaming jambalaya. In fact, Carmela figured that the first champagne corks must have started bouncing off the walls even as the actors were taking their final bows.

A white-faced actor shoved overflowing champagne flutes into their hands and leered at them.

"Dracula?" Ava asked, tipping back her glass.

"No, but I was in the count's chorus," the actor told them. "And I'm also the understudy for the principal understudy."

"So a *dis*count," giggled Carmela.

"Carmela, darling!" called Jekyl from across the crowded backstage area. "And the lovely Ava, too!" Jekyl scurried to-

ward them, grinning, blowing air kisses to fellow cast members, looking like *he* was the one who'd just danced the lead and mesmerized the audience.

"You were terrific," said Carmela, offering a cheek to kiss.

"Shucks, it wasn't much," said Jekyl. "Just the chorus."

"Still," enthused Ava, "you were onstage, you were a performer."

"Did you not fall in *love* with this ballet?" asked Jekyl, posturing slightly. "Was it not magnificent?"

"I'm considering getting my toe shoes out of mothballs," Carmela told him.

"Wicked, wicked," said Jekyl, shaking a finger at her.

"Seriously," said Ava, "we loved the ballet."

"Honey," said Jekyl, looking her up and down, "the way you're dressed, *you* could have been in tonight's performance. I'm head over heels for that corset." He pressed fingertips to leather, said, "Ooh, lambskin?"

"Custom made," said Ava.

"Looks it," Jekyl told her. "It's got that mistress-of-the-dark feel."

"Obviously, I'm planning to wear it again tomorrow night," said Ava.

Jekyl turned to Carmela. "What about you, love? You planning to join us at the Bondage Ball?" The Bondage Ball was part of New Orleans's Halloween scene. A crazy, whacked-out party at the Commodore Hotel where everyone came dressed in leather, studded bracelets, handcuffs, or whatever. And there tended to be a lot of whatevers.

"Pass," Carmela told Jekyl. "So not my scene." Carmela enjoyed a leather look now and again, but bondage . . . that seemed a little bit on the edge.

"You'd be surprised," said Ava.

"Surprised at what?" asked Carmela.

"At *who* turns up," said Ava, rolling her eyes.

"Hey," said Jekyl, "Sissy Fowler called me."

"What did she want?" asked Ava.

"The artwork?" asked Carmela. "She sure didn't waste any time."

Jekyl nodded. "Sissy wants me to take a look-see around her house and do a quick appraisal."

"Sissy's an art collector?" asked Ava.

"Says she is," said Jekyl, looking a trifle skeptical. "I'll find out for sure tomorrow afternoon."

"What if it's all velvet paintings?" asked Carmela. "You know, schlock."

"Or paintings of weird kids with big eyes?" put in Ava.

"I'll still give Sissy an appraisal," said Jekyl, waving to a fellow actor across the room and starting to slide away. "After all, market value doesn't necessarily mean valuable."

"*Cher*," said Ava, "you think there's a ladies' room back here?"

"Pretty much has to be," said Carmela. "Probably near the dressing rooms."

"I want to do a little primping," Ava confessed. "After which I'm going to accidentally-on-purpose run into Tom Travers."

"Sounds like a plan," said Carmela. She set her drink down on a nearby table, and the two of them pushed their way through the throng of people. If the cast numbered forty and there were another forty people working backstage, then there had to be yet another hundred people mingling here as well. So lots of hangers-on. Just like they were.

"Warm in here, too," said Ava, fanning herself.

"Probably your corset," said Carmela as they slipped behind an enormous piece of scenery that depicted the Castle Dracula in crumbling ruins. They passed Victorian bedroom scenery, leaving the party behind and creeping along in semidarkness now. And then they practically stumbled into the cemetery scenery. "Lots cooler back here," said Carmela. In fact, the depiction of open tombs with Carfax Abbey in the background was enough to give anyone a chill.

"But where are the—" began Ava.

Which is when they heard two voices, harsh and low, hissing at each other, obviously locked in an intense argument.

Ava frowned. A *What on earth?* frown.

Carmela only shook her head. Then the cemetery scenery behind them bumped slightly, Carfax Abbey vibrated, and they stumbled away into darkness.

"I wonder who was in such a tizzy?" asked Ava as they finally found their way into a tiny makeup room.

"Don't know," said Carmela. "Maybe we should have eavesdropped instead of being so well mannered."

"Speak for yourself." Ava grinned, applying a smudge of exotic dark mauve lipstick and lengthening her already-long lashes.

"Tarantula," Carmela cautioned. It was her warning about applying too much mascara.

"Yeah, yeah, I know," said Ava.

When they emerged from the makeup room, the corridor was dark. And quiet. No hushed voices locked in battle, no sign of anyone.

"Was this rack of costumes here before?" asked Ava. Somehow, a rack of dark vampirish costumes had materialized in the hallway.

"No," said Carmela. "I don't think so."

"Is this even the right hallway?" asked Ava. "Or did we just make a wrong turn?"

"Isn't that the Carfax Abbey set?"

"No, it's the parlor set. See all that fake fringe? Looks like trees, but it's not."

"Doggone," said Carmela, feeling like a doofus now.

"We *are* turned around," said Ava.

"Maybe . . . this way?" said Carmela, pointing.

They fumbled their way down a dark hallway, mindful of the myriad sets, racks of costumes, and ropes that dangled down from an overhead web of lines and pulleys.

"If we—" began Ava. Then her foot struck a piece of set decoration, and she suddenly plunged face forward. A nasty fall that wasn't quite a somersault.

"You okay?" asked a concerned Carmela, trying to help Ava to her feet.

"No!" fumed Ava, "I almost fractured a hip! This darn scratchy fake shrubbery! What dumbo parked it here?" She got halfway up, then stumbled again. This time a ten-foot-high gargoyle teetered and leered from its papier-mâché base, threatening to tumble down on the both of them.

"Watch out!" cried Carmela, putting out a hand to steady the evil-looking creature. "This place is a veritable minefield."

"Aggh!" cried Ava, who flailed for a handhold, got caught in some rigging, then tripped again, promptly falling into a web of ropes.

"This is starting to feel like a Marx Brothers comedy," breathed Carmela. *"Night at the Opera."*

"Holy crap!" complained Ava as she flailed about, com-

pletely ensnared in the theater's rigging. "It's like I'm trapped in a spiderweb and some oversized, furry arachnid is about to descend and . . ." She gazed upward, then blinked in surprise, as her eyes widened to heroic proportions. One second later, her face went slack, her head canted backward, and she let loose a bloodcurdling scream!

"Ava?" Carmela whispered hoarsely. "What . . . ?"

Like some kind of unholy yo-yo, the still-warm body of Jimmy Toups descended from above, wrapped snugly in a cocoon of ropes. Toups landed just inches in front of them, dangling upside down, spinning, his face purple and horribly puffed. Bobbing upward a few feet, he descended again. Definitely a dead human yo-yo.

Chapter 16

So much for the backstage cast party. That little soiree pretty much dissolved into chaos and disbelief once Carmela and Ava ran shrieking back to the party, babbling their horrific tale of Jimmy Toups bobbing upside down at the end of a rope, his face a bright purple.

"What? What?" came a quavering voice from across the crowded area. Then Sissy Fowler tottered toward them on four-inch stiletto heels, still holding her drink. "You say something happened to Jimmy? *My* Jimmy?"

"He's in the Lord's hands now," Carmela murmured.

"The Lord's poor Jimmy," echoed Ava, making a quick sign of the cross.

"Carmela," cried Jekyl, flying at her, then grabbing both shoulders in his hands. "This isn't some Halloween prank?"

"No way," said Carmela. "Just look at poor Ava, scared half to death!"

Ava nodded with great gusto. "Broke a nail, too."

Sissy staggered away and collapsed on a folding chair, inconsolable.

Barely four minutes later the police arrived. First three uniformed officers who tried to corral everyone, unsuccessfully, of course, with black-and-yellow crime-scene tape. Then Edgar Babcock came sauntering in.

"Don't tell me," were his first words to Carmela.

She held up both hands, pantomiming innocence. Ava and Jekyl watched their exchange with curiosity.

"Another dead body," said Babcock. He sounded incredulous. "You're like a magnet for violent crime."

"Hey," said Carmela, "I only *find* dead bodies, I don't actually have a hand in their demise."

"Ha-ha," said Babcock.

More officers came running in, and two were assigned to venture into the dark recess of the theater to check on Jimmy Toups. They emerged some forty seconds later.

"He's hanging back there all right," said one officer, an African American whose nametag read *Billings*. "Bobbing around like a catfish on a hook."

"Nice," Carmela told Babcock. "A totally professional assessment. I feel so much better now that the police are here to protect us."

"Gotta bring the crime-scene guys in," said Billings, ignoring her.

His partner, an officer named Sully, nodded in agreement. "Plus he's dressed somewhat oddly."

"A fashion victim as well as a murder victim," observed Jekyl.

"Oh jeez," muttered Babcock.

Then Sissy Fowler, black streams of mascara running

down her florid pink cheeks, pushed her way to Babcock and grasped him by the lapels. Carmela noted that it was his good Armani jacket, too.

"I have to go back there!" Sissy wailed. "I have to see Jimmy!"

"Trust me, you don't," said Ava. "He's not lookin' too good."

"We need to secure the scene," barked Babcock, and the uniformed officers suddenly snapped to attention. They hustled Sissy away while Babcock idly smoothed his jacket.

"I hope you don't need to, like, interview us or anything," Carmela said to Babcock. "Because I'd just as soon not stay here."

"Stay," said Babcock.

"All of us?" asked Jekyl.

"All of you," said Babcock.

Jekyl turned to Carmela. "You've got to tell your boyfriend to take a chill pill."

"You didn't see him," Carmela said to Jekyl. "Toups, I mean. It was awful. We've definitely got another murder on our hands."

"Maybe *you've* got another one," said Jekyl, "but I'm not getting involved."

"You're already involved," Ava pointed out.

"Noooo, I'm not," was Jekyl's quick reply. "I was out front here, swooning around with the party guests the entire time. If Jimmy Toups, with his big-mouthed swagger, ticked somebody off and got himself killed, it's none of my business."

"Even though you were Toups's big archrival?" asked Carmela. "People are going to bring that up, you know."

"Probably," said Jekyl. "But I'm alibied up the wazoo, and if a problem does come up, I'll bring in my lawyer."

"Sounds like you've got it all figured out," said Ava.

"Excuse me?" said Jekyl, frowning, "but that sounded awfully close to an accusation."

"Really?" squealed Ava, contrite now. "Because I didn't mean it that way." She turned to Carmela. "I didn't sound like I was accusing him, did I?"

"You kind of did," said Carmela, then noticed quick tears forming in Ava's eyes.

Ava flung herself at Jekyl and hugged him tightly. "I didn't mean it that way," she told him. "Really." She dabbed at her eyes.

He put his arms around her and patted her. "I know that, love."

"I was afraid you'd leave me for another man," said Tom Travers, "and I was right. Before we even got a chance to know each other." He stepped up to Ava, smiled at her, then quickly looked sober again. "Terrible thing," he murmured to the group.

Carmela and Jekyl nodded.

"Awful," said Carmela.

"Unspeakable," said Jekyl.

"We kind of found him," said Ava. "Carmela and I."

Travers looked even more shaken. "Oh, sweetie, no!" He put his arm around Ava and pulled her close. "I was out in the lobby with my brother-in-law," he explained, "when we saw all these police running in. First we thought there was some kind of medical emergency. Cardiac arrest or some poor soul having a seizure. Then people started whispering about Jimmy Toups and the . . . what would you even call it? A hanging?" He blanched, looking almost ill. "How could something like this happen? I mean, everyone came here to support the ballet company and have a nice time!"

"Almost everyone," remarked Carmela. She noticed Babcock standing some twenty feet away, writing in a spiral notebook in his cramped, back-slanted handwriting. She slipped away from the group, wanting to speak with him.

Babcock saw her coming and closed his notebook.

"I didn't mean to bark at you," were his first words. "Didn't mean to offend."

"No offense taken," said Carmela. "I know you're here to do your job, not romance me."

"Not that I wouldn't want to do that," he said, managing a faint smile. He paused, then said, "Was it awful? Finding Toups?"

Carmela nodded. "Unnerving, anyway."

Babcock scrunched up his face. "Something weird is going on."

"No kidding," said Carmela. "But at least we know it wasn't Toups who killed Fowler."

"How do we know that?" asked Babcock.

Carmela stared at him. "Uh . . . because Toups is still hanging back there in the wings all trussed up like a Thanksgiving turkey?"

Babcock shook his head. "Toups still could have killed Fowler."

"And then somebody killed Toups?" asked Carmela, her voice rising to an almost-panic level. That notion hadn't occurred to her. "A *second* killer? But . . . who?"

"That's my job to figure out," said Babcock. He retreated deep in thought for a few moments, then said, "You going to be around tonight?"

"You want to interview me?" Carmela asked. "Debrief me?"

"Debrief." Babcock smiled. "Something like that."

* * *

Carmela walked over to the bar, where two full bottles of champagne sat open. She touched the back of her hand to the green bottle of Rodier. Still cold. Okay. She took a clean flute, poured herself half a glass, and took a sip.

Ah, good. Cold and still tickly.

Carmela gazed at the crowd that still milled about. Like a dramatic scene change, the atmosphere was completely different than it had been fifteen minutes ago. Totally different vibe.

Carmela took another sip and let her mind wander. Ruminating about the past week.

All along, she'd had a faint inkling of Jimmy Toups as the killer. But now that he'd been killed, that theory seemed completely out the window.

Or was it? Babcock didn't seem to think so. But if Toups killed Fowler, then who killed Toups?

Had Sissy somehow insinuated herself into the act? Had Sissy somehow set up Jimmy Toups? Or used him? And why? What was her ultimate motive?

Carmela was also suspicious of Mills Taggart, Glory's unsavory investigator. He'd been here tonight with Glory. Had Glory's semitrained watchdog slipped his collar and killed Jimmy Toups? Again . . . why? Had Toups somehow been involved in Fowler's financial mess?

Of course, Tanya, Fowler's girlfriend, could also be lurking in the mix. Carmela hadn't seen her at the party, but that didn't mean she wasn't slinking around somewhere. If Tanya suspected Toups as her lover's killer, seeking revenge would have been a powerful motivator.

Ava came hurrying over to Carmela. "*Cher*, I'm gonna run

home and clean up. Then Tom's taking me to Galatoire's for a drink."

"You look great already," Carmela told her.

Ava looked horrified. "Oh no! My eye makeup is smeared and my hair looks straggly." She reached out, grabbed Carmela's champagne glass, and helped herself to a quick sip. "I want Travers to see me at my absolute best. Face perfectly made up, extensions clipped into my hair, dress cut low and tight, wearing an even better push-up bra."

"The real you," said Carmela.

Ava gave a radiant smile. "Exactly."

Carmela and Jekyl settled for a postballet drink (or postmurder drink) at Mumbo Gumbo. This was one of their favorite haunts as well as being Quigg Brevard's more casual restaurant, located just a few blocks from the theater and also in the French Quarter.

Formerly the Westminster Gallery space, Mumbo Gumbo never failed to make Carmela feel relaxed and welcome. Crumbling red bricks crept halfway up interior walls, and then the ensuing smooth plastered walls were painted a cream-and-gold harlequin pattern. A large bar, the color of a ripe eggplant, dominated an entire wall. Above the bar, glass shelves displayed hundreds of bottles of top-shelf spirits. Heavy wooden tables with black leather club chairs were snugged next to antique oak barrels that held glass and brass lamps. Potted palms and slowly spinning ceiling fans added to the slightly exotic atmosphere. The music was zydeco interspersed with haunting Cajun ballads and an occasional riff of jazz.

"I do love the menu here," said Jekyl, cozied into a club

chair, studying the multipage accordion piece that Carmela had designed last year.

"Are you referring to the design aesthetics or the food?" Carmela asked.

"Both," said Jekyl. "Since I know you did the creative work. But for now I'm focused on food . . . I'm absolutely craving a good gumbo!"

"You'll find more than enough permutations here," Carmela told him. Indeed, the menu offered chicken andouille gumbo, seafood okra gumbo, crab and oyster gumbo, and even lobster gumbo. Of course, Mumbo Gumbo also served entrées such as crawfish pie, red beans and rice, and alligator piquant.

"I'm going with crab gumbo tonight," said Jekyl. "And a nice glass of white wine."

"Wine," said Carmela, thinking about her wine trip tomorrow to St. Tammany Vineyard. "Yes, they do have a cellar full."

"So," said Jekyl once they'd ordered, once he had a glass of wine in front of him and had taken several calming sips. "What's your take on Jimmy Toups's murder?"

"Not sure," said Carmela.

"I saw you whispering with your hotshot detective. He must have a few ideas spinning around in that obsessive-compulsive brain of his."

"By that, you mean he's focused?" Carmela asked, a little put off by Jekyl's mean-spirited criticism.

"Ah," said Jekyl. "But is he focused on you?"

Carmela thought for a few moments, then said, "I'd say he's focused on *you.*"

Jekyl reared back. "What!" He shook his head in disbelief.

"You and Jimmy Toups have always been rivals," said

Carmela. "And the competition between the two of you hasn't always been pretty."

"What's that got to do with the price of potatoes?"

"I think it puts you in the deep fryer," said Carmela.

"Huh," snorted Jekyl. "So now I'm a *double* suspect because Fowler despised me and Toups and I were competitive?" He looked both worried and exasperated.

"Yes," said Carmela. "I'd say that's it in a nutshell."

Chapter 17

"HOW was your date?" asked Carmela. She and Ava were speeding along in Carmela's Mercedes two-seater on their way to St. Tammany Vineyard. With the sun shining down brightly, generating some welcome heat for a late-October day, they'd pushed back the top so they could enjoy a wide open view. Now the wind whipped and snipped at them as gigantic slices of bright blue spread out on either side of them. It was the blue of Lake Pontchartrain, and they were exactly halfway across the Lake Pontchartrain Causeway, the twenty-three-and-three-quarter-mile bridge that spanned the lake and was the longest bridge in the world.

"I had a fabulous night," said Ava, giving a dreamy smile. "I think I'm in love."

"Ah," said Carmela. "So soon?"

"Last night was practically our second date!"

"I see," said Carmela. Ava held the land speed record for falling in love. Of course, she could fall out of love just as fast.

"I'm going to meet up with Travers tonight at the Bondage Ball." She glanced at Carmela. "You come, too. It's going to be good, clean, kinky fun."

"Can't," said Carmela, keeping her eyes glued to the road. "Don't have a thing to wear."

"Silly," guffawed Ava. "You know perfectly well I have a walk-in closet filled with sexy stuff, most of which would be perfect on you."

"That's what worries me," said Carmela.

"Okay, how about this?" asked Ava, ever the fashion stylist. "A black leather skirt, black thigh-high boots, and a leather mask? Just a dollop of kink."

"What would I wear for a top?"

"A see-through blouse?"

"It's not workin' for me," said Carmela. "My slightly conservative bent means modesty must prevail."

"Okay, okay," said Ava. "How about a nice black silk blouse?"

"How about beige?"

"Argh," said Ava.

"Okay, black," said Carmela. "That I could probably manage as long as it's tasteful."

"So you'll come?"

"Let's just say I'll consider it."

"You could tell Babcock to meet you there," said Ava with a sly grin. "Pretend he's investigating a crime, which he really is, and you're a mysterious woman with secret information."

"You mean make a game of it," said Carmela.

Ava gave a playful little shiver. "That's what keeps relationships all fresh and sparkly."

"Babcock and I are still fairly fresh," said Carmela. She wasn't sure about the sparkly part. What exactly did that mean? Seeing stars?

"Here's the thing," Ava explained. "Every relationship is like a carton of yogurt. Blueberry crumb cake yogurt *sounds* great when you pick it up at the Piggly Wiggly, but it has a firm expiration date, a date when it starts to turn sour. That's why you have to jump at each and every opportunity. Grab the brass ring, so to speak."

"I understand the concept," said Carmela, frowning as she negotiated road traffic. She'd just passed the outskirts of Abita Springs and was now heading up Highway 435.

"Of course," allowed Ava, "keeping a relationship fresh and fun doesn't always work. Case in point, you and Shamus."

"I think it worked perfectly well for Shamus," said Carmela. "He kept things fresh and fun by seeing other women."

"Yeah," said Ava. "That did present a unique problem."

"Not for him," Carmela muttered. Glancing down at an unreadable scrawl on a torn piece of paper, Carmela added, "Quigg gave me pretty crappy directions. But I think we should hit St. Tammany Vineyard in about four or five miles."

"I'll keep an eye open," said Ava, settling back behind large, oval Versace sunglasses. She was silent for a couple of minutes, then said, "So, any new theories about last night?"

"I ran a few permutations through my brain and didn't come up with a single thing," Carmela told her.

Ava giggled. "You make it sound like your brain is one

of those big old-fashioned computers. What did they call them? Mainlines?"

"You mean mainframes?"

"Yeah, that's it," said Ava. "With all the blinking lights and beeping shit and stuff."

"I'm not sure mainframes blinked and beeped that much," said Carmela. "You're thinking of special effects computers for movies and stuff."

"Yeah, maybe," said Ava. "Oh hey! There's the sign!"

Carmela slowed her car. A large, light green wooden sign with deep maroon type proclaimed *St. Tammany Vineyard, 2 Miles Ahead.*

"Almost there," said Ava. "But . . . you're thinking about it."

"The vineyard?" said Carmela. "Computers?"

"No," said Ava, "the murder. Only now it's plural. Murders."

"Oh yeah," said Carmela. "After last night I'm even more intrigued."

Ava smiled. "Atta girl."

"You made it," exclaimed a large, friendly man in a plaid shirt and dark khaki slacks who hastened to pull open the driver's-side door and assist Carmela out. "I'm Don Dewey, the manager," he explained as he pumped her hand with genuine enthusiasm. Then Dewey dashed around to the other side and greeted Ava in the same effusive manner.

"This place is amazing," said Carmela as they strolled toward a small yellow brick building, which she assumed was the tasting room. On either side of the small parking lot were row after row of leafy green grapevines, growing up-

ward on thin wires and stretching as far as the eye could see. Behind the tasting room loomed an enormous white building. Where the grape press, fermentation, and bottling facilities were located, no doubt.

"Come on into our tasting room," said Dewey, holding the door open, "and we'll get started." They trooped into a sunny room with whitewashed walls and a reddish-orange tiled floor. One side of the room was dominated by a long, mahogany bar; the other side was basically a cute little gift shop.

"A bar," said Ava. "Oh wow."

"Every tasting room comes complete with a bar," laughed Dewey. "That's where all the action takes place. Plus we also have the de rigueur souvenirs and gifty stuff that appeals to tourists."

Glancing around, Carmela saw that Dewey was quite correct about the souvenirs. There were dozens of books on wine, denim caps and dark blue T-shirts embroidered with *St. Tammany Vineyard* in white thread, plus corkscrews, coasters, paper napkins, glass carafes, and sets of handsome Riedel wineglasses.

"That's Ardice, over there," said Dewey, waving at an African American woman who was stacking more expensive sets of Riedel Vinum Collection glasses. "She's in charge of the gift shop as well as our paychecks." Ardice was midthirties, perky looking, wearing a tailored navy pantsuit.

"I'm a bookkeeper who got bit by the wine bug is what I am," Ardice confessed as she came over to greet them. "I got fascinated by the whole wine-making process, and pretty soon Quigg invited me to be the gift shop buyer, too."

"She also runs a pretty mean tasting room," said Dewey, who obviously had great admiration for Ardice. "Knows all about wine, grapes, *terroirs* . . . the whole shebang."

"Not quite," Ardice told them. "I'm a work in progress. Once you start tasting wine and begin a small collection, you realize how much more you have to learn."

"Wine's complicated." Dewey shrugged. "Or should I say complex."

"Good one," said Ardice, pointing a finger at him. Then to Carmela, "You're the designer and marketing guru?"

"I'm going to give it a try," said Carmela.

"I saw the menus you did for Bon Tiempe and Mumbo Gumbo," said Ardice. She nodded. "You've got talent."

"Thank you," said Carmela.

"I'm the untalented friend," laughed Ava.

Ardice gave Ava a speculative glance. "Somehow I doubt that."

"So," Dewey asked, shifting from one size-twelve boot to the other, "do you want to taste wine or jump right into the plant tour?"

"We did some tasting the other night," said Carmela, "so maybe do the tour?" She glanced sideways at Ava. "Maybe afterward we can have a few sips."

"Yum," said Ava.

"Have fun." Ardice waved as Dewey led them around the bar and out the back door.

"See you later," called Ava.

"St. Tammany Vineyard," said Dewey as they tromped across a blacktopped area, "is a fairly small operation. We've got twenty acres under cultivation and just had a partial harvest last month. All the grapes carefully cut by hand and stacked in small tubs, not just tossed willy-nilly into some great big gondola." He got to the large white building, flipped a latch, and slid open an enormous door. They were immediately greeted by the prickly, spicy, almost heady

scent of fermenting grapes. "Here's the heart of the operation, where we do pretty much everything."

Carmela and Ava stepped inside, clearly fascinated.

"Over here," said Dewey, leading them to an enormous stainless steel tank, "is where fermentation takes place, once our grapes are crushed and destemmed."

"How long does fermentation last?" asked Ava.

"Maybe two or three weeks," said Dewey. "Depending. Then we transfer the wine into smaller vessels. For example, reds go into oak barrels, while whites go into stainless steel vats."

"And then how long?" asked Ava.

Dewey grinned. "That's up to the vintner. But basically, anywhere from a few months to twenty years. Depending on what type of wine you want to produce."

"What about champagne?" Carmela asked.

"Champagne's a little trickier," said Dewey. "In the case of sparkling wine, additional fermentation takes place *inside* the bottles. Carbon dioxide is trapped and after a while . . . poof . . . all those magical little bubbles suddenly appear."

"Love the magic bubbles," said Ava.

"That's a very condensed explanation for all of this," said Dewey. "Realize, there are also lots of lab tests and filtration processes that go on as well."

"Your entire wine-making process is fascinating," said Carmela. "Are you bringing tours through here yet?"

"Not yet," said Dewey. "Although that's certainly the master plan. Add tours and have a picnic grounds where folks can bring their own baskets or buy deli sandwiches from us."

"It's a good plan," said Carmela, looking around, knowing this was a highly marketable entity. The winery was com-

pact but still quite delightful, especially when you learned, step-by-step, about all the various wine-making processes. The roster of wines that St. Tammany Vineyard was producing was good quality. And the grounds were lush and inviting. She could just imagine picnic tables set up in that little magnolia grove over by the river.

"So you think you can help us?" Dewey asked. "We've had a pretty quiet launch so far, but we need to start making some serious noise."

"I've already spoken to Quigg about a major media party next month," said Carmela. "If we can get the press talking, we have a good chance at getting the public drinking."

"That's the idea," said Dewey, beaming.

Carmela jotted a few notes on her sketch pad. She also had a couple of ideas for a logo. Something classy but approachable. This wasn't Château Latour, but it sure wasn't Three-Buck Chuck, either. St. Tammany Vineyard had to have its own identity and project its own special appeal.

Maybe, Carmela decided, once distribution and sales were bumped up, new wines could be added seasonally. A Beaujolais in autumn, a spicy white wine for Halloween, mulled wine for the holidays, maybe pink champagne for Mardi Gras. A thousand ideas buzzed inside her brain until Dewey suddenly came crashing in on her thoughts.

"You had some crazy stuff go on down in the city last night," said Dewey.

Carmela gazed at him, unsure what he was referring to.

"The murder," said Dewey. "Or hanging. At that fancy theater. Whatever it was, it made the front page of the *Times-Picayune*." Dewey's low-key laugh rumbled forth, and his enormous shoulders shook. "This isn't exactly the sticks up here, you know."

"Funny you should mention that," said Ava, "because we were there."

"You don't say!" Dewey bellowed, clearly caught off guard. "You two were at that theater?" He looked at them with renewed interest.

"Afraid so," said Carmela.

"People are still crazy for that vampire stuff, aren't they?" asked Dewey. He hitched at his straining belt and said, "You ask me, it's all a little too strange. I mean, you have a Dracula ballet show and then somebody gets killed? You hear what I'm saying? There's something . . ." He grimaced, fishing for the right word. "Something *dangerous* about the whole thing."

"No kidding," said Ava.

"What's over that way?" asked Carmela, pointing toward the magnolia grove, anxious to change the subject.

"C'mon, I'll show you," responded Dewey as they headed across a wide stretch of mowed lawn.

"You have a boat dock," said Ava as they approached a small pond. "And a boat. Are you going to give boat rides, too?"

"No," said Dewey, "but you can sure take one if you'd like. Thing is, St. Tammany Vineyard backs up to the western side of the Honey Island Swamp. You've heard of that?"

Indeed they had. The Honey Island Swamp was a pristine bayou filled with wildlife, flora and fauna, and one other thing . . .

"The Honey Island Swamp Monster!" exclaimed Ava. "Is this where it lives? Really?"

"So I've been told," said Dewey, looking mock-serious.

"I've heard about this swamp monster," said Carmela, "but I don't know the local lore."

"Mighty interesting," said Dewey, leading them out onto the creaky narrow dock. "Legend holds that back in the twenties, a traveling circus train crashed on the train tracks nearby."

"Seriously?" squeaked Ava, getting into it now.

Dewey continued, his voice low and mysterious. "And an entire car load of chimpanzees escaped into the swamp."

"Okay," said Ava, clearly wanting more.

"Some of those chimps bred with the local alligator population and, over the years, the Honey Island Swamp Monster evolved."

"No way!" said Ava, slapping Dewey's broad chest.

"Way," he said, giving her an extra serious gaze.

"Sounds to me like we've got ourselves a genuine Southern-fried Bigfoot," said Carmela.

"Whatcha mean?" asked Ava.

Carmela smiled at her. "A hoax."

"Maybe so," said Dewey, still maintaining his serious attitude, "but if you two ladies would care to take a boat ride into this old swamp, you could check it out for yourselves."

"Then that's what I want to do," said Ava. "Right?" She threw a pleading glance at Carmela. "We're gonna check it out? Right?"

Carmela glanced at her watch. They were okay on time. "Sure, why not?"

"Whoopee," said Ava, clambering into the boat, which was no easy feat in four-inch stilettos and skintight jeans.

"Just pull the rope on that Evinrude," Dewey instructed Carmela, "and she should purr like a kitten."

Carmela yanked the rope and got the motor going while Ava pushed off with one of the oars.

"Take care," said Dewey, as they pulled away.

"We always do," Ava sang back.

"Cher," said Ava as they skimmed along, "is this not fun? Is this not magnificent?" Carmela had throttled the motor way back until they were gliding gently down a narrow stretch of water. Mangroves tangled the banks, the perfect hidey spot for bass and speckled trout. A few pale pink water lilies, probably on the endangered species list for decades now, poked their elegant heads up from giant dinner plate–sized lily pads.

"This is great as long as you drop a trail of bread crumbs," said Carmela. "So we remember how to get back."

"I have a fantastic sense of direction," said Ava. "No problem."

Carmela recalled driving up to Natchitoches with Ava once and getting horribly turned around in what was essentially a small town, so she knew she'd better keep a sharp eye out. Commit every twist and turn to memory. Carmela also decided to try to keep the sun on her right shoulder. Navigating by the sun, once you factored in time and movement, was fairly reliable.

"I've heard the Honey Island Swamp Monster legend for years," said Ava, "but I never knew anyone who actually *saw* him."

"Don't count on an actual sighting," said Carmela. "Because you just said the operative word. *Legend.*"

"But all legends have a grain of truth behind them," said Ava. "Look at the Dracula legend. I mean, there really was a Vlad the Impaler."

"How about the Bigfoot legend?" Carmela asked. "Fact based?"

"Oh, he's out there, too," said Ava.

"Yetis?"

"Sure," said Ava. "But not here. Just, like, where it's real cold and snowy. Some place like Minnesota."

"So the Minnesota Yetis," joked Carmela. "Clearly a naming opportunity for a sports franchise."

As the inlet they were following hooked right, they came upon a half-submerged log with a raft of snapping turtles sitting on top. At seeing the boat, two of the smaller turtles immediately dove into the water, while three older, rough-backed reptiles gave them challenging, nonblinking stares.

"Better napping than snapping," said Ava as they continued past.

Now the stream narrowed and the banks were studded with saw palmetto and tupelo gum trees. More rough-shelled turtles peeked at them from behind giant pitcher plants.

Further down, ferns and water hyacinth lined verdant banks. Ospreys and ibises sang from trees while speckled trout darted and zoomed under their boat.

"This is almost primordial," said Carmela. She felt a deep kinship with this still, dark bayou where tall trees were draped in canopies of living, growing vegetation. Her daddy had taken her into the bayous down near Pointe-aux-Chenes and Chauvin, hunting, fishing, doing a little trapping now and then. He'd been part Cajun and had taught her what to love and what to respect. Not fear, just respect.

Then he'd been killed in a barge accident on the Mississippi, and she hadn't gone back into a bayou until she'd married Shamus. They'd overnighted at his rough but charming

camp house in the Baritaria Bayou, enjoying the solitude and the life outdoors. But that was another place and time.

"This is great," Ava sang out, "as long as we don't run into any big bad snakes or alligators."

"Look over there," Carmela said in a low voice. She pointed, and they both peered at a blanket of thick green algae that bobbed on the surface.

"Nothing," said Ava.

"Keep looking," said Carmela.

They were motionless for a minute or so, and then the tip of an alligator snout suddenly rose from the algae.

"Oh no!" was Ava's hoarse response.

"Don't worry," Carmela told her. "He's just a small one."

"What if Momma's nearby?" asked Ava, glancing around nervously. She suddenly grasped the sides of the boat. "Jeez! What was that?"

"Relax," Carmela told her. "No monsters here."

"No, I think I really *did* hear something," said Ava, more insistent now, her head spinning from side to side like the kid from *The Exorcist.*

Carmela, who'd been focused on the small alligator, revved up the engine and moved out quickly. "We'll keep going if you're scared. See? The alligator's behind us now. Nothing to worry about but—"

"But the boat coming up behind us!" shrilled Ava.

Carmela frowned, spun in her seat, and inhaled with a sharp gasp. There *was* a motorboat bearing down on them.

Only whatever was driving it wasn't human!

Chapter 18

"GO!" screamed Ava. "Go, go, go! Punch it!"

"I am, I did," Carmela screamed back. "We're running full throttle!"

"Go faster!" Ava yelled, clenching her fists and pounding the sides of the boat. Her hair flew out behind her like she was on the downhill side of a roller coaster.

"Get down!" Carmela yelled above the roar of the motor. "Get as flat as you can on the bottom of the boat!" Ava complied and Carmela also scrunched down in the back of the boat, wondering to herself, *What's going on? That boat came out of nowhere! Or did it?*

Spying a tiny stream coming up fast on her left, Carmela aimed for it, swung the boat around a narrow spit of land, and managed a tricky one-eighty turn as she kicked up a twelve-foot-high rooster tail of water. Almost tipping over the boat in the process, too.

But she didn't.

A loud crack—a gunshot?—pierced the stillness of the swamp and then Carmela was zooming down the small tributary, almost running in the same direction from which she'd come, praying to high heaven that this stream wouldn't just peter out in weeds and thick muck.

They were lucky. Still running at breakneck pace, Carmela kept punching the engine for a good ten minutes, while Ava kept a close watch for anyone coming up behind them.

Finally, Ava said, "Nothing. I think we really did lose him." She clutched her chest. "Oh man, my heart is pounding like a timpani drum on parade."

Carmela throttled way back, keeping the motor idling but reducing the sound to a low level, low enough to hear if they were still being pursued.

There was nothing except the audacious squawk of an ibis.

"I think it's . . . *he's* gone," said Carmela. She wiped the back of her hand across her eyes where sweat and tears had seemingly accumulated, and said, "Whew." It was a cartoon *whew*. Like the Road Runner might utter after escaping the clutches of Wile E. Coyote.

"Oh jeez, oh jeez," babbled Ava. "It was the Honey Island Swamp Monster! I'm positive it was!"

"You sure we didn't just stumble into something illegal?" asked Carmela. "Some crazy local with a whiskey still or meth lab to protect?"

"Carmela, you saw that *thing* that chased us, didn't you?"

"Yes, I did," said Carmela. Not human. That was the first thought that had popped into her head.

"That creature, whatever it was, was hideous to look at!" exclaimed Ava. "I'm talkin' long gray hair and bright red eyes! The kind of monster you imagine might be hiding in the back of your closet!"

"Please don't say that," murmured Carmela. Closet monsters were the worst.

Ten minutes later, they pulled up to the dock at St. Tammany Vineyard. Even without her trusty orienteering compass, Carmela had found her way back. Thanks in no small part to the woods and swamp lore her father had instilled in her.

Gazing up at the blue sky, wisps of clouds floating haphazardly past, she whispered, *Thanks, Daddy.*

And that was that. For now.

Racing back to the tasting room, Carmela and Ava murmured hasty good-byes, then jumped into their car, spattering gravel all the way down the driveway.

"Holy horse pucky!" jabbered Ava. "I never want to do *that* again!"

"You wanted to look for the monster," Carmela pointed out. Her heart was still pounding, and her knuckles blanched white as she gripped the steering wheel.

"I said I wanted to *look* for him," said Ava, "not *find* him. Big figging difference!"

Carmela remained silent for a couple of minutes. Creating a quiet voice inside her would hopefully lead to a quiet mind. Then she said, "You say that thing had gray hair and red eyes?"

Ava bobbed her head frantically. "You saw it!"

"Okay," said Carmela. "What does that sound like to you? I mean *really?*"

"A scary, hairy beast? The Honey Island Swamp Monster?"

"How about a Halloween mask?" suggested Carmela.

Ava's mouth opened and closed a couple of times, but nary a peep came out. Finally she said, "You mean some a-hole fooled us?"

"That'd be my best guess," said Carmela.

"But he fired a shot," said Ava. "That was a gunshot I heard, right?"

"I'm pretty sure it was," agreed Carmela.

"So what does that suggest?" asked Ava.

"I don't know," said Carmela. But in the back of her mind she thought, *Another murder?*

Carmela dropped Ava back at Juju Voodoo, pulled into the alley, and ran into her apartment to grab Boo and Poobah. As they were taking a quick walk, which consisted mainly of barking, pulling, and sniffing for squirrels and other un-named alley rodents, Carmela called Babcock on her cell phone.

"Hey," he said, "I've been trying to get you all day."

"I've been incommunicado," said Carmela.

"No kidding."

"Actually, Ava and I drove up to St. Tammany Vineyard for a quick look-see and somebody tried to kill us." She knew that would get his attention.

"What!" he shrilled. "What are you *talking* about?"

Carmela quickly explained the situation.

"Why did you even go up there?" Babcock asked.

"I already explained that to you," Carmela told him, try-ing to be patient. "I'm doing a design project."

"For that sleazy restaurateur."

Carmela's words were explosive. "I think you're more concerned about that sleaz—about Quigg—than you are about me and Ava being chased!"

"Didn't I tell you to back out of this investigation? To stay out of our way!"

"I wasn't *in* the way," Carmela yelled back. "I was at a vineyard twenty-five miles north of here! And last time I looked, you were not the duly elected sheriff of St. Tammany Parish!" She gritted her teeth, shook her head, and said, "Listen, Babcock . . ."

And found she was talking to dead air!

Carmela shuffled Boo and Poobah back into her apartment and appeased them with chewy treats. That worked for about three seconds, so she had to appease them with more chewy treats. Then she jumped in her car and headed for Memory Mine. Not even two minutes later her cell phone rang. Babcock?

"I'm sorry," were her first words.

"Don't be," said Jekyl.

"Oh." Carmela frowned as she braked, then swung around a belching garbage truck. "It's you."

"Why is everyone treating me with such callous disregard today?" asked Jekyl. "Is it the approach of Halloween that brings out the evil in people? Even dear Sissy Fowler left a message on my answering machine, telling me not to come over today."

"For the art appraisal?" said Carmela.

"Um . . . yeah."

Carmela thought for a few moments, then said, "Let's pretend you didn't get that message."

"Let's pretend," said Jekyl. "Now we're playing let's pretend?"

"Because I want to go with you," said Carmela. *To see if Sissy has a mask with gray hair and red eyes? Or maybe just to satisfy my curiosity.*

"Your coming along suits me just fine," said Jekyl. "Are you in your car right now?"

"Rolling down North Rampart," Carmela told him.

"Fine and dandy," said Jekyl. "Just swing by my building and pick me up."

Sissy Fowler wasn't one bit happy when she opened her front door.

"Didn't you get my message?" she demanded of Jekyl.

"Message?" said Jekyl. "What message?" He blinked several times, looking seriously baffled, and, for the first time, Carmela saw what an accomplished liar he was. And it scared her a little.

"And what are *you* doing here?" Sissy asked, turning on Carmela, undisguised belligerence coloring her voice.

Carmela was tempted to say, *I'm with Stupid*, just like those goofy T-shirts sold in souvenir shops. One T-shirt saying *Stupid*, the other saying *I'm with Stupid*.

But Carmela held back and said in a bright tone, "Jekyl and I were over at the Art Institute." As if that explained everything.

"More consulting," Jekyl filled in.

"Obviously, I've been in a tremulous state of mind," Sissy told them. "Since last night."

"A tragedy," said Carmela. "I can understand that you're upset."

"*Beyond* upset," corrected Sissy. "Practically inconsolable. As you know, Jimmy and I were quite close."

"We realize that," said Jekyl. He cleared his throat. "Jimmy was . . . a wonderful artiste. So accomplished at float design, set decorations . . ."

"The sets last night *were* spectacular," interjected Carmela. She had to say something before she choked at Jekyl's string of platitudes.

"Yes, the sets were gorgeous," said Sissy, letting loose a loud sniffle. Then she sighed deeply and pursed her Cupid's-bow lips. "Well. You're here. I suppose you might as well come in."

Carmela found herself traipsing through Sissy's overdecorated living room, done in mauve and stark white, through a library with leather-bound decorator books whose bindings had probably never been cracked open, and into what Sissy called her "museum room."

It was basically another parlor, where Sissy's art collection, previously her husband's art collection, was on display.

"I keep my Chagall in the dining room and my small Renoir upstairs in my bedroom," explained Sissy, showing off a little. "But this room was specially designed to house our Asian art collection."

"You have some spectacular pieces," said Jekyl, gazing around.

"And so beautifully displayed," Carmela added. Sissy Fowler, or her dear, departed husband, had spared no expense in having lovely, museum-quality cabinets installed. Each cabinet featured multiple shelves, pinpoint overhead lighting, and glass-front doors that could be locked. Extremely professional in design, as good as any museum cases Carmela had ever seen.

"Most of these pieces were collected by my husband," Sissy told them. "But since I may be facing a certain amount of, shall we say, financial upheaval in my life, I wanted to get a feeling for what these pieces might be worth."

"This looks like a Shang bronze," said Jekyl, approaching a case. "A Ding, I believe."

"You know bronzes?" asked Sissy.

"Some," said Jekyl, who'd moved on to the piece next to it. "And a Jue with a nice Taotie mask. Excellent."

"What about those buff-colored pots on the top shelf?" Sissy asked. "Awfully dull, if you ask me."

"Dull looking," said Jekyl, "but Neolithic pots command fairly steep prices right now."

"What were they used for?" asked Carmela. "Food? Water?"

"Yes," said Jekyl, "but these particular pieces were probably used in graves. Filled with provisions to accompany the dead on their journey through the afterlife."

"Ugh," said Sissy, wrinkling her nose.

"Still," said Jekyl, "at first glance most of them appear to be in exceedingly good shape."

"So they're saleable," said Sissy, looking hopeful.

"I believe so," said Jekyl, "but probably not in our local market. Here, the big demand is for French and English antiques."

"So where?" asked Sissy.

Jekyl wrinkled his nose. "I'm thinking that your best bets would be Christie's in New York, Sumner's in Miami, or Martin's of Asia in San Francisco."

"Would auction houses or dealers buy them outright or take them on consignment?" asked Sissy.

"Depends on their current inventory," said Jekyl. "But

realize, all auction houses and dealers are going to ask for documentation on these pieces."

Sissy nodded. "That's what Jimmy advised me, too. Said we should have carbon fourteen dating, that sort of thing, done on the bronzes."

"Also," said Jekyl, "government regulations are very stiff regarding importation of antiquities after 1970. So you've got to prove these were purchased in this country from a reputable dealer."

"Oh, we've got documents," said Sissy, waving a hand. "All I have to do is go through my husband's files. My files," she amended.

"There you go," said Jekyl, sounding upbeat. "Do that and we can get things moving."

"So you'd help broker the deal?" Sissy asked.

"For a small fee, yes," replied Jekyl.

"Fine," said Sissy. She seemed ready to dump the whole lot. Then she turned to them and fluttered her eyelashes. Eyelashes that, Carmela determined, had to be fake. After all, how many women were actually born with fox fur eyelashes?

"I've also decided to plunge ahead and write that Mardi Gras book," said Sissy. "By myself."

"You're going to . . ." Carmela began, then stopped.

"A definitive tome," Sissy told them. "Filled with photos and factual information, as well as credible quotes and recollections by some of the more prominent members of the upper-echelon krewes."

"Really," said Carmela, though she knew she didn't sound convincing.

But Sissy didn't need or even want Carmela's approval. "Of course," Sissy added, "it's going to be slightly more

difficult without a co-author, but I am blessed with an extremely supportive editor."

Jekyl cleared his throat nervously and edged toward Carmela. She figured that was her cue.

"Um, Sissy?" said Carmela, in a tentative manner. "I don't know if you're aware of this or not, but Jekyl's been working on a Mardi Gras book."

"Huh?" Sissy looked at them, her eyes wide. "Really?"

"It's true," said Jekyl.

"A competition, then," said Sissy, a look of contempt stealing across her face. "We'll just have to wait and see which book comes out on top."

Carmela glanced quickly at Jekyl. The look on his face told her he wanted to strangle Sissy.

Chapter 19

"THE phone's been ringing off the hook for you," announced Gabby as Carmela came chugging through the front door, checked herself, then stopped to be civil to her dear assistant who had single-handedly held things together this week. "And things have gone from just plain crazy to insane," Gabby added.

"What do you mean?" asked Carmela. For some reason, the neurons in her brain were firing out of sync.

"Well, let me think," said Gabby, in a facetious tone. Then she snapped her fingers and said, "Channel Three called and wanted to do a piece about last night's *murder*."

"Oh no," said Carmela.

"And just when were you going to tell me about your role in that?" demanded Gabby.

"Now?" Carmela asked in a small voice.

"And Edgar Babcock called about eighty-seven times."

"Already talked to him," said Carmela. "He won't be calling back."

"The love train has jumped its tracks?" asked Gabby, with a hint of worry.

"Something like that."

"Well, we wouldn't want that relationship to go *pffft*," she said, making the appropriate sound effect.

"Not really," said Carmela.

"And Angie Boynton from the Art Institute called about her monster puppet. Wants to know if it's finished yet. I told her yes." Gabby paused. "Is it?"

"No."

"And to top things off, Quigg Brevard called. Of course, he stopped fawning once he realized he was talking to me and not you." Gabby handed Carmela a stack of pink message slips and said, "You've got some catching up to do, girl."

"Thank you," said Carmela as she sailed back to her office. "I owe you big-time."

"Yes, I think you do," agreed Gabby.

The first person Carmela called was Quigg. As soon as she had his ear, she was determined to harangue him about their Honey Island Swamp experience. Except he jumped in first.

"Carmela, what are you involved in now? I heard there was another murder last night! And that you were Johnny-on-the-spot again!" Quigg sounded both distressed and disapproving.

"You heard right," said Carmela, taken aback by his tone. "And there was nearly a third murder today!"

"What are you talking about?"

"At your vineyard, pal. Ava and I took a ride through Honey Island Swamp and ended up being the quarry! In other words, we got chased by some crazy, whacked-out swamp rat!"

"A swamp rat?" Quigg sounded puzzled. "You mean with whiskers and a long, skinny tail? What are you talking about? And what the heck were you doing in the *swamp*? You seriously take a wrong turn or what?"

"Apparently so," Carmela snapped. Was everyone being contentious today, or was she just overly sensitive? Was there some kind of bad karma surrounding this upcoming Halloween? An ominous warning?

"You were supposed to be taking a wine tour," shouted Quigg. "Dewey gave you a wine tour, didn't he?"

"Yes, Dewey gave us a wine tour. And afterward we took a little boat ride. Try to picture *Pirates of the Caribbean* at Disney World, except a bad guy actually came storming after us!"

"You're a little crazy, you know that?" said Quigg.

Carmela put a hand to her head and ran her fingers through her hair. "Everything's a little crazy right now." *And maybe if I get my roots skunked and chunked, my head won't feel so cobwebby. Hey, it's a theory. Might work.*

"So . . . you didn't get hurt or anything, did you?" Quigg asked. He sounded vaguely contrite. Or maybe he was just worried about a lawsuit.

"Mostly just scared," said Carmela.

"Gather enough information for the design project?"

"Quigg?" said Carmela. "Just back off, okay? We'll talk about it next week."

"I thought you wanted . . ."

"Please?"

"Huh," he said, abruptly. "Whatever."

Carmela hung up the phone and slumped over her desk. Barking at a paying client? Yes. A supremely stupid move? Probably.

So why had she done it? Why wasn't she busy sketching ideas and fleshing out a promotional plan?

The answer was simple, of course. She was hip deep in two murder mysteries and wasn't about to rest until she figured out what was going on. Or maybe even solved them.

Thump. Thump. Thump.

Footsteps sounded behind her.

"Gabby," said Carmela, smiling and swiveling in her chair, "I need to—" She stopped abruptly, the smile frozen on her face. Because it wasn't Gabby standing in her doorway, but Glory Meechum. Big sis. Breathing heavily and looking slightly cockeyed. Had Glory gone off her meds again? It would appear she had.

"Carmela." Glory's voice rolled out like distant thunder. Ominous and threatening, the kind that warns you a major storm is on the way and you better run for cover.

"Glory," replied Carmela, leaning back in her chair, taking a cleansing, calming breath just like she'd learned in yoga class. Only she didn't feel particularly cleansed or calmed. Mostly just jittery and apprehensive.

"I heard the most *hideous* rumor," began Glory, dumping her boxy black handbag on Carmela's desk and folding her meaty arms across her ample chest.

"About last night?" asked Carmela. "Because . . ."

"No. I'm talking about Shamus's Garden District house."

"Excuse me, you're referring to *my* house?" said Carmela. "The house I was awarded, fair and square, in the divorce settlement?"

Glory's nod was imperceptible.

"And just what was it you heard?" asked Carmela, knowing full well the storm was about to break. And it was going to be a doozy.

"I heard you were going to *sell* it," Glory said, her voice a low hiss. "Shamus's beloved house. The house I grew up in!"

"According to the letter of the law, it's my house now," said Carmela. "Which means I have a perfect right to do anything I want with it. Sell it, tear it down and build a petting zoo, or turn it into a house of ill repute if I feel like it."

Glory was both angry and stunned. "But why?" she shouted.

Carmela wanted to respond with *Because I can, that's why*. But she didn't. Instead, she said, "I've thought about this long and hard." She hadn't, but figured those particular words sounded measured and careful. "And I've come to the conclusion that it's probably just too much house for me."

"Then why did you want it in the first place?" bellowed Glory.

"Glory," said Carmela, with some bite in her voice now. "It's a done deal; all the wrangling is over. The divorce papers have been signed and filed. If you have any questions regarding the legal proceedings, I suggest you take them up with Shawna Hardwick." Shawna was Carmela's attorney, an African American woman who was smart as a whip and cutthroat when need be.

"It's just not right," Glory mumbled.

"It is what it is," Carmela replied.

And still Glory wouldn't back down. "If you're going to *sell* it, why not sell to a family member?"

Carmela blinked. That concept had certainly come zinging out of the blue. "Do you have a buyer in mind?"

Clearly, Glory didn't. She squinted and frowned, then glanced down at her sensible low-heeled shoes. The kind Ava referred to as her "squatties."

"Maybe Cousin Delmar would be interested," said Glory, finally.

Carmela remembered Delmar Meechum as an ethereal apparition at their long-ago wedding. Taciturn and aloof, wearing bizarrely high-waisted pants, Delmar had lived up in Shreveport for the last forty-five years and seldom ventured outside the surrounding Caddo Parish.

"Sure," said Carmela. "When it goes on the market I'll be happy to give old Delmar a jingle."

Glory pulled her mouth into an unflattering snarl and said, "As for last night, you *would* be tangled up in another sordid murder. No surprises there."

"All right," said Carmela, standing up. "Thanks so much for dropping by. Glad we could hash things out."

Glory snatched up her bag and spun on her heels. "You're still trash, Carmela Bertrand. Shamus is lucky to be rid of you."

"And I of him," Carmela replied in a pleasant tone.

"Jeepers," said Gabby, once Glory had lumbered out, tossing disapproving glances at everyone in her vicinity. "I thought she'd never leave."

"I thought we'd have to get a forklift to haul her out," agreed Carmela, flipping through papers on her desk. Then

she caught the concerned look on Gabby's face. "Uh-oh, we got busy, didn't we?"

"The phrase *hip deep in alligators* comes to mind," replied Gabby.

Rushing out into the shop, Carmela immediately counted ten customers, with two more women pushing their way through the front door.

"Oh man," murmured Gabby.

"Excellent," said Carmela. Customers meant business, and business equaled sales. A simple formula, nice and neat. "You handle the front counter while I troubleshoot the back part of the shop."

"Gotcha," said Gabby, bounding ahead.

And the sudden onslaught of customers really did mean business. Carmela pulled out various sheets of paper for her customers, showed off a series of new albums, dug out floral stickers, and then found herself offering a consultation to a new bride-to-be.

"Penny Joplin," said the excited girl. "Soon to be Mrs. Dix Hennesey."

"And you want to handcraft your own wedding favors," said Carmela, ruminating.

"Only the boxes," said Penny. She dug in her handbag and pulled out a handful of foil-wrapped chocolate leaves—all gold and bronze and deep raspberry red. "Maybe I could make little bags?" she asked.

"What about small bonbon boxes?" suggested Carmela.

"Can you do that? Can *I* do that?"

"Easily," Carmela told her. She opened a drawer and pulled out a thin metal template. "The basic pattern looks kind of like a pinwheel," said Carmela. "But when you trace it onto paper, cut it out, then overlap each of the four sides,

you end up with an adorable little box." She reached up, grabbed a sample box, and showed it to Penny.

"Adorable," said Penny. "And absolutely perfect." She paused. "So what about paper stock? And colors?"

"Even though you're having an autumn wedding," said Carmela, "you don't want to get too hung up on colors like rust and orange."

"Then what?" asked Penny.

"Think wheat, gold, a light cocoa brown, and pale green."

"I love it," said Penny. "And what type of paper?"

"Something with texture or shine," said Carmela. "Something luxurious."

"Funny to think of paper as being luxurious," said Penny.

"Oh, but it is," said Carmela, pulling open another flat file. "Take a look at this brocade. Or even this linen weave."

They studied the various papers, debating the merits of each one, and finally decided on a textural pale green brocade paper for the boxes and light gold for labels.

"You think just put our first names on the labels?" asked Penny.

"Or a fun phrase," said Carmela. "Like 'Falling in Love' and then your names."

"Perfect!"

"You know," said Carmela, eyeing some of her leftover fibers, "you could even tie a bit of dried grass or bittersweet on top of your boxes."

Carmela's next customer was even easier—a woman who wanted to do a Paris scrapbook page.

Carmela dug out a twelve-by-twelve sheet of paper that had almost a watercolor mauve effect with subtle swirls of

gold and a mottled sepia-tone border. In the lower left corner of the paper was a purple Eiffel Tower looking like it had been applied with a wood block. In the upper right corner of the paper was a French postage stamp and some French script.

Needless to say, her customer was ecstatic when Carmela pulled out a fleur-de-lis die cut and sealing wax and stamp.

"Like something Louis the Sixteenth might have used," Carmela told her.

The afternoon continued like that, fast and furious, until four o'clock rolled around and the shop was suddenly deserted.

"Where'd everybody go?" asked Gabby. She sounded a little disconcerted.

Carmela peered out the front window. Governor Nicholls Street looked deserted.

"Halloween parties?" asked Gabby.

"Gotta be," said Carmela. She thought for a minute. "Let's make a break for it and close early."

Gabby looked at her expectantly. "You think?"

"Sure," said Carmela. "Why not?" Besides, she had things to do and people to see. And later, a vampire tour to lead.

"I'll roll the phone to the answering service," said Gabby, leaping at the chance to leave early.

"Can you lock up, too?" Carmela asked. She wanted to hotfoot it over to Juju Voodoo and connect with Ava.

"Done!" proclaimed Gabby.

Carmela swung past Pirate's Alley Deli, picked up a couple of po'boy sandwiches (fried oyster for her, roast beef with extra mayo for Ava), then hit Juju Voodoo in record time.

And just as Memory Mine had been two hours earlier,

Ava's little shop was packed to the rafters with customers. A Halloween slam.

Standing at the cash register, ringing up vials of bat's blood, plastic fangs, exotic masks, and green glow-in-the-dark skulls, Ava noticed Carmela and gave her a what-can-you-do smile.

Carmela nodded back, then shouldered her way into Ava's office, dropped off the sandwiches, and came back to help.

Of course, even though Miguel and Talley were waiting on customers, Ava put Carmela to work instantly.

"*Cher*, can you grab me four St. Michael candles?"

Carmela located the candles, trundled them to the front desk, then was immediately asked to run and grab a pair of grinning skulls from a box in Ava's office.

Feeling like Hamlet contemplating poor Yorick, Carmela delivered the lifelike (deathlike?) skulls to Ava.

"It's been like this all day!" Ava exclaimed. "Crazy busy. Everybody stocking up for Halloween."

"You're like Macy's," Carmela joked. "But instead of selling out your inventory at Christmastime, your big holiday is Halloween."

"And thank goodness for that," said Ava, grabbing a red-and-purple evil-eye necklace for a customer.

"Are you going to have time to lead the vampire tour?" Carmela asked, worried she might have to go it alone. Or, rather, wing it. Ha-ha, a little bit of vampire humor there.

Ava rang up one more customer, then motioned for Miguel to take over.

"Wouldn't miss it for the world," said Ava. "In fact, I've been looking forward to the tour all day." She tilted her head back as if sniffing the air. "Did you bring food?"

They hungrily wolfed down their sandwiches sitting in

Ava's office, skulls and harmless demon heads peeping out at them, watching them eat.

"Mmm, this is so good," said Ava, her mouth full. "I haven't had a chance to eat all day."

"No wonder you keep your figure."

"No!" protested Ava. "I'm really packin' on the pork. Heaven forbid I have to struggle into a larger size jeans." She shuddered.

"Ava?" It was Miguel, sticking his head in the office. "Do we still have any of those big furry spiders?"

"Maybe one," said Ava, answering with her mouth full. "But you'll have to grab a ladder and climb up after it. It's hung way up in the rafters."

"Hey, you know what?" Miguel said to Carmela. "The police are *still* asking me questions about Brett Fowler." He looked plainly disgusted.

"Well, that's not going to advance their case," said Carmela, "since you weren't even there."

"Tell *them* that," said Miguel.

"We did!" said Ava.

"Jeez," said Carmela. "I'll bet the police even wanted to know where you were *last* night?"

Miguel nodded. "They sure did."

"What did you tell them?" Carmela asked, hoping Miguel really did have an iron-clad alibi. With *two* murders to solve, the police were probably like hounds scenting blood.

"Told 'em I was at La Madeira, celebrating my brother's birthday with my family."

"Your whole family?" asked Carmela.

Miguel grinned. "All forty-two of us."

* * *

"You know," said Carmela, "we've got about one more hour of work if we want to finish the monster puppet."

"Angie's been asking about it?" said Ava.

"Yes, and I really don't want to lie about it."

"Then let's go do it right now," suggested Ava, wiping a blob of mayonnaise from her lip. "We'll grab our vampire capes and fangs and hustle over to the float den and finish up."

"What time is the vampire tour supposed to start?" asked Carmela.

"Not till eight," said Ava. "So we've got time."

"Okay."

"Then what?" Ava asked, tapping a lacquered finger against her desk, looking inquisitive. "Date night . . . or what?"

"Or what," said Carmela. "With Babcock all cranky and upset, it looks like I'll be going to the Halloween Bondage Ball with you." She paused. "Happy now?" Why *not* give it a whirl, she decided. Since she was seriously on the outs with Babcock.

"Oh, *cher*," cooed Ava, "you just made my little heart go pitty-pat."

Chapter 20

"ANNE Rice must have had you in mind when she wrote *Queen of the Damned*," said Ava. "Because, whoa baby, you look hot!"

Carmela and Ava were strutting down Chartres Street, headed for the Hotel Sinclair, their vampire tour meet-up spot.

"A frilly, red lace shirt under a black cape creates such a dramatic, vampiric statement," said Carmela, flapping her arms out to the side. "But it's nothing compared to your black dress." Ava's black velvet vampire gown, all exotic lace and ruffles, looked like it had come from the costume department at Warner Brothers.

"And my killer heels add the final touch," chortled Ava. "Black patent with that little slice of bloodred leather for maximum effect."

"Are you going to be able to walk in those heels all

night?" Carmela glanced down at her own black walking shoes.

"Years of practice on the runway, *cher*."

"Years?" said Carmela. She knew of one instance when Ava had modeled. And that hadn't turned out so well.

"Think vampire years," said Ava. "Oh, I almost forgot." She reached into her shiny black purse and pulled out something white. "Here. I figured you forgot to bring yours."

Carmela turned the fangs over in her hand. "You really want me to wear these?"

"I vant to bite your neck," Ava said, playfully.

"I'll probably bite my lip," Carmela worried.

"They're a fun touch," said Ava. "And, who knows, maybe you can try them out on Babcock later on. If he's lucky, anyway."

"I doubt anybody's going to get lucky tonight," Carmela murmured. "Oh, here we are!"

The Hotel Sinclair had been owned by the Duvall family since 1947, and it mixed Old World grace and charm with today's conveniences. Three relaxing tropical courtyards figured prominently, as did two swimming pools, private balconies, and a grand fountain. All of it the perfect step back in time to set the tone for Ava's vampire tour.

Carmela and Ava waited outside, smiling at passersby and swooping their capes until their group finally convened. Ava collected money and issued black leather bracelets with dangling vampire fangs. Once they were ready to go, Ava led them into the Sinclair's elegant lobby.

"This isn't going to be a shock-'em, scare-'em tour, is it?" asked a woman who had an older woman hanging on her arm. "My mother is seventy-nine years old and has a weak heart."

Ava smiled prettily. "We'll show and tell you some pretty

amazing stories about the strange goings-on in the French Quarter. But it's up to you if you believe them or not."

"Yeah," said a young man in a navy peacoat. "It's *supposed* to be sort of scary." There was a rumble of agreement.

Ava flipped her cape and flashed her fangs as she led them through the lobby into the courtyard. "I bid you welcome," she said, giving a little bow and stopping in front of a cascading fountain surrounded by flickering white candles. "I hope you all have a clove of garlic or a silver cross tucked in your pocket, just in case." Her dark eyes sparkled in the candlelight.

"And if you don't," said Carmela, stepping forward, "you'll have ample time to purchase what you need when we make a short stop at Juju Voodoo."

"Charms, amulets, and potions," Ava purred. "Everything your heart desires." She paused dramatically. "So . . . are you ready to check into a haunted hotel?"

There were nods and excited murmurs from the group of twenty.

"This hotel was once a Confederate hospital," Carmela told them. "And more than one hundred and fifty years later, Confederate soldiers and their doctors are *still* seen wandering the corridors."

"Worse yet, they're wounded and bleeding," added Ava. "Many reach out to the guests for help. Moans and groans have been heard throughout the complex, and ghostly figures of men and women appear in rooms, then disappear as soon as a light is snapped on."

"Bloodstains have even appeared on the bedding and floor," said Carmela. "But, here now, let's go see for ourselves!"

Carmela and Ava led the tour group back into the lobby and up a circular staircase to room 211.

"This is the room where ghostly activity is at a peak," said Ava, who'd cleared the visit with Brenda Nasser, the night manager. She threw the door open, and the group let out a collective "Ahh."

"As you can see," said Carmela, stepping inside the room, "everything looks perfectly normal. Lovely floral wallpaper, a beautiful antique sleigh bed, and a mahogany armoire." The tour group followed her in and gazed around expectantly.

"But the thing is," said Ava, "no guest has ever been able to sleep a full night in this room. In fact, only a handful have been able to remain in here for more than a few minutes."

"If anyone wants to stay here," said Carmela, "we can get you a very reasonable rate."

No one did.

The tour continued as Carmela and Ava led their group down Chartres Street toward Jackson Square. The entire French Quarter was decorated for Sunday's Monsters and Mayhem event, so red eyes peeped out from windows, filmy spiderwebs spun across doorways, and rubber bats fluttered everywhere. Strings of orange lights wound around posts and columns, and life-sized witches, ghosts, and werewolves—many animated—lurked beside shop entrances.

A trick mirror suddenly activated as they passed by, illuminating a man trapped inside who frantically beat his hands against the glass, crying, "Help me! Let me out!"

"Wow," said one of the guests. "Crazy."

"This whole place is crazy," Ava told them.

"And very spooky," said the woman who was escorting her mother, as shadows and lights lent the creepy atmosphere the tour demanded.

"Why do vampires like the French Quarter so much?" a skinny man asked.

"Who *doesn't* like this place?" said Ava. "It's just bursting with history and mystery. And . . . vampires."

"Tell us more about that," prompted the skinny man.

"Well," said Ava, "vampires have always been part of our heritage. In fact, there's an old Louisiana tradition of 'sitting up with the dead.' How it worked was, a family member or close friend would sit with the dead all night long so a vampire couldn't slip in and steal him away."

There was an inhalation of breath. The crowd was into it.

"There's also a rural Louisiana tradition for plantations to install their exterior keyholes upside down," said Carmela. "To prevent entry by the undead."

"So lots of vampires in New Orleans," said one young woman. "Even before the spate of vampire novels and TV shows."

"You have no idea," said Ava. She stopped in front of the Hotel Monteleone. "Now, if you're looking for a friendly ghost, Casper might be found inside the Hotel Monteleone." Ava pointed to the entrance of the old hotel at 214 Royal Street. The white marquee had *Monteleone* in Old English script. On either side of the main doors were black crystal carriage lights. Above the canopy, strategically placed spotlights added creepy shadows to the Gothic carved stone face.

"This place was built in 1886," said Ava, "and has served as home away from home for countless movie stars, dignitaries, and political kingpins. The traditional European-style rooms are carefully detailed and guaranteed haunted. In fact, the International Society of Paranormal Research has identified twelve distinct ghosts inhabiting this hotel."

"And more keep popping up all the time," Carmela added.

"In one room," said Ava, "a jazz singer can be heard sing-

ing in the middle of the night. Some guests and hotel workers have told of encountering a little lost boy. When they try to take his hand and gaze into his sad eyes—poof!—he simply disappears."

On their way again, the group ambled a couple of blocks to the Sultan's Palace, an enormous four-story structure at 716 Dauphine Street.

"This place has a good creep factor," Ava told them. "A cruel Turk, who claimed to be a sultan, rented this building and filled it with multiple wives, family members, and slaves. Heavy drapes were hung on the windows and padlocks placed on all the doors. The place was protected by guards wielding enormous scimitars, and when doors were occasionally opened, waves of heavy incense escaped."

The faint smell of incense suddenly filled the night air, and Carmela wondered if it was the power of suggestion, or had Ava arranged some special effects? Whatever was going on, it was certainly working.

"Rumors of kidnapping started to spread," said Ava, "and then one morning passersby noticed blood dripping from the gallery above."

The group stepped back, half looking for the blood, half trying to avoid any last drops.

"More blood oozed out from under the front door," said Ava, "when police finally stormed the place."

"What happened?" came a tentative voice.

"Everyone inside was dead," said Ava. "Beheaded. Except for the sultan, who had been buried alive in the back garden, one hand extending out of the ground as if he'd tried to claw his way out!"

Everyone gaped in awe at the Sultan's Palace; a few used their camera phones to snap pictures.

"On a happier note," said Carmela, "because of our history of vampires and ghosts, the Vampire Film Festival has been moved from Los Angeles to New Orleans. Four days and nights of movies, with over fifty films from eleven countries."

Another block and they were at Ava's shop.

"This is my shop as well as our halfway stop," Ava explained. "Inside you'll find hot cocoa, tea, spice cookies, and pumpkin bars, as well as a good selection of amulets, magic potions, skull jewelry, and all things Goth." As she flung open the door for the group, mournful Cajun music drifted out. "Plus everything is twenty percent off tonight."

Ava's two employees, Miguel and Talley, also in vampire garb, poured out cups of cocoa and escorted customers around the shop.

"Is anyone reading tarot tonight?" Carmela asked.

Ava nodded. "A new guy, but he's older and a tad more academic with his predictions."

"Not like that hot young Romanian you used to have?" asked Carmela.

Ava fanned herself, remembering. "Don't I wish. Giovanni was one sweet hunk of manpower."

"Garlic necklaces and silver bracelets are over here," Miguel pointed out. "Just in case you need a little extra protection in the cemetery."

After twenty minutes of shopping and noshing goodies, the crowd slowly made their way down Canal Street. The breeze had picked up some and Carmela snugged her cape around her, glad for the extra warmth.

The St. Charles Avenue streetcar, which had been renamed the ghost train this week, waited for them at Canal and Carondolet.

"All aboard," said Ava. "Next stop, Lafayette Cemetery
Number One!"

Rough brick pillars stood opposite each other as a curve of
wrought iron arched from one side to the other. The words
Lafayette Cemetery were spelled out in curlicued black metal.
Tonight, as a special welcome to tours and visitors, the gates
yawned open to the darkness within.

Carmela and Ava gathered their guests into a semicircle.

"Just so you know," said Ava, "your money will be re-
funded only if a flash flood floats the coffins to the surface!"

Uncomfortable laughter followed, and then one woman
asked, "Why would coffins float?"

"Most of New Orleans is below sea level," Carmela explained. "So no one is allowed to bury their loved ones in the
ground. Or, if they do, the bodies are unfortunately returned
to them."

The night wind blew and rattled the old gates as they
tromped the gravel path.

"Some tombs in here date back to 1883," said Ava.
"Brigadier General Harry T. Hays of the Confederate Army
is buried here. So follow behind me and we'll see who else
is inside. With All Hallows' Eve so close at hand, some of
the spirits will undoubtedly be restless." Ava waved her cape
and the group scurried after her, like frightened ducklings
behind a mother duck.

Stone angels, some missing a wing, and melting faces
carved on crypts cast eerie shadows as they moved past. For
some reason, the hair on the back of Carmela's neck prickled
tonight, and she was finding it hard to distinguish between

shadow and light. Or was something else walking among them?

"Come over this way," said Ava, "and you'll be standing in the footprints of Brad Pitt and Tom Cruise. Both men were filmed here for *Interview with the Vampire.* This is the famous crypt used in several scenes . . . see the stone urns flanking the steps, the steps leading up to the door of the tomb?" Ava quickly climbed the four steps, paused, then murmured, "Oh yes, I'd know that touch anywhere. Thanks, Tom; thanks, Brad," and then she blew a kiss into the night.

"Anne Rice loved this setting," said Carmela. "In fact, she even staged a mock burial here to promote one of her books."

The group peeked around tombs and mausoleums, looking for what might be the Vampire Lestat's grave. Missing chunks of plaster revealed old brick, and sometimes even entire bricks were missing. A few people tried to peer into ancient grave openings, while others were terrified of what they might see.

"Over here," said Ava, "is the tomb of Marie Laveau, a voodoo high priestess. It's said she danced naked in the bayou, cast powerful spells, foretold futures, and even created zombies. Many believe her power is still in force, which is why they continue to bring offerings of coins, flowers, and playing cards to her tomb as an inducement to grant their wishes."

"Does it work?" asked a young woman, who was clinging to her boyfriend.

Ava smiled mysteriously. "Give it a try."

The crowd continued to wander around the ancient cemetery. Carved faces had melted away with weather and time,

lambs on children's tombs were barely recognizable, and stone angels with broken wings had been grounded from flying. Faced with heat, humidity, hurricanes, and the march of time, Lafayette Cemetery's crypts and tombs were slowly moldering away.

Moonlight shone through bare trees, the night wind clicking the branches together like bones. Another chill descended on Carmela. She'd wandered through here many times, but for some reason it seemed different tonight. A little lonelier, a little scarier. She also had the feeling that, for the past ten minutes, someone had been following them, peeping at them from behind graves and tombstones. Then again, it was probably Miguel, Ava's assistant, poised to pop out for the grand finale.

"The last vampire attack in this cemetery was pre–Hurricane Katrina," said Ava as she led the group into an area dominated by large family crypts. "But some believe the dead—or undead—are poised to return."

As her words echoed in the night, a dark figure suddenly loomed up in front of them. Wearing black from head to toe, a long black cape, and a black mask, the man raised his arms and roared like the king of the vampires!

The tour group screamed en masse, then scattered like dry leaves. Men abandoned their girlfriends, and people shoved and tripped as they raced away from the flapping figure.

Ava, doubled over with laughter, staggered up to Carmela and said, "Wasn't that perfect! Didn't Miguel do a great job?"

"Um . . . Ava?" said Carmela.

"He terrified everyone," Ava chuckled again. "C'mon, we better collect the group and tell 'em it was all just a joke."

"Was it?" asked Carmela.

Ava glanced at her sharply.

"Because that guy was much taller than Miguel," said Carmela.

"Now that you mention it . . ." Ava thought for a minute. "So who was that?"

Good question, thought Carmela. *Who was it really?*

Chapter 21

CARMELA and Ava whipped back to Carmela's apartment, tore off their capes, spat out their fangs, and stared at the jumble of garment bags and boxes Ava had carted over earlier.

"I swear, drag queens don't have as many costumes," Carmela said as she gazed at the various sparkled, spangled, and leather outfits.

"Where do you think I get my best things?" asked Ava.

"Seriously?" Carmela's voice rose in a squawk.

"Dead serious. RuPaul would kill to have my sources."

"Okay," said Carmela, feeling more and more hesitant. Was dressing up for the Bondage Ball really a good idea? No, of course it wasn't!

Ava pulled out a pink leather top edged with white feathers and held it up in front of Carmela. "Whatcha think, *cher*?"

Carmela cocked her head to one side. "When I think of bondage, I have an image of black leather with silver studs rather than pink-and-white froufrou."

"Well put," said Ava. She moved to a new box and ripped it open. The words *Southern Decadence* had been scrawled on the side. "This might be more your style." She pulled out a black bowler hat and riding crop.

Carmela took a step backward.

"No?" Ava pulled out a handful of leather straps and silver loops. Then she unrolled a full-length gown made from belts and loops.

"I'm really not willing to show that much skin," said Carmela.

"In other words, no skin at all?"

"Exactly."

Ava clapped her hands together, causing Boo and Poobah to suddenly sit down. "I have the perfect thing." She dug to the bottom of the box and pulled out a black leather spandex suit. "This is the same cat suit Uma Thurman wore in *The Avengers*. Kind of cool, huh?"

Carmela reached out a tentative hand. "Maybe. Awfully form-fitting, though."

Ava handed her a leather skirt. "Try this over it."

Carmela slipped into her bathroom and stripped down. Then she tugged and struggled her way into the spandex suit. *Well, maybe this will work*, she decided. Squinting at herself in the mirror, she was surprised at how it hugged and squeezed her in all the right places. And with the skirt over it to kind of cover up . . . well, okay!

She burst from the bathroom. "I think I like it!"

Boo and Poobah barked excitedly, dancing around Carmela, as if rooting for her.

But when Carmela saw what Ava had on, she did a double take. Her friend stood posed in a black leather bustier with silver studs, leather Daisy Duke shorts, a black mask, and a choker of fine black feathers around her neck.

"Jeez," said Carmela, "I feel like I'm at a photo shoot for *Maxim* magazine."

"If only," purred Ava.

Ten minutes later they were on their way to the Commodore Hotel. Carmela was wrapped up in her cape again, while Ava strutted her stuff for all to see.

"I do admire the way you just put it out there," Carmela told her.

"Most men like the way I put it out there," giggled Ava.

"But, once again, how do you walk in those boots?" Ava had pulled on thigh-high boots with four-inch silver heels.

"These boots are made for walkin'," Ava joked. "Not really a problem at all."

"Amazing," said Carmela as Ava linked an arm through hers.

"Let's cut down the alley here," said Ava. "Save a block or two."

"Okay."

"Are you sure Babcock won't be joining us tonight?" Ava grinned.

"Positive. We're seriously on the outs."

Ava kissed Carmela on the top of her head. "You deserve a good man, *cher*, and my instincts tell me he's the right guy. He'll come around to your crazy, meddling ways."

"Thank you," said Carmela. "I think."

"Besides," continued Ava, "I like the way Babcock dresses. He's a . . . what would you call him? A snappy dresser."

"He really is furious at me," said Carmela.

"No, he's not," said Ava, their footsteps echoing in the alley, along with others behind them.

"Babcock accused me of constantly butting into his business, his investigations."

"That *does* sound unfair," said Ava, "considering you're a . . . we're a . . . major part of his investigation."

"Try to make him see that," said Carmela. They slipped past the back door of Blue Moon Music, where tendrils of raucous music seemed to seep out into the darkness.

"Babcock has to understand you're not exactly running around the Big Easy, hoping dead bodies drop at your feet," said Ava. She lurched forward, said, "Ooh, ouch."

"What?"

"Caught my heel." Ava wiggled her left foot and pulled free from between the cobblestones. "Okay. A minor issue solved."

"I'm not so sure," said Carmela, whispering now.

"Huh?"

"Those footsteps we heard behind us? They stopped when we stopped."

Ava peered back through the inky blackness. "Crap," she muttered under her breath.

"You nervous?" asked Carmela.

"No," said Ava. "Yes."

"Me, too. Maybe this shortcut wasn't such a good idea."

"You mean in light of two murders?" Ava whispered.

Almost three, Carmela thought, remembering this morning's chase through the Honey Island Swamp.

"We better move our tails," suggested Ava.

They walked a few more steps, aware the footsteps behind them had picked up again.

"I have a better idea," said Carmela. Grabbing Ava's arm, she pulled her friend along as she broke into a run.

"Aiiiiy!" screamed Ava, tottering along at a breakneck pace, towed by Carmela.

Then Carmela suddenly braked, spun right, and pulled open the back door of Mr. Isaac's Music Bar. "In here! We'll duck in here!"

"Why is there always a crazy person loose in the French Quarter?" Ava shrilled. "I can barely find a legitimate date, but stalkers come crawling out of the woodwork for us!"

They stopped suddenly, Ava's chin bumping into the back of Carmela's head, as a group of men squatting on bar stools turned to stare.

"Howdy?" said Ava, managing a little wave. It didn't serve to wipe the quizzical looks off their faces.

Carmela pulled Ava forward. Mr. Isaac's couldn't be classified as a safe haven, especially with twenty or thirty men staring at them. But it wasn't a dark, lonely alley either. Besides, didn't all bartenders keep baseball bats stashed behind the bar just in case? Sure they did.

"Cute skirt," muttered one bar patron, giving Carmela a friendly leer.

"Zip it," she snapped, her bravado rising to the surface.

"You had a good idea, *cher*," said Ava, elbowing a path to the bar. "We'll hunker here, just in case he follows us in."

They didn't have to wait long. Fifteen seconds later a large, bulky man burst through the back door. When he saw the crowd, he slowed to a walk, but his hooded eyes continued to rove back and forth, searching for them.

"Mills Taggart," Carmela muttered, recognizing him imme-diately. Then, her anger flaring red, she stepped out to confront him. "Taggart!" Carmela called, her voice ringing out with a distinct note of authority. "What are you doing following us?"

Ava grabbed a stalk of celery from the garnish tray and brandished it like a sword. "Are you trying to scare us to death?" She advanced on Taggart and slapped him in the face with the leafy top.

"Did Glory Meechum hire you to follow us?" Carmela demanded.

Taggart maintained his bullish look. "No," he spat back. "Shamus told me to keep an eye on you two. Make sure you were okay."

"Was that you before at the cemetery?" Carmela asked.

Now Taggart looked confused. "Cemetery? What are you talking about?"

"Couldn't have been him," said Ava. "That guy was much thinner! This guy's a porker."

The bartender leaned across the bar. "You want me to call the police?"

"No," said Carmela. "We can handle this." She was wound up and angry now, shaking her index finger in Taggart's face. "You tell Shamus that I can take care of myself. Tell him to leave us alone. You hear me?"

Taggart gave a grudging nod. "Look, lady, I was only do-ing my job."

"To heck with your job," said Ava. "If Carmela says get lost, then you get lost."

"Yeah, right," muttered Taggart, turning away.

"He's going to run directly to Shamus and tell him every-thing," sputtered Carmela.

Ava stared at her. "So what? What's stupid old Shamus go-

ing to do? Send in the Marines? Divorce you? Face it, *cher*, he's got nothing over you anymore. Now you hold all the cards."

"Good point," said Carmela, starting to calm down. "I think I was just replaying old tapes."

"That's okay," said Ava, nodding, "I do that all the time." She put a hand up and rubbed Carmela's shoulder. "Do you think it might have been Taggart who chased us in the boat this morning?"

"I don't know," said Carmela. "Maybe. But . . . no, I don't think so. My hunch is it was someone else." *Like maybe the same person who murdered Brett Fowler at the Pluvius den? Or killed Jimmy Toups in the back of the theater? Because there definitely is a crazy person loose in the French Quarter!*

"Are you ready?" Ava asked as they paused outside the double doors that led to the Commodore Hotel's Grand Cotillion Ballroom.

"Ready as I'll ever be," said Carmela, plucking nervously at her leather skirt.

A wall of music hit them as the doors opened. Zydeco techno thumped a wild, driving beat that matched Carmela's fluttering heart.

"I think I'm having a heart attack," Carmela yelled at Ava.

Ava nodded and grinned, already grooving to the music. "I know, isn't it great? Voodoo Dead is one of my all-time favorite groups!"

"Or a small series of strokes?" yelled Carmela as they stepped into the ballroom.

"Yeah!" growled Ava, totally enthralled with the Voodoo Dead.

The six-man rock group wore makeup similar to KISS, except each sported a unique painted skull face. Very hoo-doo voodoo. They also wore three-piece suits with red bow ties that blinked and strobed with the music as they performed with manic enthusiasm. The musicians were a drummer, bass guitar player, electric guitar player, fiddler, accordion player, and even a rub board player.

"You actually *know* these guys?" Carmela asked. She was starting to recover from her initial shock.

"I've partied down with them a few times." Ava smiled, then said, "C'mon, let's get ourselves some liquid refreshment."

They pushed their way past women in leather dresses, men in leather pants, and women in evening gowns with all manner of chains, manacles, and leather bracelets.

"Aren't you glad you dressed up?" Ava asked.

"Are you kidding?" said Carmela. "Compared to most of these characters I look like I'm on my way to Sunday school."

The bartender wore a German uniform and had a fake scar running down the side of his face. "What'll it be?" he asked.

"What have you got to offer?" Ava asked, flirting.

"How about a Vampire's Kiss?" suggested the bartender. "Vodka, gin, vermouth, tequila, salt, and tomato juice."

"What else?" asked Ava.

"A Neon Voodoo?" proposed the bartender. "Apple juice, vodka, and Mountain Dew."

"Perfect," said Ava. "Two Neon Voodoos."

They sipped their drinks as they strolled around the ballroom.

"Isn't this a crazy scene?" Jekyl Hardy exclaimed as he

came bouncing up to them. "Don't you just love it?" Jekyl was duded up in his red sequined devil suit, carrying a glittery black pitchfork and wearing tiny devil horns glued to his sleek head. It was one of his prized costumes.

"Take a look at that guy," said Ava. A man strolled past with a blue feather mask covering his entire head. He wore black leather pants and boots, with rings of blue feathers around his wrists and ankles. "The bluebird of happiness."

"I was going to wear that," said Jekyl, "but he beat me to it."

"I'm glad you showed up," Carmela told Jekyl. "I was afraid I'd see parts of people I didn't even know."

Jekyl sniggered. "Do you know Amanda Devereaux? From Alligator Antiques?"

Both Carmela and Ava nodded.

Jekyl waved a hand, pointing her out. "She's the one with the neon pink jumpsuit and leather choker."

"Oh my," said Carmela. "I'll never look at her andirons the same way again."

They settled in then, dancing when invited, reconvening with each other, giggling at all the outlandish costumes. Carmela had to keep reminding herself that it was Halloween and this was a Bondage Ball. So . . . anything goes. Well, almost anything.

Thirty minutes later, Carmela and Ava were tired from their wild dancing and more than a little thirsty.

"Time for another drink?" Ava asked. Somewhere along the line she'd picked up an admirer, a guy in a vinyl Zorro costume, who followed her around like a love-struck puppy dog.

"You want to try a Headless Horseman?" Ava asked as they made their way to the bar.

"Remind me what's in that?" said Carmela.

"Vodka, bitters, ginger ale, and orange juice," said Ava.

"Sold," said Carmela.

Suddenly, someone pushed his way rudely between the two of them.

"Hey!" Ava cried as Roy Slayback slapped his hand down on the bar.

"So which one of you is spreading rumors about me?" Slayback asked in a nasty, nasal tone. "Just because I was Brett Fowler's partner in Emerald Equities doesn't mean I was involved in his financial schemes. And it sure doesn't mean I killed him!" A cloud of strong alcohol hung in the air above Slayback, who wore an expensive-looking red silk Peking Opera robe.

Ava leaned back and waved her hand in front of her nose. "Whew! Drink much?"

Carmela took another avenue. "What *should* we think?"

Slayback hunched his thin shoulders and threw her a hazy, pinched look. "I already *told* you I was cooperating in the investigation! I told you that when you so rudely accosted me at Fowler's funeral!"

"Okay," said Carmela, seeing an opportunity. "Is there someone who maybe wanted to set you up for a fall?"

"Fowler already did," Slayback said in a morose tone. "My reputation in the business community is ruined. I'm done for."

"Not if you can *prove* your innocence," said Carmela. "Can you do that?"

Slayback's shoulders sagged. "I don't know how. I'm already doing everything I can to get money back to investors. Of course, the police have confiscated most of our company records, and the assets are frozen, so it's a daunting, almost impossible task."

"Sorry to hear that," said Carmela. She watched as Slayback ordered a Jack Daniel's rocks, then slammed it down and staggered off. If he was innocent, she felt sorry for him. If he was part of the Ponzi scheme, then he'd just staged a pretty good act. Too bad she couldn't consult one of the crystal balls Ava sold at her shop for answers. That would solve everything rather neatly.

"Ladies," said a male voice behind them. They both turned and found Tom Travers grinning at them. He wasn't in costume, but he sure looked fine.

"Hello, baby," Ava purred.

Travers eyed her up and down, then grabbed Ava and spun her around as she squealed with delight.

"Take it easy," Ava cried, slapping at him playfully.

"New boyfriends can get away with so much," said Carmela, slightly amused by their antics.

Travers widened his eyes and mouth in mock surprise. "Is that what I am?"

"Looks like," said Carmela.

"Then I'm prepared to sweep this fair lady off her feet," said Travers. "Take her away from all of this."

"Ooh, is that my cue?" asked Ava, all wide-eyed and innocent.

"Go on, you two. Hit the dance floor," Carmela ordered. "Or, better yet, get out of here."

Ava ducked forward and kissed Carmela on the cheek. "You don't mind if we take off?"

"Go," Carmela urged.

"But you stay," said Ava.

"No way," said Carmela. "Just not my scene."

* * *

Twenty minutes later, Carmela was home, her costume puddled on the floor. Dressed in flannel pajamas, she cozied up with Boo and Poobah on the bed.

"Snuggle puppies," she told them, planting a kiss on each of their furry foreheads as they lounged together. "This is the life." She sighed, letting the residue of a hectic day gradually seep out of her. And just as she was finally feeling relaxed and calm, was about to turn out the lights, the phone jangled.

She answered it reluctantly. "Hello?"

"Carmela," said Babcock.

"What do you want?"

"We need to settle this, once and for all."

"It's settled," said Carmela. "I do what I want and I talk to whoever I feel like talking to." She drew a deep breath and said, "Doggone it, Babcock, you've got to stop acting like Shamus. You've got to stop trying to control me!"

"You don't want it to end like this," said Babcock, a pleading tone in his voice. "For gosh sakes, I sure don't."

"So romance flourishes and everything's cool as long as I mind my own business?"

"You just can't keep asking questions all over town. Carmela . . ." His voice called to her.

But she'd already hung up the phone.

Chapter 22

"MY poor head is still spinning," complained Ava. She sat at Carmela's dining room table, head in her hands, massaging her temples, looking slightly morose.

"You want an aspirin? Coffee?"

Ava waved a limp hand. "Already had both. Didn't make a dent."

"You drank champagne last night," said Carmela.

"Uh . . . yeah," said Ava.

"But you had a good time? With Travers?"

That brought a broad smile to Ava's face. "The best. I like Tom. I mean, I *really* like him." She paused, letting loose a small groan. "Ohhh."

"Now what's wrong?"

Ava slid a hand down and rubbed her stomach area. "It feels like my liver is doing a tap dance."

"What?"

"Or maybe it's my spleen," said Ava. "Anyway, I just feel crappy." She moaned. "What do you suppose that means? Think I could have contracted some rare tropical disease?"

Carmela poured Ava a cup of coffee anyway. "You're sure you still want to go treasure hunting? I mean, if you don't feel well . . ." She was kind of hoping she could weasel out of the whole treasure thing.

"Oh no," said Ava, suddenly rousing herself, "we're *going* treasure hunting. I *need* that money!"

"Frankly," said Carmela, "it's going to be a long shot. There must be thousands of people looking for that treasure medallion, and I'm just not sure where to begin."

Ava held up an index finger and flipped open the Saturday *Times-Picayune*. "There's a new clue today. So another chance for us."

"Another chance for everybody."

"But not everybody is as smart as we are," said Ava. She touched an index finger to the side of her head and made a clicking sound.

"If we're so smart, how come we haven't figured out the two murders?" Carmela asked.

That stopped Ava for about ten seconds. She wrinkled her nose, thinking. "You make a good point. But treasure hunting is different. It's more . . . intuitive."

"And nailing down a suspect isn't intuitive?" Carmela figured that was how most investigators worked. Experience coupled with intuition. After they'd amassed a few telling clues, anyway.

"It's different in other ways, too," continued Ava. "If we find the treasure, there's a cash payoff. If we solve the murders, there isn't."

"No payoff except justice," Carmela murmured. "But, whatever, I'm game. Read us this latest clue so we can decide where we're headed. But fair warning, I have to stop by Memory Mine this afternoon."

Tugboats churned gamely along the Mississippi, tooting and splashing, while an enormous red-and-white paddle wheeler carried visitors on a loudly narrated sightseeing tour. For whatever reason, visitors still wanted to hear the story of Hurricane Katrina and view its residual effects firsthand.

"You really think the treasure's hidden around here?" Carmela asked as they strolled along River Walk heading for the French Market.

"I'm convinced the treasure's hidden in the French Quarter," said Ava, digging in her handbag for the crumpled clue. "Listen again. 'Red beans and bones, and venerable old homes.'" She paused. "So maybe in the French Market or even one of the small museums or historic homes that are open for visitors."

"Maybe," said Carmela, still skeptical.

Looking a little frazzled, Ava stopped and blew a strand of hair from her face. "Woof, I'm suddenly running on vapors. Maybe we should take a breather at Café du Monde?"

"Now you're talking," said Carmela. Café du Monde was a French Quarter landmark, a little café that had practically invented café au lait and served deep-fried beignets smothered with powdered sugar.

They ordered at the counter, then were lucky enough to find a small table beneath the distinctive green-and-white-striped awning.

Ava munched happily as she glanced down at her high-

heeled sandals. "The soles of my Valentinos are covered with powdered sugar," she observed.

"You're lucky," Carmela told her. "It's still early. In another couple of hours this place will be ankle deep with powdered sugar."

"Seems like they should recycle the stuff or something," said Ava.

"Let's hope not," said Carmela. She was starting to enjoy the morning, sipping her café au lait and listening to a trio of musicians out on North Peters Street playing some Miles Davis–type jazz. But heavy on the sax. And that single impromptu concert reinforced for Carmela one of the great charms of the French Quarter. Because the French Quarter was a place where throngs of beginner and veteran street musicians could entertain for dollar bills, and where cadres of street artists, street magicians, and even card players with more than a few tricks up their sleeves engaged and delighted people from all walks of life.

"Will you look at who just showed up!" exclaimed Ava. "It's Mr. Bones!"

"Him again?" Carmela frowned and squinted at the skeleton-costumed man who was working his way slowly through a sea of tables. "He certainly seems to turn up everywhere." It wasn't lost on her that Mr. Bones had also turned up the night of the murder at the Vieux Carré Repertory Theatre. Coincidence? Or was Mr. Bones not what he appeared to be? Could Mr. Bones actually be a dangerous character?

Ava was up and waving, beckoning Mr. Bones over to their table.

"You sure you want to talk to him?" Carmela asked.

"Absolutely," said Ava, suddenly enthused. "He might give us another clue. Hey! Over here!"

"Or he might give us misdirection," murmured Carmela. She wasn't one bit thrilled by the masked skeleton who was today wearing a threadbare black sport coat over his costume.

"Ladies"—Mr. Bones grinned as he neared their table—"I don't mean to crash your little party, but my invitation must have landed in the dead-letter office."

"Ha-ha," said Carmela, clearly not amused.

"How about a clue?" Ava asked Mr. Bones. "We're a couple of working girls who'd love to find that treasure."

"Easy," Carmela cautioned, "we don't want him to think we're *that* kind of working girl!"

But Ava was totally fixated on Mr. Bones. "How about it?" she coaxed playfully. "Got a clue for me?"

Mr. Bones tipped his fedora at her and dug into his jacket pocket. Pulling out a shiny gold doubloon, he tossed it into the air, where it flipped over and over, catching the light. Then he caught it in his hand.

"I should take that as a yes?" Ava asked.

Mr. Bones nodded as he palmed the coin, making it disappear. Then, a few seconds later, it magically reappeared between his fingers. Finally, he handed Ava the coin.

"Thanks!" called Ava as Mr. Bones danced and jigged away. "I mean it, thanks!"

"What's it say?" asked Carmela.

"It says . . ." Ava sat down heavily, squinting as she turned the coin in her hands."

"Eat at Joe's," said Carmela.

"No, smarty, it says, 'If it's treasure you seek, don't overlook an antique.'"

"What does that mean?" asked Carmela. "Go root around the antique shops on Royal Street? I'm sure the owners would

love that. Excuse me while I peer under your Ming vase or lift the cushion on your ten-thousand-dollar fainting couch."

But Ava was not to be deterred. "What if it refers to one of those little museums I mentioned earlier?"

Carmela took another sip of coffee. "Maybe you should go be a tourist while I head over to Memory Mine. We're going to be crazy busy today. Seems like everybody waits until the last minute to buy craft supplies for decorating pumpkins or making masks for Halloween. Plus, I've got to run over to the Art Institute and connect with Angie."

"Yeah." Ava sighed. "I better hustle my buns to Juju Voodoo. Today's our big push, too."

But when Carmela arrived at Memory Mine, she found that things were well under control.

"You okay?" she asked Gabby.

Gabby nodded. "Nothing I can't handle. Just the usual run on black and orange paper, Halloween-themed rubber stamps, and black ribbon."

"Excellent," said Carmela. "So you don't mind if I zip over to the Art Institute?"

"Goodness, no," said Gabby. "In fact, Angie called maybe ten minutes ago. I told her you were still planning to drop by."

"Thanks," said Carmela, who was already halfway out the door.

The New Orleans Art Institute had to be one of Carmela's favorite places: a large, granite building with long echoing corridors, an international galaxy of framed oil paintings

and drawings hung floor to ceiling, and a sculpture garden to boot.

"Carmela!" said Angie, jumping up from her desk. "You didn't waste any time getting over here."

"That's me," said Carmela. "Speedy Gonzalez."

Angie gave an expectant look. "You brought the puppet with you?"

"No," said Carmela, "the Crunch Monster is still safely stowed away at the Pluvius den. Ava's assistant, Miguel, will fetch him tomorrow night, then bring him over to the parade."

"Perfect," said Angie, grabbing a sheaf of papers from her desk. "We can have our photo op then." She grinned, then said, "Walk with me. I have to deliver this budget report to the director's office."

They walked out of the nest of curators' offices and down a corridor lined with wooden cases filled with ceramics.

"Some of our curators want to have their photos taken with the puppet," Angie explained.

"Why not?" said Carmela. "That's what Halloween is for. Do crazy stuff you can regret later. Or am I thinking of Mardi Gras?"

"That, too," Angie laughed. "We've even got a couple of donors who want to pose with the puppet. So I thought, why not?"

They strolled past a case of Greek vases that practically took Carmela's breath away. "These are new!" Carmela exclaimed, gazing at a group of delicate black pots. Around the midsection of the pots were bands of painted figures done in reddish-brown paint that had oxidized to an almost golden hue.

Angie nodded. "A monetary gift from the Sheffield

Family Foundation made those possible. I understand the amphora was deacquisitioned from the Getty, and the two hydrias came from a Madison Avenue dealer in New York."

"Spectacular," said Carmela. They strolled along, Carmela gazing at all the exquisite objects. "Oh," she said, stopping in front of another case of tall, buff-colored pots. "You've got some new Chinese ceramics, too."

A small furrow appeared between Angie's brows. "Those were given to us maybe three months ago by Brett Fowler."

"Hmm," said Carmela. "Is that going to be a problem?"

"Don't know," said Angie. "I suppose if the state proved he used ill-gotten funds to purchase them, they might get . . . I don't know . . . get confiscated?"

"A clawback," said Carmela.

"Excuse me?"

"Clawback," repeated Carmela. "That's the term used when the state or the Feds retrieve profits that were realized in illegal financial dealings. You know, like in a Ponzi scheme or when fat cats don't pay their taxes and use the money instead to buy Miami beachfront homes and Ferraris."

"In that case," said Angie, "I'm going to keep my fingers crossed."

"Do that," said Carmela, thinking of Sissy Fowler's other Chinese pieces. Would they end up as part of a clawback, too? Could happen.

"Are you going to Baby Fontaine's party tonight?" Angie asked.

"Sure," said Carmela. "You, too?"

Angie looked wistful. "I was invited. Baby's in our Silver Patrons Circle, so I've really gotten to know her. But we also have a donors' dinner tonight. These days, even curators

have to sing for their supper and try to woo donors. So . . . no go."

"Too bad," said Carmela. "I think it's going to be a heck of a party."

Chapter 23

GLOWING orange jack-o'-lanterns lined almost every street in the Garden District. This pumpkin luminary sensation began some ten years ago on just one block by a group of gung-ho Halloween-loving neighbors. Over the years, it had spread like wildfire.

"This is magical," exclaimed Ava. "Oh jeez, watch out for that kid! Seems like everybody's out tonight to get an eyeful of this."

Carmela slowed her car to a crawl as they rode past hundreds of glowing pumpkins. "I'll be careful."

"And the cool thing is," said Ava, still spellbound, "all these pumpkins are different." Indeed, there were tall thin pumpkins, chunky monster pumpkins, and smaller pumpkins, all sporting grins, grimaces, smirks, and snaggle-toothed smiles.

"Quite a Halloween welcome," said Carmela. "They really set the tone for Baby's party."

"Are you ready to party down?" Ava asked, giving her charm bracelet a shake.

"Suppose so," said Carmela. "Since I seem to have transitioned from vampire to dominatrix to flapper. In fact, I can't believe I'm wearing yet another costume!" She glanced down at her red fringe dress and black nylons. "Three costumes in three days? That must be some kind of record."

"Isn't Halloween grand!" Ava exclaimed. "And by the way, that black bobbed wig looks utterly smashing on you."

"You think?" Carmela glanced in the rearview mirror and caught a glimpse of a woman she barely recognized. *Is that dark-haired girl really me? Well, I guess it is.*

"You're a completely different woman with dark hair," Ava purred. "More mysterious, more adventurous, more . . ."

"Scratchy?" said Carmela, poking a finger under her wig band.

"I was going to say *dangerous*," said Ava.

"Exactly what I had in mind," laughed Carmela as they cruised by Baby's Garden District home. Every light in the place was ablaze as soft, enticing music drifted out, beckoning them in.

"Party's in full swing," Ava noted.

"Baby always invites half the neighborhood," said Carmela, finally finding a parking spot a block away. "Plus tons of people she knows from the museum and symphony."

"Must be nice being rich," said Ava. "I sure hope none of those fat cat ladies came as Cleopatra tonight." Ava's gold tunic slid seductively up over her knees, and her long, jeweled Nefertiti earrings swung gracefully against her neck.

"They wouldn't dare," said Carmela. "Considering the fact that nobody rocks a costume like you do."

"And just wait until I wiggle my asp!" giggled Ava.

* * *

Baby was waiting for them at the front door, dressed as Scarlett O'Hara.

"Well fiddle-dee-dee, Rhett, look who's come a-calling at Tara." Baby smoothed her crushed velvet hoop skirt dress and grinned. A smart, green riding hat with a black feather was perched atop her head, a thick, golden tasseled rope wrapped about her slender waist.

Baby's husband, Del, the perfect Rhett Butler to her Scarlett, extended his hand. With a Southern gentleman's leisurely twang in his voice, he said, "Frankly, my dear, I'm glad you could make it." His high-waisted pants and pin-striped suit coat appeared custom made. His hair was slicked back and a penciled-in mustache covered his upper lip. A wide, yellow silk tie with a sparkling diamond set off his costume.

"Oh my gosh," exclaimed Carmela, "you're both so perfect." She turned to Ava. "Aren't they perfect?"

"As if they just strolled off the Metro-Goldwyn-Mayer lot," said Ava, administering air kisses to both Baby and Del.

"And you with the wig," Baby cooed to Carmela. "I almost didn't recognize you. Such a temptress with that dark hair!"

"Say now, Miss Cleo," said Del, peering up at Ava in her four-inch-high, golden gladiator sandals, "how tall are you, anyway?"

Then Carmela and Ava were caught in the swirl and crush of the party. Greeting old friends, being introduced to new ones, and oohing and ahhing over Baby's home, which seemed to have been redecorated yet again.

"Is that brocade paper on the walls?" Ava asked, fascinated by the silver-and-blue fleur-de-lis motif.

"I think it's silk," Carmela murmured.

"And those chairs over by the marble fireplace that you could probably roast an ox in . . . are they pricey Louis the Sixteenth replicas?"

"I think they're the real thing," said Carmela.

"Well, hoo-de-doo," exclaimed Ava. "Then we better get ourselves a glass of champagne, because they're probably serving Dom Perignon or Cristal."

"Only the best," agreed Carmela as they both grabbed a champagne flute from the silver tray of a passing waiter.

Carmela sipped slowly as bubbles tickled her nose and the champagne slid down her throat. "Wonderful," she pronounced.

"It does go down easy," Ava agreed.

"You be careful," Carmela cautioned. "You don't want to be fuzzy-headed for tomorrow. Tomorrow's your all-time fave holiday."

"Halloween!" cried Ava.

As they clinked their glasses together in a toast, Tandy suddenly ran up to greet them. Duded up in an Annie Oakley costume with a fringed suede skirt, matching shirt, string tie, and cowboy hat, she also had a rifle slung over her shoulder.

"I hope that thing isn't loaded," were Carmela's first words.

"What's the point of carrying a gun if it isn't?" said Tandy, patting the rifle's wooden stock.

"Seriously?" said Ava.

"I hail from a long line of gun-totin', varmint-shootin' people," laughed Tandy.

"And you can really shoot that thing?" asked Ava, slightly mesmerized by Tandy's firepower. "And *hit* something?"

"Oh sure," said Tandy. She shrugged a shoulder and shifted the gun into her hands. "If you want me to . . ."

"No, no," said Carmela, suddenly alarmed. "No demo needed. In fact, let's adopt a strict disarmament policy tonight. In other words, put the gun down slowly."

"Well, you're no fun," said Tandy as Carmela leaned the rifle, oh so carefully, in the nearest corner.

"Food," suggested Ava. "That's what we really need."

"Now you're talking," agreed Tandy.

The three of them pushed their way through the costumed crowd into Baby's elegant dining room. Normally, her dinner table sat a sedate sixteen, but tonight it was laid out with an elegantly catered buffet-style feast. Caterers in white shirts and black vests stood behind heaping platters of raw oysters, piles of bright red steamed crawfish, wedges of rich Brie and Camembert cheese, and a row of gleaming silver chafing dishes.

"Hot stuff first," said Tandy.

"Always," Ava giggled.

They helped themselves to crawfish étouffée, crab cakes, and champagne-poached trout with pecans. Then they loaded up on blackened fish, red beans and rice, and chicken gumbo.

"Try this rémoulade sauce on your crab cake," said Tandy, licking her fingers. "It's to die for."

"And the Jezebel sauce on the Brie cheese," said Ava. "My personal favorite."

"It would be." Tandy grinned.

"I can't wedge another thing onto my plate," Carmela worried.

"Then take two," said Ava, "like I did."

They tottered to the screened porch at the back of the house and plopped down in plush easy chairs arranged around a zebra wood table.

"This is the life," said Ava as another waiter dropped off fresh glasses of champagne.

"I look forward to Baby's party every year," Tandy admitted.

"Say," said Carmela, "where's Darwin tonight?" Darwin was Tandy's husband.

"Oh, he's up north on a business trip," said Tandy. "Chicago, I think."

"He doesn't know what he's missing," said Ava, between bites.

"But that brings up another question," Tandy said, peering at Carmela. "Where exactly is *your* sweetie?"

Carmela and Ava exchanged a quick glance.

"Uh-oh," said Tandy, "trouble in paradise?"

"Babcock thinks Carmela meddles too much," said Ava.

Tandy was a good sport and pretended to look taken aback. "Nooo." She paused. "Really?"

Carmela and Ava both gave serious nods.

"Now that you mention it . . . ," said Tandy, a wicked twinkle in her eye.

Carmela felt the need to explain why she seemed to be stuck in a puddle of glue. "You realize that Jekyl *asked* for my help. Right after Brett Fowler was killed with that awful Minotaur head." She took a sip of champagne. "And then things kind of escalated from there."

"Like Jimmy Toups getting hanged at the *Ballet Dracula*," said Ava. She paused, a bite of crab cake halfway to her mouth. "Hanged? Is that right? Or is it *hung*?"

"Whatever," said Tandy. "The thing is, Jimmy Toups is dead as a doornail now."

"I like the way you cut to the chase," said Ava.

"And now Carmela's up to her eyeballs in investigating," said Tandy.

"That's a pretty accurate assessment," said Ava. She turned to Carmela. "Wouldn't you agree?"

"Please understand," said Carmela, "I don't exactly go out *looking* for murder victims."

"Dead bodies just sort of drop into your lap," quipped Ava. Then she made a face and said, "Ewwww, that doesn't sound so good, does it?"

Twenty minutes later, Carmela and Ava hovered at the dessert bar, where cakes on crystal stands and warming dishes filled with bananas Foster and all manner of other treats beckoned.

"Bread pudding," said Ava, "with brandy sauce. The kind that's so rich and sugary sweet it makes your teeth hurt."

"And chocolate pecan pie," said Carmela. "Plus blueberry cobbler and apple cinnamon crepes. I wish I had room for all of this," she moaned. "I wish I could take some home."

"Give us all your desserts in small unmarked crepes," joked Ava.

"Ladies!" a male voice boomed behind them. "Contemplating a sugar high?"

They spun around to find Boyd Hodney grinning widely at them. He wore a caped *Phantom of the Opera* costume, all shiny and black. A white mask dangled around his neck on a black cord.

"If it isn't the phantom himself," said Carmela, wishing

he would crawl back to his underworld. But Hodney's eyes conveyed interest that was focused solely on Ava.

"Ava," said Hodney, edging closer to her, "you're looking particularly delectable tonight as queen of the Nile. And that costume shows off your curves to perfection, although I wouldn't mind a slight wardrobe malfunction." He winked at her, as if sharing a little joke.

"And where is Mrs. Hodney tonight?" Carmela asked.

Hodney frowned, and one hand crawled up to fidget with his mask, a gigantic emerald ring winking on his finger. "Unable to attend, I'm afraid." He cleared his throat nervously, then seemed to recover some of his dignity. "Can I fetch you ladies something from the bar?"

"What are you drinking?" Ava asked.

"Sazerac," Hodney told her. A mix of bourbon and bitters, Sazerac was reputed to be the first cocktail ever invented.

"Pass," said Carmela, grabbing Ava's arm and snatching a dish of bread pudding in the bargain. "We're just on our way to say hello to someone."

"We are?" said Ava as Carmela propelled her away from Hodney.

"Jekyl's here," said Carmela. "So we gotta say hi. Plus, Boyd Hodney is not suitable dating material for you. Think about it; do you want to blow it with Tom Travers?"

"Not really," said Ava. "I like the elegant Mr. Travers a whole lot. Fact is, I promised to hook up with him later tonight at Club Carpathia."

Carmela did a double take. "Club Carpathia?" In a town jam-packed with night clubs, saloons, jazz joints, and after-hours bars, this was a new one on her.

"It's a club that exists only for this week," Jekyl told her as he sidled up to them and planted a quick kiss on Carmela's

cheek. "At a special-event center managed by Club Godot. But for Halloween it's been all jazzed up—vampire style!"

"We surely can't miss that," said Carmela in a dry tone. "I mean, I seriously don't think I've fulfilled my vampire quota yet."

"Sarcasm doesn't become you, darling," said Jekyl. "Besides, it'll be fun. We'll all go there, get a big table, have ourselves a giggle."

"Love it," said Ava, who was slightly giddy from the champagne. Rocking unsteadily on her high heels, she swung around to grab another glass of champagne from the tray of a passing waiter, and instead screeched, "What are *you* doing here?"

Chapter 24

CARMELA and Jekyl both turned to see who'd caught her attention.

"Babcock!" gasped Carmela, shocked to see her earnest-looking police detective boyfriend standing just three feet away from her.

"Cheese it, the cops!" exclaimed Jekyl. "Fun's over now. Lock up the absinthe and ditch the weed."

Edgar Babcock remained patiently focused on Carmela.

"Excuse me," said Carmela, "but the question remains, what *are* you doing here?"

"He's off duty," Jekyl said, in a snide tone. "Probably working security at the front door."

"I'm an invited guest," Babcock said quietly. His blue eyes stared at Carmela, searching for some sign of acknowl-edgment that they might be able to meet each other half-

way. When he didn't find it, he moved toward her and put an arm around her.

Carmela stiffened. "Please don't do that."

"We need to talk," said Babcock.

"Aggh," sputtered Ava. "Those have to be the most hideous four words in the English language."

"Always precipitates a rousing fight," said Jekyl, blithely sipping his Ramos gin fizz, reputed to be Huey Long's favorite cocktail.

"Do you mind?" asked Babcock, raising his eyebrows at Ava and Jekyl. "We'd like a little privacy, please."

"It *is* a party," said Jekyl, but he and Ava gave nonchalant shrugs and moved away.

Carmela faced Babcock. "So Baby invited you."

"Yes, she did. A most gracious lady."

"Maybe too gracious," said Carmela.

"Carmela . . ."

"So have some fun," said Carmela, who felt like she was on the verge of tears. "Go pig out at the buffet. Don't let me stop you."

"I'm fine. I ate earlier."

"A drink, then?"

"I really stopped by to talk to you."

"I'm not sure we have much to talk about."

"Fine," said Babcock, his voice hardening a little. "Have it your way. Make this difficult."

"Babcock," said Carmela, choking back tears now, "I'm not a difficult person. What you don't seem to understand is I'm an independent person."

"Why are you constantly mixing apples and oranges?" Babcock demanded.

"I'm not!" shrilled Carmela. "Why do you have to be so . . . so obtuse!"

"Obtuse?" said Babcock, taken aback and obviously stung by her harsh characterization. "Is that what you think I am?"

"Sometimes, yes," said Carmela. She was already regretting her words.

Babcock was about to say something, but then he reconsidered and his mouth snapped shut. He clenched his hands, then opened them, his fingers splayed out flat. "Apologies," he said, in a hoarse whisper, then walked away.

"What was that about?" demanded Ava, hanging over Carmela's shoulder now.

"Breaking up, I think," said Carmela.

"You know what?" said Ava, mustering enthusiasm. "You can do better."

"We can all do better," said Jekyl, joining in. "Off to Club Carpathia for some serious moving and grooving?"

"Let's do it!" agreed Ava.

"Why not?" whispered Carmela. "What have I got to lose?" *Except, perhaps, the love of my life.*

Carmela drove slowly down Toulouse Street, Ava chattering away in the passenger seat, Jekyl jammed behind them in the jump seat.

"There it is!" exclaimed Jekyl. "There's the sign!"

Carmela glanced out the driver's-side window and caught the red neon sign that proclaimed *Club Carpathia* in dripping letters. It hung on the facade of an old stone Gothic building that had once been a church and then a meeting hall. The place had been for sale ever since being abandoned after Hurricane Katrina, but it had just recently been re-

habbed and turned into an event center. And what an event it held tonight!

Pushing open carved wooden double doors, Carmela, Ava, and Jekyl walked into a large room with a high-beamed ceiling, filled with comfy, wine-colored sofas and club chairs. Four pool tables sat at the rear. A small bar had been set up and about thirty people mingled and drank as techno music pounded away.

"This doesn't look very vampirey," commented Carmela.

"Downstairs," said Jekyl. "We have to descend into the depths of the place to find Club Carpathia. Come on, Mouseketeers, time for us to enter the . . ." He let loose a wicked cackle. "Dungeon!"

They headed for an archway in back, where another neon sign, an arrow with the word *Dungeon*, pointed downward.

Ava grabbed Carmela's hand as they descended the stone staircase. The stairs twisted around and around with blue runner lights leading the way. Dance music, louder even than upstairs, assaulted their ears.

"This is gonna be crazy!" predicted Ava.

And it was.

The stairs opened onto a sunken dance floor with a DJ booth set in the middle. Beyonce's "Single Ladies" ripped and roared from the speakers as dancers writhed and shook. Burning torches hung from the walls; old-fashioned, flat-topped coffins served as cocktail tables in the lounge area; and strobe lights mixed with fog added even more atmosphere. Along one stone wall, a long bar was stocked with colorful bottles and tended by female bartenders in vampire costumes.

Carmela, Ava, and Jekyl strolled up to the bar and were

greeted by a fang-wearing, gold contact lens—wearing blonde. "Help you?" she asked, her fangs slightly impeding her speech.

"Three Witch's Cauldrons," said Jekyl.

"I love your contact lenses," added Ava.

"Thanks," said the vamp, "but they make it a little difficult to see." She mixed up a pitcher of drinks, then poured out the amber liquid into three tall glasses. As her hands worked magic over the drinks, a small puff of steam rose off the top.

"How did she do that?" asked Ava. She leaned toward the bartender, entranced. "How did you do that?"

The vampire smiled. "Trade secret."

At which point Tom Travers seemed to magically appear as well.

"You're here!" screeched Ava, still no match for the sound system.

"Told you we'd hook up." Travers gave her a quick kiss, said "Hiya" to Carmela and Jekyl, then pulled Ava away from them and onto the dance floor.

"Hey!" said Jekyl as they were quickly lost in the writhing crowd.

"They'll be gone for a while," said Carmela. She took a sip of her drink and gazed around, wondering if the church-basement ladies ever figured their potluck suppers and craft fairs would give way to this?

When Carmela turned back, Jekyl was gone. Mingling, no doubt.

Oh great. Alone again. Which prompted a wave of sadness.

"Hey, sexy lady, are you here by yourself?" A man in a Robin Hood outfit, his green leotard revealing muscular legs, smiled at her. He was young, handsome, and obviously looking for female company.

"I'm with someone," Carmela told him. "But thanks anyway."

"He keeping you waiting?" asked Robin Hood.

Carmela managed a faint smile. "Something like that."

"If he stands you up, I'll be around. My name is Dimitri." He extended his hand.

"Carmela," she said as she felt his warm grasp.

He brought her hand to his mouth and kissed it lightly. "Enchanted."

Carmela blushed and moved on. But in her haste, she collided with a leather-clad barbarian.

He turned to her, bare legs and shoulders sticking out of his animal-hide costume. A horned Viking helmet rested on his head, and he wielded a large, curved sword. "Care to join me back at the cave?"

"Sorry, Conan," said Carmela, "but I'm holding out for a modern-day hero."

The barbarian grinned and moved on.

Carmela pushed through the throng of costumed revelers, noting the high proportion of vampires. Even though she'd completely lost sight of Ava and Tom on the dance floor, she was hoping to reconnect with them. Club Carpathia just wasn't much fun when you were wandering around all by your lonesome. On the other hand, she *had* been hit on a couple of times . . .

Carmela craned her neck, turned, and promptly stumbled into a witch, causing the witch to spill her bright red drink.

"Oh, excuse me!" Carmela stammered. Then, upon second glance, was stunned to find Tanya Perdue, Brett Fowler's girlfriend, glaring daggers at her. Tanya, dressed in a witch costume complete with pointed hat and black granny boots, certainly looked the part.

"Watch it!" Tanya snarled. "This isn't your personal space, you know."

"Really," said Carmela, "I do apologize."

"Wait a minute," said Tanya, looking bleary-eyed and slightly hammered. "Don't I know you?"

"I don't think we've ever actually met," said Carmela.

"I *do* know you!" Tanya screeched. "I remember your picture from the newspaper!" She shook her head as if to clear it. "You're the one who found my poor Brett! At the Pluvius den!"

"Afraid so," Carmela admitted.

Tanya seemed to stagger back then, and a cunning look came into her eyes. "He say anything before he died?" she muttered. Tanya reached out, grabbed Carmela's shoulder, and squeezed it hard. "Did he?"

Carmela shook her head slowly. "I'm sorry, he was already gone."

Tanya's mouth pulled into an ugly grimace, and then she released her death grip. "Whoever is responsible is going to pay," she said, slurring her words. "I swear, I'm going to get even!"

"Perhaps you should let the police handle things," Carmela told Tanya, then felt like choking on her own words. Wasn't that what Babcock had been driving at all along? Wasn't that the crux of their disagreement? That the police should be the only ones investigating?

"Cops don't know nuthin'," Tanya muttered. She hooked her thumb and touched it to her chest. "But I know a few things they don't."

Carmela peered at Tanya. "Seriously?"

"And I'm gonna make the killer pay!" Tanya jerked away

from Carmela, gazed unhappily at her empty glass, then staggered off.

Carmela watched her go and thought to herself, *If Tanya really is stalking someone, who'll be the next to die?*

Chapter 25

"Go on, Boo!" Carmela yelled, with what she hoped was upbeat doggy mom encouragement. "You can do it!"

"Atta boy, Poobah," cried Ava, standing next to her. "Show that prissy, pink collar–wearing poodle who's boss!"

"Don't you feel like soccer moms at the playground?" Carmela asked. They'd brought Boo and Poobah to the Howl-o-Ween party at Audubon Park and were watching the little darlings compete in the graveyard dig. That is, snarf around in a pile of dirt, looking for buried bones and rawhide chews.

"We're like moms who drag their kids to T-ball," agreed Ava, "screaming like crazy and obsessing if they miss." She stopped, scanned for Poobah again, and screamed, "Dig faster, sweetheart! And watch out for that sneaky bulldog! He's trying to make an end run! Gnaw on his leg if you have to."

"Do you think the dogs are enjoying this?" Carmela asked.

"Are you kidding?" said Ava. "Flying around like bats outa hell, nipping each other's ears, tumbling in the dirt and grass? It's a flippin' picnic for your dogs."

"'Spose so," said Carmela as Boo suddenly flopped down in the grass, legs splayed out, sides heaving.

"Uh-oh," said Ava, "looks like Boo might not be in tip-top condition for the chase-the-squirrel competition."

"She might have to take a pass," Carmela agreed as they stood together, leaning against the fence of the temporary dog park, enjoying the late-afternoon rays.

"Sun's going down," observed a gleeful Ava. "Almost time for All Hallow's Eve!"

"I hope Miguel doesn't have any trouble getting the Crunch Monster puppet down to my shop," Carmela fretted.

"Don't worry, he's cool. He knows what to do."

"I can't wait to see it in the parade."

"I can't wait *for* the parade," said Ava. "Going to be glorious. Hey, guess what?" She nudged Carmela with her shoulder. "Travers promised to fly me to Las Vegas for a romantic little escapade!"

"Lucky you," said Carmela.

"Yeah," said Ava, burbling with excitement now. "We're probably gonna stay in some fancy high-roller suite at the Wynn Hotel and dine at all the hot, trendy restaurants. Hit a few table games, too. You know, roulette, blackjack, baccarat."

"You know how to play baccarat?" Carmela was suitably impressed.

"I've watched old James Bond movies," said Ava. "I've seen how it's done."

"Seems like mini blackjack," said Carmela. "Instead of twenty-one you draw to nine?"

"Yeah," said Ava, chuckling, "but the really important thing is how good you look. You gotta dress like those careless, rich babes from Beverly Hills and Palm Springs. You know, tight designer jeans, skanky top, Manolo Blahnik heels, and a Louis Vuitton bag."

"You can do upscale skanky," Carmela said, encouragingly. "You've got that cool LV doctor's bag you found at the Latest Wrinkle resale shop on Magazine Street."

"You got that right," enthused Ava. "When I set my mind to it, I can even out-posh Posh Spice with my eyes closed. I was *born* to it."

"And you've got better hair than she does."

"And I eat actual food," said Ava.

"Just don't go bonkers and let Travers carry you off to one of those all-night wedding chapels," Carmela warned. "You don't want wedding pictures of you and Travers getting married by an Elvis impersonator in a pale blue suit with matching ruffled shirt."

"Don't worry," said Ava. "I might lose my heart, but I won't lose my head."

"Or your money," said Carmela. "Hopefully. So when are you two lovebirds planning to take off?"

"Next weekend," said Ava. "After tonight, my busy season's behind me, so I'll be free as a bird. Of course, if we could get a bead on that treasure, I'd have a tidy little gambling stake to take with me, too."

Zydeco music blasted through Jackson Square as strings of glowing, rainbow-colored lights held the dark night at bay.

Costumed revelers pushed and shoved in a good-natured display of fun, and the air was redolent with the smell of deep-fried alligator, spicy jambalaya, funnel cakes, and beer.

"Oh yeah," said Ava as they clip-clopped past a food stand. "Onion mums, gotta get me one of those." Ava pulled a few dollars from the velvet purse that swung from her shoulder and pushed it toward the cashier. She'd opted to wear her long black vampire dress again, while Carmela had donned black jeans, black T-shirt, and a black leather motorcycle jacket. Not a costume per se for tonight's Halloween gala; more like an outfit with an edge.

"And rémoulade sauce," said Ava, pointing at a twenty-gallon vat of creamy sauce. "Drizzle on a couple good gobs." She shoved her paper tray with the gigantic deep-fried onion mum at Carmela. "Help yourself. Don't you just adore deep-fried onions?"

Carmela helped herself. After all, Halloween, like the aptly named Fat Tuesday, was one of those days when you received special dispensation for eating candy and junk food. All was allowed, any notion of fat grams banished.

"So crowded," observed Ava as they pushed their way up Chartres Street, heading for Memory Mine. "I don't know about the monster part, but there certainly is mayhem." Paradegoers in all sorts of costumes capered around them—ghosts, goblins, Venetian lords and ladies in velvet dress, *Star Wars* characters, political figures, a contingent of gospel singers, and a huge number of vampires.

"A real *fais do do*," said Carmela, using the Cajun word for *party*. Then she glanced at her watch. "There's so doggone much going on tonight, isn't there? The Day of the Dead candlelight parade, then the monster puppets, then the hearse cavalcade."

"With a few miscellaneous bands, flag twirlers, and floats thrown in for good measure," said Ava.

"And lots of action in the bars," said Carmela.

"Can't forget the bars," agreed Ava. She popped another bite of onion in her mouth. "Jekyl's gonna meet us at your shop?"

"That's the plan," said Carmela. "But with Jekyl, you never know. He usually has his own agenda."

"I told Travers I'd meet him at Galatoire's after the parade," said Ava. "In their cozy bar."

"You two have really clicked, haven't you?" said Carmela.

"I think so," said Ava, a satisfied smile stealing across her face. "You know, a girl searches all her life for Mr. Right and—bam!—suddenly he appears out of nowhere."

"Sometimes that's the way it works," said Carmela. "A guy just gets dropped in your lap."

"Ouch," said Ava, clapping a hand against the side of her head.

"What's wrong?" asked Carmela, "you get poked or something?" The carnival atmosphere was morphing into a madhouse as people lurched past them carrying their ubiquitous *geaux* cups. Definitely a high-octane, liquor-fueled evening!

"My hairpiece came unsnapped," complained Ava, fidgeting with her hair.

"Seriously?"

"You didn't think this was the real me, did you?"

"One never knows," said Carmela.

"I hear Jessica Simpson wears six separate hairpieces when she's in concert."

"How many do you have in?"

"Seven," said Ava. "Here, help me get this thing snapped."

Carmela slipped a hand into Ava's wild mane and found the clip. She fumbled with it, then felt it click back into place. "Okay, got it."

"You're a lifesaver," said Ava.

"What are you gonna do when you go to Vegas? Leave your extensions in all weekend?"

"Oh sure," said Ava. "Beauty always comes first, even if your head does feel like a burning pincushion."

They turned left and headed up Governor Nicholls Street, the crowds growing thicker by the minute. When they reached Memory Mine's front door, Carmela was relieved to find the lights on.

"He's here."

"Of course, he's here," said Ava as they pushed their way in to greet a smiling Miguel.

"You're here," Carmela said again. No sign of Jekyl, though.

"Me and the Crunch Monster," said Miguel. He grinned. "You want to get me into this thing?"

"He looks great," Ava said, gleefully. "Doesn't he look great?" After a good ten minutes of lifting, tugging, snugging, and giant head fitting, Miguel was fully costumed and ready to march.

"We do good work," Carmela agreed.

"*You* do good work," said Ava. "You're the one who conceived this crazy, twisted monster puppet in your brain. And, by the way, missy, where exactly do your crazy ideas bubble up from?"

Carmela thought for a few moments. "Gotta be the New Orleans influence?"

"Has to be," Ava agreed. "Since we're the Mardi Gras, Halloween vampire, mudbug-eating, daiquiri-drinking capital of the universe."

"Oops," said Carmela, "can't forget this." She grabbed a white silk banner that proclaimed *New Orleans Art Institute* and settled it around the puppet's long neck.

"Now what?" asked Ava.

"Now we lead Miguel to the meet-up point," said Carmela, finally feeling a sense of accomplishment. "For the Monsters and Mayhem parade."

But that was easier said than done.

"How many people are milling around the Quarter anyway?" complained Ava. She was on one side of the giant puppet, Carmela on the other, but they were having a tough time tugging Miguel through the press of rowdy people.

"Thousands," said Carmela. "Maybe tens of thousands."

"Ouch!" said Ava, sounding annoyed, "somebody just pinched me. I think it was that guy in the green elf costume." She spun around, grouchy, looking for the offender. But he'd already melted into the crowd. "Too bad," complained Ava. "What I wouldn't do to him!"

"Don't feel bad," said Carmela, "I just got propositioned by a guy in a clown costume."

"Does a clown trump an elf?" asked Ava, giggling.

"No idea," said Carmela. She was suddenly aware of someone else walking closely on her heels. So she did what any normal, curious, ticked-off woman would do. She stopped, spun around quickly, and yelled, "Gotcha!"

It was Mills Taggart.

"Taggart!" Carmela cried. "You're following us again?"

"And dressed in a cowboy costume," said Ava, immediately joining in the harassment. "Who are you supposed to be? Hopalong Cassidy?"

"I think Hoppy wore all black," Carmela pointed out.

"You're right," said Ava. "Hoppy would've never worn a purple cowboy shirt with a yellow bandana. He'd get drummed out of the TV cowboy corps."

"Give me a break, will you?" said Taggart. "I'm on duty."

"On duty?" Ava sneered. "For what? Grand marshal of the stupid costume parade? The OK Corral?"

"No," said Carmela. "He's just dogging us again." She stared tiredly at Taggart. "You're following us again, aren't you." It was a statement, not a question.

Taggart sucked air through his front teeth, then reluctantly replied, "Yes."

"Do Shamus and Glory know what a terrible PI you are?" asked Carmela. "Because, clearly, every time you tag after us, we figure it out."

"Which makes you a clueless schlump," said Ava.

"And you two are stupid," snarled Taggart, "because you don't get it. You don't realize you're probably being watched."

"We can take care of ourselves," said Carmela.

"Right on," echoed Ava. "So buzz off and leave us alone!"

Chapter 26

CARMELA and Ava escorted Miguel to the meet-up point on North Rampart Street near Louis Armstrong Park, then tucked him into the middle of the slowly forming Monsters and Mayhem parade. Right behind the contingent of Day of the Dead candle walkers, directly in front of the cavalcade of hearses.

"Think he'll be okay?" asked Carmela as they scurried away. They were planning to go back to Jackson Square, where the parade would conclude with a big finale.

"He'll be fine," Ava assured her. "All Miguel has to do is stand there for another fifteen minutes, then start walking when they give the high sign. Besides, there are lots of parade starters and marshals to help out. You see all those folks in the black-and-orange vests?"

"I just don't want any hiccups in the program," said Car-

mela. "I want it to be perfect for the Art Institute. For the photo ops and all."

"When the parade ends in Jackson Square," said Ava, "we'll hustle him back to Memory Mine just like we planned. Meet up with Angie and her friends for their little photo session." Ava put a hand on Carmela's shoulder and gave a gentle squeeze. "Just relax, okay?"

Carmela nodded. "Okay."

Ava's head whipped around. "Holy smokes, will you look at that!"

"What?" said Carmela.

"Over by the Andrew Jackson Museum," said Ava. "There's a guy wrapped up in a straitjacket crawling into a coffin!"

"I read about this," said Carmela. "It's an escape artist who's going to be buried alive."

Ava looked skeptical. "They're going to bury him six feet under?"

"There's a hole dug in the ground," said Carmela. "So . . . looks like."

Ava gave a little shudder. "Sure hope he makes it out alive. Remember poor Houdini? He had a whole bunch of close calls."

"I don't exactly *remember* him," Carmela laughed.

"But you've heard about what he did," said Ava. "The straitjacket, the locked trunk, the whole river thing?"

"This guy was probably hired by the merchants association," said Carmela, "so I'm sure they'll see fit to retrieve him in time." Carmela paused. "Since we're near Mumbo Gumbo's food booth, I think I'm gonna grab a cup of shrimp chowder."

"Sure," said Ava as they started across the street together. "Ooh, careful," she cried, pulling Carmela back. "You almost walked into an entire brass band complete with flag-twirlers."

They watched the marching band high-step it past them, and then Carmela hustled across to the food booth.

"Hey, hey!" said Ava, waving and trying to catch Carmela's attention again. "Mr. Bones is here!" But Carmela was already at the food stand, placing her order.

"What?" said Carmela, hearing her name called, turning for an instant, then losing sight of Ava. She shrugged, then focused on the cup of hot, steaming chowder being shoved across the counter to her, paid her four dollars, then stood on tiptoes, searching for Ava. After a few hectic moments, she finally located her.

"Guess what?" said Ava as Carmela hurried toward her.

"You got pinched again, and this time you creamed the guy."

"Naw," said Ava. "But I did run into Mr. Bones."

"Oh, him. He's getting as annoying as Mills Taggart."

"No, he's not," said Ava as a cat-that-swallowed-the-canary grin suddenly spread across her face. "He gave me another clue." She held up a folded piece of paper in her hand.

"What's it say?" Carmela had pretty much given up on the treasure hunt. With all the people that had come to see Monsters and Mayhem, there was no way she and Ava were going to find the treasure medallion tonight.

Ava unfolded the paper and read it. "Check the dial and find noontide. It's all downhill, an easy ride." Ava's eyes widened at this last part, and then she hastily folded the clue and tucked it down the front of her dress. "Oh my gosh," she mouthed.

"What?" said Carmela, still spooning up chowder, wishing she had a crusty piece of French bread to go with it.

"I know where the treasure is," Ava said in a hoarse whisper.

"Sure you do," said Carmela, sounding not quite convinced.

Ava gazed at her, excitement lighting her face. Her cheeks flared pink, her eyes sparkled, and she almost quivered in anticipation. "No, I really do!"

Her curiosity aroused now, Carmela took Ava by the hand and pulled her back onto the sidewalk. They walked about fifteen feet, then stopped in a little alcove outside the Hotel Ivy. "Are you serious?"

Ava nodded furiously.

"Where do you think the treasure's hidden?"

Ava didn't bat an eye. "Not even four blocks from here! In St. Louis Cemetery Number One!"

Surprised, Carmela took a step backward. "What makes you think that?"

"The last line of the clue." Ava grinned. "'An easy ride.' Get it?"

"Not really," said Carmela.

"*Easy Rider*," said Ava. "That's where they filmed the druggie scenes from the movie *Easy Rider*. In St. Louis Cemetery Number One."

"Oh my gosh," said Carmela, suddenly catching Ava's excitement. "You might actually . . . be right."

"I know I'm right," Ava chortled. She glanced around, as if fearing someone might overhear them. "Which means we've got to hustle over there right now."

"And maybe miss the Monster parade? When we worked so hard on—"

"If we don't grab that treasure, somebody else will!" Ava

was not only jazzed, she was insistent. "This is the final night! Mr. Bones is probably gonna be handing out clues like crazy! The *same* clues!"

Still Carmela was reluctant. "It's a huge cemetery," she worried. "And not terribly safe at night. And how exactly are we going to pinpoint this thing?"

"Simple," said Ava, her enthusiasm ratcheting up even more. "Because 'check the dial' and 'noontide' are also clues."

"You mean like a gravestone with a carved sundial or something?" said Carmela. "Or the number twelve?"

"I love that you're so smart," said Ava.

Carmela thought about the clue Ava had just recited. As well as the notion of discovering the treasure. It was certainly possible the medallion had been hidden in the nearby cemetery. And there were, after all, gravestones with all manner of images and carvings. She'd seen doves, lambs, angels, books, kittens, even horses carved in stone. So why not a sundial?

"Come on, *cher*," said Ava, grabbing Carmela by the hand. "What have we got to lose?"

"I . . ." began Carmela, then pushed back any feelings of worry and tossed what was left of her chowder into a trash can. "Okay."

St. Louis Cemetery No. 1 was dark, spooky, and practically deserted. It was also difficult to navigate. Most of the crumbling old tombs were tall and vertical and jammed together, versus the lower, rounded tombs found in Lafayette Cemetery.

"We should split up," Ava whispered.

"Negative," said Carmela. That was the last thing she wanted to do. "We have to stick together. Safety in numbers."

"There's only two of us," said Ava.

"Better than one," muttered Carmela.

They stood paused at a kind of cemetery crossroads, where two narrow gravel roads, barely wide enough for a hearse, intersected. Whitewashed aboveground tombs stretched in all directions, making the cemetery look exactly like the boneyard it was.

"Okay," said Ava, "what does your intuition tell you?"

"To get out of here?"

"Seriously," said Ava.

Carmela tried to conjure up a vibe, she really did. She tried to picture the treasure medallion hanging on one of the tombs, just waiting to be plucked. But her vision felt . . . hazy at best. Finally, she pointed a finger in what she assumed was a westerly direction and said, "That-a-way?"

"I wish you sounded a tad more confident," said Ava as they struck off.

"Believe me," said Carmela, "I wish I did, too."

They searched for a good ten minutes, gravel crunching underfoot, slipping behind tombs, sometimes hearing faint voices, but never really seeing actual people. Thin moonlight streamed down, lending an otherworldly glow.

"This isn't working," said Ava.

"Let's go back," Carmela urged. "There's still time to catch the parade."

Ava frowned and bit her lip.

"Okay," said Carmela, seeing Ava's distress. "Five more minutes. But that's it."

They worked their way back along a narrow walkway. Discovered tombs that had a carved bird, a butterfly, and what might have been a vase of roses.

"This feels right," said Ava. "We're so close I can taste it. There's even a jittery feeling traveling up and down my spine."

"That's your blood sugar signaling you didn't eat enough," said Carmela. "Face it, we're searching for a needle in a haystack. And how often do you—"

"I see a stone sundial," said Ava.

"Ha-ha," said Carmela. "Nice try."

"No, really," said Ava, standing very quietly and pointing.

Carmela gave a casual glance over her shoulder, then did a double take. "Good gravy, it *is* a sundial!" She sounded shocked. Beyond shocked.

The sundial sculpture was freestanding, about three feet high and set atop a canted rock.

"Told you we were hot!" Ava chortled.

They both bent low over the sundial and poked at it gingerly with their fingers. Then Ava said, "We gotta check for moving parts."

Carmela ran her hands lightly across the face of the sundial. The sculpture felt cold and concrete. And totally immobile.

"Anything?" asked Ava.

Carmela shook her head as her fingers skittered across the back of the sundial. "There don't seem to be any moving parts."

"No," said Ava. "There have to be."

Carmela shook her head again.

"Maybe we need to hit a secret spot or something," Ava suggested. "Like those crazy library shelves you see in scary movies."

"A sweet spot," Carmela murmured as she ran her fingers over the sundial yet again. But nothing happened. No secret compartment swung open on a perfectly balanced fulcrum, no medallion suddenly popped up to reveal itself. "Nada," she said.

"Rats," said Ava. "I'm positive this is it!"

Carmela thought for a couple of moments. It was a sundial, and it fit the clue. Or did it? "Ava, let's check your clue again. Just to make sure."

"No," Ava murmured, more to herself than anything, "I'm positive we have it right."

"Indulge me," said Carmela.

Ava stuck a hand down the front of her dress and pulled out the clue. She handed it slowly to Carmela. "It's kind of crumpled. From being . . . well, you know. Stuck down . . ."

Carmela unfolded the clue and studied it. "This is written on a piece of Chinese money," she said, squinting. "Looks like a . . . a yuan? What is that, like a Chinese dollar bill or something?"

"Yeah, probably," said Ava, giving an eager nod.

"But not like the other clues," Carmela said slowly. "Not in the newspaper, not printed on a doubloon."

"Probably because this is the final clue," said Ava.

"Hold everything," said Carmela, a warning note beginning to ping in the back of her brain. "Something's a little off here."

"You're right," said Ava. "We are. We're off the mark somehow." She made a slow circle around the sundial, kicking at it with her toe.

"And you got this clue from Mr. Bones?" Carmela asked.

Ava nodded. "Yup."

"The guy in the skeleton suit."

"Well," said Ava, thinking, "it was a slightly different skeleton suit tonight. Maybe a little . . . shinier? And he wasn't wearing his usual hat. It was more like a baseball cap."

Carmela stared at Ava as moonlight filtered through bare trees, hitting their faces and bathing them both in a ghostly glimmer. "What if somebody gave you that clue for the sole purpose of leading us to this spot?"

Ava scrunched up her face. "You mean like accidentally-on-purpose?"

"Something like that, yes."

"And the reason would be . . . what?"

"I don't know," said Carmela, her heart suddenly taking an extra thud. "For the time being, let's—"

"Oh crap," said Ava, in a hoarse voice. "Somebody's here."

"A car," said Carmela, suddenly picking up a low rumble. A car was indeed plowing its way up the narrow path that led through the cemetery.

Except it wasn't a car at all, but an enormous black hearse with dark, tinted windows. It lurched out of the darkness, suddenly blocking their path and cutting off their retreat.

"What on earth?" Carmela muttered, the hairs on the back of her neck prickling like crazy. And then a thought burbled up in her head, like long-lost dinosaur bones finally erupting from a turgid tar pit. *Danger. There's danger here. We've got to get away!*

Which was precisely when the driver's-side door creaked open and Mr. Bones stepped out.

"Mr. Bones?" said Ava, in a whisper. "What are you . . . ?"

Her voice trailed off into a harsh wheeze as she suddenly saw the gray snub-nosed revolver clutched in the skeleton's hands. Then Mr. Bones reached up and clawed his mask off. And, suddenly, it was Tom Travers who was pointing the gun at them!

Chapter 27

"TOM?" Ava quavered. She sounded like she was about to pass out.

"Climb in back!" Travers snarled at the both of them. "Don't ask questions, just do it!"

"This can't be happening," Ava moaned.

"Get in the car!" Travers repeated.

"No!" Carmela snapped back at him. She'd just been handed an ugly surprise and had no clue as to what might happen. But she realized that climbing into the back of the hearse wasn't going to improve their plight. She'd read plenty of newspaper stories about kidnappings. Knew that once you submitted to your kidnapper's demands, let him transport you to a *different* location that he controlled, your situation became a hundred times more dangerous.

"I said move!" Travers flicked his gun again, indicating the hearse.

"The police are on their way," Carmela bluffed. "Edgar Babcock knows exactly where we are."

"Edgar Babcock knows nothing," Travers sneered, seeming to take great pleasure in nullifying her statement. "And neither do you. Now stop wasting my time and get inside this hearse!"

Still full of false bravado, Carmela grabbed Ava's arm and said, "No. Not on your life!"

Travers offered a thin smile, then shifted the gun toward Ava. "Then how about hers?"

Reluctantly, they climbed into the back of the hearse.

"Why are you doing this?" Ava implored. Travers had raised the privacy window and was seemingly immune to their pleadings. They could see him through the tinted glass but were unable to communicate.

"Save it," said Carmela. Seated cross-legged, she gripped Ava's shoulders, trying to pull her back from a hysterical crying jag and get her to focus on their immediate and disastrous situation.

"But . . . he told me he loved me," sniffled Ava, who was still beside herself.

"I know, honey, but try to put that out of your mind for now. We've got to figure this out."

"He lied," whimpered Ava.

Carmela pulled Ava toward her and held her. "I know," she whispered into her hair. "I know."

Ava cried and sniffled some more, then finally heaved a deep sigh and said, "Where are we?"

Carmela peered out the window. "Just coming out of the cemetery. Onto Basin Street."

Ava wiped at her tears. "What are we gonna do?"

"Only one thing to do," said Carmela, determined to keep a positive attitude. "Escape."

Ava stared at her with red-rimmed eyes. "Did Travers kill Brett Fowler? Did he kill Jimmy Toups?"

"I think so," said Carmela.

"Then he'll kill us," said Ava, hopelessness creeping into her voice.

"No!" said Carmela. "Listen to me! We're going to get out of this!"

"How?" asked Ava.

As if in answer, Carmela began pounding the side window of the hearse with her fists. And because her pounding seemed dulled, she also yelled and screamed. "Help! We're being kidnapped! Call the police!" She waved frantically to people they passed by, hoping, praying to grab their attention.

Ava joined in, too. "Get us out of here! Call the police! Fire! Call 911! Anybody! Just call!"

They caught the attention of two vampires who watched them go by, but the vampires just smiled and waved back, thinking it was part of the Halloween festivities!

"Wave at the nice people," said Travers, his voice booming across the intercom, sounding almost gleeful. "Smile at them. It's the last chance you'll ever get."

"You jerk!" Ava screamed back. "You . . . murderer!"

"The price of doing business," said Travers, and now his voice was cold as ice.

"But . . . why?" wailed Ava. "Why?"

Carmela thought for a minute, recalling the clue scrawled on the Chinese yuan. And suddenly the China connection slipped into place. "The artwork," said Carmela. "That'd be

my guess. Travers has been slipping in and out of China, so he's probably been importing Chinese fakes along with his Mardi Gras heads and clothing contracts." She glanced up and caught Travers's eye in the dim yellow light of the rearview mirror. "Isn't that right?"

"Took you long enough to figure it out," Travers snorted.

"And you did this . . . why?" asked Carmela.

"Money." Travers grinned. "Lots and lots of money."

"You sold Chinese fakes to Brett Fowler," said Carmela.

"No," said Travers. "Mr. Sam Li of Dynasty Imports in Hong Kong sold the fakes. Delta Imports merely brokered the deal, then transported them."

"And took a healthy cut," said Carmela.

"Well, of course," responded Travers.

"When Fowler was indicted, you were afraid he was going to roll on you," said Carmela. "Because he was donating fakes to museums and getting a fat tax write-off. And you also got nervous about Jimmy Toups. He was Sissy's confidant and had enough know-how to figure out the Chinese artworks were fake."

"Then you started snooping around, with your contacts at the Art Institute," said Travers. "You and your friend Jekyl, the art dealer. And things got way too hot."

"But Jekyl didn't know the art was fake!" cried Carmela.

"He would have recommended carbon testing or thermoluminescence dating at some point," said Travers. "But now it doesn't matter," Travers added, sounding indifferent. "Too late for all that. Too late for everything but the cleanup."

"Too late for Las Vegas," murmured Ava.

"Sorry, darlin', it just wasn't meant to be," said Travers, which sent Ava into a series of hiccupping sobs.

Angered by Travers's callousness, enraged by his blasé sociopathic explanation, Carmela renewed her efforts to escape. She slammed the back door with her feet, batted at the windows. Nothing happened, nothing broke, nothing moved. They were still prisoners!

"Doggone!" she screeched, slamming her hand down on the floor of the hearse.

Ava gazed up at her with red-rimmed eyes. "What would Houdini do?" she whispered.

"Good question," Carmela whispered back. Pulling herself to her knees, Carmela eased herself toward the front of the hearse, her fingers searching for something, anything, that would help win their freedom. She pushed panels, batted at windows, tried to pry her fingers under the coffin table. And just when she was panting and exhausted, about to give up, her fingers scrabbled across a panel of buttons. Frantic now, Carmela began pushing buttons willy-nilly, hoping to crack a window, slide open a door, do something!

Then, suddenly, as if by magic, the electric casket table began to move beneath her. It creaked, jiggled, then oh-so-slowly groaned backward, pushing against the back door.

"What are you doing?" screamed Travers, his crazy, high-pitched voice coming across the intercom. "Stop it!" He fumbled for his gun. "I'll use this!"

But the electric casket table pushed relentlessly against the back door. First a jagged crack appeared in the back window, followed by a loud wrenching of protesting steel. Then the back door flew open and the coffin table slid out like a long gray tongue, carrying Carmela and Ava on top of it!

Travers jammed on his brakes, shrieking and babbling at the top of his lungs. But Carmela and Ava had already scrambled out!

* * *

Bobbing and weaving their way through the crowd, hanging on to each other for dear life, Carmela and Ava dashed toward the Monsters and Mayhem parade.

"Is he behind us? Is he behind us?" Ava chattered.

Carmela risked a look over her shoulder. "Yes. Wait, he stopped. Now he's jumping back into the hearse."

"Then he's coming after us," shrilled Ava. "What are we gonna do?"

"Head for the puppets!" yelled Carmela. "Look for Miguel!"

"I don't see him!" yelled Ava as they threaded their way through the cadre of slow-moving hearses, finally catching up with the last row of marching monster puppets.

"Keep going," yelled Carmela. They were inside the parade of monster puppets now, looking like screaming idiots. But she wasn't about to give up. "Faster!" she told Ava.

They renewed their efforts, jamming past an enormous purple sea monster puppet with bobbing tentacles, elbowing a green alien puppet out of the way.

"There he is!" yelled Ava. "I see the Crunch Monster!"

Carmela risked another glance over her shoulder. And what she saw chilled her to the bone. Travers was skillfully weaving his way through the fleet of hearses and was bearing down on them.

"Miguel!" yelled Carmela as they dashed to the middle of the parade. "Wait for us!"

Inside the Crunch Monster puppet, Miguel stepped hesitantly, then paused as Carmela and Ava finally caught up to him.

"Change of plans," said Carmela as she grabbed the puppet head. "Ava goes in, Miguel comes out."

A stunned Miguel held the head above him, allowing Ava to squirm inside.

"Now me, too," said Carmela, climbing inside the puppet.

"What about me?" asked a puzzled Miguel.

"You call the police!" Carmela instructed as she pulled the final flap of fabric down over them. "Get Edgar Babcock down here right now!"

"Did Travers see us?" asked Ava as they marched along, monster puppets bobbing all around them.

"I don't think so," said Carmela. "So we should be safe for the time being."

"Will Edgar Babcock come?" asked Ava.

Carmela grabbed her friend close. "I don't know. I hope so."

They marched one block, then two, crowds screaming wildly at them.

"Do you think Travers gave up?" Ava asked hopefully.

"Don't know," said Carmela. "Here, let me take a look." She put her hands up into the puppet head, turned it slightly, and peered sideways.

There, running alongside, to their left and slightly behind them, was Travers in his long, black hearse. He seemed to be intently scanning the puppet contingent, searching for them, but unsure exactly what puppet might be hiding Carmela and Ava.

"He's trying to figure out where we are!" said Carmela.

"Oh crap," said Ava. "Now what?"

What indeed? wondered Carmela. She searched frantically as they marched, hoping for Babcock, knowing she'd settle for any police officer who could help.

Her eyes scanned the Day of the Dead marchers out in front of them. No help there. Her head whipped to the right, taking in the throngs of people who lined the streets, cheering the puppets. Nothing.

Unless you counted . . . Mr. Bones! Standing casually by a wrought-iron lamppost, gazing into the fray of the parade.

The *real* Mr. Bones? Should she take a chance that he could help? Or continue marching and worry that Travers would eventually figure out where they were and cut them from the herd?

Grabbing Ava by the arm, Carmela said, "C'mon! We're going to make a break for it."

"What!" But Ava bumped after her anyway, the puppet flexing and squirming, the giant head bobbing like crazy.

"Mr. Bones!" yelled Carmela. "Mr. Bones!" She struggled to free an arm and wave at him as they skittered across Dauphine Street, where Mr. Bones was poised on a curb, one arm curled around the lamppost.

At hearing his name called out, Mr. Bones searched the crowd and saw the Crunch Monster puppet heading right for him. That's when he sprang into action and ran to meet them.

"Mr. Bones," Carmela cried, ducking her head out so he could see who she was. "We need help! There's a man in a hearse who . . . Well, it's Tom Travers . . . and he's . . ."

But Mr. Bones had already reached into his hidden pocket and drawn his police-issued pistol. And was suddenly completely focused on the rogue hearse that slid alongside the marching puppet brigade.

"Mr. Bones?" said Carmela, stepping aside as he rushed toward the hearse.

"What happened?" asked Ava, popping her head out.

"He's going to help us," breathed a relieved Carmela.

Ava grinned. "A man who can rescue two damsels in distress!"

Carmela could only nod her head in agreement. Clearly Mr. Bones wasn't who she thought he was.

Chapter 28

HE was, in fact, Bobby Gallant, Edgar Babcock's associate and one of the detectives Carmela had met the night of Brett Fowler's murder. All this was explained to her after backup arrived in the form of four screaming police cars and Edgar Babcock himself.

It was amazing, of course, how Gallant had rousted Tom Travers from the hearse, handcuffed him, and held him down on the pavement, his foot planted squarely on Travers's back. Carmela would have preferred his foot planted somewhere else, but that was just revenge thinking.

And when Edgar Babcock swept her into his arms, Carmela could only think of one thing to say. "I'm sorry, I screwed up, I got in your way," she mumbled tearfully."

"I'm amazed," Babcock told her. "You flushed out the killer. And at great risk to yourself."

"Clearly not my intention," said Carmela. She hic-

cupped, let loose a few hot tears, then added, "The risk part, I mean."

He nodded. "I know that."

Then Carmela called Jekyl on Babcock's cell phone, and he arrived a few minutes later to minister to the devastated Ava.

"Poor you," said Jekyl, putting both arms around Ava and giving her multiple friendly pecks.

"Poor me," repeated Ava as Carmela and Babcock looked on.

"But your hair still looks good," said Jekyl.

"Does it?" said Ava, brightening. "Really? You're not just saying that?"

"Never better," said Jekyl. "Like pageant hair. Very full and lush."

"That's good, huh?" sniffed Ava, managing a weak smile.

"Look at that," Babcock said to Carmela, the sides of his mouth twitching, "your friend is starting to bounce back already."

"Give her another ten minutes of compliments and she'll be ready to sashay into Brennan's for a couple of drinks," said Carmela.

"Good to hear you laugh," said Babcock.

"Good that you showed up," said Carmela.

"Now what?" asked Babcock.

"Maybe we should have that talk, after all?"

Babcock held up an index finger. "Give me five minutes."

It took Babcock only four minutes to give orders and get things moving again. Then he and Carmela peeled off from

the crowd and wandered down Dauphine Street, their arms wrapped tightly around each other.

There were crowds, but they didn't seem to notice them, so focused were they on each other.

"So Delta Imports was only a front," said Carmela. "For importing fakes."

"Oh, Delta Imports is quite real," said Babcock. "They do real importing and handle really good fakes. Roy Slayback mentioned the art thing to me a few days ago when we were probing Emerald Equities. I guess he was suspicious of Fowler's growing collection and had an idea that the art could be sold and the proceeds used to pay back investors."

"So he didn't know the art was fake, either?"

"Slayback figured it might be stolen," said Babcock. "Or smuggled out. So that sent me looking into the FBI's art theft database. When nothing turned up there, I thought the trail had dead-ended. Then I got a callback from them late this afternoon. Found out that a ton of fakes have been coming out of Hong Kong. Some place called Hollywood Road where there are legit antique stores right alongside forgers' studios. By then, of course, I couldn't find you. I didn't know if you'd jumped on this art lead as well." He paused. "What's worse, I couldn't warn you because I couldn't *find* you."

"But Travers found us," Carmela murmured. "Through a bit of conniving."

"Yes, he did," said Babcock.

Carmela put a hand to her head as if to silence her whirring brain. "So other art collectors purchased the works," said Carmela, "thinking they were legitimate?"

"To a point," said Babcock. "Because Travers also sup-

plied certain collectors with fake papers, so they could donate their pieces to museum collections and take huge tax deductions."

"And Ava's boyfriend was a fake, too." Carmela stopped suddenly in her tracks, looking ashen and more than a little shaky.

Babcock peered at her, looking worried. "I think you're experiencing a mild case of shock," he told her. "You need something to bring up your blood sugar right away. Orange juice or something to replace electrolytes." He led her into the nearby Chantilly Hotel and out into the courtyard. When they were seated at a table, he hastily ordered orange juice for Carmela, a black coffee for himself.

"This is where the macaws live," Carmela murmured.

"Hmm?" He put a hand to her cheek and stroked it gently.

"The macaws," said Carmela. She pointed. "Over there in that cage."

"Beautiful birds," said Babcock.

"They're for sale, you know," said the waitress, setting a tray on their table and placing a tall glass of orange juice in front of Carmela, a silver pitcher of coffee in front of Babcock. She shook her head. "Nice birds, but just too much trouble, I guess."

"Wish I could take them," said Carmela.

Babcock put an arm around her and said, "I'll buy them for you."

Carmela took a sip of orange juice and shook her head. "It wouldn't work. With two dogs there's not enough room for birds, too." She sounded profoundly sad.

Babcock's heart went out to her. "I have an idea. What if we keep them at my place?"

"Really?" Carmela's melancholy seemed to evaporate like a puff of morning fog off the Mississippi. "Would I . . . would I have visiting rights?"

Babcock grinned at her. "Anytime you want. Twenty-four-seven. Full access, day or night."

"Full access," said Carmela, snuggling closer to him. "That sounds awfully nice."

"Okay, then," said Babcock, looking pleased.

"And what if the macaws wanted their freedom one day? Wanted to go back to Honduras?"

"Is that where they're from?" asked Babcock, looking puzzled.

"I don't know," said Carmela. "Maybe Brazil."

"Tell you what," said Babcock. "If you ever want to set them free, we'll just FedEx them down to Brazil. Back to the rain forest."

"Really? You can do that?"

"Of course we can."

"That would be perfect, then," said Carmela. "Really perfect."

Scrapbook Tips & Tricks
from Laura Childs

Nifty and Gifty

Make your own gift card holders. Take a stiff sheet of paper, fold it in half, then cut it out to fit your card—allowing an extra ½ inch or so on all sides. Stitch or glue your holder on three sides, leaving one end open. Now simply embellish your gift card holder with letters, charms, stickers, bits of paper, and so on.

Collectible Candles

Metallic rub-on designs and letters transfer beautifully to candles. Choose large white pillar candles, then carefully add your rub-ons. Give them extra zing by adding strategically placed silver or gold metal brads. Ribbon or raffia lends an elegant finishing touch. Hint: These make great gifts!

Holiday Glassware

Use your stamp rollers to create continuous patterns on beverage glasses and even mirrors. Think ghosts at Halloween, leaves

at Thanksgiving, ornaments for Christmas. Just use your stamp roller and colorful stamp-pad ink, which can be easily removed with ordinary glass cleaner.

Family Tree

Use a die-cut tree image to create a family tree scrapbook page. Use circular-cut photos and place the senior relatives at the top, youngsters at the bottom. Or mount the photos on die-cut apples. A fun headline: *The apple doesn't fall far from the tree.*

Easy Mini Photo Albums

Make an instant mini album using clear plastic badge holders from an office supply store. Just slip photos into the badge holders, then use ribbons or raffia strung through the top of each badge to hold your book together. You might want to give your mini album a theme and scrapbook a special cover.

Art Smart

Children's drawings are adorable, but what's the best way to show off their many projects on a single scrapbook page? Solution: Take six to nine pieces and shrink each one down on a color copier. Now cut each piece into a square and arrange the squares in a grid style. Tip: Artwork, any artwork, looks better when it's reduced!

Pillow Boxes

Using a pillow box template, create your pillow box using an 8½-by-11-inch sheet of gold brocade card stock. Once your box is assembled and glued, wrap a 2-inch strip of red-and-gold paper around it, then tie the paper in place with red ribbon or

raffia and add a small gold charm. Pillow boxes are perfect gift boxes for handmade soaps, jewelry, or scarves.

Aged to Perfection

Want to give your photos, documents, or favorite recipes an aged, instant artifact look? Copy them onto beige or parchment paper, then tear around the edges. Now sponge on a little bit of tea—it's the instant ager used by forgers for centuries! Let dry, crumple slightly, then smooth out. Your photo will look like an eighteenth-century daguerreotype!

Favorite
New Orleans Recipes

Pralines

1 can (5 fl. oz.) evaporated milk
¾ cup granulated sugar
½ cup brown sugar
1 tsp. vanilla extract
2 tsp. butter
½ cup pecan halves

Combine the evaporated milk, granulated sugar, brown sugar, vanilla, and butter in a saucepan over medium to high heat. Once the mixture boils, reduce to medium heat and cook for about 10 minutes until the mixture is thick and bubbly (soft-ball stage). Remove from the heat and whisk for a few minutes until the mixture dulls in color and thickens slightly. Add the pecan halves and stir well until the mixture

thickens even more. Drop onto wax paper in 3-inch circles. Allow the pralines to harden at room temperature for about 1 hour. Enjoy!

Carmela's Cajun Shrimp Bake

2 lb. large, fresh shrimp

½ cup butter

2 Tbsp. chili or cocktail sauce

2 Tbsp. Worcestershire sauce

1 Tbsp. Creole seasoning or Old Bay seasoning

1 Tbsp. lemon juice

½ Tbsp. chopped fresh parsley

½ tsp. paprika

½ tsp. dried oregano

½ tsp. ground red pepper

Preheat the oven to 400 degrees F. Spread the shrimp in a shallow foil-lined pan. Combine the butter, chili sauce, Worcestershire sauce, Creole seasoning, lemon juice, parsley, paprika, oregano, and red pepper in a saucepan, stirring over low heat until the butter is melted. Pour the sauce over the shrimp and chill for at least 2 hours. Bake uncovered for 20 minutes. Serve with French bread for dipping.

Black-Bottom Banana Bars

½ cup butter, softened

1 cup granulated sugar

1 egg

1 tsp. vanilla extract

1½ cups mashed ripe bananas

1½ cups flour

1 tsp. baking powder

1 tsp. baking soda

½ tsp. salt

¼ cup cocoa powder

Preheat the oven to 350 degrees F. Cream the butter and sugar, then add the egg and vanilla and beat until combined. Blend in the bananas. In a separate bowl, combine the flour, baking powder, baking soda, and salt, then stir into the creamed mixture. Divide the batter in half; add the cocoa powder to one half and stir to combine. Spread the chocolate batter into a greased 9-by-12-inch baking pan. Spoon the remaining batter on top and spread evenly. Bake for approximately 25 minutes. Cool the bars and cut into 24 pieces.

Pork and Sweet Potato Bayou Casserole

1½ lb. cubed boneless pork

6 medium sweet potatoes, peeled and cubed

1 medium onion, sliced

2 or 3 carrots, sliced
1 cup tomato sauce
1½ tsp. dry mustard
¼ cup white wine (or water)
Salt and pepper, to taste
1 cup barbecue sauce

Place the pork in a 3-quart slow cooker, then add the sweet potatoes, onion, and carrots. Combine the tomato sauce, mustard, and wine and spoon the mixture over the meat and vegetables. Add salt and pepper. Cover and cook on low heat for 6 to 7 hours, until the pork and vegetables are fork tender. Stir in the barbecue sauce and warm the entire mixture.

Spunky, Funky Black Bean Chicken

1 Tbsp. olive oil
½ lb. smoked sausage, sliced
1 lb. fresh skinless chicken pieces
1 medium onion, diced
1 red bell pepper, seeded and diced
1 Tbsp. chili powder
Salt and pepper, to taste
1 can (15 oz.) chopped tomatoes
1 can (15 oz.) black beans, drained and rinsed

Heat the oil in a medium-sized pot over medium heat. Add the sausage and sauté until browned. Add the chicken and brown on all sides, 5 to 6 minutes. Add the onion and bell pepper and

sauté until soft, about 6 minutes. Add the chili powder, salt, pepper, tomatoes, and black beans. Mix thoroughly, then cover and simmer for 20 to 25 minutes, until the chicken is thoroughly cooked. Serve in bowls with crusty bread. Serves 4.

Jezebel Sauce

1 jar (10 oz.) apple jelly
1 jar (10 oz.) pineapple preserves
1 jar (10 oz.) orange marmalade
1 jar (5 oz.) horseradish, drained
1 Tbsp. dry mustard
½ tsp. black pepper
2 bricks cream cheese or large round of Brie cheese

Beat the apple jelly with an electric mixer until the pieces are broken up. Add the pineapple preserves and orange marmalade and mix thoroughly. Stir in the horseradish, mustard, and pepper. Mix well, then chill.

When party time rolls around, spoon the sauce over bricks of cream cheese or round of Brie and serve with your favorite crackers.

Juju Voodoo Chicken Wings

5 lb. chicken wings
1 jar (10 oz.) apricot preserves
1 packet dry onion soup mix
1 bottle (12 oz.) Catalina-style salad dressing

Preheat the oven to 375 degrees F. Cut each chicken wing in half to make two drummies. Place on two lightly greased baking sheets (this makes a lot!) and spread the apricot preserves over wings. Sprinkle the dry onion soup mix over the wings, then pour the salad dressing on top of that. Bake for 1 hour. Serves 20.

Neon Voodoo Cocktail

Apple juice
Vodka
Mountain Dew

Mix equal parts apple juice, vodka, and Mountain Dew. Pour over ice and add a pink rock candy swizzle stick.

Candied Fruit Banana Bread

2½ cups all-purpose flour, sifted
3 tsp. baking powder
½ tsp. salt
1½ cups mixed candied fruits
¾ cup chopped nuts
⅓ cup raisins
½ cup shortening
¾ cup sugar
3 eggs
½ cup mashed banana
½ cup orange juice

Preheat the oven to 250 degrees F. Sift together the flour, baking powder, and salt. Stir in the candied fruits, nuts, and raisins. In a separate bowl, cream the shortening, then add the sugar and beat until fluffy. Add the eggs, one at a time, beating the batter after each one. In a third bowl, combine the mashed banana and orange juice, then add to the creamed mixture. Now stir in the dry ingredients. Pour into a greased 9-by-5-inch loaf pan and bake for 1½ hours.

Dr Pepper Tickle-Your-Ribs Spareribs

4 lb. spareribs
1 can (12 fl. oz.) Dr Pepper
1 cup ketchup

½ tsp. salt
½ tsp. black pepper
2 Tbsp. Worcestershire sauce
¼ cup vinegar
1 tsp. chili powder
1 cup chopped onion

Preheat the oven to 400 degrees F. Cut the spareribs into pieces, then place them in a shallow, foil-lined pan, meaty side up. Roast for 30 minutes. While the meat is roasting, combine the Dr Pepper, ketchup, salt, pepper, Worcestershire sauce, vinegar, chili powder, and onion in a saucepan and simmer for 20 minutes. After the meat has roasted for 30 minutes, spoon the sauce over the ribs. Reduce the oven temperature to 340 degrees F and continue roasting for another 30 minutes, basting frequently.

Turn the page for a preview of Laura Childs's next
book in the Scrapbooking Mysteries . . .

SKELETON LETTERS

Available in hardcover from Berkley Prime Crime!

Chapter 1

CARMELA Bertrand stepped into the dark interior of St. Tristan's Church and uttered one word. "Spooky." Not only was this historic pile of stones tucked discreetly into New Orleans's freewheeling French Quarter, but it lent a note of Gothic sobriety. Dim overhead lights spilled muddy puddles of light down the center aisle. An ornate wooden altar with a large gold cross and tabernacle loomed at the far end, flanked by two red lamps. Tucked down both sides of the church were small chapels and prayer nooks where flickering vigil lights cast dancing shadows across the faces of painted, peeling statues, giving them an uncanny animated look. All around were the rustlings of unseen people as beads rattled, doors closed softly, and footsteps whispered on slate floors. Choir practice had just concluded, and it felt like the final notes of "Abide with Me" still hung thick in the air.

Blinking rapidly, Carmela fought to adjust her eyes and take in the vaulted arches, dark confessionals, and gigantic pipe organ, which all seemed to impart an air of monastic seclusion and deep solemnity. "It's almost like something out of *Phantom of the Opera*," she murmured to her friend, Ava Gruiex, who was a step behind, juggling a large hand-lettered poster.

"Or *The Hunchback of Notre Dame*," Ava offered. "You remember that poor, twisted creature scrabbling around in the bell tower . . . ?"

"I remember," said Carmela, and wished she hadn't. St. Tristan's had a bell tower, too. A tall, spindly structure with ancient bronze bells that clanged out their soliloquy above the French Quarter three times a day.

"Still," said Ava, gazing about the church with an almost beatific expression on her face, "I love it here. It's particularly meaningful now that I'm volunteering with the Angel Auxiliary."

Carmela, a youthful blonde of not-quite-thirty, directed a skeptical sideways glance at her best friend, whose va-va-voom figure was sheathed in tight black leather slacks and a plunging yellow T-shirt with a sequined court jester motif on the front. She herself was dressed in Republican beige and had worn sensible low-heeled shoes, quite appropriate considering her churchy errand today. But Carmela, who fancied herself conservative and worried that she was plain in a city where moonlight and magnolias were the norm, was really quite lovely in her own right. Her skin glowed with a peaches-and-cream luminosity, her blue-gray eyes mirrored the color of the Gulf of Mexico, and she projected an upbeat air of barely contained mirth and energy. And, upon certain occasions, generally a fanciful Mardi Gras ball, Carmela

wasn't afraid to fling caution to the wind and jack her five-foot-six-inch frame onto tottering four-inch stilettos to hang out with the tall gals. And the tall guys, naturally.

Still, the fact remained . . . when Ava strutted her stuff with the assurance of a peacock, Carmela sometimes felt like a little brown wren.

Got to ratchet up the sizzle, Carmela told herself. *Buy a Wonderbra or a purple silk teddy. Spritz on a cloud of Chanel No. 5. Keep that boyfriend of mine on his toes. Although maybe I shouldn't be thinking about all this . . . in church.*

"People don't realize," said Ava, dipping two fingers into a marble holy water font, crossing herself, then turning innocent, practically guileless eyes on Carmela, "that I'm a very strict Catholic."

"Really." Carmela's tone was purposefully flat. No question intended, no judgment made. Just a bushel basket full of curiosity. Like . . . had the church elders ever dug into Ava's background? Did they know she was the proprietor of the Juju Voodoo shop? Carmela thought not. But, seriously, what *was* the harm in a voodoo shop owner working as a docent in church? Nothing really. Because Ava was Ava, a retired beauty queen who partied her brains out and was known to enjoy a romantic fling or two. Or eight or nine.

"It's so peaceful in here," said Ava, as they slipped silently up a side aisle and stopped in front of a low wooden table scattered with books, hymnals, and pamphlets. "And I can't thank you enough for hand-lettering this poster." She reached behind the table, slid out a wooden easel, and plunked the poster onto it. "A perfect display," she declared.

Carmela pushed aside a hunk of artfully honeyed blond hair and directed a smile at Ava. "Always glad to help out." She'd been brushing up on her calligraphy like crazy any-

way, gearing up for an upcoming seminar at her scrapbook shop, Memory Mine.

Ava set about straightening the little stacks of pamphlets, while Carmela gazed up at a stained-glass window that depicted a tall, stern-looking angel cradling a lamb. What should have been resplendent panes of red, blue, and yellow glass, with thin November sunlight streaming through, only looked dull and muted today. Rain poured down outside, as it had for the past three days, encasing all of New Orleans in a soggy gray amorphous cloud. Even in here, Carmela could hear rain drumming against the roof and gurgling down drain spouts. For a moment, Carmela wondered if, way at the tippy-top of the roofline, St. Tristan's might not have gargoyle drain spouts, much like the great churches of Europe?

And why not? This was an old church built at the turn of the century—not this century, but two gone past—by the hands of the same type of good and God-fearing men who'd supervised the construction of landmark cathedrals and abbeys. Using the tried-and-true Romanesque plan of long nave and short transept, they'd built this fine edifice, established an adjoining graveyard, and buried their noteworthy followers in crypts beneath these very same floors where today's worshippers now walked.

A sudden soft clunk focused Carmela's eyes on a nearby confessional. Was someone in there? A penitent and priest, conferring over some sins that required forgiveness?

Had those purple velvet draperies stirred just a touch? Or was someone else padding about the church? There was a sense of emptiness in St. Tristan's; the rustlings and bustlings of a few minutes earlier seemed to have faded away. And yet . . .

Carmela touched a hand to Ava's shoulder. "I think we should—"

Like ragged gears scraping against metal, a bloodcurdling scream suddenly ripped through the church. It rose in ghastly screeches, spiraling into high-pitched shrieks.

Ava spun around and caught the eyes of a startled Carmela. Then both women whirled in tight concentric circles, fearful, searching, trying to ascertain where that ungodly scream was coming from.

Ava lifted a hand and pointed across the church. "There!"

Squinting through the darkness, Carmela saw two figures locked in a rough-and-tumble embrace.

"No!" came another piercing scream. Now it was distinctly a woman's scream, a woman who was terrified. "Not the—" came her words, and then she broke off in an agonized keening.

Carmela dashed forward a dozen steps, then pulled up quickly. What was going on? Dare she get involved? Was it a robbery of some sort? Was there even anything here to steal?

She was about to leap forward, try to thwart whatever was happening, when Ava suddenly grasped her arm.

"Be careful!" Ava hissed.

Then the woman across the way moaned low and deep.

Ava quickly touched a hand to her mouth. "Oh man, I think she's . . ."

Carmela saw a swirl of brown robe as a cloaked figure forced a smaller figure to its knees. A flash of silver shone in the hooded figure's hands as he swept his arm backward, causing a four-foot-high statue to teeter precariously, then slowly topple from its perch. The statue crashed forward, and

the woman dropped to the floor like a dead weight as chunks of plaster burst everywhere, knocking over candles, spewing rivulets of hot wax. Then the figure in the hooded robe leaped away and seemed to melt into darkness.

Carmela and Ava dashed between pews toward the small altar, where the woman lay like a tossed and discarded rag doll.

"Call 911!" Carmela shrilled. Ava fumbled frantically in her velvet hobo bag for her cell phone as Carmela sprinted into a turn and smacked her left hip hard against a wooden pillar. Without breaking stride, she careened her way to the wounded woman.

Eyes wide in disbelief, Carmela pulled up short and let loose a startled, "Oh no!"

There, splayed out in front of the small altar like a sacrificial offering, was Byrle Coopersmith, one of her scrapbook regulars!

What? Byrle? Her mind could hardly grasp this horrendous discovery.

Ava skidded to a stop behind Carmela, immediately recognized Byrle, and shrieked at the top of her lungs, "Dear Lord, it's Byrle! It's Byrle!" She gibbered for another couple of seconds, then caught herself and said, in trembling tones. "What *happened*?"

Carmela was already down on her hands and knees. "Knocked unconscious, anyway," she said, tersely. Byrle's head was bleeding profusely, her neck was ringed with purple splotches—almost like fingerprint impressions—and her eyes had rolled so far back in her head that Carmela could see only the whites. Worst of all, Byrle didn't seem to be breathing.

"Do something!" Ava implored. "Maybe . . . chest compressions?"

Carmela nodded with the mechanical movement of a bobblehead doll. She laid her hands flat against Byrle's chest and tried to dredge up every morsel of know-how she had regarding CPR and chest compressions.

"Breathe," Carmela willed, as she pressed her fingers against Byrle's chest, up-down, up-down, working to establish a rhythm, trying to stimulate the poor woman's heart and force some air into her lungs. "Come on, honey, you can do it!" she cried to the woman who was quickly turning a horrible shade of blue. "You *know* you can!"

"Help her!" Ava implored. She squeezed her hands open and shut, as if working in concert with Carmela's efforts.

Carmela's knees scraped against rough stone as she continued to work on Byrle. "Ambulance coming?" she asked. She was filled with panic and starting to tire.

"On its way," said Ava.

"Can you . . . ?" She kept up her constant mouth-to-mouth breathing and repetitive motions of push, push, pump. "Can you . . . spell me for a couple of minutes?" Carmela asked Ava.

"Ooooh!" Ava wrapped her arms tightly around herself.

"Never mind," said Carmela, trying to wipe her damp face against her sleeve. She renewed her efforts even as her back muscles burned, and shouted out loud, "Come on, Byrle, *breathe*!"

"Anything?" Ava wailed, as Carmela, resolutely but with hope failing, continued to pump, pump, pump.

"Doggone," Carmela muttered through clenched teeth. Because the poor dear wasn't responding at all.

She was too far gone and, undoubtedly, in the Lord's hands now. As hard as Carmela was trying, she was no miracle worker.

"This is *awful*!" Ava whispered. "Beyond belief!"

Carmela could only nod in agreement. Byrle Cooper-smith, their friend and fellow scrapbooker, who'd not long ago bought a pack of pink mulberry paper from her shop, now lay lifeless and cold on the unforgiving stone floor of St. Tristan's.

Chapter 2

CARMELA stared into the earnest hazel eyes of the young detective who had arrived amid a blat of sirens and a brace of uniformed officers. Yet another shocking intrusion into what had been an oasis of calm and contemplative spirituality.

"Blunt-force trauma," was his quiet pronouncement.

"What?" Carmela asked in a hoarse whisper. Had she really heard Detective Bobby Gallant correctly?

"From the statue," Gallant told her, giving a downward bob of his head. He was young and earnest-looking, with dark curly hair and hazel eyes. Because of the cool weather, he was dressed in a black leather jacket and chinos.

Ava, hovering directly behind Carmela, increased her viselike grip on her friend's shoulder. "The killer smacked Byrle over the head with St. Sebastian," Ava sobbed, trying to be helpful but failing miserably.

"Saint . . . ?" Carmela began, as Ava suddenly released her hold and pointed toward the flagstone floor, where shards of plaster lay scattered. The statue, the one Ava had positively identified as Saint Sebastian, lay facedown amid the rubble. Most of its head was missing. Pulverized from the blow, she supposed.

Byrle's body lay prostrate at the foot of the saint's altar where she'd fallen, looking like some kind of unholy martyr who'd given life and limb for the church. And, in a way, she had.

Carmela let loose a deep and shaky sigh. She knew she had to get a grip and pull it together. After all, she'd been a sort of witness. So maybe she could be of some assistance in the investigation? On the other hand . . .

Making a half spin so she faced Bobby Gallant, Carmela said, "We need Babcock on this." Her words came out a little more hoarse and a little more demanding than she'd actually intended.

Gallant barely acknowledged her statement concerning his boss. "I'm the one who got the call out," he murmured.

"The thing is," Carmela said, gesturing toward Byrle's lifeless body, "we know her. She's a friend."

"From Memory Mine," Ava added. "Carmela's scrapbook shop."

"I'm very sorry to hear that," said Gallant. And this time he did sound sorry.

"So we need to do everything in our power"—Carmela gulped—"to find whoever did this."

"Which is exactly what I intend to do," said Gallant. He glanced around and noticed a uniformed officer standing off to the side, staring at Byrle's dead body. "Slovey!" he barked. "Get something to cover her up!"

Slovey seemed suddenly unhappy. "What do you want me to use?" he asked.

Color bloomed on Gallant's face. "I don't care," he snapped. "Use your jacket if you have to!"

"This isn't happening," Carmela murmured to Ava. Holding on to each other, they staggered over to the church pew that faced the small altar and collapsed together on the hard seat. There, they huddled like lost souls, trying to make sense of it all. At the same time, like some bizarre soap opera, the beginnings of the police investigation played out right before their eyes.

The crime-scene techs arrived, set up enough lights to make it look like a movie set, and began to photograph Byrle's body as well as the damaged saint statue and everything else within a twenty-foot radius.

Uniformed officers were given assignments and hastily dispatched to interview possible witnesses and take statements.

And finally, two EMTs arrived with a clanking gurney to carry Byrle away. Probably, Carmela decided, they were going to transport her to the city morgue. And wasn't that a grim thought!

"Babcock should be here," Ava said in a low voice. "Working this case."

Edgar Babcock, homicide detective first class of the New Orleans Police Department, was, to put it rather indelicately, Carmela's main squeeze. As Carmela had wrangled through her divorce from her former husband, Shamus, the two had gazed longingly at each other. When Carmela finally separated from her philandering rat-fink husband, she and Babcock finally started seeing each other. And now that

Carmela's divorce was signed, sealed, and delivered, they were most definitely an item.

"Don't worry," said Carmela, "I'm going to call Babcock." She hesitated. "But Gallant does seem to be doing a credible job."

"Credible is only good when it comes to talking heads on TV," said Ava. "For this investigation we need a grade-A detective."

"Sshhh," said Carmela. Gallant was suddenly headed straight toward them.

Stepping lightly, Gallant slid into the pew directly ahead of them, settled onto the creaky seat, and swiveled to face them. Only then did Carmela notice the tiredness and deep concern that were etched in his face.

"Something tells me this isn't the only case you're handling," Carmela said.

Gallant shook his head. "Two drive-bys last night and a floater in the river."

"Tough job," said Ava.

"Tough city," said Gallant.

"What . . . what's happening now?" asked Carmela.

"Well," said Gallant, "we've got the church and outside area pretty much cordoned off, and my officers are interviewing everyone who was hanging around the church. Plus, we're canvassing the neighborhood."

"I think some people left before you got here," said Ava.

Gallant leaned forward. "Did you get a look at them?"

Ava shook her head. "Not really. It was more like hearing them." She looked suddenly thoughtful. "You know how when you're in church you're *aware* of people nearby, you hear their voices and shufflings and such, but you don't really look at them?"

"I suppose," said Gallant. He seemed keenly disappointed that Ava wasn't able to give him a complete description. He directed his gaze at Carmela. "You said earlier that you thought the killer was wearing a brown robe?"

"He definitely was," said Carmela. "Like a monk's robe. Dark brown with a deep cowl and hood."

"With a white rope knotted around his waist," Ava added.

"There's a bunch of those robes hanging in the back room on a row of hooks," Gallant told them.

"That's a problem, then," said Carmela. "It means anybody could have grabbed one and thrown it on."

Gallant shifted on the uncomfortably hard pew. "What's the story with the garden and graveyard outside—all the digging and stakes and ropes and things? Either of you know?"

"It's an archaeology dig," Ava told him. "Been going on for almost four months now."

"Do you know who's in charge of it?" asked Gallant.

Ava shrugged.

"I'm pretty sure it's the state archaeology board," said Carmela. "With assistance from students at Tulane." She paused. "At least that's what the article in the *Times-Picayune* said."

Gallant jotted something in his notebook. "They find anything?"

"Ten feet down," said Ava, "they discovered the ruins of the original church. The one Père Etienne founded back in 1782." Père Etienne had been a Capuchin monk who'd been a much-beloved figure because of his tireless work with the sick and the poor.

Gallant looked mildly interested. "Ruins, huh. Anything else?"

"They also unearthed an antique silver-and-gold crucifix," said Ava, "believed to have been the personal crucifix of Père Etienne."

"Which was stolen during the murder," Carmela said suddenly, almost as an afterthought.

Gallant reared back. "What? A crucifix was stolen?"

"From the saint's altar," said Ava. "Where Byrle was killed."

"I think," said Carmela, "Byrle was struggling with her killer, trying to wrest the crucifix back from him."

"Why didn't you mention this sooner?" Gallant demanded.

"Because," said Carmela, "we thought it was more important for you to dispatch your men immediately to hunt down suspects."

"So a robbery and a murder." Gallant stroked his chin with his hand. "I wonder . . . was this crucifix terribly valuable?"

"Byrle thought so," said Carmela. "After all, she gave her life for it."

Laura Childs

TRAGIC MAGIC

A Scrapbooking Mystery

Carmela, owner of Memory Mine scrapbooking shop, and her best friend have a big project—converting an old mansion into an unforgettable haunted house. But when the owner's flaming body comes crashing through a tower window and "welcomes" them to the mansion, Carmela must crop out a killer from the throngs of people flocking to New Orleans.

penguin.com

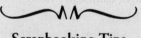
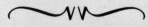
M315AS0510

Don't Miss the Next
Scrapbook Mystery

SKELETON LETTERS

Things are humming along at Memory Mine as Carmela offers lessons in calligraphy and plans a huge wine-tasting party. But the discovery of a strange handwritten note shakes things up and points her in the direction of an unsolved murder.

Also Watch for the Next
Cackleberry Club Mystery

BEDEVILED EGGS

After a "read dating" party at the Cackleberry Club, mayoral candidate Chuck Peebler is shot to death with a crossbow. Two days later, a sheriff's deputy is found murdered on the historical society's Quilt Trail. As Suzanne Deitz, one of the club's founders, and Sheriff Doogie try to unravel clues, they have to contend with rescued dogs, a prison break, dirty politics, and a spookier-than-usual Halloween.

Don't Miss the New
Tea Shop Mystery

SCONES & BONES

As Charleston's Food and Wine Festival gets under way, Theodosia and the Indigo Tea Shop gang introduce the hottest new culinary trend—tea and cheese. But with a shocking murder, a raft of suspects, and a bungled investigation, something smells funny. And it's not just the Gorgonzola!

Find out more about the author
and her mysteries
at www.laurachilds.com.
Or visit her Facebook page
and become a friend.

SAVOR THE LATEST FROM
NEW YORK TIMES BESTSELLING AUTHOR

LAURA CHILDS

SCONES & BONES

· *A Tea Shop Mystery* ·

Indigo Tea Shop owner Theodosia Browning is lured
into attending the Heritage Society's Pirates and
Plunder party. But when a history intern is found
murdered—and an antique diamond skull gets plun-
dered in the process—Theodosia knows she'll have to
whet her investigative skills to find the killer among
a raft of suspects.

M734T0710